LOVE NOTES (THE WILDER BOOKS #3)

SAVANNAH KADE

Published by Griffyn Ink

www.griffynink.com

For ordering information or special discounts for bulk purchases, please contact Griffyn Ink at Mail@GriffynInk.com.

Thank you to my Daddy, who has always supported me, always loved me, and always been there for me.

CHAPTER 1

He ached everywhere. But mostly his head hurt. It felt like he was coming off the mother of all benders, his brain pounding out his punishment. TJ started to reach up to clamp his hands alongside his head, but his arms ached, too.

He tried to squint so the light wouldn't hurt so much and he could tug himself up and into the kitchen to get a little hair-of-the-dog. But squinting made him feel like someone had taken a baseball bat to his face. He didn't go anywhere.

"Ahhhhh." He wasn't much for complaining about what he did to himself, but this morning he just needed to moan a little of it out.

"TJ?" The voice was soft and female, and contrary to what he expected, he recognized it.

What he couldn't figure out was why his brother's wife was in his bedroom.

"Hhhmmmmm?" He tried again to squint, and again was rewarded with a crank up on the headache-o-meter.

"TJ. Oh, thank God." Her fingers touched his, but he really didn't want that. He pulled away. Lately his brother and his beautiful wife had begun to wear on his nerves.

"Kelsey?" It sounded thick and slurred, even to him. But that was just another good reason for Kelsey not to be in here. From behind his eyelids he could tell that she had turned on the light. "Turn off the light and go, I'll call you later."

"TJ. You need to wake up."

"No, I need to go back to sleep." He tried to roll over, and when that didn't work he just lay still, wondering where the hell what's-her-face had gone to.

"Dammit, TJ!"

That voice he recognized, too. The gods were angry at him.

"JD, get the hell out of my bedroom."

The gods always sent JD to him. JD was their favored son, and in exchange he was given the responsibility of telling TJ when he'd screwed up. The voice was still angry; the gods were still pissed. "TJ, open your eyes. You aren't in your bedroom. You're in the hospital."

Son of a bitch.

He cracked his eyes, ready to face the daylight, if only to tell his brother to stuff it. But, when the pain of light hitting nerve endings receded, he saw that he was, in fact, in the hospital. Well, that explained a lot of the pain. "Shit."

"That's all you have to say for yourself?"

"Oh, God, spare me." TJ actually managed to get a hand to his head this time.

JD's expression went grim. "He usually does. You've been charmed, little brother. You've escaped scrapes that I would never dream of trying out. I'm going to have to let the doctors explain this one, but God didn't spare you this time."

That got his eyeballs all the way open. Taking in a quick perusal of the bed, he saw that all four limbs remained intact, and he heaved a great sigh of relief.

"By the way,"

Uh-oh. From that tone, something horrible he'd done was

about to get thrown at him. He just hadn't decided yet if he cared.

"The girl who was with you, Marcia Winters, was fine."

"Good to know." Although whether it was good to know she was fine, or just to finally know her name, he wasn't sure.

His brother grabbed his hand and squeezed it. "We're going to go. The doctors will be by in just a few minutes to talk to you."

He squeezed the hand back.

Kelsey came right up beside the bed, placing her hand on his shoulder. "I love you, TJ."

He didn't want to say it back, but he had to. "I love you, too, Kelsey."

He had to love her. She had handed Wilder everything they needed to break out of the un-signed rut they'd been in six years ago. She'd also given his brother the sun and the moon, the way JD told it. But, damn, if she wasn't the one focal point of how JD was still the gods' favorite. The beautiful wife who greeted his brother at the end of every tour with open arms and a warm bed. A very warm bed, if the three children they'd cranked out since they'd married were any indication. As they left the room hand in hand, TJ realized it was a good thing he didn't want anything like that, because he was certain the gods would deny him.

When the room was blessedly empty, he attempted to roll his head from side to side. Some joint limbering was part of his usual after-indulgence routine. This time it didn't work and the pounding in his head combined with his presence in the hospital seemed like a good sign that he shouldn't be doing it.

He blinked a few times, orienting himself in the private room. The bed jutted out into the middle of the room. Machines and poles lined one side of the bed, and if he followed the wires and tubes he could see that several were connected to him. Something dripped from a clear bag into his arm, and another machine pulsed a green line in time with his heartbeat. He was no doctor, but it looked pretty good.

On the other side of him was a moveable table, pushed to hang partway over the bed, with a pitcher of ice water and a pink plastic cup. He reached out for it, only to realize that he had died and gone to hell. The water was just beyond his reach. He laughed a hollow sound at himself. Normally, Glenlivet was his drink of choice on mornings like these, but now, even the stupid water was out of range.

He grabbed at the wires and was contemplating yanking them and just sitting up when the doctors came in.

"Oh, no. Don't pull on those." The oldest doctor was trailed by two younger ones.

TJ looked at all of them warily. "I don't really need this. I can feel that my heart is beating just fine. So I'll just get a drink and be going."

He reached again for the wires.

The doctor placed his own hand over TJ's, again stopping him. This time the hand seemed far more grandfather than dictator. "Let's talk first."

TJ just nodded or tried to.

"I'm Doctor Sanbourne." He held out the weathered hand, and reluctantly TJ shook it, though the ache of his hangover had made even his arms sluggish. He proceeded to listen through the introduction of the two other doctors, one dark and Indian, the other female and shy-looking. TJ dismissed them mentally and promptly forgot their names.

Dr. Sanbourne pulled up a swivel stool and seated himself, while his lackeys just hung back and watched. "Do you remember the accident?"

TJ blinked. *Accident?*

He shook his head as a little memory filtered back. "I really just remember that there was one. A semi rear-ended me, right?" In his head he could see it, in the rearview mirror, orange and large . . . and getting larger by the second. But that was all that came through.

The doctor nodded. "Luckily, you have good airbags. They saved your life and that of your passenger."

TJ didn't take the prompt. Didn't ask after whatever her name had been.

Dr. Sanbourne continued. "Unfortunately, you were in a convertible and you didn't have your seatbelt on."

TJ raised his eyebrows. *Tell me something I don't know,* but he didn't say it.

"You suffered a crushing blow to the base of your neck. The C-6 vertebrae," he pointed it out on his own spine, "was cracked."

TJ frowned and reached up to his own neck. He was shocked to find it encased in a hard collar. Well, that explained why his head wouldn't turn. His brain cranked through the possibilities. He flexed his fingers in front of his face.

"You've already had a surgery to put pins in to hold the pieces of bone together. The pins will remain for the rest of your life, but the collar will come off shortly, and the bone will heal."

The sound was dull and dry even in his own head, where he left it. *Whoo hoo.*

"However,"

Oh, shit.

"There was damage to the nerves themselves. Nothing appears to be completely severed, but we can't be sure. Your responses prior to surgery were lacking."

He found his voice, "What do you mean, *lacking*?"

"You were missing basic reflexes in your legs. There was no response. We had hoped that after surgery, after we relieved whatever pressure the cracked bone was placing on the spinal cord, you would regain sensation. It doesn't appear that you have."

What?

He felt fine. TJ flexed his toes, looking just beyond the little table, but nothing happened.

He flexed again. *Nothing.*

It had to be the water table blocking his view.

He gave it a good shove, sending it toppling. The two attendant doctors flinched. Sanbourne did nothing of the sort. He simply watched.

TJ felt his ribcage constrict. He couldn't breathe either. He couldn't bend his knees or curl his toes. After a few tries he decided that it was his brain that was broken, even just thinking about moving his leg felt wrong.

Sanbourne nodded. "Your brain works, son. It's your legs that aren't responding."

TJ pulled back, then realized that he must be having a perfectly normal response to finding out that your legs don't work. Sanbourne wasn't a mind reader. He was a doctor.

And TJ was an invalid.

JD's words came back to haunt him, *God didn't spare you this time.*

His breathing increased rate while the room closed in on him. His hands clutched at the sheet clumsily, gathering fistfuls and squeezing without his usual strength. At least driving his fingernails into his palms would have offered some measure of relief, but it looked like that wouldn't happen either.

Sanbourne stood closer, getting his face into TJ's. "Let's do a few tests and see what the damage is. We'll know how to proceed from there."

How to proceed?

But the blunt statement worked. TJ managed to find air and bring it into his lungs. He nodded as well as he could in the collar.

Dr. Sanbourne turned to his assistant who shook her shy head at him.

No, *what?*

But Sanbourne didn't tell TJ.

He did run his pen up the sole of TJ's foot.

At least it looked like he did. TJ saw the sheet pinch from the pressure. Saw the pen disappear behind his foot. But he didn't feel anything. He thought for a moment that the doctor was playing a cruel trick, but then remembered that he hadn't been able to make it move himself. He saw the doctor try again, and realized that he should have at least been able to feel the sheet pull and tug, because he could sure see that it was moving.

Sanbourne tested various spots on both legs. The doctor tried different pressures, from obviously poking him to running the pen along the leg.

Nothing.

"Let's try your hands."

"My hands are fine." TJ was thanking God for small favors.

"C-6 injuries often involve fine motor control of the hands."

TJ flexed all his fingers, grateful that something worked. "Just fine."

"Good." The doctor held out two fingers. "Squeeze."

TJ squeezed.

"Hard as you can."

He added extra force, but didn't feel any difference.

The expression on Sanbourne's face wasn't good.

"Now do this." Sanbourne held up both hands, then touched his first fingers to his thumbs.

TJ did the same, somehow managing a cocky expression at that.

The expression slipped as Sanbourne demonstrated touching each finger in turn, and none of his others worked individually. Either they all went or none did. TJ discovered that he could move his thumbs to touch each fingertip, but couldn't make the fingertips go to the thumb.

"All right." That was all the doctor said.

"What does that mean?" TJ wasn't sure he really wanted the answer.

"There's some loss of fine motor control in the hands." Sanbourne pulled back the sheet revealing the traitorous legs that no longer looked like they belonged to him. They certainly bore a striking resemblance to his own, but they couldn't be his. "Let's do one more test."

He and the other two doctors carefully positioned TJ upright. Since he didn't have a clue what they were doing, he let them. They moved his legs and dangled them off the bed, then asked if he could stay there by himself.

He managed it, although he had to brace his hands out because his body wanted to slide over.

Sanbourne watched, then pulled his rubber mallet out of his pocket. He whacked at both knees, but TJ couldn't watch.

"That's good news." Sanbourne perked up.

"What?" He needed any good news he could get his less-than-functioning hands on.

"Your patellar reflex is intact in both legs."

"Speak English! What does that mean?"

Sanbourne took no offense. "Those nerves are working."

"How do *I* make them work?"

The doctor shook his head. "You can't, you don't. They're reflexes. We have no control over them."

"Then why is it good news?" He wanted to grab the white lapels of the stitched lab coat and shake the doctor. But he couldn't; he'd already figured out that he'd fall over if he moved his hands.

"It means the nerves may heal."

"*May*?"

"May."

CHAPTER 2

TJ felt the walls closing in. The one thing he wanted to do was bolt. But, in great mockery of his feelings, his legs still refused to work. He had stared at them, exerted every last drop of will, and still they wouldn't move. The only thing he could do was grab and lift them like heavy logs. And, like logs, they fell immediately back to the bed.

If he wanted to escape, he'd have to hijack a wheelchair and make for the elevator. The whole thought was so demeaning that he simply lay there, resigned.

The doctors had left him there, the one guy hadn't said anything the whole time, but just before he left he picked up the bedside table and pushed it closer. The girl had disappeared into the hallway and returned with a fresh pitcher and cup. She reset the table without a word. After they left, he wondered if it hadn't been a cruel joke. His hands hadn't grasped the pitcher as tightly as he had thought and it slipped.

The water puddled on the table top and ran across the side to drip a pancake size pool onto his sheet. It took three tries to get upright and pull the thin blanket from the bottom of the bed to sop it up. He was now pushed to one side, not that he could feel the cold spot.

Using two hands, like one of Kelsey and JD's little kids, he poured himself a drink. At least he got some liquid down his throat.

Pain pushed at the backs of his eyeballs. He remembered the sensation from childhood. He was on the verge of tears, but they didn't come. TJ figured his body had forgotten how.

He had nothing but time to think.

There was no band with a lead singer in a wheelchair. Wilder had pushed boundaries from day one, combining country and punk genres. But a wheelchair was a boundary that wouldn't get crossed. Either this year's tour was over before it started, or the guys would have to find a new front man.

And he played guitar. Not as well as JD or Craig, but he added music onstage and he'd started working on his piano skills. Playing was the only thing he could think of, besides being on stage, that he truly enjoyed.

And it was over. His fingers wouldn't function independently.

"Hey." The voice cut into his thoughts. He knew it like he knew his own heartbeat.

"JD."

In the space of a breath, JD was beside the bed, seated, and leaning his elbows onto the mattress. "I'm so sorry."

"Don't." TJ raised his hand, stalling the "but you brought it on yourself" that he was certain wasn't coming, but everyone was thinking.

JD nodded. "The doctors said there's hope—"

"Hope for what?"

"A full recovery, TJ."

It didn't sound as good to his ears as it obviously did to his brother. "There's also a good possibility that I'll work my ass off and get nowhere."

JD nodded. "That's true."

He didn't say anything else, thank God. Then TJ remembered that God had let him go. No wonder. He would have cut himself loose long before this.

JD's hands went into his hair, something both brothers did when they were frustrated. But TJ only did it when he was alone.

JD's voice cut through his thoughts. "You can come live with—"

"No." He squashed that before it could get started.

Kelsey and JD had six kids, from Daniel at twelve down to newborn baby Amy. There wasn't enough money in the universe to get him to live in that house. Holidays were enough. He loved every child, but after a while there was just something about being there amid the chaos and noise that rubbed him the wrong way.

JD simply nodded. "Then what are you going to do?"

TJ shrugged. At least that still worked.

"They've got you slated to stay for observation for another week."

TJ wanted to nod, but couldn't.

"Then we have a week to figure something out." His brother gave a half-smile, the face so like his own. JD was older by two years, but these days no one could tell by looking. TJ partied hard enough to age himself beyond the actual difference. TJ was always guessed to be younger, but that was because he was a free-wheeling loose cannon with a new girlfriend every few months.

"What are we going to do about Wilder? I can't go on tour."

JD just shrugged.

"Don't replace me." He didn't know where the urgency came from, only that it was necessary. "I'll . . . *you* do it."

"No." His brother protested in the only voice that could truly replace his own. "I'm not a front man."

"I can't have someone else taking my place."

There was a sad headshake. "No one could. There won't be any tour. I notified Brenda. She agrees."

TJ was shocked that their manager thought so, but he didn't want to argue it. Wilder was cohesive if nothing else. Every last note on those albums and in concert had been played or sung by one of them. Some of the guitar work had been his own. His fists clenched.

"We are out of the game for a while, little brother."

Again the pressure came at the backs of his eyes. Again, nothing else happened.

A nurse came in just then, making the space between the brothers less obvious. She gave TJ a round blue pill that he swallowed without question. She took his blood pressure, frowning a little. TJ was simply happy that the mercury in the meter didn't explode out the top. She also took his temperature, for the seventh time today.

"What's with the thermometers?" He mumbled around the one in his mouth.

She smiled, although her words offered no comfort. "Patients with C-6 injuries often have trouble maintaining their body temperature. We want to be certain that yours is stable."

She futzed around the room a little more, then left.

TJ sighed. "At least I can still sing, right?"

"Actually . . ." JD drew out the one word, the look on his face grim.

"You are shitting me!" There was no way his vocal chords were injured, his voice sounded fine. He was half tempted to belt out a few choruses right there on the spot.

JD filled in the pieces. "I've been reading up. You're probably lacking strength and fine control in your hands."

TJ flinched.

"And you won't control your diaphragm with any strength either. You probably can't get or push big lungfuls of air."

There it went: the only thing he'd ever been the best at. The pressure returned behind his eyes.

"It's important to Kelsey and me that you're well taken care of." JD's hands went down into his pockets. "I know you don't want to stay with us, but I really want you to reconsider."

"No."

JD sighed at him.

Too bad. That house made him uncomfortable. And he'd be even more so in a wheelchair.

A wheelchair.

The pressure increased.

"There are facilities—"

"No."

"Are you going to outfit your entire house for what is hopefully a temporary condition?" JD was getting huffy with him. At least that one thing was still normal.

"No."

"Then what?"

"I don't know!" How was he supposed to decide these things now? "I really just need to be left alone."

JD nodded. "Craig's coming over to stay tonight."

"No." Did it never end?

"*Yes.*" JD gave as good as he got. "If it was Craig, you'd be there, even if he didn't want it. So welcome back to the world."

TJ shook his head. Or tried, the damn collar was in the way.

"I'll be back tomorrow." JD nodded at him once, then left.

The room held an eerie stillness, and for a moment, TJ decided he was waking up. That he didn't know about the accident. That he still believed he could move.

It was a lie and he knew it. But right now, it was a pretty one. So he closed his eyes and believed.

CHAPTER 3

Norah threw the blanket over the gelding's back and followed it with the saddle. Reaching under his belly, she pulled the strap across and buckled it tight. She patted Thunder's nose and his neck. Then when he wasn't paying attention, when he'd just breathed out, she grabbed the belt and pulled it another notch. Thunder was an old pro at holding his breath so the cinch wouldn't go tight and bother him.

Of course, in that case, it would slide right off and she'd slide with it.

But Norah got it tight and grabbed the reins in her left hand. She didn't need a mounting block, no matter what her grandfather had insisted. She was tall enough and flexible enough that she could just swing over.

In a second, and without thought, she was astride. She rocked back and forth a little. Grandpa may have been wrong about her needing a mounting block, but she missed her grandfather every time she mounted up.

The horse could go fast enough to give a real wind-chill factor and she was grateful for the long-sleeved shirt. She shook out her hair, the heavy black mass trailing down her back too long to show any of its natural curl.

She didn't care. The natural curl meant nothing in the face of the tangles she was about to make.

Slipping the reins up tight and using her pinkies for control, she added a light kick of her boot heels to get Thunder going. Walking him to the fence, Norah blinked in the late-afternoon sun. She trotted just a moment then cantered to the edge of their property. They knew all their neighbors here, and she didn't hesitate to bend low, give the extra kick, and enjoy the flight and roll of horseflesh beneath her as Thunder cleared the fence.

He took off over the hill. The horse knew every stone and pothole far better than she. He may have even enjoyed the run more than she did. She couldn't really call her own feeling enjoyment; it was more simply release.

Tension flew out behind her and lay scattered amidst the tall grass. Norah held herself in perfect position, low over Thunder's neck, legs held solid but not squeezing the horse. You only make that mistake once, she thought.

Her heels pushed down, keeping her toes planted in the metal framed stirrups. And she let her body outrun her thoughts.

After a while Thunder stopped of his own accord. But Norah didn't mind. She breathed in deep. She loved the fresh air, the four seasons, her new life.

Or so she kept telling herself.

It was a good life.

Her father had invited her out here after—

She didn't finish the thought. He had simply invited her when he needed her. Her mother had remarried, remaining in Texas, staying tight with the old biddies in the church and lording it over everyone.

Norah didn't need to be lorded over. And it turned out her

father wasn't the ogre her mother had painted him to be. He was a good man, who maybe was a little too open-minded. Maybe his idea of right and wrong hadn't meshed so well with her mother's entrenched beliefs.

She set Thunder to trotting again, and she posted, standing and sitting in accordance with his stride. It was a casual reflex for someone who had been riding since she was three months old.

The pace was slower now, and her thoughts caught up.

The dance school wasn't doing as well as she had hoped. It had seemed like a good investment of her grandfather's money. Seemed far better than just being a teacher there. The school had a steady clientele and teachers.

Norah was more than qualified. But somehow it hadn't suited. She hadn't liked the kids, although she didn't know why. She'd loved teaching kids when she was younger, but now they all rubbed her the wrong way. Her choreography was uninspired. She was good, but . . .

Maybe that was part of growing up: finding out you weren't as good as you thought you were.

She sighed. She wasn't up to snuff as a professional anymore, but surely she should be able to turn that silly dance school around. Her credentials alone should have pulled more people through the doors. Then again, maybe her marketing skills weren't up to par. There was a lot of bookkeeping, too, even though old Mrs. Kenner was still doing most of it.

Underneath her, the world slipped away. Thunder let out a shriek, and without any other warning, he shifted. His front hooves lifted, pawing the air, and he gave no concern to the woman on his back.

Norah clung to him, wondering why she hadn't worn a helmet and whether or not she was going to break her neck. On pure adrenaline, she held the saddle. Thunder planted all four feet on the ground, and she sighed, relieved, only to have her breath ripped from her lungs again as the horse then jumped sideways. Involuntarily, her hands jerked the reins. Her heels pressed down, and she fought for control over a beast that outweighed her by a ton.

Her rear end lifted from the saddle, her feet losing contact with the stirrups. As she came crashing back into contact, she felt her spine compress and come close to snapping.

Then, as quickly as it began, it ended. Thunder pawed the grass once and stopped.

Her neck ached. Her back and butt were sore. Norah groaned. Only then did she see the movement in the grass, the snake slithering away.

She could have died. She could have been thrown from the most docile horse she had ever known. She didn't have a helmet on, and for a brief second, her hand came up and felt her head, just to be sure it was still attached.

She turned Thunder for home. Wondering if she should tell her father about this.

He would muse about whether this was God reminding her that life could change on a dime. But she didn't need reminding. That lesson had stuck. Even after all these years.

Her body ached as she posted in the saddle, up and down, with Thunder's now perfectly normal trot. In the distance she spotted the farmhouse, gleaming in the fading sun. The red shutters matched the barn that sat in classic style off to the left of it. The road wound by a short distance beyond. Norah leaned low, in spite of the new aches, and gave Thunder the signal to race for home.

CHAPTER 4

"Look." Kelsey handed the printout to him. "I called our real estate agent and asked if she knew of anything."

TJ took the picture of a mostly normal looking cottage. In big letters the printout read "Wheelchair accessible". He forced himself to read it.

But Kelsey didn't really let him. "It's in beautiful country, on one of the outer roads, and the whole house was built for a handicapped man. You really can't get much better than that."

Yeah, I can. He thought wryly. His own house with his own legs would be so much better.

"We're going to hire you a nurse."

He groaned inside, and wanted to tell them to go to hell. TJ neither conceded nor fought.

The pounding in his head had receded to a dull ache, but the pressure behind his eyes was building. With each passing moment he was more hemmed in by the walls, the feeling compounded by the fact that there was nothing he could do about it.

He rolled his head to the side, grateful for even that movement. The plastic collar had been removed just that morning, his bones declared all right. But what did he care if he couldn't make his legs work? And when he looked straight ahead from where his head had rolled, he saw only the intertwined fingers of his brother and his wife. They'd been married six years. Shouldn't they be over this by now?

TJ rolled his head the other way.

Kelsey's voice carried to him. "You need to comb your hair."

What a stupid thing to think about. He hadn't brushed his teeth until yesterday, because he hadn't eaten anything since the night of the accident. Apparently even going to the bathroom was being taken care of for him. His eyes threatened to roll back into his head.

Now Kelsey wanted him to fix his hair. TJ didn't really have the will to argue, so he took the comb she held out and started on his hair, yanking at tangles, but not caring. Kelsey walked calmly into the bathroom and grabbed something, returning with it in her hands. Only as she held it up did he realize that it was a mirror. Like he cared.

But the reflection made him jerk back.

The hand with the comb stopped its movement.

It wasn't his face in there. But it was. Somewhere under the swelling and the bruises was what was left of him. The eyes were his—the clear, vivid blue somehow looking more damaged than the battered skin around them. He looked like he had wound up on the swinging end of a baseball bat. Purple, green, and yellow all fought for dominance on his face. Half of his mouth was swollen. Funny that he hadn't felt that until he saw it.

In a moment of pure fear, his hand found the side of his face and touched everything. He winced as callused fingertips connected with growing whiskers and bruised flesh, but he was grateful for the feeling. His hands felt his whole head, finding a knot on the side about the size of a microphone. His eyes flitted away from the mirror, making contact with his brother.

JD nodded, "You had a concussion, too."

Again TJ waited for it, but it didn't come. "Where's the 'we were hoping it would knock some sense into you'?"

Again JD shook his head. It was Kelsey, only three feet in front of him who answered. "Oh TJ, we're just glad you're alive."

"Come on. Where's the lecture? I know you don't approve."

Again JD just shook his head at him. "No lecture. It never worked any way."

"I guess this is my come uppance."

"No! It's just something that is." His brother's hands found his hair again, setting it on end. He looked down at TJ, not realizing that even just his standing there bordered on insulting to someone who might never do it again. "I only ever wanted you to be happy."

"Like you."

JD shrugged as TJ realized that his brother couldn't see beyond his perfect little world. "However you want to do it. You weren't very happy your way though."

He sucked in breath, his words coming out as more of a yell than he intended. "JD, I'm not like you. I'm never going to be like you."

"You aren't. You don't have to be. But why do you have to move so fast? Why do you have to break every rule? Close every party?"

"You don't get it, JD." TJ sighed. "And you never will."

CHAPTER 5

In perfect cadence with the last notes of the music, Norah's arms floated down to an arc framing her torso. In the mirror she saw fifteen students attempt to do it as well as she did; none succeeded. But they were improving.

"All right girls. That's it for tonight. Thank you for coming back, and I'll see you next year."

There was a round of applause, both from the girls and from the parents just beyond the door. Norah didn't blush, it wasn't really for her, it was for the girls. A few showed promise, but these girls were likely too old to go pro, and that wasn't Norah's goal for them anyway.

The girls all broke form, a small swell of colorful leotards and leg warmers parting and moving for the door, almost like a school of fish. The parents came in to talk to her, to ask what classes each girl should be placed in the next year. These girls were going into junior high, and she was going to promote all but a few of them to pointe. That meant parents ranged from concerned to excited—and unilaterally ignorant.

She answered questions, and answered them again. And smiled.

One girl hung back, until all the others had been gathered up by moms or dads.

Only three weeks ago, at the recital, had Norah met Andie's father. Before then she had only seen the mother, and only briefly. On those few occasions Norah noted that the two had no looks in common except for brilliant smiles. But at the recital, Andie's Dad had come backstage to give his daughter flowers, and Norah had silently blessed the gods that it was after the show instead of before.

She was used to good-looking men. Her students' fathers could be found crawling all over the dance studio on a regular basis. Some of them hit on her. Of course, she always said no; she had a strict policy not to get involved with anyone associated through the dance school. But she hadn't been prepared for the blow when Andie's father had introduced himself.

Her gut had twisted when he turned, and she was facing JD Hewlitt. The boy she'd idolized from age eight to sixteen. She'd fancied herself in love with him then, but later learned that it had been nothing more than a good crush.

The worst moment had been that he had recognized her, too. "Lilah?"

Norah had shaken her head, not surprised at all that he'd thought she was her sister. He hadn't even noticed her or her silly infatuation while they'd been growing up. Why would he? He'd been seven years older, mature to her gangly child. And he'd been dating Lilah. Norah looked enough like her older sister that, given the years, the mistake was more than understandable.

JD did a double take when she told him who she was, probably shocked that she wasn't still the stick-skinny kid who was all big eyes and too-wide smile. They'd spoken just a few sentences, then he'd gone.

Now mother and daughter approached her, the last ones lingering on the last night of class before summer.

"Hi, Norah. I'm Kelsey." The woman with the kind face had a tiny baby tucked in one hand and the other extended out for a welcoming shake.

"I remember." She smiled. At least JD looked to have found someone good for him.

"I wanted to talk to you about a few things."

Uh-oh. That never had meant anything good in her past. But she nodded and smiled as though she couldn't wait to hear what was coming.

"We had Andie's portraits done here at the studio this winter when you offered them."

Norah simply nodded, waiting for the point. The portraits had sucked, but she'd gotten a cut of the meager profits, and she needed every penny she could squeeze out of this school.

"They were passable."

That was a kind word for it.

Kelsey continued, realizing that Norah wasn't going to step in. "I do portraits. I'd like to bid on next year's job."

That brought on a few blinks. It certainly wasn't expected. "Okay." It was all she could think of to push out of her mouth.

"On a separate note, I understand that you know my husband."

There you had it.

"We'd love to have you over to dinner." The words gushed out, not giving Norah near enough time to process all of them. "You should get a chance to catch up with JD. I have examples of my work at the house. And TJ is in town. Although, if you've paid any attention to the entertainment news then you know that TJ isn't his usual self. But he might be over."

Again Norah nodded, meaning only that she'd heard, but Andie was jumping up and down, clapping and squealing. "I'm so glad you'll come."

There was hardly any way to say ‘no’ after that. Even though she hadn’t really meant to say ‘yes’.

CHAPTER 6

TJ looked around the place from his vantage just above his usual waist height. After two weeks here it seemed even less like home and more like some alien land. Sadly, he owned it. The whole house screamed his condition, from the ramp up the front walk to the low queen-sized master bed.

The kitchen was the worst. It was the most obviously 'handicapped.' Every door and drawer opened with a full handle —no knobs to slip through weakened grasps. The counters were low and hung out beyond the cabinets underneath, so TJ could wheel his chair up and work. Like he was ever going to prepare a meal here.

Even the cabinets were hung low. The paths throughout the house were wide enough for the chair. There were so many silver rails in the bathroom that it looked like the plumbing had gone nuts and come through the walls.

His room was large enough for him to maneuver the chair around each side of the bed, and the side tables simply jutted from the walls as most counters in the house did. It was a necessity for someone who would never stand to work at the surface.

The back room was outfitted for the live-in nurse. Probably the worst feature of this whole set-up.

Kelsey had arranged the first nurse when he moved in. TJ was grateful that he didn't have to call and find his own babysitter. She was a big matronly woman who didn't seem to understand that he needed help, not a mother. When his plate had slipped through his grasp, shattering and sending shards of china skittering across the smooth floor, she hadn't understood his deep need to pick up each additional plate, and smash it alongside the first. They had shattered so completely against the slick silver refrigerator, the wall, the floor. The cups had been picked off their hooks one by one and flung to wherever they would make the best end, the last crashing on the countertop and sending a burst of tiny slivers into his arms and neck.

He hadn't noticed much. But Nurse Ratchet sure did. She had hmmphed, wiped the blood off him while he sat there shaking, swept the floor, then told him in her imperious tones that she would have the agency send someone else.

JD had arrived in the interim, and hadn't said a thing.

TJ had no idea what was boiling inside him, only that it was. JD and Kelsey were about the last ones standing where he was concerned. Craig and Alex already told him to go to hell.

A repair-man came to fix the broken kitchen window that TJ hadn't noticed he'd caused. He had watched the whole repair job, thinking how easy it was. Then TJ realized he was now perfectly incapable of doing it.

A second nurse had come and said nothing when he watched endless reels of himself on entertainment shows. Pictures of his face in better days flashed on screen. The talking heads reported that he was expected to make a full recovery. He laughed. They said it was speculated that drugs were involved in the accident. He contemplated calling them up and telling them that *no, it had just been alcohol, but clearly that was enough.*

That was when he realized that he wasn't as famous as he thought. While cards, flowers, and gifts poured in, no paparazzi followed him. For the first time he was glad not to be bigger than he was.

When the shows changed to more pressing news, all of three days later, he turned the TV off. Instead he watched his feet, hoping for some sign of life, some twitch or jerk that would signal that this nightmare would end. He refused to go to physical therapy, purposefully oversleeping and missing appointments. It was worthless and heart-breaking to watch someone else move his limbs.

On her day off, nurse number two went out. She didn't come back. He was later told something about non-cooperation.

Nurse number three was male, and by far the best of the lot. But still intolerable. He ate healthy breakfasts sending smells of wheat germ pancakes and turkey bacon all through the house. Though good-natured, he constantly told TJ the effects of the cigarettes he'd started smoking, the pizza and Cheetos he ate, the beer he drank. To add further insult, the man sang in the shower. Bad songs. Poorly. And at a volume that TJ could no longer achieve.

The man had to go.

Still he showed up in the living room right on time, in blue scrubs. The too-bright kind that made it clear the man in the wheelchair was out with his assistant, not a friend. "Are you ready?"

TJ just stared. TJ was bathed, a phenomenal chore that took up a good portion of his mornings. He was dressed, yet another thing that took fifty times as long as it used to and was yet another demeaning experience. He was ready.

He didn't want to go to JD and Kelsey's. All he really wanted was to be left alone, and there would be so many of them. All five kids would walk better than he did. They would run around the backyard in the early summer air, screaming and chasing each other. They might as well take kitchen knives and stab him repeatedly. No, he wouldn't ever really be ready.

CHAPTER 7

Norah followed Kelsey around the house. Apparently they'd moved in a while ago, needing a bigger place. That made sense; JD and Kelsey sure seemed to be working on stuffing it to the gills.

She had followed Kelsey upstairs, checking in on kids doing the last remnants of studying for the last few days of school. She thought maybe she should have kept the dance school going a little longer. Instead, she simply closed for the end of the year at the same time as the previous owners had, never giving it a second thought. But already the money was being missed—a few extra weeks would mean more of it next year.

"This is my in-house workshop." Kelsey opened the door to walls covered with photos. Portraits, candids, black and whites, all casually perfect to Norah's eyes. Though she was untrained, like most people she knew what she liked. And she liked these too much.

"I love it. I think you'd take excellent portraits at the studio, but I'm afraid most of our parents can't afford you." *Which was a damn shame,* she thought to herself.

"Don't worry about that. I won't work for my usual rate. It's something I'd like to do." Kelsey talked and gestured, casually aware of the sleeping infant in the crook of her arm. Norah wondered about this woman with so many children, who could hold her baby so easily.

Norah offered another conciliatory smile. "That would be even worse. If you lower your prices, then there's no room for the studio to take a cut." She sighed. "I have to, or I'd give you the job. But we aren't making a real profit yet and I have to take what I can to keep it open."

"I understand." She pulled out a folder of prints. "I'd still like to do it. I did these for Daniel's soccer team last fall."

Norah flipped through the pages, seeing smiling kids caught in action, looking victorious, and all of them portrayed with a clear eye for whichever child was in them. Norah had no doubt that each kid looked his or her best.

Kelsey smiled at her. "We'll set a reasonable price list, and we'll offer a lot of options, and we'll split the profit. I'll even give you a minimum."

Norah closed the folder and handed it back. "When you make offers like that, it's hard to refuse. It's yours."

Kelsey beamed. "Thank you."

JD's voice called up from downstairs. "Dinner's ready."

"Well," Norah gave a small smile, ready to get out of confinement with the baby. Luckily, the little girl hadn't woken up and tried to look at her. "I guess we'll hammer out the details later."

With that Kelsey led the way back down the stairs to a strange whirring noise Norah had just then noticed. She wondered what JD was doing to dinner when she saw the man sitting in the wheelchair at the base of the stairs watching her come down. His mouth hung open.

The voice that fell out of it was so like his brother's. "Lilah?"

"JD?" She shot back.

He jerked his head back, and this time when he spoke his

eyes were wider. As she reached the bottom of the stairs, he looked her up and down in full surprise. His voice was filled with wonder this time. "*Norah*?"

She couldn't help but enjoy his shock. She was a long way from the awkward pre-teen he'd known. She was sure her smile was too near a laugh to be polite. "Hey, TJ. I didn't know you were coming."

JD poked his head out of the kitchen to join the conversation. "Yeah, TJ, get this, she's Andie's dance teacher."

Kelsey cut in, helping out. "Actually, she owns the studio."

Norah so wanted to hate the woman who'd bagged the most sought after boy from her corner of Houston. But it was hard to do. And JD was clearly in love with his wife.

TJ looked up at her. "Did you just move out here?"

"No. I taught at the studio for a year before I bought it three years ago."

He looked affronted. "And you didn't call us up?"

Norah laughed. "You're famous. What was I going to say, 'hey do you remember me? The little sister of the girl your brother used to date in junior high?'"

He had the grace to look sheepish.

Kelsey and JD called everyone to the table, and there were several minutes of shuffling. The baby had to go into her crib, then the toddler got strapped into his high chair and was handed his own dinner of finger foods. Ari, at five, had a cute little regular chair with a seat higher than the others. The older kids sat in their own seats, and easily made room for TJ at the end.

Norah watched all of it in a kind of sick fascination. She and her father just pulled out chairs and sat. But Kelsey and JD were obviously in their element, they worked in concert making sure everything happened.

TJ was more like her, just an observer. Suddenly quiet, he sat in his place at the end of the table, seemingly made of plaster, only his eyes showing any movement. Tucked there where he was, it was almost impossible to distinguish that he was in the wheelchair.

After the shuffling stopped, dinner was served, and Norah was caught up in what it was like to be part of a large family. Andie had taken the place to her right, and TJ occupied her left side. Thankfully, the smaller children were nearer to their parents. Her own childhood had never been like this. It was a very organized chaos.

In minutes the conversation turned to other topics. Daniel's final baseball game. How much Andie liked the dance studio. That Norah had agreed to let Kelsey do the portraits at the studio next year.

Kelsey had one hand in her toddler's face holding food and the other stopping Daniel from interrupting his little sister, but she looked happy. "Norah, I'd love to do some dance portraits of you over the summer. At several different times, so they look like they were taken over more time, and you can have them. But I was thinking copies could go up at the studio with my name on them, so by the time portraits come around the parents will know what to expect and have an idea of what they'll be getting."

Norah nodded, and it was decided. As usual, the details would be worked out later. Even she wasn't going to whip out her day-planner at the dinner table.

JD spoke down the long table to his brother, "How's Arlen working out?"

TJ sighed. "Aside from the fact that his name is Arlen?"

They all waited.

"He's getting fired."

That was it. Everyone was talking on top of each other. "When?" "Why?" "What will you do?"

For a moment Norah took pity on him. They wouldn't leave him alone. They didn't see that he was in a bad place they couldn't bring him out of. Even though he joined in at the dinner table, Norah knew how fresh the wound was. Hell, the whole world did. And she remembered the boy he'd been. This wasn't TJ. Not like she'd seen in the music videos, or in interviews.

"He's better than the others. At this rate I think we'll have it figured out by the tenth one."

Norah didn't miss the bitterness that peeked through the covering of irony.

TJ continued, "Aside from being generally intolerable, he sings in the shower."

Huh? She almost said it, but the words came out of Kelsey's mouth. "That's a fireable offense?"

Her own husband answered with a solid "Yes."

It was the expression on his face, the compassion for his brother, that made Norah realize that the singing wasn't some old Hewlitt thing, it was an affront to TJ's situation. She was startled to realize that his career might be over. That his singing voice might have been damaged.

As the conversation turned again, Norah was willingly led along.

Dinner's end was punctuated by a baby's cries and Kelsey popping up from the table, her already slim form dashing down the hall to get her youngest. No wonder the woman regained her figure so quickly, she didn't have time to put food in her mouth.

JD led the oldest kids to clear the table, then sent them all out back to play in the yard. He led Norah and TJ out there as well, with TJ's chair barely fitting through the doors. It had gotten stuck on the threshold out the back door, and quietly, almost unnoticeably, JD had simply lifted the wheels over the slat of wood. TJ had noticed, and he stiffened at the help.

In the fading light, they all sat and waited for Kelsey. JD asked about TJ's therapy. "It goes," was the only response he was given, before TJ turned the conversation to Norah and her dance studio.

She explained that she'd joined the Houston Ballet after her second year of college, leaving her with an unfinished degree, but an amazing opportunity. She toured with the company, then came to visit her Dad and just never left. The job at the dance studio opened up. The owner was looking for someone to hand it off to, and then her grandfather died, leaving her the bulk of his estate. So she had his horses, and a huge collection of antique saddles, tack and a sleigh and buggy of all things. She also had a lump sum of cash that she decided to use to buy the school.

Just then Kelsey emerged with a bright and happy Baby Amy. Norah stiffened at the sight of the small child watching the world around her. But, as she was a female, she was naturally the first one Kelsey turned to, "Norah, can I ask you to hold Amy for a minute or two?"

Her hands went up, palm out, to ward off the little creature Kelsey was already holding out. "I can't."

"Sure you can—"

But TJ was looking at her face, and whatever he saw made him volunteer. "Give her to me, Kelsey."

The baby was settled into his arms, and he looked like an old, if reluctant, pro at it. He didn't coo at the baby or talk to her. Mostly he held her as he would a valuable vase, with care but not communication.

Kelsey pulled her husband off into the back room, and Norah looked up. "What? Did they just go off to make out?"

"Probably." He shifted the baby. "They do that periodically. They've been married too long for this shit."

He didn't even flinch or apologize for swearing in front of the kids.

Her voice was soft with her next question. "Is it bad?"

He didn't ask what she meant, just looked straight ahead at

the backyard. Norah wasn't sure what he was seeing, but it wasn't the kids. "Yeah."

She nodded. "People will tell you that it gets better."

"Does it?"

She shrugged. "You'll find a rhythm."

Kelsey re-emerged with JD in tow and a grin on her face. "Thank you both, for keeping an eye on the kids for just a moment."

It was JD who picked up his youngest daughter, smiling at her, making eye contact and holding her above his head.

Norah saw TJ flinch and wondered if he was thinking that was as dangerous as she did. Babies vomited.

But Kelsey laughed and wrapped her arms around JD's waist. For a moment their world included only the three of them.

Norah's stomach clenched. She stood up, "Thank you for dinner, and for doing the portraits next year. It's been wonderful seeing both of you again." She smiled at JD and down at TJ. "I need to get going. But give me a call and we'll schedule some time for those portraits."

Kelsey nodded at her.

"Me, too. I'm calling it a night." TJ turned the chair and was once again quietly assisted over the threshold by his brother. But Kelsey and JD stayed behind talking.

Norah overheard them.

"Was Lilah as beautiful as Norah?"

Then JD's answering laugh. "She was fourteen—the hottest thing at Sam Rayburn Junior High. And she does not begin to hold a candle to you, baby." Then softer, "No one does."

Norah thought her stomach might turn at the gooey love. She gathered her purse and the lightweight jacket she brought. From behind her came a snort and an under-the-breath, "One of them needs to get something tied."

Norah laughed. It was rude, to be sure, but it captured her

own thoughts entirely. "It sounds like they're on their way to number seven."

"Spare me." He pulled out his cell phone and placed a quick call. But then he didn't move.

She cocked her head to the side, and he explained. "Waiting for my ride."

"I'll wait with you. Want to sit out front?" Quickly she prayed that the porch was level and not a mass of stairs. She hadn't been thinking about wheelchairs when she came in.

"I thought you had to go."

"I had to *leave*," she corrected, "doesn't mean I had anywhere to be." She asked again. "Want to wait outside?"

He shook his head. "Threshold's a bitch. I'm good."

"No you're not. I'll help."

"You can't lift me and this chair." He looked at her like she was nuts.

So she laughed at him. For a moment he looked like the TJ she remembered. "Not over my head, no, but over that threshold, yes."

"No, you can't."

"Then get your butt over here, wheel boy. And we'll just see." She set her purse down and opened the front door for him. He might be right, but the challenge determined her.

She did it. It took everything she had and then some, but she did it. JD had made it look so effortless. But she didn't say that. Not when TJ clearly didn't want help, and just as clearly needed it.

TJ positioned himself to watch the sun sink beyond the hills, and Norah took up point, sitting on the top step.

"Your hair is so long."

"What?" Only as she turned did she realize that he had some of it in his fingers. "Oh, too long."

"It's pretty."

"It's messy. It has curl, but you can't tell."

He nodded at her, clear blue eyes trying to focus on the conversation about the hair, and not notice that he was stuck in an untenable situation. "That I'd like to see."

She grinned. "Maybe next time. I think I can afford a haircut."

"That a problem?"

She looked away. "Yeah, the dance school isn't doing as well as I had hoped. I don't love it like I thought I would."

She waited until his van pulled up, then she said good-bye and climbed back into her old sedan, sad that it was too late for a horseback ride.

The following day she got a phone call.

"Norah, it's me, Kelsey."

She stifled back the sigh that threatened. Who knew what the woman wanted now?

But she didn't have long to wait. "You didn't seem comfortable watching the baby."

"No." *Where in hell was this going?*

"What about grown men?"

"Excuse me?" But even as she asked, Norah understood who Kelsey was talking about. "He doesn't need a babysitter."

She was in the process of hanging up, not thinking about the loss of three students, or the portraits, when the voice pulled her back.

"You're exactly right. That's what makes you perfect."

CHAPTER 8

TJ sat in the middle of his living room staring at his brother. Pissed that JD was staring back. Pissed that JD had the good grace to sit and stare him down at his own height.

"Norah? You are shitting me."

"No, I'm not. She's available, she needs the job. You don't need a real nurse. In a while, you won't need anyone." His brother broke the stare to rest his head in his hands. He looked like he was nursing a foul headache. TJ knew that he was the source of it but didn't think now was the time to give in. "You talked to her the other night. Like *you*. Like you haven't talked to any of the rest of us since the accident."

TJ roared. "That doesn't mean I want her here!"

"You got a thing for her? You've never been attracted to anyone like Norah."

"No, I'm not." He didn't add that JD was wrong. His first serious crush had been on someone very much like Norah: Lilah. "None of this means she should be here."

"Then who?"

"Craig." He didn't know why that fell out of his mouth. He knew and understood JD's protest even before he said it.

"You and Craig would kill each other in a breath. And he's got Shay and the boys. He shouldn't even be here."

"Norah's not strong enough to lift me. If I needed anything, you think I'd holler down the hall for her?"

"I think she'd be great. I think she needs the money. And I think we're running out of options." JD looked him square in the face again.

Son of a Bitch.

"Fine." Maybe she'd run off on her own like nurse number two.

JD just pulled out his cell and called, but unexpectedly he handed the phone to TJ. "It's ringing."

"What?" But her voice was in his ear, and asking "Hello?" before he knew what to say.

"Norah?"

"JD?"

"No, it's TJ." He took a deep breath in. "JD told me they talked to you about living here."

"Well, only for a while. End of the summer at the longest."

"Yeah, something like that." He hoped that would be the end of it.

"If you want me to." She paused. "I don't want to be shoved down your throat."

He took just a moment to appreciate that. She was the only person in this whole mess who seemed to care what he wanted. Not what was best for him, but what he *wanted*. The next words came much easier. "I think it's the best option. Let's try it."

"When do I start?"

"When can you get here? I fired Arlen this morning. He was singing Air Supply. Off-key."

She laughed. "Your property's fenced right?"

He didn't know what that had to do with anything, but he answered. "Yes."

"An hour or two."

He hung up, handing the phone back to JD. His brother fixed grilled cheese sandwiches, and they ate a quiet lunch together before JD left him to wait for Norah by himself.

For an hour he was the only one there. It happened so rarely that it was a wonder. Inside of fifteen minutes he was bored, and he began to watch his feet for twitches. Somehow this was more interesting than anything else. Even though nothing ever happened.

He heard the gate at the end of the drive. It creaked something awful, but it wasn't like he was going to get down there and fix it. And he wasn't going to ask Norah to be his handy-man.

Looking out the window he got a shock. Norah had arrived, atop a brown and white horse. The hooves made rhythmic clops on his paved driveway, and Norah stayed her saddle with a gentle sway in time with the horse's gait. When she reached the front, she dismounted in one smooth motion. Her foot lifted gracefully from the stirrup, and he understood, of course it did, she was a dancer.

She was tall enough to easily lift her bags from where she had tied them behind the saddle, then she led her horse around to the side. With curiosity, he watched as she undid the saddle and slipped off the bridle, leaving the halter in place. Then she pulled a brush from one bag and began combing down the horse. It had a look on its face of a petted dog. She gave the horse a nuzzle and a pat on the rump before she turned to grab her bags and come inside.

She was startled to see him watching her out the window. "Oh, TJ. I hope you don't mind my transportation. You're fenced, and he eats grass. I'll pick up after him, I should have asked first, I—"

He held up a hand. "It's fine."

He showed her to her room, even offering to carry her bags

for her. He was far too pleased when she let him. And he laughed when she crinkled her nose at the back room. "Oh, I can't do this. I can't live in here."

She made it sound as though she was going to leave, and he laughed.

"No, TJ. I think I'm serious. That's disgusting. All those ruffles. Uhhhph."

"You can do whatever you want with it."

"Really?"

At his nod she waltzed into the room, and pulled down the ruffles riding the tops of the windows. She peeled back the comforter and shoved it under the bed. She pulled a sham off a pillow before tossing the other two at him to do the same. He obliged while she plucked the doilies off the dresser tops. The cross-stitch eagle came off the wall.

He threw the now naked pillows back onto her bed, and offloaded her luggage there, too. Finally she stopped and looked around. "Okay, maybe I can stay. At least I won't have nightmares now."

He laughed again.

She made dinner with the things Kelsey had stocked in his fridge. Meatloaf with peas and French bread. She found them both trays and insisted they eat on the front porch, watching the sunset. Norah sat below him, on the small edge next to the front ramp.

Only as he finished the meal did he see it. "You cut your hair."

She nodded. "Told you it had curl."

It did, big loopy ones, even though the hair still brushed her shoulders. It was a true ebony with hints of blue, not like his own deep brown. He would have thought she colored it, but he remembered her and Lilah as kids having that same hair. "It's a really beautiful color, too."

"Thank you. I'll tell my mom, she's the one who gave it to me." Norah paused. "Of course, she gave it to Lilah first."

He laughed. "I never thought of it that way. But I know what you mean. I look so much like JD."

"Nah. I can see where people would mistake you, but you're so different."

He changed the topic. "How is Lilah?"

Norah's response shocked him. "She's a slut. Like always."

"What?" He blinked. "Lilah was the sweetest girl."

"Oh, please." She even turned to look at him for that one.

"She was not a slut, she dated JD for three years."

Norah had been raising her glass of milk to her mouth, and almost managed to drop it. "Oh my god. You don't know. Does JD?"

"Know what?"

"Lilah only dated him because Mom made her. Mom wanted her dating a good Catholic boy. She wanted them to get married, and make her and your mom grandparents together. But Lilah only did it because it kept Mom off her back. She was running around on your brother the whole time." She did manage to take a sip of her drink this time. "I thought everyone knew that Davidson girl was a slut."

"*That Davidson girl* could also refer to you, you know."

Norah nodded. "No real harm in the truth."

TJ was shocked. Those two girls had been at church in white dresses in the front row every week. Their grades had been perfect. Lilah and Norah had both excelled at ballet. "You, too?"

This time she was sheepish. His world shattered.

But she called him on it. "Come off it TJ. Even together we haven't done the same damage as you. Your slut exploits make the news."

He laughed. "True."

"Speaking of, where's Anna Lee?"

Norah deserved the unvarnished truth. If for no reason other than simply being real.

"Nowhere to be found. She was just a date for events." He laughed. "And another notch on my bedpost."

"See? You are a slut."

CHAPTER 9

Norah had been doing her research on TJ's spinal cord injury. And it was either surf the net or go stark raving mad from boredom. It wasn't like she was even taking him to his therapy. He refused to go.

She hauled TJ out to go grocery shopping one day, more for fun than for food. That's how bad it was.

What she was learning from her research was that TJ was making his own life worse. He needed to be in therapy. He had a chance at a full recovery. She was armed to the teeth a week later when she confronted him. She waited until he was ready and they were on the porch, then grabbed the keys to the handi-van, as he'd dubbed it. "Let's go."

"Where are we going?"

"Therapy."

"Yours?" He looked at her with that blank look like he knew what she was doing.

"Yours."

"Sorry." He turned away.

"TJ you need to go. You can get your old life back. You just have to work at it."

His jaw was steel. "And if it doesn't work?"

"Then at least you'll be able to say that you tried!" *What was wrong with him?*

What was wrong with her? For the life of her she couldn't figure out why she cared. So Norah simply left him there on the front porch. She dropped her keys and her purse and left them where they fell. Walking down the front ramp she decided that she'd just saddle Thunder and ride away.

He called to her back. "It's not your life, Norah."

Damn him. Damn him for making her mad. She turned back to face him. "So you're going to waste yours just to prove that point to the rest of us?"

His tone of voice was a mockery of the words he spoke. "Handicapped people can be a useful part of society nowadays."

"You need to go to therapy. You don't have to be in that chair. You can sing with Wilder again. So what if therapy sucks? These sessions will make that possible."

"Therapy doesn't work if I don't cooperate." His tone again told her he was simply repeating what he'd been told. He'd completely disengaged from the conversation.

She didn't know where it came from. Only that she was angrier than she had ever been in her life. And she'd been as angry as him once. "How dare you!"

She stormed up the ramp, an avenging angel, or more likely demon. "How dare you waste this chance!" When she was within striking distance, she did. She hauled back and slapped him across the face the hardest she'd ever hit anybody in her life. "You have no idea how much I wish I had another chance. I wish I was you! I *wish* I was in that chair, that I could fix what was wrong."

He opened his mouth but she steamrolled him.

"I had a husband and a baby! And they got killed. I would give anything to be able to fix that." She motioned to his chair even as the tears formed. "I'd take that in a heartbeat. I'd give my legs and my arms, forever, for one more day, one more hour. So you shut up about how bad it is. You stop sitting here and feeling sorry for yourself, you get your sad ass to therapy and fix your problem!"

She was practically screaming. And she was shaking.

He'd even stopped rubbing his jaw.

But she had to get herself together. It had been so long since she'd had any kind of outburst, since she'd said or done anything to acknowledge that part of her life. She stalked off, thinking again how nice it would be to saddle Thunder and ride away.

TJ's voice pulled her back. "I'd take what you have in a heartbeat."

That stopped her and made her blood run cold. "No you wouldn't. You lost your legs. Get over it. I had my heart ripped out. And it's never come back."

"That's just it. You had someone who loved you. For how long?"

"Five years."

"Whatever pain you're in, it's because someone loved you for five years. I've never had that—not for a day. So you can go to hell."

He was turning to go inside. But the porch wasn't wide enough for a graceful exit, he had to turn and maneuver a couple of times. Norah came back to the porch, breathing deeply, tears running down her face.

"Don't go." She didn't wait for his reply, just sat herself back down on the edge of the porch, where she usually watched the sunset.

She felt his hand in her hair before she heard him. "We're a sad pair aren't we? Just drowning in our sorrows."

He still didn't speak, so she grabbed his hand and held her cheek against the back of it. His skin was smooth and warm, and she closed her eyes. Her father was the only one who'd been able to comfort her. She wasn't even sure if this was comfort now.

But she took another breath and tried again. "TJ, I want you to go to therapy. Please."

"Why?"

Somehow she knew that her answer mattered. That what she said would change things, one way or another. "Because this isn't you."

"You don't know me."

"Yes, I do. I hear your voice on the radio, and I remember what you were like."

He sighed. "What if I fail? How would you handle it if you'd tried to rescue them and you'd failed?"

She nodded. "I wouldn't be able to live with myself. But I wouldn't be able to live with myself if I'd had the opportunity and never tried. Trying and succeeding is the only survivable option. But not trying is guaranteed failure."

She looked up at him. Again wondering why she'd gotten involved. "Why would you fail? TJ, you've never failed. You made everyone in school do whatever you wanted. You got a punk-slash-country band on the radio, crossing over into the pop market. The world has to watch out when you decide what you're going to do. It's in the basket."

He laughed. She wondered what he'd decided. And why it mattered.

CHAPTER 10

TJ watched as another truck appeared at the front door with yet another medical logo on it. The neighbors had to wonder what the hell was going on out here. Another man in another uniform got another big box out and dollied it up the front ramp.

Norah, as usual, met him, signed for it and looked excited. She had done far more to heal him than he had. But he had logged the hours, and the hours were excruciating. Some of the exercises were ridiculous, some embarrassing, and some downright painful. But he did them.

Sometimes therapy was awful because it was so boring. He spent hours each day in a hot pool with a therapist bending and flexing limbs that didn't work. With Norah's help, of course, he was laid out on what they affectionately referred to as 'the rack' and tilted at various angles. He was hooked up to wires and given electrical stimulation to each of his muscles. Where he could see, if not feel, them twitch.

All of this was designed to keep his muscles limber and his blood flowing, so that when the feeling returned, he'd have something he could use.

So far, nothing had returned.

The therapy was also to keep him healthy while he was paralyzed. He'd been doing his own research. This process was all about keeping unused limbs from getting sores, blood clots, infections, or any of a host of other problems.

He liked Norah's assessment of him: that he could take on the world and it had better watch out. He didn't know if she was right, but he chose to believe it.

And Norah had stuck.

Far superior to any of her three predecessors, Norah seemed to understand. She had empathy. And no wonder. In the end, he figured he really did have it easier than she had. Although the only comparison he could muster was imagining if his brother lost Kelsey. That thought alone was enough to bring him almost to tears for what JD would go through. For all he hated putting up with their hand-holding and nuzzling and hiding in a corner to make out, he loved his brother, and his brother *loved* Kelsey.

Norah had endured another plate smashing. She had walked in right after he'd broken two and was throwing the third. He had frozen as she appeared in the doorway, time slowing as he watched the plate sail against the wall, all of a foot away from her. She flinched as it hit, shattering and spraying shards. But she was Norah, and she simply wiped away the smears of blood on her leg, and walked over to where the plates were stacked on the counter.

She picked up the top one and held the rim in her fingertips, as though it were an old record. She turned partly away from him, holding the plate out as though it might bite, and let it go.

It wasn't the strong, physical release he had gotten from flinging them. But a quieter, softer letting go that told him worlds about what was still inside her. When it shattered at her bare feet, spots of blood showed where the shards had nicked her again, but she didn't care. She simply picked up another plate and handed it to him.

He handed it back, the desire to break something had fled the instant blood welled on her legs.

Norah broke the remaining two plates without a word. Lifting each one high and just letting it go. She seemed more interested in the physics of it, in watching the shards skitter and jump, than she did in letting off any steam. There was no steam in her—just a quiet desire to watch things shatter.

Later, they swept it up together. She had handed him the broom, and taken up the dustpan for herself.

That was when he realized what was better about Norah than any of the nurses. She just assumed he was capable. There were none of the preformed ideas about what patients with his condition could and couldn't do. She just gave him her bags to carry, or asked him to fetch her something, or handed him the broom.

She had even laughed later that evening when she fixed dinner, only to realize they had nothing to eat on. They went plate shopping, with his money of course, but Norah still rejected several styles simply because they didn't look like they would break well.

And now, she jumped up and down like a kid because some big box had arrived for him.

He sighed, wondering what kind of torture device he'd gotten now. He was partly grateful that he and his brother were wealthy enough to afford all these sick playthings. He could have been doing this at the mercy of the state or insurance adjusters. "What's in the box?"

"A stander."

"The stander, huh?" He wasn't sure what to make of the thing. It was exactly like it sounded—a robotic stand-up wheelchair.

Sitting in his chair was bad; he was shorter than everyone else, and he was used to being a tall man. If he was standing, he'd regain his usual height, and then some. It would be just as awkward, but taller.

Norah was already cutting the box open in the middle of the living room, simply hacking at the sides rather than tipping it. He worried sometimes about the things she lifted. But she was much stronger than her willowy frame gave hint to.

She handed him a box cutter, and while they were hacking at it another delivery truck arrived. "Get that, will you?"

He put down the cutter and opened the front door to a man with a pristine folded wheelchair. The man didn't wait for a question or 'hello.' He must have taken one look at TJ in his chair and known he was delivering to the right place. "Sign for this?"

As soon as he did, the man disappeared back into his truck, leaving TJ with the chair and no good way to carry it. Eventually he got it lifted and settled, then backed his own chair into the living room. "Norah, what is this?"

She glanced back at him, "Lightweight chair."

"Thank you." His sarcasm said he could see that much. "Why?"

She grinned, her full lips and wide smile showing just how excited she was over his new wheelchair. "Look!"

She popped the thing open with just a flick of her wrists. Somehow the chair managed to look both technologically new and old-fashioned at the same time. "It's skinnier, you'll fit more places."

"It's manual." He countered.

She threw him the most taken-aback face he'd ever seen on her. "What? You're not strong enough to work this thing?"

Then, with no warning, she hopped in it, propped her feet up, and raced away from him. She was gone around the back, and he couldn't keep up. He was at the mercy of the battery and the layout of the house. There were no straight open paths to build up any speed.

He heard the crash in the back room and laughed. Until Norah shouted. "Ow!"

He arrived to find her near tears and nursing her elbow, but really none the worse for wear. "I think that right there is a really good reason for me not to use that thing." But he pulled her arm away and looked over the elbow. She hadn't broken any skin, but she probably would sport a bruise by tomorrow.

True to form, she frowned at him. "What are you afraid of, getting buff?"

"I'm plenty buff." Of course, the moment it was out of his mouth, he realized it was an old reaction. His legs weren't, not anymore. His arms were okay, but not what they had been.

Norah's cocked head and her clear gaze told him she realized exactly that. She reached out from her chair to his and grabbed his biceps. "This powered chair is turning you into a girly man. You could be ripped."

He hadn't been lifting weights, it was dangerous with his weak grasp. And he wasn't powering himself around except with the little joystick at the arm of his chair. He sighed. "JD and I discussed this. People get their fingers caught in the spokes all the time. I might recover, but then not have use of my crushed fingers."

She sniffed and rubbed her elbow. "I know, that's why I ordered this one." Reaching down, she demonstrated, flipping the two handles out and back in flush against the side of the chair.

With a look, he realized that he could either use the circular railing that ran along the rim, or use the handles, to power the wheels. "All right, we'll try it. Back in the living room so we can trade."

"Sweet." She grabbed the wheel rims, unconcerned for her own fingers, and raced off more like a kid than a grown woman, bruised elbow forgotten.

CHAPTER 11

"Wow."

Norah looked up, startled by the voice. "I know, but it's how I dance. And Kelsey said this one was supposed to look like practice." She knew she looked odd to anyone who hadn't danced more than casually.

TJ looked her up and down, trying to figure out what she was wearing. Just a sleeveless plum leotard, with gray thick-knit leggings that folded over at her waist and puddled around her ankles for the best warmth.

"What's that shirt?"

"Old dancer's trick." She held her arm out for him to finger the fabric of the clingy sleeve. "It's tights."

He blinked. "I clearly don't know anything about ballet, but I'm confident tights go on the other end of your body."

The laugh just came out. "Not when you're a dancer. Anything goes anywhere it needs to for easy movement and warm loose muscles. See?" She explained how you just cut the legs off the tights at the knee, then cut the crotch out in a big circle, turned it upside down, and voila, shirt with a built in bra. "Warmth without heat, built-in stretch for movement. This is good stuff. What's funny is that the dance stores sell them for about ten times the price of cutting your own."

He fingered the fabric a little more before she reclaimed her arm, "Come on, let's go."

He had therapy to get to, and she was meeting Kelsey at ten thirty.

But he stopped her again. "What's with the pants? It's ninety outside."

"I know. But it's not ninety in the studio. This is what I dance in. And," she added, "I haven't worked out in a while, so I need to be plenty warm before I get there. Let's get."

He conceded, using the new manual chair to get down the front incline and up the access ramp into the van. When they arrived at the treatment center, Norah simply stopped at the curb and waited while he let himself down. It would be faster if she came around, but she got the impression from him that he didn't want the help.

So she smiled when he pushed the access ramp back up and closed the door. Then she felt guilty because she was glad to not go with him today. She knew it was her job, and she knew she was keeping him motivated when she went. But he often fell. Each time she and the therapist would watch him drag himself back up and try again. Each time he did, more determined than the last.

The first time the therapist had held her back from reaching for him, her heart had broken. She still felt guilty about yelling at him on the porch that day, because on some level he was right. Maybe it was better to be her. She would heal eventually, wouldn't she? But he didn't know if he would. And she'd had no idea, when she slapped him and told him to 'fix his problem,' just how much back-breaking, heart-breaking labor went into getting better.

So far they hadn't seen any progress.

He was stronger. He was healthier.

But she'd caught him trying to touch his fingers to his thumbs and not able to do it. His feet still didn't twitch. Periodically, she would bump or touch his leg, on purpose, to see if he would notice. He never did.

She parked in front of the dance studio, shoving thoughts of TJ out of her head. There was a summer camp having practice in one of the rooms. At least it made her some money.

It also meant that the air conditioning would be on. Which was good, because TJ was right and the thick knit pants were making her blast the air in the car as the sun beat down.

Quietly, she let herself into the unused studio room and flipped the lights. Instantly the room looked ten times larger, the lights illuminating not only the room itself but its reflected counterparts on three walls. Barres lined two, and Norah breathed deep. There was rosin for the pointe shoes, a lingering scent of leather and satin, and wood from the floor. The specialized floor was built with a wood plank surface pressed down over several feet of foam and bolted there. If you laid on your belly at the doorway you could see the slight upward bow in the middle of the room, and when tap classes all worked in time, the whole floor bounced.

Norah smiled. It was hers.

She set down her bag and dug out her ponytail holders. With a few quick flips of her wrist, she had her hair up. She turned her music on, situating herself in the middle of the floor as she pulled on worn ballet shoes.

Just sitting there, she realized that she hadn't been here since she'd taken the job with TJ. And that had been too long. She warmed up, wondering what she'd lost while she hadn't been paying attention. She started with simple ballet stretches and exercises.

At ten, when Kelsey didn't show, she practiced turns. Then leg lifts.

"Holy shit!"

Norah jerked at the sound of the voice, and found Kelsey standing in the doorway, her camera in hand and looking already used.

Kelsey spoke again. "I am so sorry I startled you, I was getting the best shots, but damn, I don't think you could push my leg that high, let alone have me just lift it and hold it there."

That was typical Kelsey, it seemed. No wonder JD loved the woman. She was taking pictures unbeknownst to her subject, but she just made it all okay. "I was a principle dancer with the Houston Ballet for three years. It's a requirement."

"Well, I am damned impressed."

"You swear a lot for a woman who looks as wholesome as you do." Norah motioned to the Ellie-May style pigtails and jeans.

Kelsey shrugged. "There aren't any kids around."

"Actually, there's a summer camp in the next room."

"Oh, crap."

Norah laughed.

But Kelsey shook it off. "Can you do that again?"

"Of course." Norah turned to the mirror out of habit, her feet automatically locking into a clean fifth position, and her arm held out for balance. She lifted her right leg with her toe at her knee, and then extended her leg out sideways and lifted, ending with her knee nearly touching her shoulder.

Kelsey snapped photos.

Norah held.

She was used to this, she had posed for calendars and ads and stills when she was with the ballet. Although it had been a while, it came back. The major difference was that Kelsey was not a dance photographer. She didn't know the terminology, and didn't know how to get Norah to do what she wanted without resorting to "like the last time" and "that thing with your leg back". So Norah began educating her in the phrasing.

That way when Kelsey came back to work with the students, her life would be much easier.

Kelsey had her re-do the warm-ups, finding some of that photo-worthy. Then went through most of the routine again with her pointe shoes on. The morning was punctuated by a few little 'Jesus's and 'wow's from Kelsey.

Norah held back her grins. She hadn't atrophied too badly while at TJ's. For the first time in a long time, she simply enjoyed the stretch of muscles under her skin. She was grateful for her own body—that it responded to her commands and did it gracefully.

She shut down the photo session at one. She was hungry and she had to go get TJ, she explained. Kelsey stopped her and fished in her purse for a moment, before producing a check. "I don't know what you've done, but it's working."

Norah fingered the check, she didn't really like getting paid for it.

Kelsey saw. "Feeling guilty about taking the money?"

Norah nodded. "I took the job for the cash. I need it. But what I'm doing is being a friend. It seems wrong to get paid for that."

With a nod, Kelsey started setting her stuff down. She plucked the check from Norah's fingers and, before a protest was even possible, shredded it and pocketed the evidence. "You're right. It is wrong to get paid for that."

Norah was stuck in limbo. She felt better that she wasn't getting paid for it. It hadn't seemed right. But she needed the money, and technically it was owed to her.

Then Kelsey pulled out her checkbook. "You're right. You're the best at it because you aren't doing a job. You're a good friend. You expect things out of him and he does it." She kept talking while she wrote, but Norah didn't know what was coming. "JD and I couldn't get that out of him, and we love him more than you could know. Probably more than he could know.

There isn't enough money in the world to thank you for what you've accomplished."

She handed it to Norah. "I know you'll stay while you can. And I don't mean that as pressure. It's just who you are. Thank you."

With that, Kelsey said good-bye and gathered her things. Norah didn't look at the check until she had turned out the lights, waved at the camp director through the room window, and climbed into the car. While she waited for the air conditioning to take effect, she unfolded the slip of paper.

The check was for a larger lump sum than the whole summer should have paid her. In the note line were three scrawled words: *late Christmas present*.

CHAPTER 12

If TJ had been thinking up tortures for a man in a wheelchair he would have automatically come up with 'make caretaker an exotic beauty'. He wouldn't have thought to add that she should smell like warm sunshine and something that made him think of sex. Of course, part of the torture was that he didn't function below the waist anymore.

He had been in therapy for a month and a half, and he hadn't felt the first sensation or seen the first movement. He spent his days in the hot pool and hauling himself around sadistic jungle gyms, but he never would have thought up the torture he was enduring now. And no one was torturing him. Not on purpose. Either she'd only recently started doing it, or he only just noticed it now.

Norah was dancing around the house. He'd gotten up one night for a drink, and found her with her foot on the kitchen counter, stretched over her long, lean leg while she waited for toast.

All the floors in the house were wood—smooth surfaces for the wheelchair to function better. Also, apparently, for Norah to practice her turns. She stretched in the mornings. She could pull her leg up and hold it over her head with the opposite hand. It lacked that undefinable quality that made people flinch at contortionists. On her it was graceful.

She would sit on the floor with her legs out almost to the side of her. What had made his jaw drop was that her torso was flat on the floor, too. When he'd questioned her, she had simply turned her head sideways, peeking out at him, and talked to him as though this were a perfectly comfortable position.

He didn't think he'd ever had a woman who could do that.

Aside from the fantasies it was spawning—fantasies that he was incapable of doing *anything* about—it was making him jealous. What better torture for a paraplegic than to live with a dancer? Her limbs were lean, strong, and healthy, and responded to her wishes.

And TJ suffered.

On the one hand he was grateful that her dance school reopened in another seven weeks. On the other, he wondered what he'd do without her.

"Jesus, Norah."

She was on the living room floor, in jeans, in the splits. And apparently the splits alone weren't enough. So here was a twenty-eight year old siren, on his wood floor, bent first over her front leg, then tipping back to touch her head to the sole of her raised foot.

She made it within an inch, and growled in frustration. It was all he could do to tone the bark down to a laugh. She gave him a dirty look, and switched legs. The thing was, she didn't so much switch legs as simply leave them where they were and just swivel to facing the other direction.

This time her foot and head made contact, with the toe of her sock touching her forehead. "Ah-ha!"

"Christ!" That hurt just watching her. He watched his own

feet for a minute. He'd have been happy if they just responded to a single wish. So he changed the subject. "How did you get started dancing?"

"Lilah did."

"That's it? You were a principal dancer with a ballet company because your sister did it?"

"She didn't get that far." Norah pulled herself up off the floor, looking like the stretches hadn't affected her any. "Whatever Lilah did, I did. Dancing, getting good grades, even lusting after JD."

"Oh, that's sad."

"Please! I saw you panting after her. You should have said something. She probably would have been glad to give you whatever you wanted."

He decided to drop the conversation of Norah wanting JD. It bothered him somewhere south of his stomach. "You based your whole life off what your sister did?"

"No! And that's the pot calling the kettle black."

He jerked as her statement hit him.

Then he nodded. "Does that make me the pot or the kettle?"

Her eyebrows went up. "You're the pot, I'm the kettle."

A week and a half later he woke up screaming in the middle of the night. He grabbed for his calf, the pain crushing. In his dream, the truck had rolled over his left leg.

Footsteps pounded down the hallway, lights were thrown on in time to the feet. His door crashed open and Norah appeared silhouetted in the hallway light.

He fought for control but lost. A harsh sound pushed through his teeth, and that brought her instantly to his bedside.

She flung back the covers with no measure for propriety, his blue boxer briefs the only thing on him. But he was with Norah, and this was no time for niceties. It felt like his leg was being shredded. In rough words, he told her so.

"I'll get your medication." And she was gone, footsteps pounding their urgency down the hardwood floors.

His fingers clenched on his leg as Norah returned. She moved so fast she was in danger of spilling the water she had brought. She thrust the pills and the cup to his hands, but he refused.

She attempted to put them into his mouth herself, but again he shook his head, refusing.

"TJ?"

He gulped for air, unable to remember any pain like this. "My leg hurts. I can *feel* it."

In her surprise, she dropped the water. Luckily it bounced off the side of the bed and went onto the floor. But Norah didn't go after it.

She gulped air herself, then squealed like a school-girl. "Oh my God!"

For a brief moment she threw her arms around him in glee. But, between breaths, he pushed out more words. "It hurts—I don't want medication—don't want to make the feeling go away—but it hurts."

She peeled his hands away and replaced them with her own. In seconds she was sending shooting pains up his leg. His stomach clenched, but his brain was grateful for the sensation.

Norah pushed him onto his back while she worked. She massaged the whole leg, her fingers small but strong against his skin. That he could feel her touch through everything else was a wonder as well.

When she had massaged every muscle she could reach, and some he hadn't known existed, she grabbed his foot and started rotating his ankle and bending and flexing his knee and hip.

TJ gulped. That sent another pain shooting up. He hadn't

realized that some of the pain had subsided until it shot up again. Still, Norah kept working with steady hands against his too-solid muscles, and never complained.

By now they both knew that muscle spasms, where the muscles just clenched and stayed taut, weren't uncommon to his injury. He just hadn't thought they'd feel like this. But her hands were sure and skillful, and TJ took a moment to be grateful it was a dancer in his house. That was probably how she knew what to do. Surely she'd had her legs seize up on her after a full day.

He tried to breathe.

He didn't realize she'd been at it for an hour, or he would have stopped her. What he did realize was that her hands were all over his leg. While it wasn't sexual, it wasn't impersonal either. She wasn't his therapist, and didn't act like it.

For the first time, in the light from the hallway, he saw that she was mussed. Her hair made a messy halo around her head. Her shirt had gathered up at one side, exposing smooth olive skin. She was wearing men's boxers. They didn't reach all the way to her waist, revealing that she had one. It had been easy to mistake her build for skinny, but her height allowed her to be both slim and curvy. And her hands were slowly massaging their way up his leg.

TJ bolted up and brushed her hands off, replacing them with his own. As she slid away, flexing her own fingers to work out the kinks, her shirt shifted again, covering exposed skin and revealing new. She also looked down and realized she was only half clothed, but she didn't blush or fluster. "I'm going to go grab my robe."

He nodded, still working the kinks out of his leg.

Standing, the sleep clothes clinging, she walked out of the room. The last thing he saw of her as she disappeared through the doorway was long, lean legs and a sweet ass.

A bolt of lust hit him hard. And he felt it where he hadn't felt anything for a while. Looking down, he saw that he was indeed rock solid. It wasn't just his leg that had come back.

Norah, it seemed, was a miracle worker.

But he pulled the covers across and hid his erection.

It was a wise decision as she reappeared in his doorway all of five seconds later. He'd expected her robe to be terry cloth and bulky. Instead she was in a shimmery, silk-like fabric that belted at her waist and fell to only halfway down her thighs. She seemed to think it was appropriate, so he didn't say anything.

Norah cleaned up the spill on the floor, then fetched them both ice water. He enjoyed the feel of the sheets on his leg, and of Norah poking him periodically. Her face lit up when he reacted.

"I've been poking you for weeks. This is the first time you've noticed."

"You have?"

"It wasn't working so I didn't say anything."

He nodded. Then jumped.

She giggled, and held up the ice cube she'd touched to his skin.

"You!"

"You felt it!"

He sighed, it was hard to be mad at her.

She massaged his leg for him again as the night wore on. But neither of them went back to bed, she stayed perched at his bedside for hours.

It was close to dawn when he started feeling his body pull him toward sleep, and he was almost there when Norah nudged him. "TJ look."

She pointed at his foot.

He didn't feel anything. He didn't see anything happening to his foot that he should be feeling. And he still couldn't make it move. So he lay his head back down.

"TJ."

"What?"

"Watch."

Sure enough. His foot twitched.

CHAPTER 13

Norah stood over TJ. She wanted to be upset, but he was asleep and there was something boyish and sweet about it. With the return of sensation in one leg, TJ renewed his attack on therapy. When he got home he often hauled himself out of the chair now, sitting on the couch and unwinding, rather than being stuck.

He had no more control over his body than he had the week before, but he had more hope, and more determination. Norah figured 'hope' wasn't a word TJ was familiar with; he just plowed ahead, and believed.

Now he was curled on the sofa and passed out cold. Dark lashes fanned his bronzed cheeks and a five o'clock shadow made him look a little disreputable. Not that he needed any help in that department. While the brothers looked enough alike to make people believe they might be twins, JD had always looked wholesome, and something about TJ said he was the one your mother warned you about. It was there, even when he was asleep on the couch.

Still, she had to wake him, TJ insisted that they go to JD and Kelsey's for dinner, and that they show up early. So she reached out, making contact with his bare arm. Her brain caught as she felt the muscle underneath. She'd told him to use this opportunity to buff up his arms. In true TJ fashion, he'd used that suggestion only as a starting point. In a number of weeks the man had become ripped.

She tried not to notice. "TJ?"

When he didn't respond, she shook him harder.

His hand batted hers away and went back to what it had been doing. She hadn't realized it at first, but his fingers were playing guitar in his sleep.

She blinked and looked closer. It was funny, him playing air guitar in his sleep. She laughed, and he shook himself, blinking sleepy eyes at her. "What time is it?"

His words had that hazy quality of unpolished brain.

"Time to go, if you want to get there early."

He nodded and his vision cleared a little more.

He levered himself into his chair, then rolled to the bathroom to brush his hair and his teeth, before showing up at the front door and declaring himself ready. Norah barely had time to grab her purse.

He was faster into and out of the van than he'd been even last week. The bumps in the sidewalk meant nothing to him now; he just powered over them.

When JD greeted them at the front door, ready to pull his brother up the steps, TJ refused, surprising both Norah and JD. But his words were more shocking. "We're going for a walk first, just around the block."

"Okay." She didn't know why they'd come to the door then, but TJ wasn't done.

He turned to his brother. "Will you take Norah's purse inside? And will you bring us Amy? I think she'd like to come along."

"Amy?"

Norah wasn't sure if it was her voice or his brother's that

uttered that. But TJ nodded, certain of what he was doing. She was just along for the ride, she realized.

JD didn't understand either but did as asked, fetching the baby and handing her over. This time when TJ held her, he made real contact with his niece. She replied in the form of a bubbly smile.

He struggled with holding the baby in one arm, and operating the chair with the other. But he made it all the way down the drive and out beyond the hedges onto the street. Norah walked silently beside him.

TJ waited until they were well beyond the front gate. "Norah, Amy wants you to hold her."

"No." It came so easily. "I don't do babies."

"Yeah, that's a problem."

She didn't see where it was. But it was TJ, and he managed to stop her dead in her tracks. "Were you a good mother?"

Her breath stopped in her chest and it took a moment to formulate even a simple answer. "I guess so."

"Then why don't you hold babies?"

"Don't be stupid, TJ." She wouldn't look at him, just started walking away.

"Norah, you have to come back. It's your turn."

"I don't need a turn holding babies." She was actually calculating how far it was to walk from here to TJ's house. She could make it.

"It's your turn for therapy, Norah. I have to do it, and so do you."

"No, I don't."

"Why not? You're just as broken as I am."

Her eyes closed. *Maybe more so.* The man knew where to hit her, and he didn't pull punches. "You're not being a very good role model for me."

"Who said I was your role model?" Her hands clenched into

fists. She wasn't an idiot, she knew that was just a sign of how much this scared her.

"I do."

"Well that's just stupid." She still harbored some hope that she could talk her way out of this. The thought alone was making her heart beat faster.

"If you don't do your therapy, I won't do mine."

"You're a bastard, TJ."

"Yes. Come hold the baby."

Her eyes opened. He'd come down to blackmail. Part of her was so tempted to just walk away. Let him stop going to therapy. His decision, not hers. But her fingernails were biting into her palms, and her chest was tight. So she forced herself to walk toward him and Baby Amy.

The poor thing was being held up by her uncle like some little sacrificial lamb. But Norah put her hands out.

The weight of the infant settled into her palms, but she felt it everywhere. For some reason Amy trusted her. She looked up with eyes the shade of deep blue that most babies came with, and she grinned.

Norah felt it flood her. She knew what to do with babies. She'd had her own for so long, and for so little. Her chest clenched and she put Baby Amy to her shoulder, bouncing her and talking to her.

"I hate you, TJ."

"Why? Because you obviously like this. You are good at it."

She bounced the baby a little more. "Because I was right." She breathed in the soft clean smell that only babies have, and she was flooded again. "I didn't avoid babies because I don't like them, I avoided them because I know I'll get attached." She snuggled Amy in closer. "Apparently this is really all it takes for me."

She patted the little back that wasn't as wide as her hand. "I see Kelsey with all her kids. She just keeps having them, because she doesn't know. She's never had one ripped away. She's so casual with them."

A car drove past them. Norah heard it, but it didn't break past the boundaries created by her and the baby.

"Come here. Sit down."

She opened her eyes to see TJ indicating his lap. She almost couldn't move. When she finally sat down, his hands came up and brushed at her face smearing the wetness there. She hadn't realized that she'd been crying.

Eventually they walked back to the house. Norah held Amy most all of the evening. She thought she'd caught TJ saying something to Kelsey and JD, but she wasn't sure, and they didn't try to take the baby away.

She made it through handing Amy over at the end of the visit. She couldn't ask TJ to drive, so she managed to keep it together on the way home. He asked her a few more questions when they got in, but she was exhausted from being so tense all evening, and upset that it had been so hard to hand Amy back. So she told him good-night and closed her door.

She dreamed of Jordan's blue eyes, so like her own. She dreamed of his small giggle. She felt his little hand curl into hers as she walked ahead pulling him along and not paying enough attention to him. And she woke up as red-eyed as she went to sleep.

Norah showered and tried to hide her yawns. Mostly she tried to ignore TJ and his questions. By noon he had given up asking them, as she had successfully avoided him most of the morning.

Until she heard a loud, horrid chord and something that was a cross between an off-tune ping and a sharp twang. It could only be a guitar string breaking.

Norah headed into the living room, wondering what he'd done.

Sure enough, he sat in a dining room chair, facing away from the table, the guitar clenched so hard she was surprised it was only a string that had snapped. The offending wire stood out at both ends in bent escape.

"What's wrong?"

"I still can't play. I've been working my fingers, trying to make them respond, but they don't move separately. I thought maybe I could get some sound out of it even with these hands, but I can't."

Norah didn't comment. She understood that his definition of 'sound' was different than other people's.

As he set the guitar aside, she saw that she was a fool. She'd watched him play in his sleep yesterday and never realized that his fingers had moved individually. Apparently, he hadn't realized it either. "TJ, you can play."

"No, I can't. Not yet anyway."

"You can. I—" She didn't know why she didn't tell him what she had seen.

"You what?"

"I know you can." How did she get TJ to let his fingers work? It had to be some kind of mental block, because he'd done it while asleep. The nerves had to be connected. "I'll bet you they work."

"You're going to bet me what?"

"Five hundred dollars."

"Norah."

"Five hundred dollars says your fingers work."

He held up his hand and twitched the fingers for her. The final three moved only in concert. "They don't. You lose."

"Funny." She frowned at him, glad for something to distract her from the big hit of baby lust that had swamped her last night. "I have twenty-four hours to make your fingers work. I win, you owe me five hundred dollars. I lose, I pay you."

His brows raised. "This is a bet? If I win, I get money, which, to be honest, I couldn't give a crap about. But if you win, my fingers work. I'm in."

Her mind was occupied for the rest of the day. She tried everything. She made him chop vegetables. She made him try braiding ribbons. She set him at the table and made him mock playing the piano. Nothing worked.

He either failed at the task or did it exceptionally well—using only his first two fingers. He was thoroughly disheartened, and so was she. He knew she didn't really have five hundred dollars to spare. She just had to figure out how to make it happen.

They both went to bed frustrated.

In the middle of the night Norah woke up. She knew how she'd do it, and she laughed.

CHAPTER 14

TJ sank down on the couch. It was pretty obvious that Norah had given up on his hands. She'd seemed sure enough to make him wonder what she knew. But nothing last evening worked and she hadn't even given him any silly tasks this morning.

The problem was, she didn't seem upset. He would have wondered what she had up her sleeve, except she didn't have any sleeves on. It looked like some old dance top, and it was slit right down the middle to exactly between her breasts. He kept getting glimpses, thinking that at any moment she might come entirely out of that shirt. It distracted him, but still, five hundred dollars wasn't going to cut it. Seeing Norah naked might begin to ease his pain. She wasn't as chesty as the girls he usually chose, but then again, she was Norah. She wasn't just a set of breasts. Although he had to admit that, if she were, they were damned near perfectly formed.

Maybe he was just suffering a severe case of wanting to celebrate the return of his johnson. He hollered out, "Hey, Norah. What's the likelihood of me being able to find a woman willing to have a go-round with a guy in a chair?"

She appeared in the doorway between the living room and dining room holding a dishtowel and laughing. "Pretty good. Women are more sympathetic to men in wheelchairs than vise versa. Add in that you're rich, famous, and good-looking and you won't have to go far."

"What about you, Norah? Would you do a guy in a chair?"

As soon as the words were out of his mouth he felt his face flush beet red. He had meant the question as simply a matter of *would she?* not *would she with him?* At least he thought he'd meant it that way. It sure wasn't how it sounded coming out of his mouth.

He squeezed his eyes shut for a second, knowing that if his legs worked, he would have been long gone by now. Instead he was stuck here with his eyes shut tight.

He heard her laugh. His breath let out a notch. At least she wasn't horribly offended.

TJ let his eyes open a crack, and sure enough she was laughing at him. And walking closer.

"You're blushing. Maybe you *are* a good Catholic boy under there."

He felt another wash of color climb his face. "I haven't been a good Catholic boy since I-don't-know-when."

His eyes opened all the way so he could apologize, but she had a funny look on her face. It was a grin, a wicked grin, and he didn't know where to place it.

"So," that single word in her soft tones held a world of weight. "You want to find out if I would?"

All thoughts fled as she planted first one knee then the other on either side of him. Instantly turned on, he reached up, grabbing her hips to hold her there. His hands looked large on her delicate structure, and they spanned almost the whole width of the small skirt she was wearing.

She laughed again, "So find out."

Jesus.

He grabbed her behind her neck to pull her down for a kiss, but she refused him, pulling against his hand. Instead she wrapped her fingers around his palm and turned it away from him. In a move he would never have seen coming in a million years, she led his hand under her skirt and tucked his fingers inside the band of what he could just see was lacy, blue underwear.

TJ needed no further instructions.

He pushed his hand down to where he could feel what she was offering. She was warm and soft, and as he touched her his fingers flooded with wetness. Her hips moved, bringing her closer and pushing her against his fingertips. He was certain he was going to bust the zipper on his jeans.

Because he didn't want to stop, and because Norah didn't seem to want him to, he slid one finger inside her. He barely noticed that her hands found his shoulders for balance. He definitely noticed the sigh he forced out of her throat, and that she pushed against him again.

"More."

With a ragged breath, he obliged.

He didn't remember the last time he'd felt this. This desire that sucked the air from him and demanded every ounce of his attention. Reaching up with his free hand, he slipped his fingers around the back of her head, trying again to kiss her.

Again, she refused, this time rolling her head, and forcing his focus to where his hand joined her. Her hand snaked down, covering his. Through the thin layer of lace she gave him instructions on exactly how she wanted him to touch her. The sounds that she made told him he'd done it correctly.

Nothing had ever been quite as right.

Then she smiled at him, and grabbed his hand, pulling it out of her underwear and away from the heaven they'd both enjoyed. TJ awaited his next set of instructions while his lungs labored.

Norah leaned in close. "You are *very* good at that."

He didn't respond. He couldn't. He just waited.

She stepped away, planting her feet on the floor and letting go of him. He waited for her to peel away her shirt or her underwear. But she did neither.

With a deep breath in, she focused and her eyes cleared. "And you owe me five hundred dollars."

"For a *feel*!?!?" It was out of his mouth before he could think. Not that he was able to think at all. She'd completely addled his brain, then stepped away and demanded money.

"Your fingers work." Norah fled the room.

He heard her in her own bedroom then slamming out the back door. He figured she'd gone off riding on her horse, but TJ just stared at his fingers. The tips were still wet, and he knew with what. Somehow, now that he'd done it, he was able to move each finger in turn. But he wasn't so interested in how he'd been moving them as *where*.

It had been a while for him. Though he *had* hit his head in the accident, he hadn't gone stupid. She'd been hot for him, then she stood up and stepped away. No qualms. She'd apparently been able to turn it off at will. So maybe she could turn it on the same way. Maybe she hadn't wanted him.

She was a self-proclaimed slut. Then again so was he. But he'd been far more involved in this one act than in many other times he'd had full-on down-and-dirty sex.

And her being a slut didn't match anything he knew of her. She taught dance to school-girls. She was a prima ballerina, though he guessed that didn't preclude being promiscuous. She had been nothing but friendly before this, in all the time she'd spent here. She hadn't been leading him on, hadn't made any suggestive remarks or gestures. At least not until today.

And today didn't match the woman last night who'd held his niece with such tenderness and tears in her eyes. It didn't match the woman who lived with her father when she wasn't here.

He looked at his functioning fingers again. At least when she'd said he owed her money it was like throwing ice water on him. It was his own damned fault, too—he'd asked her if she'd do a guy in a chair.

He could play guitar now—piano, too, but he didn't give a shit. He'd been convinced that any case where he lost the bet was going to leave him pleased as peaches. Man, had he been wrong.

With a resigned sigh, he hauled himself into his chair and went off to get the cash. He left it on her pillow, and wondered if he needed a note with it. He thought maybe just *'you win,'* but she already knew that.

CHAPTER 15

When Norah returned that evening, she came in through the back door. Strains of guitar music came from the living room. He must have re-strung it. Aside from a minor miss here or there, usually followed by a soft swear word, it was sweet sounding.

She was sweaty and grubby from riding Thunder, and some part of her knew she was hungry. But she was more sick to her stomach than anything. She didn't know what she'd been thinking. Just that it would make his fingers work. But that was TJ, for god's sake.

Ultimately, he hadn't looked all that happy about finding out his fingers worked fine. She'd played him for a fool when she really hadn't meant to. Somehow in her twisted logic last night, she'd thought it would all be detached, and it would feel good, and he would be happy.

Instead, it felt better than good, and she felt it more than just where he'd touched her. And it wasn't detached. She didn't even know why she'd kept refusing to kiss him. Except . . .

She ignored the thought pestering her brain and decided instead to head for the shower. She turned on the water and peeled out of her clothes. TJ had to hear the water running, had to know she was back. But she focused instead on washing away what she'd done and how to make it right.

When she got dressed, she noticed the money on her pillow, and wondered if he'd put it there while she was showering. So he had, in essence, paid her for 'a feel' as he'd so eloquently put it.

Glad that she could still hear him playing in the living room, she grabbed the wad of cash and padded softly down the hall, practically sneaking into his room. She had a perfectly good excuse to be in there but didn't want to get caught. Not because she was doing anything wrong, but because she didn't want to face him. She just wasn't ready. She considered leaving a note with the money, and instead just folded it and left it on his pillow, like he'd left it on hers. He'd understand.

She managed to avoid him for the rest of the night. Then did pretty well avoiding him the following morning, too. She appeared just in time to take him to therapy, and they both stayed quiet the whole way there. She returned just in time to hear his therapist say that he'd attacked the job today. TJ looked like he'd run a marathon, and maybe he had.

That only made her feel worse. He was pissed, and he had every right to be. They drove home in more silence, then he showered before passing out for a while. When he emerged, she headed for her room and read a magazine until she bored herself to sleep.

The next day went much the same. Again he attacked therapy, again she left him to attack it alone. He was silent but a little more relaxed on the way home.

Only several hours later, he actually came to hunt her down. She was in the back room online ordering dance shoes, something that usually made her excited. She enjoyed seeing the new technology and what you could do with a simple leather ballet slipper. But she'd been walking through the photos, not finding anything of interest, and knowing full well why.

"Norah."

She straightened. She couldn't remember the last time he'd said her name. "What?"

He started with a sigh. "Don't do that again."

"Okay." That was easy. But she got the impression that he wasn't finished.

"That wasn't fair."

Her eyes closed and the corners of her mouth turned down, but she couldn't face him. "I know. I'm sorry."

"If you wanted to know if you can turn me on, congratulations you can."

"No, that wasn't it."

"Then what?"

She needed a deep breath. "I saw your fingers moving while you were asleep on the couch. You were playing guitar in your sleep." She still didn't have the guts to turn and face him. "So I figured they worked but you were just too caught up in making them work. That's why I bet you. I knew you could do it."

He waited. He wasn't going to let her off the hook.

"I figured if I could disengage your brain then you'd do it. I thought if I just . . . well, clearly I wasn't thinking."

"Yeah."

"I know. Not my best moment." She paused, still not looking at him. "Can you forgive me?"

"Can you answer a question for me?"

Norah could hear that he was pretty close behind her so she gave up and turned around. Answering a question was the least she could do. "What?"

"Want to go out for dinner?" He turned the chair and wheeled away.

"That's the question?" God he was confusing, but she probably deserved it.

He laughed. "Actually, no. But neither of us has cooked anything, and I'm starving. I want a huge bowl of pasta."

"That sounds good." As if to punctuate her statement, her stomach growled. She hadn't eaten much these past two days, she'd been so upset over what she'd done.

"So come on. You're driving."

She had to laugh at that. She pulled on shoes and followed him to the car. He was able to ride in her sedan now that they could take the fold-up chair. He easily levered himself into the passenger seat, and not for the first time she admired the flex and play of his muscles under his skin. He was a strong man. In more ways than one.

Just like that, they found their rhythm again.

They talked and laughed throughout dinner. TJ was true to his prediction and ate every last piece of food brought to him. He even managed to joke when she pointed it out. "Yeah, well, I had some frustrations to work out during therapy today."

But he didn't seem angry about it.

Only later when they were sitting on the couch and he had clicked off the TV did he ask her his question. He warned her he was about to do it, but that was all the warm-up she got.

"You said you were a slut, but especially after the other day I really don't see it."

"Really? I thought that was actually rather slutty of me."

He laughed. "A real slut would have followed it through. Did you just take after Lilah?"

She shook her head. And started at the beginning. "So I mentioned I had this crush on JD?"

"Yes." He was exasperated, "I know you had this *huge* crush on JD."

"Well, that ended when I was sixteen. I met Jeff. He was my first boyfriend." Her heart ached just remembering. "I know most people look back on their first loves and realize that they weren't really in love at all. But not us. We really were. Even at sixteen. We just always knew we'd get married.

"Our parents had plans for us, at ivy league schools, but we both paid out of our savings to apply to several schools in Texas where we could both get scholarships together. We knew if we went, our folks were likely to cut us off. So when I turned up pregnant right before graduation we just figured it was fate. We were both eighteen, so we went down to the courthouse and got married. I'd gotten myself the best white dress I could afford, and figured I'd surprise him by showing up in it. But he'd shown up in a tux and surprised me. We went to A&M, and Jordan was born right in the middle of Christmas break."

TJ just listened. He wasn't asking any questions, so she continued.

"I'd always been the good girl. Lilah was the one they'd had to rein in. So I think they'd told themselves it wasn't true when I said I was married and pregnant and going to a state school." She let out a little laugh. "I don't know which of the three was worst.

"Then, my junior year, I tried out for the Houston Ballet. I got into the chorus, and I wanted to go. Jeff didn't balk at all. We finally figured out that he and Jordan would stay at school for one last semester, while I started work. He could graduate early with his credits and pick up a few extra courses in Houston. We did that for two months. Then they were coming out to see me at Thanksgiving, and got hit by a drunk driver on the way."

Next to her, TJ stiffened. It was a normal reaction, no one wanted to hear about a beloved husband and toddler getting hit by a drunk driver.

"He hit the side of their car, and totaled it. Of course, being drunk, he walked away." That was what still got her. She could now calmly speak the words that her husband and child had died, but the anger still came when she spoke of the other man walking away.

She had to get rid of it, she knew, or it would eat her soul. It almost had. "Somehow I stayed with the Ballet and managed to ignore that I'd ever had a child and husband. I threw myself into the work, got a few lead roles, then made principle. After the first year, I just needed sex. That's all it's been since. No one's going to replace Jeff, so I've never tried for anything more than a one-night stand."

"And that makes you a slut?"

"I was pregnant at eighteen, and I've had nothing but one night stands for seven years now. I think I qualify." She finally turned to look at him. To watch him digest what she'd said. She didn't wait long. "So, how did you get broken?"

"Car accident."

Just those two words. After she'd told her whole story. She wasn't going to stand for that. "You'll have to do better."

He took a breath, still seeming stiff, "I was partying, and not paying attention, and this semi rear-ended the car. I should have gotten out of the way, but I didn't react fast enough."

He flinched even as he said it, and she frowned at him. Then she remembered when he'd stiffened. Her breathing sped up, and she hopped off the couch. "You were drunk!"

He nodded.

"You—" But there was nothing else to say.

CHAPTER 16

TJ hauled himself into his chair and then sped down the hall after her. She hated him, and she should. So he didn't knock, just opened her bedroom door to find her packing.

She looked up at him like a wounded deer, but her hands never stopped folding clothes and clearing out. "I can't believe I've been here, driving you to therapy and everything, when you did that."

"I didn't kill anyone, except almost myself."

She came around the bed like an avenging angel, forcing him to back up. Then she closed the door in his face.

He didn't hear it lock, so he tried again. This time when it opened he planted himself in the doorway and didn't move. He even locked the chair.

"Norah. I'm sorry. But I didn't kill them."

That stopped her. "How do you *know*? Had you never driven drunk before?"

He wanted to say no. Oh, how he wanted to, but he couldn't. "It wasn't me. I was never in Houston at Thanksgiving."

"That's your defense?"

She was right, of course. He felt like shit on the bottom of a shoe. His only proof that he hadn't killed her husband and infant, was not because he *couldn't have* but because he hadn't been in that place at that time. His voice was softer. "It wasn't me."

She just turned back to packing.

And they had just found their ground again. It was volatile, living with this woman under his roof. "Can we be even? I forgive you for being a tease and—"

She cut that one at the knees before he even finished. "Your hand down my pants is not anywhere near a comparison to you driving drunk! Drunk drivers ruin lives. I'm sorry if you had some sexual frustrations for a few days."

Then she turned her back and shut him out.

TJ stayed planted in the doorway. "Norah, you have to forgive me."

It was worse because she didn't scream or yell. "No, I don't."

He stayed planted until she had her bags packed. She marched right up to him and faced him in the doorway. "TJ, get out of my way."

"No, I'm staying right here."

"Get out of my room."

He clenched his jaw. He couldn't let her leave. "It's my house."

"I'll go out the god-damned window if I have to."

"Norah, I am the safest driver out there now. I've learned my lesson, better than just about anyone could have. I never hit anyone, though that doesn't make any of it okay. I know that. But I am the poster boy for not drinking and driving. I'm sorry I can't bring them back. If I could, I would."

He watched as she crumpled, and he caught her when she fell, twisting into her tears, her bag forgotten. He held her and tried to take some of her pain away. "Norah, I know I didn't deserve to walk away from my accident. I—"

"That's the worst part." Her voice was tinny and thin. "You

have to be bad. You have to be evil for what you did, but I know you're not. You don't deserve what happened to you."

He took a deep breath, and spoke as soothingly as he could. "Yeah, I probably do." It was the first time he had admitted that, even just to himself. "I made a mistake. A big one, and not the first. It should have only hurt me, but somehow it doesn't."

She sniffed, and her shoulders heaved. "I'm not stupid. But if you're not evil, and you just made a mistake, then maybe he did, too. Maybe whoever hit them wasn't evil either, maybe it really was a mistake. But I've held so long to hating him. I don't know if I can forgive him."

She was sniffling and crying and he could hardly understand her, but the woman made sense. "Maybe you should. Maybe you can forgive both of us, Norah."

He held her tighter, sensing that she needed it, and knowing that he wanted to. His arms were in direct contradiction to his words. "You can leave if you want. I won't hold you here."

She was curled into a tiny ball in his arms, her flexibility making her seem not much bigger than nine-year old Allie. He felt her head shake 'no' against his chest, and he was supremely grateful.

She cried for hours, and he didn't say anything. She'd held on tight, and he understood. Once again, he realized that maybe she was more broken than he was. That she had been right when she'd slapped him. His instant reaction had been that she was out of line. But the more he'd thought about it, the more he realized that he'd had it coming for a long time.

Eventually he realized she'd fallen asleep. He was grateful for his strong arms just then. He'd worked out so hard, thinking he'd give people something to look at besides his legs. But now here he was actually finding his strength useful.

He was lifting her off his lap and onto the bed, when Norah started to wake. His hand shot out to comfort her, smoothing her hair even before his brain registered it. So he simply levered himself up onto the bed next to her. It was only a full size but there was just enough room.

As he pushed with his hands against the bed, propping himself against the pillows, he felt the pins and prickles. His legs had fallen asleep.

He sighed, until it hit him.

Both his legs had fallen asleep.

Norah curled into him, sleeping soundly despite the light he'd left on. Despite the breakthrough he'd had not inches from her. He smiled to himself. Somehow when the breakthroughs came, Norah was always right beside him. Despite all the trouble she caused, she was some kind of good luck charm.

His legs hurt like hell, and it felt good.

CHAPTER 17

If someone had told Norah she would finally shed her hate for the man who had killed her family, she would have thought she'd feel free. She didn't. She felt lost. For so long she had hated this man. Believed he was a cold blooded killer of the worst sort—the careless kind. She had refused to believe he might feel remorse or pain over what he'd done.

She also felt like a fool for not seeing before that TJ had, of course, been out drunk when he'd had his accident. She'd known the Hewlitt boys since they were little. While she didn't follow celebrity gossip much at all, she followed Wilder. TJ was at every party, and he always left with the hottest girl. Why she hadn't put two and two together was beyond her.

But if she had, she wouldn't be here.

She'd woken up in TJ's arms the next morning. His face was buried in her hair, and he was tucked alongside her. Like they were lovers.

They weren't.

She didn't want to be his lover. He went through women the way most men changed underwear. Sure, he was on a temporary reprieve, but she had no doubts that, while he would be a safer driver, he would pick up right where he had left off with the female set.

Norah sighed. It's not like she was averse to casual sex. Lord knew she'd had enough of it. But she lived here with him; it could never be casual.

Waking up in his arms had been scary. She wasn't sure why, only that it was. Also, her face was all puffy from crying in his arms for several hours. He'd been polite enough not to say anything, but she didn't think he'd offer again.

So maybe it would be fine.

She took a deep breath.

Maybe her thoughts wouldn't be so scattered in another day or two. Maybe the Titanic would raise itself from the ocean floor.

At least she'd slept alone last night. She turned the doorknob, letting herself out of her bedroom, hollering exasperatedly. "TJ!? You ready?"

She had accompanied him to therapy the last several days. He was starting to regain control of his legs—a fact which made him almost too happy to be around.

He was like a five year old. 'Look what I can do!' But she didn't have it in her heart to begrudge him. And it *was* interesting to see what he could and couldn't do.

The therapist was holding him back, and TJ was pushing forward. She was glad not to be going today. Yesterday he had asked when he got to try standing and walking. So the therapist measured the output of pressure TJ could apply with his feet, then politely pointed out he would fall and crack his head in a heartbeat.

TJ followed her down the hall, "I hate you."

It was casual, but there was a bite to it.

She was going to pose for Kelsey, for the studio shots, again this morning. As she turned she saw his eyes tracking her pointe shoes.

His mouth said much the same thing. "I can't stand on two flat feet. And you're going to go put all your weight on one toe."

His sat still, and she was upset that they weren't making any progress down the hall. She was twitchy these days. Anything that deviated her from her plans made her uptight. She hadn't figured that one out either. But TJ was making her twitchy now.

"So get your butt to therapy so you can do it, too."

She turned and walked away.

His voice followed her. "I have no desire to do that. If I can get on stage and sing, I'll be happy. If I can dance and jump, I'll be beyond thrilled."

There was a lull, but she should have known that didn't mean she was safe. Far from it.

"Speaking of butts."

With a huff, she turned, nearly getting herself run over. But TJ managed to stop the chair on a dime; he was in supreme control of it. Maybe to make up for the parts of him he wasn't in supreme control of. Like maybe his mouth?

"That little skirt doesn't cover yours."

"It's not really intended to." It was a short, purple, knit, sweater skirt that just hugged her hips. It matched the long-sleeved, but very cropped warm-up sweater, and the short, tight leg warmers she was also wearing for the photo-shoot.

She turned and walked away, but didn't hear the telltale squish of his tires against floor. She turned, frustrated with him, even as she wasn't sure why.

He was sitting there at the back of the hall, grinning. "You can just turn around and keep walking. I'm discovering some benefits to this chair. I'm at ass-height."

"TJ!"

"Hey! I was given very explicit instructions to not attempt to stand up." He defended himself. "And you come out here in that very short skirt—"

"I have a dance bottom on under it!" It was just the bottom

half of a leotard. It left her midriff bare so she wouldn't overheat today.

"Yeah, I know. I can *see* your little dance bottom under the hem of that thing you're callin' a skirt."

She sighed again. Not sure if he was talking about the same 'little dance bottom' that she was. "It's not indecent. It's for dance. What's an ass but another body part? Lord, the men perform in those tights where you can tell if they're circumcised or not!"

"You have an excellent point. So you can just sashay your body parts down the hall, and I'll watch."

"I'm not sashaying!" So, stiff as a board, she marched down the hallway and out the front door.

She wanted to climb in the driver's side and steam while she waited, but she couldn't. Reaching over and flipping on the air conditioner, Norah reminded herself she'd gotten paid for this. Right now, when he was harassing her, it didn't hurt to think of the money.

He popped himself into the seat and waited for her to slide into the driver's seat. "You know, I think you gave my neighbor a good show back there, when you were putting my chair in."

"Ah!" She gave up, and turned on him, smacking at his arms while he raised his hands in mock defense, laughing at her all the time.

He didn't give up the whole way over. "I want to go with you this morning. You come to therapy with me. I want to go with you."

She held her face steady. "You'd be bored."

"Oh, I don't think so."

She reached over popped him on one of his big, bad biceps at the next stop light.

"Ow." He rubbed at the arm.

"Oh, please, you're so buff you probably didn't even feel that!" She popped him again, and he laughed at her.

They were acting so juvenile. Norah had no idea what had come over her. She expected this from TJ, but not from herself.

He bugged her all the way there, "Please, Norah, I want to go with you."

"No! You are clearly a pest. Kelsey and I are working. *Working.*"

But when she got out to unload the chair and wheel it over to his side of the car he changed his tune. "Norah," his voice was suddenly serious, "Just go straight to the studio. Don't stop for a soda or anything on the way out or back."

Where the hell had that come from?

She asked him pretty much that.

He gave her half a grin. "I know I was teasing you, but you're indecent." He merely pointed to where a handful of therapists had gathered at the window. He waved to them.

"I'll be back when I'm done."

"Just go home and change first."

She huffed off to meet Kelsey. *Damned men.*

The studio was empty this time when she pulled up, and she was grateful that today wasn't as hot as it had been last time. Still, she was trying to not work up a sweat. She pushed the air conditioner to capacity and started her warm-up. She did it without music, to just a steady rhythm she counted. For the first time in several days she felt like herself.

Even though she normally didn't dance in an outfit like this one. She rarely danced with her hair in a pony-tail, especially not when it was this length—the exact right length to whip around in a turn and give her a black eye. Even though there was no music, just being here, dancing, centered her.

She pulled herself up, her right toe pointed at her left knee, her arms automatically went into position, and she suddenly realized she hadn't ridden Thunder hell-for-leather since she'd taken up residence at TJ's. She wasn't sure why that was, only that it was.

When she had her pointe shoes on, she spent a few minutes getting accustomed to them. She thought of the junior high class last year. Kelsey and JD's daughter Andie was in that class. All the girls balked, but they spent a year practicing, pushing on their toe tips, stretching their ankles and putting weight on them. Just so they could get ready for pointe.

It made her think of TJ. He had to do his baby steps first. It must be excruciating for a grown man to have to take baby steps, just to take steps at all.

"Norah!" Kelsey interrupted her thoughts.

Norah found a smile. "Hey. You ready?"

"Sure, but you dance in the dark and with no music?" Kelsey cocked her head to the side.

That brought out a half grin. "Sometimes."

"Here," Kelsey flipped a light on and pulled out the folio she had dragged with her. Without words the two women spread the prints out across the floor.

Norah was stunned.

Each picture seemed to capture some expression in her face or body, some detail in her hands or feet. She examined the photos carefully, looking for chinks in her technique. Though she couldn't find any, even in her hand or leg there was hope or sadness.

That was damned impressive, and damned scary.

After that, they got to work. Kelsey snapped picture after picture. All the while she was wondering what she was giving away—what Kelsey would find in her today and capture in the photos.

Kelsey ran out of film before they ran out of time, and so Norah stayed, ignoring TJ's warning. She practiced her turns en pointe, working her way to a perfect quadruple pirouette. She was warm and hungry by the time she realized she was running a little late.

She stepped off the wood floor and into her street shoes

before dashing out the front door. Peeling out of the empty lot, Norah headed for TJ's rehab facility.

He gave her a dirty look when she got out of the car in her dance gear. She gave him a dirty look back.

When he hauled himself into the car he started in on her again. "You're going to get asked out a lot next week."

"That's a bad thing?"

"Well, they aren't in it for your sparkling personality."

She ground her teeth at him. "And what *are* they in it for? Do they want to see pirouettes?"

"I suspect they want to get a good look at those *dance bottoms*."

She made a growl at the back of her throat and he laughed again.

CHAPTER 18

TJ had to laugh at her. There just weren't that many options. She'd given him funny looks when she'd woken up in his arms a few mornings ago. So he figured throwing her to the ground and having his way was out of the question. Never mind the physical limitations he was operating under.

So he'd teased her. And thanks to the gods above that he had enough movement in his legs now to both hide and ease the pressure lurking there.

What the hell was she thinking, prancing around with her long midriff entirely bare? She had unmarked skin, and a tiny, perfect belly button. He didn't need to know that. That outfit had played her curves to perfection, too. *Damned women.*

He considered hiring a professional to help him relieve his 'needs,' back when this whole fiasco had started. However, if that ever hit the press, that would be beyond bad. The guys had already talked to him more than once about his escapades. It would be a mess, no doubt. And if he hired a girl, then it was bound to wind up somewhere, some day.

So he had no relief. And Norah was dancing like the devil was at her heels. He knew why he went to therapy every day.

But Norah had stopped coming with him. He found he missed having her there. Though she'd seen him fall repeatedly, she'd been watching, and that alone made him get up more than once.

Now she was always at her studio. She said she was calling clients and budgeting and balancing the books. But she left in leotards and dance gear, and she returned looking like she'd been through her paces.

He didn't see her eat much either. He wasn't sure if that was part of being a dancer, or if it had more to do with the fact that she was sad. She had been since the other night when she'd cried her eyes out in his arms. Twice he had caught her in tears with no ready explanation.

Once he heard her behind her bedroom door and asked if she was all right.

Norah had only replied with, "Go away, TJ."

That hadn't been acceptable and so he pushed. "Norah, tell me what's going on."

"I haven't worked through my five stages of grief yet. Leave me alone."

Even now he had to laugh at that one. There was something in her tone of voice that had told him she was sad but mostly whole. So he left her to cry it out as she asked.

She was more contemplative now, telling him that she had to make a decision this year about whether to keep the studio or sell it. When he'd asked her what she'd do if she sold it, she shrugged. "That's part of the decision."

She saddled up and rode Thunder more often, too, walking him down the driveway and out the gate. The Norah he knew left the yard by sailing her horse over the back fence. Then he realized that maybe he'd had it backward all this time. Maybe this was better.

So he teased her—just to lighten her up a little—and she teased back.

He pointed out that she was gone a lot.

She pointed out that she was leaving in four weeks. The summer would be over and she would move back in with her Dad and TJ would have the place to himself. So maybe it was a good thing she wasn't around so much right now.

TJ was shocked that made him so uptight.

He'd wanted the place to himself. He hadn't wanted her, or anyone, here at all. He wasn't sure when that had changed, or when she had started drifting back to a life of her own.

So when JD called and invited them over for dinner TJ accepted, only later to realize that he shouldn't have accepted for her. He found her in her room, reading.

"Norah."

She looked up, so different looking with her hair down and curling around her face. She so often wore it pulled back that this was a rarity.

"JD called and he and Kelsey invited us to dinner. I said 'yes' unless you have other plans?"

She shook her head.

That was the end of it. Another conversation where she hadn't said a word to him.

But that evening, she said she didn't feel well, but she'd drive him. He refused. He didn't want to put her out if she was sick, and they could just go another night.

Norah spent a good portion of the time in her room. He ate by himself, then watched TV until the doorbell rang.

He was actually getting pretty good at popping himself in and out of his chair. Of course these days it was much easier with a little help from his legs. They didn't just hang there anymore, dead weight fighting him. Now they moved, he could put them where he wanted them even if he still had to bear his weight on his arms.

He opened the door to find Kelsey with a huge envelope in her hands.

"Hey Kelsey. Did you leave my brother at home alone with six kids?"

She nodded. "Yes, and he loves it."

As much as he and his brother looked alike, there were some things about JD that he would never understand.

"Here. Look at these." With that, she pulled out a chair at the dining room table and started spreading out prints of Norah dancing.

His eyes were drawn to photo after photo. Damn, but the woman was graceful. He'd seen her whack her knees, elbows, and toes around here, just like anyone else, but clearly she wasn't just like anyone else.

Her head tilted at just the right angle. Her arms framed her face in an oval that was just imperfect enough to be beautiful. Her legs extended to angles far beyond human, but she made them all look natural.

One photo grabbed him. She was simply standing. But Norah never simply stood. Her feet were pressed tight against each other, one tucked right alongside the other. Her posture was perfectly straight, while somehow still looking a little weighted. Her hands were drawn up alongside her face and her eyes closed as though she had decided to nap right there in the fluffy knit of her sleeves.

"She looks sad to me." Kelsey's words echoed the thoughts in his head.

TJ only nodded. He didn't add, *I wonder what she was thinking about.* He didn't want to tell, uncertain if any of them knew about Norah's husband and baby boy.

"The rest are amazing. She's flawless." Kelsey pulled the one photo aside. "I like it, but it's not what I would hang in a dance studio."

She said goodnight and kissed his cheek—a sweet sisterly kiss that she had to bend over to give these days.

After she left, Norah emerged from her room. "Is she gone?"

TJ frowned. "Yes." But he picked up the one photo and brought it with him. "She dropped these off. She said you should start picking some out, so that she can get them framed and ready before the students arrive."

Norah just looked the photo over, somehow with no expression on her face. "She's amazing. These always seem to be art as much as portraits."

So he started it. "You look so sad."

"Yes, I do." She set the photo aside on the arm of the couch and ended it. Curling herself into a tight ball tucked into the corner of the sofa, she looked up at him. "Do you want to watch something?"

TJ ignored the question. "Kelsey said she hopes you're feeling better and she invited us over for next week."

Norah just shook her head.

"You don't think you'll be better by then."

Her smile was wry. "I'm not sick. I just can't go over there anymore."

"The baby?" Maybe he had pushed her too far.

"I've been admitting a lot of things to myself these past days." She started, staying tucked behind the knee she was hugging. "I don't forgive you for driving drunk."

He tensed, waiting for her condemnation. It would be less than he probably deserved.

She continued. "I don't have to, there's nothing to forgive. That's all about you. I'm getting there on forgiving the man who killed them."

She didn't elaborate on 'them,' she didn't need to. The breath he'd been holding let out.

She took a breath in, "And while I'm admitting things to myself, I realized that I can't be around Kelsey and JD anymore."

"What did they do?" The rest had made sense, up until that.

She looked up at him, a grin on her face even though she looked close to tears. "Don't you see it? I'm jealous."

It hit him like a fist in the gut. "You still have a thing for JD?"

She laughed out loud at that one. A laugh like he hadn't heard out of her in a while. "Don't be stupid."

The relief that flooded him was overwhelming, but he didn't question it. He was just supremely grateful that Norah thought it would be stupid for him to think she still carried a torch for his brother.

She got herself together enough to explain. "I'm jealous of what they have. All these years, I never admitted to myself that I was lonely. And those two are the worst. They've been married, what? Six years?"

He nodded. "Almost seven."

"And they still hold hands, run off and make out in the hallway, act like they just met. I'd be jealous of anyone falling in love, but they're worse."

Before he could respond she picked herself up off the couch. Saying good-night to him, she disappeared down the hallway.

CHAPTER 19

TJ's breath fought its way out of him. His weight was on his arms. They were working doubly hard pushing up on the walker because he was trying to allow some weight onto his legs. And his legs kept collapsing underneath him, leaving his arms to support his full weight, often at a moment's notice.

He threw his weight forward over the front bar, balancing and relieving some of the pressure. His arms were close to shaking. He just lay there and breathed for a few moments, regathering his strength.

He was halfway down the hall, his chair behind him. He would have to turn around and get back just before he could sit again. He hadn't thought the day would come when that damnable chair would look good to him, but here it was.

He was also alone in the house. So there was no one to call out for, no one to come fetch him if he didn't, or couldn't, make it. Granted, that person would have been Norah, and at this point he figured that would keep his mouth good and shut. He would make it back. He just had to.

TJ pushed back up, willing his legs to work. They seemed to simply quit when they got tired, and they got tired very quickly.

The first time it happened he had gone insane, thinking he'd pushed too hard and snapped something vital.

But he was going to walk again. He was going on stage with Wilder. For a moment, he simply blessed Brenda, their manager. When he'd had his accident, she started canceling the tour. He'd found out earlier today from JD she'd actually only cancelled the first four month's dates. She'd cancelled another two later. But that put him on the road in just over three months.

He had to be walking, running, and singing at full volume by then. He'd never realized what kind of physical shape that required until he'd lost it. But he was not going to have Brenda canceling any more performances.

He heard the click and slide of the key in the front lock, and knew he was caught.

"TJ?" Norah hollered for him. He was usually pretty quick in the chair. Hanging on his walker this way, snails would beat him handily.

He didn't yell back, she'd find him soon enough. It took all of about three seconds.

"TJ! Are you on that thing again?"

He didn't answer that. It had to be obvious.

She'd said she was going to the studio, but he hadn't seen her leave. She looked like she'd had a good workout. With good reason, he turned the tables. "What the hell are you wearing?"

She frowned at him. "Dance clothes."

"Are those mine?"

She was wearing men's underwear. In public.

"No!" She looked at him like *he* was crazy. She who was wearing not boxers—which he might have accepted—but boxer briefs. "They're mine."

Like that solved all the worlds ills. "Norah."

"What?"

"I live with you, and that's indecent here. I can't believe you wore that in public."

"I just went to the dance studio and back. Lots of dancers wear these, and I'm more covered than I am in a bikini. I've worn far less on stage."

All valid points. All missed *the* point. He groaned.

She parried. "Since when did you become the decency police?"

He opened his mouth.

She put words in it. "I've seen photos of you with your tongue down some girl's throat. And that girl was usually wearing far less than I am right now."

His arms hurt. His head hurt. "I just don't want people getting the wrong idea about you."

She walked away, her ass hugged by burgundy rib knit. The waistband read *Hanes* plain as day. She threw her last line at him over her shoulder. "Shut-up, Pot."

"Thanks, Kettle."

All of ten minutes later, she returned, scrubbed clean, her wet hair combed back. At least she was fully dressed in jeans and a tank top. All of it clung to her slender form.

He was half-way turned around. TJ had taken to locking his knees in order to hold his weight while he moved the walker in a semi-circle one agonizing inch at a time.

She squeezed by him. "So."

"So?"

"You're only supposed to be on that thing for ten minutes at a time." Her hands were on her hips and she was planted between him and his chair. "So, if you're going to defy your orders, you should at least plan ahead and lie to me about what they were." She held out her arms. "Come on."

He barked out a good laugh. "What? You're going to carry me?"

She rolled her eyes at him. The gesture looked so young on her scrubbed face. There wasn't a trace of makeup on her, and she looked even younger than she was. "No. I'm going to support you while you brace your hands against the wall. Then I'm going to take your walker and bring your chair to where you can sit down."

"No, you're not."

She pressed her lips together. "You'd already been at it for a while when I got here. You were worn out then. It's been another ten minutes while I was in the shower. You're done."

"Norah, I'm just going to my chair."

Her mouth set. And just like that she walked away. Only she didn't just walk away. She grabbed the handles on his chair and wheeled it down the hall away from him.

"Hey!"

But she kept going. Leaving him stranded there with nothing but the walker. Maybe it would be a good time to find the wall and slide down it.

He heard her before he saw her. She had brought the chair full circle around the house, arriving close enough behind him to practically bump him in the knees. TJ wondered if she knew that he'd locked them. That, if she did bump them, he'd collapse right into the chair.

She didn't bump him.

With a heaving sigh, he sat. He'd known he was caught the moment he'd heard her at the front door.

Norah had the decency not to do anything more for him. She just squeezed around the chair and took the walker-from-Hades away. It didn't fold up, even though it resembled an old man's frame walker. It was made for rehab, and was far sturdier.

For a moment he wished she would do more for him, his arms were worn out. They didn't want to push the wheels. Hell, he needed to go back to his motor chair. And he couldn't remember the last time he'd ridden in the thing. He let his head tip back and just tried to breathe.

Returning to the end of the hallway after putting the walker away, Norah stood with her hands on her hips. She cocked her head and faced him, making him think it was some kind of shootout. Although with his head resting against the back of the chair, it probably looked like she'd already shot him dead.

He wasn't prepared for the smile she gave him. Or for the question, "What's your deadline?"

"What do you mean?"

"You have a deadline, even if you just gave it to yourself. That's why you're pushing so hard. So, when is it?"

He hated her for being able to read him like that. She probably also saw his muscles trembling from the exertion. He desperately wanted to at least roll down the hallway with some dignity. By force of will, he straightened his back. "Just over three months. We have tour dates then."

"Wow."

He waited for her to leave, so he could slump back into his seat, but she didn't. Her hands stayed perched on her hips, and she looked like a dancer even in that pose. A small smile played across her face, and she walked up to him only to pass him by and take the handles of his chair. For the first time, she pushed him.

He closed his eyes, trying to concede defeat. But she pushed him to his bedroom, and turned back the covers. Without asking and with no further fuss, she pulled one of his arms across her shoulders and supported him over to the bed.

He was too stunned to do anything. Norah made him do for himself. Norah, who had him carry things for her and made silent demands that he be useful, was pulling off his shoes. Her fingers reached for his waist and tugged at his shirt.

Holy shit.

If she was offering herself he was going to use every last ounce of strength to scream in pure agony. There was no way he could perform now. Although if she wanted him to never overwork himself again, that would be the way to achieve it.

She pulled his shirt up and over his head with little help

from him. TJ just waited, wondering what rabbit hole he had fallen down.

Laying him out across the bed, Norah pulled his legs straight, and puffed a pillow behind his head. "I'll be right back."

The ceiling mocked him as he lay there, too exhausted to move, every muscle beyond his will power.

She waltzed back into the room with some red and blue bottle in her hand, she was already flipping the lid and pouring something into her palm. "Now, this isn't going to happen again."

He just wished to hell that he knew what *this* was.

She continued, "So don't go overworking yourself thinking you can con me into it."

"Yes, ma'am," was all he could muster. He was lying there, shirtless, wondering if she had laid him out for slaughter.

Her hands found his arm, smearing warm oil down it, fingers working into muscles too sore to even react. Something half sigh/half moan escaped his mouth and she answered it with a smile and a bit of commiseration. "With me it's usually my legs that give out. That warming oil is what I always use on them, and it does feel good."

She stopped, and he almost protested before he saw her pour another handful and walk around to reach his other arm. She didn't speak while she found knots in his muscles, and softly worked each of them.

He was grateful that she didn't poke and knead the way the therapists often did, as though his muscles were to be attacked and punished. Her hands were soft and her touch soothing. She alternated between his arms, not leaving one too long, somehow knowing when it was starting to clench up on him again.

Climbing on the bed, she parked herself on her heels, her knees and hips pressed along his torso. TJ could feel every movement of her legs in the soft, worn jeans. While he was grateful for the sensation, he also cursed it.

She spoke just often enough to keep him grounded. "Your sheets are ruined. Well, it will wash out, but you won't want to sleep here after you've showered."

"Oh." He'd wanted to nod, but even those muscles weren't obeying.

After a while, she had him turn over. He just managed to find the strength so that she didn't have to flip him herself. She put a pillow under his chest so he could keep his neck straight. Then, without warning, she threw one leg across him and straddled him like she did her horse.

TJ thanked every god he could think of that he was face down. But she didn't wiggle or do anything suggestive, other than straddle him, of course. Her hands, covered in warm oil, found his shoulders, his back, his neck. This time he moaned for real.

CHAPTER 20

Norah listened to TJ and laughed to herself. Everyone had a roommate who sang in the shower. Hers was singing a song his brother had written that was currently slaughtering records for country music and climbing the pop charts. From the sound of it, the studio hadn't fiddled with the recording that much.

She wasn't one much to go see concerts or listen to live music. But TJ had a voice that made her think not all the sirens had been female. She understood now what he and JD had meant when they'd talked about keeping Wilder's sound 'organic'.

This was new. He hadn't sung while she'd been here—almost as though that part of him had been broken in the accident. As though his loss of control of his diaphragm had meant the loss of his vocal cords. Now the shower was prime territory, whether it was dawn or midnight. And the man had a set of lungs on him, a set he was rapidly reclaiming.

The man wasn't going easy on himself. If he wasn't working his lungs, it was his legs. He needed strength and balance and all the fine motor control that no one thinks about just to stand upright. The few steps he had taken had seemed more like he was catching one fall after another, and had wound up with him landing, hands first, on the couch. At least he'd been laughing.

True to her word, no matter how much he killed himself, she hadn't offered another massage. Norah had found that quite easy to adhere to. She wasn't sure what it was, but some element of that last one had turned sexual. It certainly wasn't what she'd intended.

She didn't understand how it had gotten away from her. She couldn't count the number of times she had done that for her fellow dancers. She'd straddled them when they were face up and worked chest muscles. No one had thought anything of having their hands in each others groins. Dancers were always touching each other, and yet none of those situations had reached inside her and turned her on the way handling TJ had.

It was a good thing that school was only a few more weeks away. She'd re-open the studio doors, move back in with her Dad, and this gripping fear that was eating at the back corners of her would recede.

She tried to read her magazine, but TJ's voice kept getting through to her. So eventually she stopped trying and just listened to her own private concert.

He stopped singing—usually a sign that the shower was about over—and she laughed. Her Dad's house was going to sound remarkably dull after this summer.

Sure enough, a few minutes later he emerged from the bathroom, seated in his chair, towel slung around his hips. His legs perched on the foot rests, but they didn't succumb to gravity anymore. He looked like he'd just chosen to sit there, not like he couldn't get up and saunter down the hallway.

"Nice concert." She called out to him. That hallway bathroom was designed for a wheelchair bound person who needed live-in help. Her room, the help's room, had a small private bath that came off the back corner. His master bedroom didn't. His bathroom was easily accessible to the help, in case anything should go wrong, and it left him wheeling out into the hallway after each shower.

He grinned at her. "We're meeting in the studio tomorrow for a starter practice. Want to come?"

"That's great, but I'll be working out then." She stood and started to tell him she was leaving now and would be back in a few hours.

His frown stopped her. "Tell me you're going dancing."

"Of course. I'll be back in a few hours."

Jesus, he was going to start in with the indecency again. He did.

"Put a sock in it, TJ!" She sailed out the door.

Ten minutes later she was parked at the door to the studio. Once inside, she put on Wilder's latest album. She hadn't listened to it all summer, but now she wanted it. Maybe she'd been inspired by the music coming from the shower.

The studio was cool, and she flipped on the lights in the largest room. She practically ripped her soft sneakers off her feet. Only the first song was allotted for warm-up. After that she felt the burn to push herself and stretch her limits, so she shoved her feet into her pointe shoes.

She wasn't where she wanted to be. She wanted her Houston Ballet body back. The body that could dance from dawn til dusk and not tire until she hit her pillow. The body that never missed a step, that only rarely couldn't quite stretch or lift far enough.

Dance turned her brain off from the demons that were chasing her. Her forgiveness of the man who killed Jeff and Jordan only opened the floodgates. She'd been so locked up being angry, that she hadn't truly grieved for them.

But she wasn't in any place to truly grieve for them now either. They were so long gone. So she worked it out the way she always did—on a hard wood floor with her muscles burning.

Norah stood up and snapped at the speaker system. It was voice activated, but she'd trained it to the sound of her fingers snapping instead. Most of the time it was silly to snap at the music and have it come on, now it was just an angry motion of her wrist.

Track two opened on a hard chord, and Norah opened on her toes. It wasn't ballet music by any measure. But she'd learned along the way that pointe shoes didn't always mean ballet and ballet could be danced to anything.

She threw herself into it. Every movement held just so, the tension in her both escalated and released. She knew these songs, she'd listened to them often before the summer began. When she finished the CD without stopping for a break, she snapped her fingers and it started over again.

This time, having just heard it all the way through, she was aware of every nuance, every downbeat, every half-measure the guys made use of. She'd always been known for that—she could listen once, and hit every grace note or half-start perfectly. Now it meant that she could throw herself into the wild rhythm that much harder. She didn't falter with mis-steps; she could leap and know she'd hit ground when the chord came down.

An hour later she lay flat on the floor, panting.

She'd wrung every last drop out of it that she could.

So she cried right there—soft, silent tears for Jeff and Jordan. Then she peeled herself up and went into the ladies room to wash her face.

Her eyes were rimmed red, but it would fade before she got back to TJ's. Her skin was a little blotchy. That, too, would disappear quickly. She told herself she was cleaning out her soul. Now her eyes were clearer and the smile she gave herself in the mirror was truer.

Norah exited the bathroom, and looked around the lobby for

just a moment, taking in the new portraits. Kelsey had delivered gold. Norah was considering inviting her to photograph the classes. There might be parents who would want that even before portrait time.

Trying to see the studio through fresh eyes, she looked for the whole picture, and wondered if selling was really the right thing to do. But she had nearly six months to decide and pushed the thought away.

Slipping back into her sneakers, she shut the place down, bolting the front door behind her. On the drive home, it hit. Her feet locked.

They were cramped into position, and Norah wasn't all that surprised.

Flexing at every stoplight, she drove straight for TJ's. She couldn't work out her cramps while in the car. Her teeth ground together while she drove, the only concession she made to the pain.

Parking as close to the house as she could, Norah gingerly stepped out. She was grateful that much of the front yard was level cement. It was intended to make things easy for a wheelchair, but what it meant right now was that the ground was flat and she wouldn't have to add a twisted ankle to her wounds.

TJ must have spotted her coming, because he held the door open. "What's wrong?"

"Foot cramps." She just got the words out.

"What do you need?"

"Bananas."

He looked at her oddly, and she just was in too much pain to explain. "Potassium."

"I have that." He wheeled off to the kitchen and quickly returned with two white pills and a cup of water. Norah stopped rotating her feet long enough to swallow them.

A half-smile lingered on TJ's lips. "You know I owe you.

Where's that massage oil?" He was already halfway down the hall.

She barked at him, "No! It'll burn."

He swiveled the chair. "It didn't burn me."

"You didn't have open skin."

"And you do?"

She nodded, still rotating her feet with her hands.

"Norah."

She looked up at him. He was now right in front of her, and demanding her feet.

Without much input from her, he pulled her legs onto his lap, carefully untying the laces on her left shoe before pulling it off. "Jesus, Norah."

She just shook her head, trying to pull her foot, still in the sock, away and getting ready to explain that that's what it was to be a dancer.

But he beat her to it. "Does your other foot look like this?"

"Probably." She sighed.

TJ left her for a moment and returned carrying a bin of gauze bandages and tape. The stash was for him; they expected him to sustain cuts, scrapes or burns just because he hadn't been able to feel anything to protect himself. Luckily the kit had gone largely unused.

Gingerly, he reclaimed her feet, which were still cramping enough to make her lock her jaw, and carefully peeled away one sock. She saw that it came away bloody. She was used to it, but realized from his face that he wasn't.

"Norah." It came out sad and hurting.

"I'll be fine."

"I hope so." He sighed, then got to work. Gently he used the betadine swabs to clean each crack, each spot where she had simply rubbed the skin off. Then he cut and fit gauze, and taped each one into place. She practically had mummy feet when he finished. But she grabbed each one in turn—still working it, still trying to loosen clenched muscles.

"Do you want them massaged?"

"Yes."

That was all it took. Trying so hard to avoid the cuts, which were just about everywhere, he took one slim foot in his hands until it unlocked. Then he turned his attention to the other foot.

"Your poor feet." He breathed in a sigh of pity. "How do you do this? It looks like you didn't even feel the pain that was telling you to stop. You just wore the skin off in some places."

"That's about it. You just take off your shoes and go 'oh, look, it's bleeding.'" She shrugged. Now that her teeth weren't locked, the massage felt good.

He worked her toes, then her ankles, and for a moment she got embarrassed and tried to pull away.

"Uh-uh." He shook his head and recaptured her feet.

"They aren't pretty feet. They're too abused."

"On the contrary, they're very abused, beautiful feet. I think only dancers have this." He traced the fluid curve of her ankle, then back up her arch. He massaged her calves, and she laid back, thinking it felt like heaven.

He took up the conversation again. "I don't know what you were dancing to, but you should destroy it."

She couldn't help the laugh. "I was dancing to Wilder."

"In your pointe shoes?" The look on his face said it all. "Well, there's your problem."

"I was just taking out my aggressions."

"On our CD?" He stroked her feet, and something knotted inside her.

Quickly she reclaimed them. "No, on my feet."

"You got a lot of aggressions to get out?" He looked at her sideways, as though the different vantage point would yield answers.

“No, that was the end of them.” She stood and winced as her feet made contact with the hard wood floor. “Ow.”

“Duh.”

“I’m getting old. This never used to hurt like this.”

He laughed and the sound followed her all the way down the hall.

CHAPTER 21

TJ hauled himself into the chair Norah pulled out for him. Still standing on the sidewalk when he turned around, she refused to come in. He wasn't sure if that bothered him or not. "Suit yourself."

Her grin at least let him know she wasn't upset with him, maybe she just didn't want to come see him. Giving a mock salute, he rolled himself through the front doors of the building that housed HeartBeats recording and practice studios. It was handicapped accessible and he didn't think much of the impression he made wheeling down the hallway.

Maybe he shouldn't have invited her. It wasn't like JD was bringing Kelsey or Alex would bring Bridget—who should have had that baby by now. Then again, the tour hadn't been re-tooled around any of them either.

Brenda spotted him. "Hey, how are you?" She didn't sound quite pleased to see him.

"Good, why?"

She stopped walking. "I thought you said you were up and around. I may need to cancel more tour dates."

"Oh, no you don't!"

She grinned. "That's the attitude I like to hear, but if you aren't ready . . ."

"I'm good." He pushed with his arms, standing up out of the chair for just a moment. "But I can only go a few steps right now. I just lost all my strength. I'll be back in time."

"All right." She wished him luck and went off down the hall, stopping to talk to someone else not ten steps later.

He pushed through the wide doorway into the studio. JD was already there, tuned up and singing something TJ hadn't heard before. Listening for three bars was all that was necessary to determine that it was a love song—surprisingly not for Kelsey. This one pined for the girl next door, in one verse as a kid, in the next as an adolescent, and finally as an adult.

When the last note ended TJ looked at his brother, knowing that even JD, as focused as he got when he played, couldn't have missed the fat wheels of his chair sitting inches away. "You told Kelsey that one isn't about Lilah, right?"

"It kind of is."

"You had feelings for her after junior high?"

JD shook his head. "Nope, just made for a better song."

TJ started to open his mouth, then held back. For the first time he had something over JD and he didn't need it. JD didn't need to know that Lilah had run around on him. That would ruin his few good memories before their parents practically disowned him for throwing away his stock analyst job to come do something as low-class as be a musician.

TJ had no pride or happiness at the knowledge either. With that thought came a flood of shame. He'd wronged the brother who'd done so much for him. He'd grown up simultaneously worshipping and hating JD. Jealousies had eaten at him: that he'd never be the golden child his big brother was, that he wasn't a brilliant musician, he wasn't a capable career man, he wasn't a family man. JD did it all. Well.

TJ never had. He simply wasn't as good as JD, in so many ways.

At that moment he looked at his brother and saw him as human, and TJ felt more comfortable in his own skin. He didn't miss the irony that skin that wasn't responding to his commands was the most comfortable he'd ever been in.

Alex arrived, looking nervous. "I'm here, but I'm going to bolt the minute we finish, and if she calls then one of you has to drive me."

His eyes were wide with pre-panic as he glanced between the brothers. "I take that back. JD you're going to drive me. No insult intended TJ."

He laughed. "Of course."

Craig arrived next, looking simply content. But then again Craig usually did. He'd been that way since he'd found Shay two years ago. Though their partying-together days were past, Craig still spoke to him straight. "You can get out of that thing, right?"

TJ nodded and wheeled over to where they had a bar stool set up for him in front of the mic stand. Using his arms for leverage, he stood, balancing on unsteady legs. He managed to get onto the high seat with some level of grace, and tucked his feet up on the foot rail. "Let's go."

The others tuned up. TJ didn't, he saved his energy.

They started with a slow one for him, and he sang it, giving it everything, wanting to impress them with what he could do. He ended up impressing himself. By the fifth song he had one foot against the ground for balance, and a quick glance down told him he looked like he belonged there perched atop the stool.

He didn't once envision screaming fans. Before, it was always how he knew what to say. This time he sang for himself and wondered how he had missed something so terribly obvious all along.

They were midway through a rough rehearsal of JD's new piece when Alex got *the call*. Bridget's water had broken.

"Oh! I didn't need to know that!" Craig made a face like someone had just shoved liver at him.

Alex went instantly insane, shouting into the phone. "I'll be right there!"

"I can hear you, honey." They all could hear Bridget laughing. "Get someone to drive you."

"I got him, Bridge!" JD hollered out, and he hauled Alex outside, even as he blustered, "They said they were going to induce her tomorrow. She can't wait until tomorrow?"

JD had the grace not to laugh at his friend. "It's not her. Babies come when they feel like it. It's your time, bud."

With that, the voices faded from the hall.

Craig looked up at TJ. "You look better. I've missed hanging out."

TJ was startled to realize that he missed his friend, but not his rowdy nights. He'd been so busy getting back in gear that a bar or a willing woman hadn't really crossed his mind.

Craig laid out the guitars in their cradles, and eyed TJ. "You need help?"

"Nah." Then he changed his mind. "Hand me JD's Fender?"

Craig nodded. TJ was the only one who could get away with touching any of his brother's guitars. He waited for Craig to leave him there, alone in the studio.

His fingers picked at strings, enjoying the feeling of each reacting, the sounds of individual notes. His left hand occupied his attention as it picked off chords, moving up and down the neck.

Shifting, he used one arm to push back up onto the stool and settle the guitar across his legs. He sang into the mic, at a decidedly lower volume than before, sometimes with his eyes closed, enjoying the idea that no one was listening.

The piano caught his eye. Before the accident, both he and

JD had been trying to hone their piano skills. They wanted to add some pieces to the next album with it, but neither of them played well enough to do it, and they weren't going to get anyone else. JD had probably gotten better while TJ was hauling himself through rehab hell. The thought didn't twist his gut anymore.

TJ wanted to walk over to it and contemplated making a beeline for it. But he knew better. If he didn't make it all the way, crashing into the piano would hurt. More than that, it would jostle the instrument. So he levered himself off the stool and down into the seat of his wheelchair, traveling the seven feet, then scooting over onto the bench.

His fingers caressed the keys and he tried a song from the old album. It was usually played with guitars and drums, but he wanted to hear it this way. He laid into the keys, only just then understanding the sway some had when they played. He'd always played straight-backed, more for the looks and the praise than the sound.

But this time he closed his eyes, his fingers picking out the tune even better than he would have guessed. If he just let himself play, and didn't *think* about it, it came. TJ gave the song a longer than usual intro, then added his voice over the piano strings. He'd read some critic once who described his voice as "honeyed whiskey;" TJ mostly ignored it at the time, thinking only that *honeyed-whiskey* meant sexy. Now he went for exactly that sound.

This Ordinary Man, like everything else since he'd been able to get out of that chair, suddenly made more sense. It was one they teased JD he should call: *Song I Wrote for Kelsey.*

TJ realized that he'd never done the song justice. He'd given a show, and he'd slowed down and looked out into the audience, making eye contact with as many of the women in the front as possible. But he'd never *felt* any of the pieces. He wasn't sure why he felt this one now.

Maybe he'd just needed to wash all the alcohol out of his system, clear his brain. Maybe it was the sense of accomplishment—for once in his life he'd really done something right. Not just had it happen to him or around him, but something he'd worked for.

He sang the chorus one more time through. A sigh came from behind him and he jerked around to find Norah leaning against the door, her eyes searching the ceiling for God only knew what. He deserved to have someone watching him, simply because he'd thought he was alone. It had probably looked odd, and maybe sounded worse—

"God, TJ, I love that song, but it's a good thing you didn't record that version. People would be having traffic accidents every time it was on the radio."

His fingers still stroked the keys even though he coaxed no sound from them. It didn't matter if she didn't like it. It hadn't been for her. "That bad?"

CHAPTER 22

She laughed, a deep burbling sound. "Just the opposite. I'm a puddle over here. You're going to have to drive that chair over and peel me off the floor." She looked at him and laughed again, "Then you're going to have to tell me dirty limericks or something to snap me out of it before I get behind the wheel. If I drive like this—"

She cut herself off, jerking straight. He could see her thoughts veer toward the accident that had taken her family.

TJ stood, reaching for her as the clouds crossed her eyes, and knowing he'd never make it. "Norah, don't."

She waved him away. "I was just wondering, if maybe he was celebrating something, and it all went horribly wrong. He would have more trouble sleeping at night than I do."

A nod was all he could muster in response, before her mood shifted again. "It's a shame we don't have a piano at the house."

He hadn't even thought of it.

She nodded at him, but he could see she was thinking about something else. Without thinking, his legs bent and he sat back down on the piano bench, the trail of a song itching in him. He knew where it had to go, it had to change keys in crazy ways and yet stay true to the core. Words found him, while his fingers silently walked black and white bars. *Her moods / shift like the wind, when she's gone / I don't know where she's been, when she leaves / I never know / if she's coming back again.*

TJ didn't know how long he sat there, tracing the keys, only that Norah was watching him. He could feel her eyes on him, and he wrote that in. That he didn't really know what she expected of him, and that she would be leaving soon. When he had the framework he blinked and turned to her. "You just stood there this whole time?"

"I didn't want to interrupt. I usually choreograph on my feet, but I've done it in my head." Her smile was genuine, "I've never seen what it looked like before this though. Play it for me."

Something deep took hold of him, a recognition that Norah would see herself in the song, and that would give her some power over him. He'd seen his brother hand it over to his wife, willingly, time and time again. He'd never seen it as taking guts before. So he played Norah her song.

She spoke even as the last note faded. "It beautiful. It's haunting and I think it's a little sad."

He agreed. "It needs work."

"Of course."

That shocked him. It did need work, but he'd expected platitudes and fawning. Or at least a polite rebuff. He didn't fish for more by adding that it was the first thing he'd written that he'd ever played for anybody.

He'd written music for Wilder before. But he'd never gotten it past his bedroom door. He was smart enough not to think he'd written a masterpiece when he hadn't. His pieces came out trite and stupid sounding. But as he looked back it made sense: he'd been living a trite and stupid life.

It was too much for one day. Part of him was itching to get

the music committed to paper. Another part of him realized that his hands would remember what he'd written and the words would stay in the back of his brain. And he was worn out. He told Norah so.

She tossed the keys and caught them, "Then let's go, cowboy."

He made his way back into his chair, then out the door, offering to peel her off the floor if necessary. She didn't say 'no,' she just laughed and walked off.

The car was parked curbside, the light of mid-afternoon blinding. They grabbed burgers and ate them on the couch, where TJ promptly passed out after he finished.

He woke to kinks in his neck and embarrassment that he didn't remember the conversation ending or anything. His body had just given up and gone to sleep. The light had faded and he sat up, only then realizing that he had company, and that she, too, had passed out cold.

Norah was curled into the far corner of the couch, facing in against the cushions. TJ just looked. Her hair had been pulled back that morning into a clip that kept the top half of it out of her face. Of course, a handful of rebellious wisps had escaped and formed heavy curls around her eyes and chin.

Her feet were encased in white socks, the kind a school-girl would wear. Under them he could read the lines of tape and gauze. She was wearing only a t-shirt and shorts in the late summer heat. Sleep showed her curves defined by length and muscle. Her thigh was slim enough around that he feared a hit could snap her, but a delineation between the muscles ran up the side, betraying the quiet strength in her. He wanted to reach out and trace it, but he knew he'd wake her. So he sat back and looked his fill.

She seemed so young, breathing peacefully, curled into his couch, and he felt so old. Still he'd learned something from

Norah. When she'd slapped him she'd also said that the world had to watch out when TJ set his mind on something. What would she think if she knew she was the next thing he'd set his mind on?

He wouldn't wake her.

He did need to do something though.

So he rolled off the couch and started doing crunches.

He was going to make Norah fall in love with him, and he was starting now. It didn't matter that he was still in that damned chair. She'd want him either way. She'd get an able man, but he wanted to know that she'd have him if he wasn't.

He counted fifty, and took a ten count break before starting in again.

Norah had become his gold standard. This was why he'd never been able to get into any of the bouncy blonde things he'd dated or simply screwed. He'd needed a tight, slim, exotic *Norah*.

He counted a ten beat break at one hundred, only to find Norah awake and watching him. He should have taken off his shirt. His abs had filled back in nicely.

"How many are you doing?" Her voice sounded sleepy, and he hoped he might get to hear that just-woke-up sound from her in a better circumstance. "A thousand?"

He grinned, thinking about it. "How'd you know?"

"Because your therapist said your limit was five hundred. And why'd you smile at me like that?"

"Like what?"

She shook her head. "A crocodile smile."

He didn't answer. *Note to self: Norah can read you like a book.* God, he loved it. But he wasn't about to turn himself over yet, so he just asked another question. "You know I'm not adhering to my limits, but you never ask me to stop. Why?"

She put her feet on the floor and he winced when she did. But she turned on a few lights, brightening the dullness that had come with dusk while they were sleeping. "First, it wouldn't have done any good. Second, it's your life. Nothing to do with me. Third, I remember watching you one of the early days at therapy, every time you fell you got back up. Every time, no matter how much of a beating you'd taken. You impressed the crap out of me, and I said so to the therapist. That I was a dancer and thought I knew something about making your body work when it wasn't made to. I said I'd never seen anything like you. Never seen anyone get up with more determination each time."

TJ waited for the end.

"He said he had. That once in a while you got a patient like that. And you didn't stop them, because every one of them eventually walked."

He nodded and started on the crunches again, liking that he'd impressed her. It meant a lot.

He had just decided to peel his shirt off, when the phone rang. Norah popped up from where she'd just settled herself on the couch to get it. "Hello? Mmm Hmm, he's right here."

She put her hand over the mouth piece and whispered. "It's your mother."

Oh, shit. He took the phone. "Hi, Mom."

Norah had never asked why his parents hadn't shown up after the accident. But she'd known his parents. She'd probably figured out that he and JD had downplayed the severity of his injuries, hoping to avoid any of this.

Right now his mother couldn't care less about his spine. "Who was that girl? She sounded sleepy!"

"That's because she was asleep."

"At your house!"

"She lives here, Mom."

"Ahhh!" It was a deeply affronted sound. But TJ thought the woman could take her plastic principles and stuff them. "Then you'd better tell me about her."

It was a command. If the woman was sleeping in his house, then his mother expected a wedding invitation within the month. "She's a dancer, Mom."

Norah watched him sideways, making no pretense about eavesdropping. Her eyebrows rose.

"A dancer!" Again his mother was affronted.

Suddenly, he realized. He spoke it out loud for Norah's sake. "No, Mom, not a stripper, a *dancer*. Formerly with the Houston Ballet."

Norah did laugh at him.

"Still." His mother managed to be upset that he had a prima ballerina in his house.

"I'm a musician, Mom. It makes sense." They could be *low class* together. Only by his mother's rules was being famous in a band or being a dancer with a Ballet low-class. There was always that snotty air of 'we don't *perform*.'

He fought the urge to yell at her *it's Norah Davidson, and she grew up hot!* Because then it was likely to be all over that he was seeing Norah Davidson, when in fact he wasn't. *Yet.*

Suddenly it occurred to him that there were other people who lived by his mother's rules: particularly Norah's family.

After hanging up, he finished his crunches and took a shower, emerging with only his towel around his hips. Norah was nowhere around.

He changed into plaid pajama pants and decided it was time to start. Leaving the chair behind, he tottered down the hallway to her room. He leaned heavily on the wall, and locked his knees on more than one occasion.

Still, halfway there he realized he wasn't going to make it. Turning, he leaned his back against the wall and took a breather. When had he taken it for granted to just walk twenty feet?

Norah peeked out of her room, wearing another pair of men's boxer briefs and a t-shirt.

He grabbed hold of that. “See, those aren’t dance clothes, they’re pajamas.”

She rolled her eyes at him. “Taken to lurking in hallways, have we?” She made no comment that he was on his feet.

He ignored her back. “Maybe that’s why you’re low-class.”

She stopped in front of him, laughing. “No, I’m pretty sure it’s because I eloped at eighteen, pregnant. Lilah became the good one then.”

“Lilah, huh?”

Norah nodded. “She married a doctor. In the church. Never mind that she’s a mild alcoholic who smokes a pack a day when she thinks her kids aren’t watching.”

“Jesus.” He looked her up and down. Healthy, beautiful, wonderful. “I am so glad you didn’t follow in Lilah’s footsteps on that one.”

“Me, too.” Her grin was infectious.

His arm snaked out and around her before he could stop it, hauling her closer. His stomach pulled as he realized what he intended to do.

His mouth closed over hers, and she didn’t stop him.

Keeping it soft, his hands searched for and found that mass of black silk she called hair. He buried himself in her scent, wondering if any other kiss had ever been this good.

She kissed him back, and that gentle pressure was enough to make him gasp.

So he stopped there, pulling away. Only because he knew if he didn’t, he’d go too far. Too far for a first kiss. Too far to keep it from maybe feeling cheap.

For just a moment he looked in her eyes, expecting heat instead of the bewilderment he saw there. In a last ditch effort not to ruin everything before he even started, he found his voice. “I’m really glad you weren’t the good one.”

He disentangled his hands from her hair. “I’m going to bed.

Good night." He planted one last kiss on her nose, not sure why he'd done it, just that her nose had looked cute there.

Turning away, he faltered back to his own room, leaning heavily on the wall. He just wasn't sure if his legs were giving out from under him because his legs didn't work, or because his brain was overwhelmed.

CHAPTER 23

Norah didn't know what to make of it. TJ was on his feet again. Not well, mind you, but up and around. What he did couldn't be called walking. She would watch him find his balance then stumble to the nearest solid object that could support him. Even so, he was getting better at it day by day.

Currently, he was leaning against the upright grand he'd rented and installed in the dining room the day after she picked him up at the studio. He was grinning at her like a shark.

She didn't know what to do with him. He'd kissed her in the hallway that night. Then kissed her again the following morning, just a peck on the mouth before he went into therapy. He hugged her, he touched the corner of her mouth at dinner, and looked at her like she *was* dinner. He set her on fire.

Part of her brain laughed at her—she *did* know what to do with a man like that. But the other part of her brain argued back. This wasn't like what she'd known before. It wasn't a one night only deal. It wasn't true love either.

Norah was smart enough to realize she was the only one in line. TJ still wasn't up to his usual self, but he might figure Norah would have him. As soon as he could walk out of here, he wouldn't look back. Okay, she adjusted her assessment, maybe that was a little mean. He wouldn't be drinking like he had before, and he probably didn't screw every willing female. He had enough of them that he could be quite discriminating.

It didn't change the fact that she wasn't chosen, she was merely available. It also didn't change the fact that she wanted him.

She never thought that watching a man fall down would make her fall for him. But TJ made it happen. The way he got back up, every time, even when he seemed defeated, spoke of the strength that was in him, even when he wasn't strong. She'd never seen him cry, but she'd seen him let go, and seen him get it back together afterwards. He'd recently gained a maturity she hadn't seen in a single interview or TV clip in all the years since they were kids.

And he wanted her.

Norah didn't have any doubt that he would say yes if she offered. Then again, he wasn't legendary for refusing women.

His voice cut through her thoughts, "Why are you looking at me like that?"

She fudged. "Just wondering what your therapist thinks about you toppling around like that?"

He grinned again. "That I should just use the walker."

"Yeah, that's gonna happen." She knew he hated it.

"That's my girl."

She didn't know if she was *his* girl, but she knew how he thought. "You know next you get a cane—and not a nice one. One of those silver ones with the four legs at the bottom."

His hands grabbed for his heart and he mimicked being wounded.

Norah laughed at him. "You'll be ready to go?"

He nodded, already focused on the piano keys in front of him, and Norah went off to change. She returned twenty minutes later, in her leotard and tights, her hair up in a looped-through ponytail, sneakers on her feet. She didn't say anything, she just walked up and stood beside him, wanting to see how long it took him to see that she was there. He played on, and she waited.

TJ didn't seem to notice her at all. Until she realized that he was messing with her. He'd focused on his left hand, playing scales, and she hadn't seen the right hand creep across the piano bench. Then she felt his fingers against the back of her thigh. She just stood there, wondering what he'd do if she didn't seem to notice. But she wasn't really given that option.

The hand crept up until he stroked her ass, and he couldn't keep the grin off his face.

She called off the dogs. "Give it up, TJ. You know I'm here. I know you know. It's time to go."

"Damn. I was enjoying that."

She turned and realized that his chair was nowhere near him. He swiveled himself away from the piano and she could see him calculating his path. He spotted the corner of the table. Then the arm of the couch. An upright chair.

Her mouth moved without her permission. "How are you going to do it?"

He grinned that crocodile smile she'd seen more of lately. He must be recovering. "I am going to beg. Sweet Norah, you'll help me, right?"

Her tone was dry. "I'll get your walker."

"Ugh!"

Good, he sounded like TJ again.

"I'll get your chair?"

He heaved a sigh.

She fetched it and was wheeling it back to him, only to discover him waiting at the edge of the couch. On his feet.

Stopping where she was, she offered up the wheelchair, "Well, come and get it then."

The look he shot her was pure steel. Going across the room

could wear him out, but she'd never given him quarter before and didn't see why she should now.

TJ came at her, practically falling into the chair with a grunt. She held it steady until he was in it, then she slung her bag over her shoulder and walked out the front door.

He called out behind her as he caught up on the front porch. "Are you going dancing?"

"No, I thought I'd play golf." It was her only defense against him when he was like this. The turned-on charm turned her off, but this she could never refuse. So she was sarcastic and wry.

"Norah, your feet can't be healed yet."

"They're healed just fine."

"They're still covered in gauze. They need more time."

Turning, she leveled a gaze at him. "Listen, Pot, I've had just about enough of *you* telling me to 'respect my limits.' If I were to go by your standards I would have danced on them yesterday."

"Norah."

She didn't answer. The trouble was her name sounded wonderful from his mouth, it looked good on his lips. So she steeled herself and waited for him to get in the car.

He did, and sat quietly while she folded the chair and tucked it behind her seat. She cast a glance at the handi-van, parked off to the side of the driveway. They hadn't needed it in while, and with luck he wouldn't again.

The drive was short, but seemed longer for the silence in the car. They did everything in reverse when they arrived at the rehabilitation facility, Norah getting the chair out for him then waiting while he got out of the car. "I'll be back for you in three hours."

She started to walk away, but felt her arm catch. TJ had her by the wrist. She turned, exasperated, "What?"

"Kiss me?"

CHAPTER 24

"Kiss me and make the guys jealous?" He grinned at her, that sweet, I-love-you, eyes-shining grin that worked on every female heart but hers.

Casting a glance over at the window, she saw that the front desk had a clear view of the two of them, and that several of the male therapists were hanging out there.

She smiled, and leaned down closer to him, her face right near his. When she was almost there, she reached up and patted him on the head before turning to walk away.

He caught her wrist again.

This time, when she turned back she was mad.

He was caught off guard by it. "What? What did I do?"

"Don't give me that crap, TJ. Don't try to charm me, it doesn't work. I was there when your legs cramped so bad in the middle of the night that you couldn't keep your mouth shut. I was there when you smashed plates in your kitchen. So don't give me those worn out grins, they're insulting."

Oh, Dear Lord. She might as well have just said, *Don't treat me like everyone else, because I want to be the one.* She'd just handed him a loaded gun and told him where to aim.

He nodded, his expression serious and honest.

She just nodded back at him and walked off, only to find her wrist shackled in his fingers for a third time. "Norah."

"What! What do you want, TJ?"

"Will you kiss me?"

"TJ—"

"Because I want you to." This time there was no grin, no cocky attitude. Plain as day, written all over his face was his uncertainty whether or not she would.

That bastard. He had her.

She sighed. "Move your feet."

He looked at her, not sure of what she was doing. *Good.* But he took his feet off the rests. She kicked them up, and moved in between his legs. She slipped one finger through her key ring before taking his head in her hands and tilting his face to meet hers.

She didn't know how she did it, just that she was bent over and her lips were against his. Her eyes fell closed as his mouth moved against hers, his lips searching, his head tilting.

Norah felt his arms encircling her shoulders and she jerked back. "Be good."

She gave him a quick glance up and down, trying not to notice the glaze in his eyes, or that he didn't move other than to nod at her. Then she got in the car and bolted.

Pulling into the parking space at the studio, she wondered how she had arrived. Her brain was still back on the sidewalk in front of the rehab building with TJ. She wondered if she'd spot it sitting there when she went to get him.

She opened the studio and danced in the big room. That kiss siphoned her brain cells and made choreography impossible. So Norah gave up and ran old routines.

The problem was that her body knew the patterns and, once started, would run the entire dance. She watched in the mirror and checked her form, but her brain wandered back to TJ no matter how much she tried to rein it in.

She stopped periodically to help sign up students who came in through the doors. A bell would ding when Mrs. Kenner at the front desk needed backup, but Norah wasn't certain how much she actually helped. Mrs. Kenner pointed out Norah had signed a three-year-old into the high school class, and a boy into pointe.

She gave up early and parked the car at rehab. On the way in, she merely waved to the folks at the front desk and headed into the sadistic jungle gym, as TJ referred to it. Instantly, she spotted him, off to one side with his trainer, doing leg presses. He pushed far more weight than she'd seen the last time she was here. But probably still not what she herself could do.

She wanted to hang back and watch. But rules were rules. You couldn't watch unannounced. Whoever you were visiting had the right to know you were there. So she made her way over and waited for a break before tapping him on the shoulder, "Hi."

His head popped up and he smiled at her. A real smile. All TJ, all glad to see her. Norah felt her heart simultaneously melt and break. She shouldn't let him get any closer. She was moving back in with her Dad in five days. And TJ would be moving back into his own world not long after that.

He looked over his shoulder at her. "I'm not done yet. Are you hanging out?"

She merely nodded.

He gave her a small frown like he knew something was up, but he chose not to pursue it. For that, she was grateful.

She stayed, she coached, she laughed when the therapist told him to try to be up and out of his chair as much as possible. At least Tim, who was barking the orders today, knew enough to laugh at that one himself. Then he told TJ, "Congratulations. You graduate."

"What?" Norah wasn't sure if it was his voice or hers.

"Twice a week. Put your time in at the studio and give me a signed copy of the next album for my wife." He grinned.

TJ laughed at that, then hopped into his chair and led Norah out the door.

They made it home with reasonable conversation, rambled in through the front door and showered at separate ends of the house. Norah simply kept her door closed when she got out of the shower. Telling herself she would only sleep for fifteen minutes or so, she lay down, only to startle awake several hours later.

She dressed in jeans and a pullover shirt, taking care not to do anything too sexy, realizing that she needed to start distancing herself now, while she still could. She found him at the piano, in jeans and a t-shirt that showed everyone just how much he'd improved his arms in the past several months. Those same arms were playing the piano with a gentleness that tugged at her. The same song he'd composed in the studio the other day. He stopped and scribbled something on pages he'd spread out across the front. Without looking at her, he invited her out for pasta, his favorite choice after working himself to near exhaustion.

"Okay." She told herself it was because she craved garlic sauce and not his attention.

At dinner, TJ waited until they were seated in a back booth, before he asked her what had been bothering her earlier. Norah evaded, and for some reason he let her.

But he tried another route. "JD and Kelsey have been asking when they'll see us for dinner again. Anything you want me to tell them? Or should I make something up?"

"Tell them whatever you told your mother. That seemed to work pretty well. She was more concerned that some *dancer*," she whispered the word, "was living in your house, than that you'd had a crippling accident."

"That won't work on JD and Kelsey. It only worked on my mother because she hated me from the moment I was born."

While it was delivered with a disarming grin, the statement was too searing to ignore. "TJ."

"It's true. I have proof."

Norah doubted he could have that proof; the woman had doted on those boys.

"You know what JD's full name is, right?"

"John Darcy."

"Uh-huh. He's named after Jane Austen's leading males."

Norah set down her fork. "I'm not sure that that proves anything other than JD likely got teased in tenth grade."

"Do you know my full name?"

She shook her head.

TJ didn't speak. He just quit eating for a moment and reached under the table to fetch his wallet. His Tennessee State Driver's License skidded across the table to her.

Thomas Jefferson Hewlitt showed in capital letters.

"Proof." He resumed eating.

"How is this proof? Thomas Jefferson was a fine president."

"He owned slaves and has hundreds of descendants he disowned." TJ shook his head.

"He had that neat house."

"You aren't going to convince me."

Norah handed the driver's license back to him. "Did you ever stop to be grateful that she didn't name you George Washington or Abraham Lincoln?"

"Where were you when I was in third grade? I could have used a little humor about it then."

"I think I was still in diapers." She was stuffed and finally forced herself to set the fork down. It didn't help that TJ managed to consumed his entire meal, making her look like she just wasn't trying. "TJ suits you."

"Sure, but I think I spent the first three months of every school year being called 'JD' by my teachers."

That she understood. "By second grade, I learned that if I made a big production at the beginning of the year and demanded to be called 'Lilah,' they always took it upon themselves to correct me and they never got it wrong."

"Very smart." He paid the bill and had her pasta wrapped up for her. On the way home he started a different conversation. "Are you going to still drive me around after you move back in with your Dad, or do I need to find someone else?"

"I can do it." Even as she spoke the words, she wasn't sure why she committed to it. It was just prolonging the agony. "Your schedule will be about the same right? Except you'll be going to the studio more?"

He nodded. "Thank you. You've been a godsend."

"I'd really rather I was just a friend." She thought about the lump of cash sitting in her savings account. It didn't feel right to take money for lusting after him. It didn't feel right to get paid when she was getting kissed. Kissed by one of the hottest bachelors on the chart. Hadn't he made the People sexiest men list a few years ago? She'd been kissed by TJ Hewlitt. *Thomas Jefferson* Hewlitt she reminded herself, as though that might clear some of her wayward thoughts.

She let him lock the front door behind them while she put her food in the fridge. When she straightened up and closed the door on the cold, putting out the fridge light, he was silhouetted in the kitchen doorway. He'd gotten out of his chair and stood up.

"Norah?"

"Good night, TJ." She ducked and fled, out the other door from the kitchen, around the back of the house and into her room.

She successfully avoided him the next day, until she had to drive him to the studio. Norah congratulated herself on keeping the conversation to a minimum. Luckily, he didn't ask for a kiss this time.

She sorted paperwork at the studio, not even trying to dance today. When she left five hours later, she was relatively certain that she'd placed each student in the right class. Then she headed back to get TJ, ready to avoid getting caught in any conversations again.

He was helpful, making only unimportant small talk until they were in the car with doors closed. He'd no sooner clicked his seatbelt shut, than he turned to face her. "Norah, why are you avoiding me?"

She lied through her teeth. "I'm not."

"Uh-huh."

So what if he didn't buy it? It's what she was selling.

When they got home she shut herself in her room for most of the remainder of the evening. Then she congratulated herself on a job well done. Four days left to go.

CHAPTER 25

Norah was emerging from the bathroom the next morning, the taste of mint toothpaste still in her mouth, when a crash came at her door. Jerking into action, she raced the five steps around the bed and threw open the door, only to have TJ come falling through at her.

Startling again, she grabbed for his arms and realized she wasn't capable of supporting his full weight. With as much thought as she was able to muster, she supported what she could and guided him to the edge of the bed.

He laughed. "All the way around the house, and still upright."

"Not so much. You came crashing through my door."

"But not because my legs gave out. I just lost my balance."

Like that made it okay. But Norah just smiled at him. He seemed so pleased, and, in truth, so was she. He'd be driving again soon and on his own. Turning away, she set the washcloth still in her hand on the nightstand, only to feel his arms slip around her waist.

Her stomach sucked in. He tugged her down onto the bed. The top and boxer briefs she'd been sleeping in didn't quite meet and his hands had slipped between, touching bare skin.

Without a word, he settled her beside him, and she scooted back.

"Norah."

She didn't nod, couldn't answer.

"You do realize I'm a man, right?"

She laughed, relaxing just a little bit. "It's hard to miss."

"Good." He looked at her a little sideways. "You know that I'm fully functional, and have been for a while?"

There went that relaxation. She nodded.

"So when you run around dressed like this, you totally turn me on." He gestured to the briefs and top she wore.

The t-shirt was the same one she'd worn the day she'd showed him that his fingers worked. Only after she'd fled the scene did she see in her own mirror just how low the slit in the front went.

TJ's cerulean blue eyes found hers, and she wanted to look away, but found she wasn't capable. His voice still held a conversational tone, only his face didn't look casual. "Are you trying to turn me on?"

"I wasn't *trying*." She protested, but whether she protested him coming at her or her own reaction, she didn't know. "I'm in my own bedroom."

He nodded, but reached out his hand, his finger tracing the edge of the neckline on her shirt. "This shirt is cut so low," his finger followed the curve of the top of one breast, effectively stopping her breathing, "that you look like you're going to fall out of it." His finger dipped down in between her breasts, making the point that the shirt was indeed too provocative. His eyes followed the path his finger was taking, up and over the curve of the other breast.

All of her control fled. She sat, rigid as a statue, enthralled by his touch. She didn't move as his finger found her collarbone, then followed a path back down between her breasts.

Of course she wasn't wearing a bra. She'd been asleep. TJ's

finger hooked into the slit of the shirt and tugged. "And I want you to fall out of it."

She had no choice but to move nearer or let him pull the shirt out far enough to see down it. That wouldn't take much. Her brain didn't decide, but her body did. She followed the tug of the fabric and the pull inside her, until she was right next to him, until she couldn't get any closer.

His eyes left the front of her shirt, searching her face, leaving her unsure of what he found there. His hand opened, all fingers following skin, up between her breasts and around the back of her neck. They laced into her hair, and her mouth fell open knowing what was coming.

The faintest grin crossed his mouth before it found hers. His kiss sent streamers of heat out through her, undoing the frozen muscles she'd held so tightly in place. Where before she'd been stiff, she now moved against him, her arms coming up to hold him, her mouth taking his with an abandon she hadn't felt in forever.

She held him there, kissing him until his mouth left hers. His lips traced paths along her jaw, up to her ear and back. Her head tipped, giving him better access. If they stopped, it wouldn't be because of her. Her fingers searched the front of his shirt, grabbing at the soft fabric and wanting it gone, wanting the feel of hot skin beneath her fingertips.

With a small chuckle, he leaned back, breaking contact and pulling the shirt off in one fluid movement. He waited, maybe wondering what she thought. But she thought he was magnificent, all muscle and lean strength. Her fingers found his chest, curling in the light dusting of hair there, loving the texture of him.

For a moment he watched her look and touch, and he'd gotten tired of waiting. One of his hands came under her arm and up behind her head, able to brace her where he wanted. Her fingers still played with him, going only by feel as his lips found hers again.

This time the kiss was hotter, more demanding. His tongue slipped inside her mouth and she opened wider to him, giving as well as she got and wanting still more. She felt his fingers at her neck while she kissed him trying to convey all the flames inside her. His hand traced down over her collarbone and found its way inside the front of her shirt, cupping one breast.

A startled gasp escaped her and TJ licked it off her lips, just as his fingers found her nipple. Norah leaned into his touch, not sure when she'd ever been this on fire, ever wanted someone with this drive for completion.

He smiled that half-smile again, his eyes hot as blazes, as he left her mouth, kissing down her neck and over to where he'd tugged her shirt to expose just the nipple on one breast. She realized what he was doing only as he did it, and she let her head fall back as the sensations of his mouth closing over the tip rocketed through her.

She was putty when he leaned back and stripped the shirt over her head. Breathing heavily in cadence with him, she watched as he paused. She expected steam and sex, she wasn't prepared for the reverence in his tone. "God, Norah, you're beautiful."

She started to breathe in, the clutching in her heart radiating out, making her want to think, to wonder, but he didn't let her. TJ dove back at her, touching her everywhere, fondling her breasts, running his fingers along the indentation of her waist. His mouth followed, lavishing attention on every exposed inch of her, while she reached for him, wanting to touch him, to feel him beneath her fingers.

She didn't realize, until he found her, that he'd slipped his hand under the waistband of her boxer briefs. His fingers touching her, lighting her on fire, making her gasp out his name.

His own voice came out under tight rein, "Oh God, you feel so good." As his fingers plunged inside her, he caressed her, shrinking her world to only the places where he touched. Without removing his hand, he stretched out beside her, his mouth finding hers again. He stroked her, holding her in this suspended state of frenzy, not letting her come down. She was simply a breathing, writhing body, totally at his mercy when he removed his hand and made short work of stripping the last of her clothing from her.

She lay there panting, wanting, and too wound up to wait. Coming up on her knees, she reached out to him, following the line of hair down his chest that plunged into the waistband of his pants. She unzipped him, needing his help to get him as naked as she was.

He pulled her against him, both of them on their knees on the bed, his mouth searching hers as her hands traced the curves and planes of his hard body. She moved against him, savoring the feel of man—of *him*.

TJ pulled his mouth away from her, for just a moment in the middle of all the frenzy and the reaching he found her eyes. "Say 'yes,' Norah. Please."

The last word drifted out on a sigh, begging more than polite.

"Yes."

He kissed her once, hard and demanding, before breaking away. He leaned over to the nightstand where his pants had fallen, fumbling for his wallet.

Finally having access to him, she found his swollen shaft and caressed him while he attempted to work the packet he'd pulled out. He groaned as she pushed against him, then kissed her while he sheathed himself and sat back on the bed. He lifted her, holding her over him. Norah felt him, more than ready, probing her, and she pushed against him, onto him, the feeling of him entering her robbing her of the ability to watch his face.

He pulled her to him, making a sound of sweet yearning at her ear, and he held her tightly, moving the two of them together. There was only him. Only the feel of her skin on his, of him deep inside her, trying to get deeper. She held on tight while she felt the waves of release overtake her.

CHAPTER 26

TJ felt something shift, and he fought for control. He fought for the ability to watch as Norah came apart in his arms from his loving. And he loved her.

Her body tightened in perfect rhythm around him. It took every ounce of determination not to follow her, but to continue and give her more. With a wrung-out sigh she started to relax in his arms, trembling. Nothing had ever felt sweeter, but he leaned over her, laying her back, keeping himself fitted inside her where he belonged and, with his weight on his arms, began to move again.

At first she protested, as though her body couldn't take another onslaught. He stroked her until a small moan escaped her as her hips started moving against him again. He murmured to her, words of encouragement until she clung to him, moving as frantically as he did. Together they fought for another release.

Her hips locked her onto him, and this time she took him with her—the grip of her orgasm a storm he couldn't help getting tossed in, triggering his own fierce waves of pleasure.

A sound ripped out of his throat and he collapsed against

her. His body worn out from the exertion, his mind numb from what had just happened. Realizing that he was crushing her, he rolled to the side, taking her with him.

It was, he knew, the first time he'd ever done that. He was one of those men who did not want to be touched after sex. He would find the strength to stand or at least roll away every time. But right now he wanted to stay here, inside Norah. He couldn't hold her tight enough, couldn't get close enough. He breathed in the scent of her hair, felt her skin touching his, felt the wetness on her skin and his.

He smiled to himself. They would both need a shower, and God what he could do to her in a shower.

Her hands pushed against his chest, feeling small and sweet. "TJ, let go."

He shook his head, even knowing that she couldn't see him. "Stay."

"We can't. The condom."

He held her tighter, knowing what he had felt while making love. Something *had* shifted, and he suddenly realized what it was. He didn't look forward to telling her, so he pulled her tighter and thought maybe she wouldn't be upset.

"TJ, you have to get up." She shoved against him again, harder this time.

"Just stay, Norah. Please. It's too late to do anything—"

She interrupted him, not letting him get all of it out. Pushing against him, she struggled for real, and he knew he had to let her go.

She was angry at him. "You know, condoms don't work if you don't use them correctly."

"Norah, the condom broke. I felt it."

She disengaged like a bolt of lightning had hit her, and he used her frantic movements to his advantage. He peeled the remnants of the busted condom from himself and flung it into the trash he'd seen tucked under her nightstand.

Norah was worried, he understood that. He held his arms out to her, knowing it wasn't like him and knowing that she was what was different. He'd hold her, tell her he loved her, and they'd make things right.

But she shoved away and off the bed. On her feet, she looked at him once with frantic eyes. He started to speak, almost getting sidetracked by Norah standing straight in front of him in all her naked glory. But she was upset and he needed to help her.

This time when she looked at him, she was mad. "Why didn't you stop?"

"I didn't know what I felt until afterward. I never had sex without a condom before. I never had one break." Her anger didn't change with his words. She didn't crawl back into his arms and ask him to make it better. The words tumbled out of his mouth, begging her to forgive him. "I didn't know."

"But—"

He waited for something more but it didn't come.

"Norah?"

She didn't look at him, just walked almost blindly to the bathroom. Uncertain what was going on right in front of him, he waited. He heard the water running, and he lay back figuring she needed a moment alone. He would fix things when she got out.

But when she came out a moment later, her eyes still looked glassy. She didn't look upset, but she didn't look calm either. She started over to the old bureau and opened drawers, grabbing jeans and a bra and a t-shirt. She started pulling on the clothes.

"Norah."

She shook her head, not turning to face him.

"Norah, what's wrong?"

That at least startled a reaction from her. Just not the one he expected.

"What's wrong is that the condom broke." She slipped the bra on and the t-shirt over her head.

TJ started to rise up to get her, only to discover his lack of energy was going to last a little bit. Being with Norah had drained him and his legs didn't want to support him. He settled for sitting up behind her and reaching out.

She evaded him even as she slipped into a tiny pair of underwear and then jeans.

"Norah, where are you going?" He was starting to get worried. She wasn't even in there.

"I'm going to go take care of the problem."

"Can we talk about it?" She hadn't made eye contact with him once, just mechanically went about getting dressed. "If you get pregnant it will be okay, Norah—"

"It *won't* be okay." She practically yelled it, cutting him off and showing the first emotion she had since leaving his arms. "You don't know anything about being a parent. It isn't going to *work itself out.*"

"Norah, we'll figure something out together. I have plenty of money, that's not an issue." He reached out for her, his fingers reaching the denim of her jeans, only to be slapped away with a vicious, stinging swing. "Ow, Norah!"

"*We* won't figure anything out. *I've* got it taken care of." She walked out the bedroom door and down the hall.

Alarmed, TJ shoved off the bed to follow her, only to discover his legs still refused to hold him. "Norah!"

She didn't come back.

A second later he heard the front door shut, and a moment after that her engine and the sound of wheels on smooth pavement.

CHAPTER 27

Norah tried to breathe while she drove straight to the clinic. She'd make them work her in. She couldn't get pregnant. She couldn't get pregnant.

She repeated it like a mantra.

The problem was she knew from experience that she *could* get pregnant, and the bands tightening around her chest with every minute told her just what a bad idea that would be. He had so casually thought it would be okay, that he could just throw his money at her.

But she wouldn't let him. It was her fault just as much as his. In all these years, with all the one night stands, just looking to slake some need, she'd never had a condom break.

Her hand reached up and wiped at the tears that had fallen down her face without her permission. She made all the appropriate turns and stops, and prayed that the doctor would work her in.

TJ.

Of all the people for the condom to break with. It would be the one she shouldn't have been with in the first place. Her heart was frozen, pumping icy blood throughout her system. Even though it was the last of the hot summer days, she cranked the heater, but couldn't get warm.

She parked in the lot and ran up the stairs. Stopping at the front desk, she explained in hushed tones what had happened to the woman in the berry pink scrubs. She received a sympathetic smile and a clipboard with several pages attached. She was asked to wait.

It was all she could do not to stare at the pregnant woman in the waiting room. There were usually pregnant women in here when she came for her checkup, but she usually had time to prepare herself before she came. She never sat here, staring at the walls, wondering if she might be pregnant.

She tried to focus on the questions on the page and filled them out as best she could before waiting nervously on the edge of her seat.

What seemed like an eternity later, Norah was called. The doctor was sympathetic, she always had been. She knew about Jeff and Jordan and wasn't surprised when Norah asked about morning after pills.

Norah thought she had bordered on demanding them.

The doctor looked through the files. "Let's see, you were in almost two months ago. Is anything different?"

All she could do was shake her head, and try to keep her fingers from twisting.

"All right, then we don't have to give you an exam."

A knot loosened inside of her. The idea of an exam had seemed so violating. But she would have done it.

"Norah." The doctor waited until she made eye contact. "I'll prescribe you the pills—"

"Oh, thank you. Thank you, I'm so sorry." She gushed, the words tumbling out of her.

"I wasn't finished."

Norah nodded her acquiescence to whatever it was, waiting.

Finally the doctor continued. "These aren't birth control, and I usually only give them out on one condition."

"What's that?" She didn't add *I'll do anything, I just can't get pregnant.*

"That you find a more permanent alternate form of birth control. I would recommend the pill, or an implant, an IUD."

Norah waited, her hands and heart still twisting. After a moment she realized the doctor wanted her to make a choice. "The pill."

"I'm writing you two prescriptions."

Norah listened intently to the instructions, when to take the pills, what it might make her feel. What should make her call the office tomorrow morning, what shouldn't.

Then she took her prescriptions and bolted.

The pharmacy line was too long. The workers too slow. Norah knew that all the pharmacy workers knew what her prescription was for. If they were unsure, then the additional first time prescription of the birth control pills screamed that she'd been having unprotected sex.

She blinked back tears. She sat and fidgeted. She waited, stalking the magazine aisle, but couldn't find anything of interest. Finally, they called her name.

Rushing to the counter, she handed over her credit card and gratefully took the small bottle with one lone pill rattling in it and the pill case with her next method of birth control.

She fled the scene, stopping only long enough to purchase a bottle of water on the way out. Sitting in the car, she pushed and cranked at the stubborn pill bottle top, finally getting in. Then, with a gulp, she washed it down.

Relief settling over her, she pulled out of the parking lot. At the first stop light, she shoved the pill pack down in her purse. At a fast food restaurant she pulled through to the back of the lot and threw the pharmacy trash into the dumpster. TJ rode in this car all the time. It wasn't like he wouldn't know what she'd done, but something about having evidence upset her.

By the time she was halfway home she was shaking uncontrollably. She was almost not safe to drive. But she couldn't call TJ to come and get her and no one was on the road.

She felt tears splashing down her cheeks and dripping onto her shirt.

TJ would be there when she got home. There wasn't anywhere he could go, but there wasn't anywhere else for her to go either. She couldn't go to her Dad's, it was too far from here. Besides she wasn't a coward, and her problem had been solved. But her stomach churned, and she knew it wasn't from the medication.

Norah turned the sedan into the driveway, acting like she wasn't sick and shaking. Then she forced herself out of the car and up the front porch ramp.

TJ met her at the door. He was showered and dressed and propped in the door.

That he'd showered angered her for some reason. That he hadn't sat around wanting to be certain that he could beg her forgiveness. She pushed it to the back corners of her mind.

"Norah," His arms reached for her, the frown on his face one of concern. "Where did you go?"

"Away." She pushed past his embrace. "I took care of it."

She was walking down the hall, but his voice chased her. "Damnit, Norah, I can't follow after you and you know it. What did you do?"

He did follow after her, just not fast enough to catch her. When she spun around, he was at the end of the hallway, his face contorted. It wasn't rage, or anger, or even flat-out concern. She couldn't place it, and she didn't have time.

"I got a morning after pill. I won't get pregnant."

With that delivery done, she turned and fled to her room. Closing the door behind her, she locked it as she heard him crashing down the hallway. His voice carried through the wood. "Norah!"

She didn't answer. She couldn't.

She had taken the pill as a response to her fear. All that waiting in the doctor's office, all those nerves at the pharmacy, she had toughed it out. But she hadn't *thought*. And thinking was churning her stomach.

It was *her* baby. Even if it wasn't yet. And she wasn't capable of destroying it. Or even of destroying the possibility of it.

His fists pounded on the door and he called to her.

She managed to get out a few words, "Leave me alone!" before she bolted into her thankfully private bathroom and vomited.

Her stomach heaved out the pill and the shaking quieted.

Sitting on the floor of the bathroom, while TJ yelled for her through the door, her hands stilled, and her heart did, too. It didn't matter that she was more terrified of having another baby than of anything else in this world. She would have to play the cards she was dealt and level the rest with TJ later.

He was still calling to her through the door when she stripped down and climbed into the shower.

CHAPTER 28

TJ sat on his couch staring into space. In all the days since the accident, he'd never been less motivated. His thoughts were punctuated by shuffling sounds coming from the back bedroom. Norah was packing.

She'd taken Thunder back yesterday, her father driving her back here. TJ had stood at the doorway and waved at the man when he dropped his daughter off. He remembered Norah's Dad. Of course the man looked older now, and the last time TJ had seen the man he hadn't been wanting to say, "I'm in love with your daughter."

So he had just smiled and waved at Mr. Davidson. He wondered why Norah hadn't changed her last name when she married, or if she had, but changed it back. He asked her, hoping it was so far off topic that she might respond.

She didn't.

Norah wasn't talking to him. It wasn't as childish as refusing to speak to him. That actually would have been better, because he could have called her on it. Could have yelled and told her to grow up. No, it was more like she simply didn't have anything she wanted to say to him. She answered his questions, sometimes with only a dirty look, but usually with a couple of meaningless words, then she would walk off.

She'd driven him to therapy yesterday, silently. Still the fool, he tried several times to start a conversation, and was quietly rebuffed each time.

TJ played a few games of his own. He worked late at therapy, forcing her to come inside to get him. He was grateful when Tim told him it was time to start distance walking. Preferably at a track, as he needed a flat smooth surface, one with a fence lining the inner perimeter, in case he stumbled or needed support. Norah agreed to drive him, and Tim made her promise to stay with him when he was there.

TJ had almost jumped up and hugged his therapist right there. He needed a way to Norah, and Tim had handed it to him.

Still, she had said very few words on the way home.

TJ sought her out later, trying again to start a conversation. He'd found her in her room last night, where she stayed for most of these past few days. He wondered if she regretted her decision, but as she wasn't talking to him, he had no chance to find out.

A slow anger had started to boil alongside the discouragement. That Norah had been so adamant about not getting pregnant ate at him. He didn't want children, he hadn't even considered it. It was always one-of-those-things, it would happen when it was right. But part of him wanted Norah to want it. Or to at least be sad about what she'd done. That she'd rapidly thrown away any chance at it was more painful than he wanted to admit to himself.

"Norah." He stood in her bedroom door, having learned quickly that if he wanted it open, he would have to open it himself. TJ braced his hand on the knob, both for support and to keep her from closing it in his face.

She didn't look up, but she knew he was there.

So he just started talking. "I called JD and we wanted to start early at the studio. Can we leave soon?"

"When?"

"Whenever you're ready."

She nodded.

He left.

In that whole exchange she'd said one word. He sighed, turning, and stumbled down the hall to his chair.

She appeared, ready to take him, keys in hand, in just inside five minutes. They drove along in silence, TJ trying to figure out how to make her come up to get him afterward.

JD met them at the front of the studio, guitar case in hand. Norah smiled at him. "It's good to see you, again."

"When are you coming for dinner?"

She shook her head, looking for all the world like she was so sad that she couldn't make it. What a beautiful liar she was. "Oh, I'd love to but I'm moving out this afternoon."

JD laughed. "You're still invited to dinner."

"I'll see." And she drove off.

In two minutes with his brother she'd spoken more words than in the three days since she had fled, leaving him in her bed.

JD waited until they were in the studio, but as soon as the door clicked, he spoke. "I've seen that face before."

TJ's eyebrows rose. Since he'd never felt like this before, he had no clue where his brother might have seen 'that face' before. Even though he didn't ask, JD answered. "In my own mirror, when I couldn't get things right with Kelsey."

That had been over six years ago, and TJ winced now that he had teased his brother mercilessly about falling in love with his neighbor.

"What happened?"

TJ gave the short version. "We made love, the condom broke, she fled."

"So she might be pregnant?"

TJ shook his head. "No, she made certain that she got a morning after pill within a few hours. Apparently the thought of being pregnant by me made her shake and vomit."

JD winced at that one. Then he took a breath and spoke again. "You know, you're giving up awful easily. It's clear that you're in love with her. You waited a long time for this."

TJ didn't point out that he hadn't been waiting, and he certainly hadn't wanted *this*. Still he nodded, realizing his brother was right. He wanted Norah, and he got what he wanted. He would have to be more careful, more thoughtful, but he wouldn't give up.

He tucked that thought away and changed the subject. "So I have this piece of a song in my head—" The look on JD's face stopped him cold. Then he laughed. "Yes, I decided to try my hand at writing."

It felt good to laugh. It would feel better to have Norah, but he tried to keep his thoughts on task. "I need guitar for it. That's your job."

They'd never written together before. Hell, TJ thought, he'd only ever written the one thing before. But they knew each other, and TJ cranked up the mic so he could hear what his one line sounded like. "*It just always seems it goes / that the one you can't have is the one you want the most.*"

JD listened. "That's fairly hard."

"Well, we have to keep up our punk side. It's getting harder to do with all that mushy crap you write for Kelsey." He didn't mention his own 'mushy crap' that he'd been fine tuning the last week.

Thankfully his brother laughed at him, then thought for a minute before pulling a string of notes and chords out of his brain. TJ nodded, it was exactly what he'd wanted. They tried it together. JD added a line of lyric. They tried it again. TJ added to it.

It still wasn't quite there. Alex and Craig passed by outside the small window, then turned the handle entering the room. TJ and JD just played what they had, and Alex nodded, pulling out his sticks. He added a drumline to it, and Craig then also picked up a set of sticks and, standing over Alex, added more drums around him.

TJ looked around. He'd never been part of this before. JD and Craig were the writers, Alex occasionally added, and he himself had changed lines here and there. But he'd never been part of synthesizing a piece before.

JD pointed at the ground, "Go lower on that last part."

They played and tuned and tweaked and only managed to run a few of their old songs. TJ stayed on his stool, not ready to go crashing around the studio. But his lungs didn't give out anywhere near as fast as they had previously.

Three hours later they packed things away. Alex was already anxious to get home to Bridget and his new daughter. Craig was anxious to get away from Alex and his wallet full of baby pictures. TJ wanted to get back to Norah. He had work to do.

JD hung back after the others had left, "Are you going to go after her?"

"I guess I have to." TJ shrugged as though it would be that easy.

"I'll stay here. I'm parked at the curb and I don't want to intrude on your time."

TJ nodded and stuck himself back in the chair, grateful that his brother was a better man than he had been, and hadn't given him hell about falling for Norah.

She pulled up just as he pushed through the front doors. With more efficiency than was necessary, she popped his chair closed and stuck it in the seat behind his. He stayed on his feet while she did it, then slid in.

About a block away, she started talking. At first he was just grateful for the sound of multiple words at one time. But then he heard what she was saying.

"I'm just dropping you off. All my things are at my Dad's now. I'll be back to get you to the studio tomorrow morning. Ten, right?"

And that was it. He said 'yes' because she had steered the conversation to his one-word answer and then closed down again.

He watched her while she drove back to his place. Her hair was unbound, a blue-black shimmer falling just past her shoulders. A few big, loopy, wild curls defied the slick brushing she'd given it. Her aquamarine eyes stared straight ahead at the road, in open defiance of his perusal. Her nose was straight and stubborn, her mouth set against him.

He had his work cut out for him.

When she pulled into the driveway he allowed her to help in ways he no longer needed. He climbed out of the car and let her pull the chair from behind his seat. He could do it, but most likely she did it because she was used to it. Norah probably wouldn't have gotten out of the car at all if she'd realized.

When she held the chair open for him he ignored it, instead stepping around and taking her into his embrace. She stiffened, but TJ chose to ignore that. He put his mouth next to her ear, hoping she felt any portion of the rush he got being this close to her. "I'm going to miss having you here, Norah."

She didn't respond verbally. But for just a moment he thought he felt her relax in his arms. He couldn't help the reaction from his body. His arms tightened around her and he breathed in the smell of her.

She stiffened and pulled away. Offering a forced half-smile, she hopped into the car. She left him standing there in the driveway as she practically left rubber on the pavement in an attempt to get away from him.

TJ didn't know whether to be encouraged or disheartened.

CHAPTER 29

Norah pulled into her own driveway, nearly crying. Her father should be home any minute now. She fled through the front door, tears starting as she fumbled the key.

The old farmhouse should have screamed 'home' at her, but it didn't. She could see the old couch more for what it was. She could see photos of Lilah and her doctor husband and kids, photos of Norah, dancing. And one lone photo of herself, with Jeff and Jordan, happy at a picnic. Her father insisted on keeping it up, even though she hadn't been able to bear the sight of it.

Now she could.

She blinked at it for a minute before realizing that it didn't hold her attention one way or the other, and she fled up the stairs to her room as fat tears fell.

When she heard footsteps on the wooden planks of the front porch and the key in the old lock, she jumped up. Her feet carried her back down the stairs where she flung herself into her father's arms.

He dropped his briefcase and hugged her back. "Honey, what's wrong?"

She shook her head against him, not able to talk.

His hand stroked her hair, and for a minute he just offered the parental comfort of a hug. "Did you fall in love with the hunk?"

She nodded, still not looking at him.

He smiled. "It's about time."

She knew he was referring to Jeff. That there had been no one since her husband. But she had expected that when it finally happened it would be because she met someone and dated, and they fell in love *together*.

"No, Daddy, it's bad."

"Can you tell me?"

She sniffed, arrows piercing her heart, but she had to tell someone, and her father was the best. "I might be pregnant."

"Is that good?" He led her over to the couch, now that she seemed to have it a little more together and was talking.

"No."

He waited her out.

"Daddy, I can't have another baby. I'm too scared."

"Sounds like it may not be your choice. What about him?"

"He's a playboy. I was the only one around and I still fell for him." She sniffed again, thinking of that morning in TJ's embrace. But it didn't make her face flush, that she saved for at night, when she gave up and simply let her mind remember how he'd touched her. Like she was precious.

Her Dad searched her face and she wondered what he saw.

She didn't have to wait long.

"Norah, you're not stupid. There must have been something there on his part."

"Yeah, he made me feel loved. But Daddy, I must be number ten thousand, seven hundred and ninety-two. I'm sure he knows how to make a girl feel special."

Her Dad didn't pull punches. It was one of the things she

liked best about him. "He's not that small a number on your list either."

Norah winced. She had only ever been with Jeff, until a year after he died. Then she'd gone crazy, seeking companionship in the form of sex whenever she found a suitable partner. Her Dad knew about that, too. She didn't answer.

"He's different."

She snorted. "He's different because the condom broke."

"He was different before that, Norah. I didn't say anything, maybe just because I was so shocked. I guess I'd given up on you ever coming around."

Her father had given up on her coming around?

He continued, "I thought maybe you would never fall in love again. But when we went out to dinner after you first moved out there, you talked about him all evening. About how he always got back up, about how he got himself back together, wondering if you'd made the right decisions expecting things out of him. Your face lit up, honey. I haven't seen that since you were a kid."

Norah cried earnestly then.

"And you *were* a kid then, Norah. A kid with a big heart, a good boy, and some really bad luck."

It didn't help to have her father pointing out that she'd had these feelings for TJ all along. For a minute he let her sit there with her tears.

"Honey, I imagine he feels more for you than you think. I've never known you to throw yourself at anyone."

Norah shook her head, the tears still falling. Her father was sweet, but clearly biased. He'd never understand how someone *couldn't* fall in love with his baby girl. Norah could. "He's used to getting whoever he wants. I'm not what he chooses when he has his pick."

"Maybe that's a good thing."

She wanted to laugh, but her chest was too tight. "He likes

me as a friend, and if he found me attractive then I put the two together wrong. Loving someone and having sex with them doesn't mean that you're *in love*. It doesn't mean that you want to be with that person."

This time it was her Dad that snorted. "Don't I know that."

It didn't make her feel any better about TJ, but it did make her laugh. Her father had been pursued by a string of girlfriends since he moved here. Norah knew her elopement with Jeff had been the final straw in her parents' marriage; her mother had wanted to disown her and her father had wanted his grandchild. She also knew enough now to not start that conversation again.

Her dad got up off the couch, picked up his briefcase, and gave her a minute to compose herself. Then he wandered into the kitchen. "I guess we should eat here, so you can tell me about this baby you're going to have."

She followed him. "I don't even know yet if there is a baby. I have to wait."

"All right."

Her chest worked, and she needed to get it out. "I went to the clinic. Well, I *ran* to the clinic, and got a morning after pill. I took it."

Her Dad frowned as he filled a pot with water for rice.

"I started shaking when I realized what I had just done. I went right back home and vomited it up."

He nodded absently as he turned the stove on. "When are you going to tell him?"

"He thinks I took the pill. I told him I did. So I guess I'll say something if—" She really couldn't push the words *I'm pregnant* out her mouth again. Saying *I might* had been hard enough. "If there's something to tell."

Her father added a scoop of rice to the pot, along with various other things he found in the fridge. The one-pot-dinner was his specialty, and Norah wasn't much of a cook herself. But the stiffness of his actions while fixing her dinner told her that he didn't approve of her waiting to tell TJ. She gulped air in.

"Daddy, I'm so scared." She broke down right there in the middle of the big, old-fashioned kitchen.

Her father's arms found her and enfolded her in another hug. "You'll be fine. You're stronger than you think you are."

CHAPTER 30

Norah picked TJ up three days later for their first walk at the track. She had managed only a little physical distance since she'd left. Her heart still ached.

She wasn't sleeping well. There was the possible baby, which occupied a lot of her brain space. When she finally managed to push those thoughts away, her brain wandered to her morning with TJ.

That was a bad place to wander. It made her want it again, want *him* again, even while she was still reeling from the effects of the last time. The man was a potent drug.

She still wasn't speaking to him much. Not because she was being juvenile, but because she didn't know what to say. So she put the car in park and waited while he got out. She would have offered support, but she knew what would happen if she had him lean on her. She'd smell him and touch him and, well, only bad things could come of it.

In the end, she had to help him. Though the track was on level ground, it was at the bottom of a half flight of stairs. It was just the terrain in this part of the state. If there was a flat space big enough to put a track, then the land wasn't flat around it.

Holding his hand, she braced him on one side while he let the railing take the bulk of his weight. His movements were jerky, but he still managed to get down the steps. What he lacked in fine motor control he made up for with sheer determination.

At the bottom of the steps she released his hand, not wanting to maintain the contact. He could walk well enough on flat ground. She was only here in case he fell or over-taxed himself, and to help him back up the dangerous turf of the stairs at the end.

Norah surveyed the place. It was vacant in these hours. School was in, the early morning practices had been here but gone. The track was just far enough from the school that kids weren't walking by. A copse of trees stood sentry at the back side, but the flat, reddish pavement was just what he needed.

She opened the chain link gate, leading him to the inside of the track and forcing herself to set his hand on the fence and stop touching him. "Ready?"

He nodded.

She walked away. She wasn't going quickly, but TJ didn't catch up.

Looking over her shoulder, she couldn't resist. "Have you had a relapse? I'm supposed to keep an eye on you, how can I do that if you're behind me?"

He gave her a lazy smile. "View's better back here."

She clasped her teeth together. That's what she got for speaking to him. Not *Norah, I love you*—which was really hoping for too much, she knew—but *nice ass*. She made a mental note not to wear spandex again.

"You have a great ass."

As though she hadn't gotten that part the first time.

"I speak from experience."

"TJ! Now you can get up here, or I can leave you to crawl

back home on your own." She turned around, grateful that he was proving himself. It would help her get over him faster.

She waited while he came up beside her, and she stepped aside to give him the inside track. Without a word—those had gotten her in trouble with this man more times than she could count—she resumed a steady pace.

They were halfway around the track when he spoke. Though it wasn't accompanied by a charming smile, she was wary. "You lied to JD the other day, just pretty as you please."

She didn't respond.

"What have you lied to me about, Norah?"

All at the same time, she melted at the sound of her name from his mouth and her heart crumpled in response to the words. He assumed she had lied to him, and worse, he was right.

She bit her tongue. She was in too much of a state of limbo already without adding him and his worries to the mix.

"Norah." His voice interrupted her jumbled thoughts. "Tell me, please."

She shook her head, and tried to veer the subject a little. "What do you think I lied to JD about?"

He bit. "You said that you wanted to go. I know for a fact that you don't."

"But see, I *do* want to go. I just can't."

He let it drop then. Or at least it seemed that way for another quiet half lap. When she didn't volunteer, he pressed again. "Norah, what did you lie to *me* about?"

"I didn't lie."

"You're lying now. I can see it, and it's worrying you. Maybe I can help."

She almost laughed out loud. *You've already helped enough.* "You can't."

"You won't know until you tell me."

He stopped, leaning on the fence, but she didn't realize it

until she was a good ten feet beyond him. Norah turned and backtracked. "Had enough for today?"

"No." His hands were braced on the fence.

Hers found her hips. "Don't forget, you have to get back up those stairs. I can't carry you."

He nodded, and she figured the matter was settled. So she waited for him to either give the signal to start walking or to head to the car. He did neither.

He'd been staring at the track surface between his braced arms, but he turned his head to look at her. "We aren't going anywhere until you tell me."

"You aren't in any shape to make threats like that." The words came out of her mouth easy enough, but it twisted inside to say them. She didn't like making threats against him, as if she would actually leave him here. In running shorts and a t-shirt with the sleeves ripped off he had no place to hide a cell phone.

TJ nodded. He turned his back to the fence, and used his hands to climb down, lowering himself to a sitting position. He leaned back against the chain link, looking like he'd just run fifty laps. His face looked defeated. "I got rid of three nurses before you. I liked that you were always honest with me, and there's a hell of a lot more between us now. If you aren't going to tell me, then leave."

Damn him.

Norah stood there. Deciding. He'd called her bluff—she wasn't going to go anywhere. But she wasn't about to tell him.

For long minutes neither of them spoke.

Finally, not knowing what to do, Norah walked off. She kept a pace much faster than they had together. She wasn't much for jogging, but it was so mindless that she loped into a better rhythm, and it let the steam off better than just a fast walk.

She kept speeding up until her feet pounded the track. The lanes lay out in front of her, and she ate ground until TJ came back into view as she rounded the last corner. She slowed as she approached him, breathing heavily.

He sat, patiently waiting until she stopped a few feet away from him. "Made any decisions?"

"I'll tell you within two weeks."

He frowned. "What the hell happens in two weeks?"

She could see the gears in his head working. He was mentally thumbing through events and plans, trying to figure it out. But if she told him one thing, he'd figure the whole thing out, and she couldn't live with that.

Her hands braced on her knees as she looked at him. He was confused and worried about what she would say. But she couldn't give any more. "Take it or leave it."

"In two weeks, this will all be cleared up?"

"I don't know if it will be cleared up, but I'll be able to tell you about it." She stretched, imagining that the conversation was over.

TJ spoke again, his voice soft but full of dread. "Are you sick?"

Her head snapped to him. God, she couldn't let him think it was cancer or something like that. "No."

"Are you—"

"Don't ask me anything else." She snapped. "I didn't agree to *Twenty Questions*."

He nodded, conceding, and pulled himself up the chain link. Norah wanted to hold out her hand to him, but the feel of his skin on hers, his hand holding tight to hers, would push her. Her balance was too precarious already. Her Dad's disapproval of her decision didn't help. But she *was* going to tell TJ. Just not yet.

Of course, the first thing he did when he stood was hold out his hand to her. She wanted to refuse, but there was only open space and seven steps in front of him. She had been around him all summer. She knew that if his legs were going to go out from under him it would be right after he'd exerted himself. Falling on the track would be painful from the burns from the rough asphalt alone, but if he fell on the staircase . . .

TJ looked at her, both of them knowing that she couldn't refuse him.

With a sigh, she grasped his hand from behind, just like Tim had shown her at rehab. It looked like a casual hand-hold, but with a flick of her wrist she could brace his arm, and do it the second he started to buckle.

Closer than she wanted, but not as close as she wished, they made their way along the fence, then up the steps. He didn't falter once.

She walked him through the parking lot to the car, around to his side, and waited until he was in before jogging the last few steps around the hood and slipping into the driver's seat.

"Can I ask you a favor?" The words were out of his mouth even as she buckled her seatbelt.

"I suppose you can ask." *God, she sounded bitchy.* And for a moment it panicked her. Maybe it was hormones running away with her because she *was* pregnant. She tried again. "What do you need? I'll do it if I can."

That earned her a genuine, heart-stopping smile—the kind that made her wish she weren't the only of-age female around. Kelsey had once called TJ a charm-shark, and Norah so understood that. He was beautiful, but deadly. Even knowing that didn't change the way her heart told her to take whatever chance she could, that, just maybe, she could win him. Her brain told her that she was being silly. He was TJ Hewlitt, and he had women throwing themselves at him on a regular basis. Or he had. And he would again, very soon. There was really no way for Norah to compete.

"Can you drive me by my house? I need to get some things."

She frowned. "I was going to drop you off at your house. Is there somewhere else you need to go after that?"

He laughed, the sound rich and full of the liquid voice that had made him famous. "I meant I need to go by my *real* house. The one I used to live in, and will move back into in a few weeks probably."

"Oh." That made sense. She remembered he *did* have another house, a non-wheelchair accessible house, "Where is it?"

He made a face. "On the other side of town. But you probably have things to do at the studio and . . . never mind."

This time she laughed at him. "I *do* have things at the studio, and they can wait. I'll call Mrs. Kenner and let her know I'll be late."

"No, it's okay. I'll get the stuff later." He waved a hand at her.

"Just get in my purse and find my cell phone, cowboy." She took a turn toward his current house, and immediately wondered if she'd gone the right way. "How do I get there?"

"Oh, jeez. You've never been there, have you?" It seemed surprising to him, although she couldn't fathom why. She hadn't crossed paths with either of the Hewlitt brothers even though they'd lived in the same town and JD's daughter attended her dance school for several years.

"I've got it." He held the phone out to her, then told her to turn right at the upcoming light.

Norah speed-dialed the studio and told Mrs. Kenner not to expect her anytime soon.

TJ winced, and Norah sought to calm him. "I'll be there until around ten tonight, so if I don't show up before noon it's no big deal at all."

He kept giving her turns, and the houses and businesses kept getting nicer and nicer as they drove. Norah began to wonder what kind of house this man lived in when he chose for himself.

He directed her to a closed gate with a brick booth sitting just in front of it. Her car seemed suddenly older and clunkier sitting there at the ornate entry. The security guard frowned at her as she stopped. No wonder, this place didn't look like it had many older model sedans pulling in.

TJ leaned across as she lowered the window. "Hey, Brett."

"Good to see you again, TJ." The guard smiled as his fingers went automatically to the brim of his embroidered hat. He started to open the gates, but TJ didn't lean back.

"This is Norah Davidson. I'd like her added to my list. She can come and go as she pleases." TJ waited until Brett nodded, then pushed himself back into his own seat. "This will take a minute."

Norah just nodded, thinking she'd ridden horseback to his other house and even jumped the fence. She wondered now what he must have thought of her.

Brett asked her for her driver's license, and she happily handed it over. When he asked for her signature, she gave that, too. Then he asked her to sit back for a photo. That was when she protested. But not to Brett.

"TJ! You should have told me I was getting my picture taken. I was just at the track!" Her hair was in a ponytail, and she had on only some tinted sunscreen and a trace of sun block lip-gloss, if any of that remained after the walking and running. She wasn't supposed to get a photo taken.

He smiled. "It doesn't go anywhere. Just here, and it's just so all the guards can type in your name and ID you. If you don't do it, then Brett will be the only one who can let you in."

"Fine by me."

"Come on, Norah. I'm giving you a set of keys, too. You need to be able to get in. Besides, you look beautiful."

"Yeah, that's a little late." She huffed, but she agreed.

The guard snapped a photo that Norah was certain was mug shot quality, then commented. "All the women on Mr. Hewlitt's list are quite beautiful, you'll fit right in."

Her heart felt slapped, but she raised her eyebrows at TJ and tried to cover the hurt. She wasn't fast enough.

"Don't look so insulted." Then he looked up at the guard. "Tell her the names of the females on my list."

Brett laughed and pulled up a list on his computer screen, he read them off. "Kelsey Conklin Hewlitt, Anderson Hewlitt, Allison Hewlitt, and Anna Lee."

TJ leaned across her again. "Take Anna off the list."

The guard tapped a few keys, "Done," and the gates opened.

Norah pulled through. TJ may have thought he saved himself with that short list. But it only showed that he was fairly prompt about deleting names. She reminded herself she'd be wise to keep that tucked away.

He gave her directions, leading to the top of a hill. The houses here were large with the little space in between filled with tall fences and shrubbery. Each had clearly been built for size and impressiveness. Norah tried not to look like she was gawking.

He had her turn up a driveway to a tastefully butter-colored mansion. It probably wasn't much bigger than her Dad's Farmhouse, but it screamed wealth from the arches over each window, to the pull-through in front of double front doors, to the three car garage.

Norah felt silly parking in the driveway, but TJ didn't have the garage opener. Picking his keys and wallet out from under the seat where he'd tucked them, he climbed out of the car and came around to her side. His things held in one hand, he stretched the other out to her. Again, she took it.

They climbed the stairs together, TJ not needing a smidge of support from her. He unlocked the door and motioned her through.

Norah made it two steps before she stopped dead. TJ pushed by her, scratching the back of his head. "It's a bit much, isn't it?"

"You could say that."

Norah was three feet from a fountain taller than she was. Water splashed down four tiers of sculpted basins. The entire front entry-way was round: the fountain, the marble flooring radiating out around it, the stairs that clung to the left side, winding up to the second floor.

She could see large, dark wood doors leading to rooms off the upstairs landing. Down below she could see through to a huge kitchen sporting floor-to-ceiling chrome. She'd thought her father's kitchen was a waste of space for a man who didn't cook, but this was ridiculous. "Are you a gourmand when you're here?"

He winced. "Nope, mostly spaghetti with sauce from a jar and sandwiches."

"You forgot macaroni and cheese." She couldn't peel her eyes away, it was just too incongruous.

"Yeah." He tugged at her hand, re-locking it with his since she'd dropped the hold the second they'd reached level ground. "My room's on the second floor."

She nodded, letting herself get pulled away. She flanked him up the stairs, her brain churning fifty miles an hour imagining what might be awaiting her up there. The rest of the house had that feel that a professional had 'done' it. This was more a showpiece than a place to *live*. Then again, the bedroom might be all done up S&M. Just because he hadn't tied her up didn't mean he wasn't into kink.

Again she tugged her hand from his when they reached the landing.

"This is my room." He pushed open a wide door revealing the one thing she hadn't suspected.

Her mouth fell open. "Did you design this?"

"The designer did the rest of the house, except the music room. But in here, I picked what I liked."

Norah could only nod. The huge room was done in shades of deep, but cool, blue. The carpet was soft and squishy, even through her running shoes, and the sheers hanging to either side of two tall, tall windows matched the color. The bed was big enough to suit the room and she wondered briefly if he had to get the sheets made. The wrought iron head and foot board scrolled gracefully but only touched ground in one spot. It was exquisitely crafted but physically impossible.

She tipped her head sideways.

"Yeah, it's pretty cool, huh?" He reached out a hand and fingered the iron work. "I found the bed, then I made the designer match everything else to it."

Her voice sounded breathy. "It's amazing."

"It's supported underneath." He turned away and began rummaging through drawers painted in butter-cream shades with black iron drawer pulls that echoed the bed.

Norah just looked around, blinking. She didn't remember what she'd expected, but then again, maybe she *should* have expected this. She'd been living with the grown-up version of the TJ Hewlitt she'd known in school. Only in the back of her brain did it really register that he wasn't that man. He was this one.

He talked to cover the silence. "When I had the designer do the place, she actually tried to talk me into doing a room for a baby. She said it was a bachelor thing. Apparently when looking for a wife, having a baby room ready is a big draw."

Norah was standing still by the time he looked up.

"Oh." The word just fell from his lips. "That was the wrong thing to say."

"Is it true?"

"Yes." He had to say it. She wasn't turning around to look at him.

"Then it isn't wrong. It just is." She looked at him then, seeing that he was upset. Ten-to-one said he thought he'd blundered because of Jordan and then the morning after pill. He didn't know that it made her freeze because maybe he should have let the designer put that room in. She just smiled, "Is there anything I can help with?"

He took the opening she offered. "Yeah, there's a leather duffle bag in that closet, can you get it?"

"Sure." She wondered what else she would find in the closet. It was all pretty normal, except most men with a wardrobe of jeans and t-shirts probably didn't store them in a place this opulent. She pulled out the bag, and handed it to him. "Anything else?"

He shook his head. "I just need a few minutes to gather things. You should try out the bed though."

She raised her eyebrows, indicating that she wasn't going to docilely walk to his bed and invite him to join her. Tempting though that was.

He had the grace to blush. "I just meant that it's the most comfortable place to relax."

And he turned away, ducking into the bathroom to gather a few things.

CHAPTER 31

TJ climbed into the driver's seat of the van. It was the only car available to use for driving practice. Also, JD was due any moment, so if TJ wound up causing an accident at least his brother would find him and get him help.

Unfortunately, the handi-van was huge and uncomfortable. The emergency brake, which he'd been counting on, was foot-operated instead of hand-operated. The reason he still wasn't allowed to drive was that he might need to stand on the brake and he couldn't count on his legs. So an emergency brake at his right hand would have been perfect. But no, the handi-van offered no such solution. If his legs went out, both brakes were lost to him.

He swore to himself for a moment, then decided the van was all wrong anyway. The seat was too high, the pedals huge and stiff, and the vehicle was so heavy it wouldn't stop if it ran into anything.

His own car was totaled, probably now a small cube in a landfill. He'd loved that car, but like most things he hadn't thought much about it, hadn't thought ahead. At least it was replaceable.

Climbing down from the van, he decided to head back inside to wait for JD. He'd surf the net for cars, and get something delivered.

He wanted to call Norah for dinner tonight—to see if she would drive him, and maybe he could make her come with him. But she was working. School was in its second week and Norah was in full swing as well, teaching dance classes four nights a week.

She'd showed up this morning in running clothes, startling him and making him think he'd gotten his days backwards. But she'd laughed at him, and said she was cutting the tension with running. He made no remark about the tensions she was working out, or that they might work out better if she'd share them with someone. Like him.

TJ settled himself at his computer, thinking how glad he was that he was allowed to live by himself. Only the house felt horribly empty without Norah. He pushed that thought away. He'd see her. He'd work his way around to her. But he had another week and a half to go before she told him what was going on, and he wasn't about to profess undying love while she was holding that over his head.

He clicked up Google and was looking at sports cars in no time. He'd found a fifth car he liked when the front door clicked. "JD! Come back here."

His brother appeared in the doorway, "What?"

"Look, I've got to get a new car. What do you think?" He clicked the pages and photos.

His brother just shook his head. "I think I left Kelsey at home with things boiling on the stove and six kids running around."

TJ pushed the chair out and stood. JD was more the SUV-with-car-seats type anyway. He'd ask Norah what she'd like. "You know if you could keep it in your pants, you wouldn't have this problem."

"I love this problem, and we had three kids before we even

started." JD was out the front door and leading TJ to his family car. Four of the six seats had child restraint devices strapped into them. TJ would bet the next album sales that the car had scored the highest in the crash test ratings.

Maybe he should check that on the cars he was searching.

JD turned right at the end of the driveway, "Norah's teaching? Is that why she couldn't make it?"

TJ just nodded.

"Then we'll have to have the next one on the weekend. But you have to keep coming over. Kelsey cooks with a little something extra for you."

"Me?"

JD laughed. "Yeah, like you're company or something. But she makes my favorites for you, so it's a good deal all around."

"Six kids, career, hired help, and she cooks. Add in that Kelsey's kept her figure, and I'm surprised she doesn't get regular hate mail."

His head thrown back, JD laughed so hard he almost missed the last turn to his own house. "She loves it. She has energy to burn and a history of having to take care of everyone around her." He paused. "There's something you should know."

It sounded casual, but that phrase always meant something bad. TJ braced.

JD continued. "Women don't get their figures back after they're pregnant. Kelsey will tell you that they just get a new one and you hope it's a good one."

"Why are you telling me this?" They were sitting in the driveway, but he didn't know why.

"Because you've lost a lot of your restlessness lately. It's like you're growing up or something." JD said it with a sarcastic tone, and TJ had thought the exact same thing just a while ago. But it didn't stop him from bristling.

"Besides, I've seen the way you look at Norah. I know that look."

"Like I want to get her pregnant?" TJ threw that one out before he thought about it. *Bad move.*

Keys in hand, JD unbuckled but made no move to get out of the car. "It bothered you that she bolted to take that morning after pill."

"Yeah." His brother had him pegged. He usually did. Maybe it was just part of the territory of being the younger one. He tried changing the subject. "Kelsey looks the same to me."

"Nah, she's different, better."

Oh God, save him from his brother waxing poetic about his wife. No wonder Norah couldn't come.

TJ climbed out of the car and headed up the front steps, hand firmly gripping the railing. The chair was a thing of the past.

Daniel met him at the front door. "No chair? Are you normal yet?"

"Thanks, kid."

Daniel scrunched up his face, looking like Kelsey did when she made that same expression. "Don't call me *kid*."

"Don't ask me if I'm *normal*." He went into the living room and sat down. There were a lot of stairs up the front porch, and he'd been tense throughout his conversation with JD. "And no, I'm not normal. I have to stop and rest a lot, but no more chair."

"What are you going to do with it?"

He quirked his mouth, he thought he smelled pork chops and probably broccoli. "I was thinking I'd get it bronzed."

Allie was suddenly there, plopping on the couch beside him and bouncing a little from the force of it. "You should sell it."

"Hmmm." There was some sense in that. He'd ask Norah.

Kelsey called them all to the table, and they all helped set the places and bring out the dishes and silverware. TJ seated himself and fielded an onslaught of questions about Norah. He fought against the constant urge to yell out, *I don't know! She's barely speaking to me.* But he wasn't giving that one away, either.

JD went and told Kelsey that TJ had said she looked the same since the baby, so Kelsey started in on trying to lose the extra weight. In an effort to change the topic, TJ threw out what Norah had said about going to the track again. He was only supposed to go every other day, but Kelsey might keep her company on his off days. He had no idea if Norah wanted company or not, and he regretted it after he'd said it.

About two thirds of the way through the meal he started to get uncomfortable. Like he didn't really belong here. Like they weren't his family. But they were. Every last one of them.

For a moment, he pulled back and looked at them with new eyes. They were united against the world. They didn't all look alike—the two oldest kids had come from Kelsey's brother and JD's ex-girlfriend. But there were no distinctions here. TJ knew they wanted him in that circle, and for that he would be forever grateful. He knew he was loved, and it did make all the difference.

But even here, it was about JD. TJ was loved because he was JD's brother. Kelsey would always take care of him, the kids would always be there. Because he was JD's brother.

He figured he was getting a taste of what Norah felt when she was here.

Good, old-fashioned envy.

He begged off after the meal, saying he was worn out. And he was, just not that much. Kelsey made him promise to bring Norah next time. He managed to promise to *try*, and hoped she didn't notice the distinction.

He had his brother drop him at the front gate and he walked the long driveway enjoying the setting sun and cool air. In the distance, on an adjoining property, he saw a horse and rider. Stopping, he hoped that the horse would turn his way and sail over the fence. But it didn't happen. Norah was teaching dance tonight anyway.

It was noticeably darker when he made it to his front door,

and the driveway wasn't that long. It was just the way the sun set in this part of the country. For a moment he thought of the very few times he'd enjoyed any of his travels, and one had been his amazement at the sunset over the west coast the first time he'd seen it. The sun had taken forever to go down. Maybe that was part of why he'd never felt at home in L.A. with Anna.

He'd been far more comfortable here, in the handi-house, than he'd been in a lot of other places, and that worried him. The smell and feelings of 'home' assaulted him as he opened the door and he realized that he owed Norah a call.

As expected, he got her voicemail. She was probably still in class. He confessed what he'd told Kelsey and told her to call back, even late, if he'd made an error. He'd fix it if she wanted to run alone. He signed off with, "I'll see you tomorrow morning."

TJ decided not to dig too deep into his psyche and what he'd wanted to say into the phone, and went back to the computer, calling up the cars he'd chosen. This time he pulled up the safety ratings, wondering why he hadn't looked at them before.

He winced. Some of the cars didn't even have a single star out of five possible. What had he been thinking?

Sighing to himself, TJ admitted that he hadn't been thinking.

Story of his life.

CHAPTER 32

TJ had decided that when he had been driving for a week, he would move back into his house. But nothing was going according to plan. Norah was still picking him up in the mornings. Maybe because he wanted her to, or maybe because he needed it.

He hadn't seen the progress he'd seen earlier. Of course, for once, he'd been doing what he was told: the track every other day. He wanted to do more. Just over a week had gone by, and that was far too long for him to suffer no real advancements.

Norah was still going to the track every day. Whatever aggression she'd been working out had driven her to it. He considered joining her, but Kelsey was going on his off days and the two women were jogging. Kelsey had brought Baby Amy exactly twice—TJ knew because he'd had to hear about every moment in deep detail from Norah.

Handing her that baby had not been the best thought out move of his life. He just hoped it was the right one for Norah.

TJ decided to hit the gym on his off days. He wouldn't crowd Norah, which usually would have seemed like a fine idea, but lately didn't. He would get in his extra workouts and get out of this stagnant limbo.

His car had been delivered. He'd settled on a sedan with clean lines and a certain cool appeal and excellent safety ratings. Once he'd started checking, anything less than four stars made him break out in a cold sweat. One glance at the motorized wheelchair sitting in the corner reminded him why.

He heard the engine when Norah pulled up out front. Her door slammed shut, but he didn't hear her at the front.

By the time he'd made it to the front door, she had just finished circling the car and was peering inside the windows. "Hey, Norah. You like it?"

"It's pretty. Still new-car-shiny."

"Yeah," he smiled. "Come in for a minute?"

She nodded her consent, clearly a little wary, and he had to wonder if she thought he was going to ravage her. He *wanted* to, but he wasn't *going* to. At least not until she told him her dirty secret.

She came up the steps, looking lighter than she had. Her smile came a little quicker and she spoke more. All of those were good things.

When she brushed by him, where he held the front door, he could smell her hair. For just a moment, it brought on a powerful sense memory of their morning together. It was like he was there, inside her again. Like she was holding him, her legs wrapped around his waist, her body moving with his. He could hear her and taste her and . . .

TJ bit back a groan. His body reacted and wanted to rescind his earlier decision about not attacking her.

Norah walked by, oblivious. "What did you want?"

Note to self: keep nose away from Norah until you are *ready to ravage her.*

He directed her to the dining room where he had all the torture devices lined up. Side by side they sat—the motorized wheelchair, the lightweight chair, the stander, the tilt rack, the walker. There was no cane. It was the only implement missing from the line-up, because he'd refused to get one, insisting that Norah stay by his side instead. "What do I do with it? Can I auction it? Should I sell it with the house?"

She was standing beside him looking at the machinery. There was so much that there was no more room at the table and he couldn't get to the piano at all. TJ cast a sideways glance at her. Just in time to see her wheel on him. Her mouth was open and her brows pulled together.

"TJ Hewlitt! I know you weren't raised by wolves. I expected better of you than this." She shook her head like she couldn't believe what she was hearing.

He didn't respond, not sure what he'd done to make her blow up. "Norah! You've got to help me out here. I have no idea what you want from me."

"Compassion."

He didn't know who this compassion was supposed to be for.

"Intelligence?" She tried again.

He hated to be at a loss on that one, but he truly was. "Norah, tell me."

She came back to him, heaving a sigh of the damned. "First, you're being stupid if you think you're ready to get rid of the racing chair and the walker."

He frowned at her, so she kept going, like she was explaining to a child. "The whole point of us going to the track, which we are now late for, is to push you to your limits, to make you stronger. Small relapses are expected. It's unusual that you haven't had one before now."

"Okay," He conceded, "I still need the chair and walker on hand . . ." He trailed off, knowing that wasn't the whole reason she was mad.

She huffed again. "TJ! You just point-and-clicked a top-of-the-line Mercedes Benz to your driveway. And you don't know what to do with this stuff?"

He saw what she was getting at, and he felt like a heel. "I'll donate it."

"Damn straight you will." She shook her head, looking like she was going to give up on him, but then she turned back for one more go. "Lots of people can't afford any of this stuff. They don't heal as well as you did because they don't have the money that you do. And what happened to you happens to plenty of people who didn't deserve it."

Ouch!

But there was nothing he could say. He'd played his way right into his injury, and had just been damned lucky that he'd only bruised his spinal cord. Another millimeter and Norah wouldn't be looking up at him to berate him about his equipment.

Suddenly it didn't matter that he was leaning on the couch to conserve his energy for the track. He'd had a remarkable recovery. He owed all of it to Norah, who had expected him to act like a man even when no one else did. If she thought he should light all of it on fire in his front yard he'd probably do it.

Of course, instead she was full of righteous sense.

He nodded. "I'll donate the house, too."

Her eyebrows lifted at him in surprise.

And he thought that was appropriate. A house like this -not just retrofitted, but *built* for a person in a wheelchair—was worth a tidy sum. He'd paid good money for it, expecting to reclaim most of it when he sold. But the money didn't really matter anymore. It was easy to think that way when he was on his own two feet, ready to go to the track and walk as far as he could.

He nodded, heading to the front door, having caught that remark about them being late. "I'll call Tim when we get back and ask who it should go to."

TJ realized he'd reached the front door, but Norah hadn't. She was still standing at the edge of the dining room. "TJ, I'm sorry I yelled at you. It was uncalled for." Her voice was only a brush above a whisper, and she looked upset with herself.

"It's okay. It hadn't even occurred to me to donate it." He would have gone back to the dining room and grabbed her hand, but he was waiting to spend his efforts on the track, and he already wasn't feeling like a speeding bullet.

She slogged her way out the door, past where he held it open, and again he was assaulted by memories of their morning together.

Silently TJ berated himself. He'd just decided not to get that physically close to her. Maybe he *was* stupid. Maybe it was some sick twisted form of passive-aggression against himself.

She climbed in her car and waited until he was in the passenger side.

He started talking again. At least the communication had gotten better between them, even if it still wasn't *there* yet. "Do you have to go straight to the studio? Do you think you could come back here one day and help me get back into driving?"

She looked at him. "Depends on what you want me to do."

"Stand on the porch and be sure to call 9-1-1 if I crash into anything." He grinned.

"And what will you be learning to drive on?" Her hands clutched the steering wheel tighter as though afraid he might suggest he use her car.

"The Mercedes."

Her mouth fell open again for a split second before she regained control. "You're going to *practice* on that brand new Mercedes?"

"I don't see anything else. I got in the handi-van and the emergency brake is foot activated." He explained all his reasoning, and he could see that she still thought he was plum crazy.

She nodded slightly, then rescinded before she agreed. "Not today, but in a few days if you still want."

There was something in the way that she delivered that last line—like he might actually not want her to—but TJ shook it off.

CHAPTER 33

They were at the track in no time, descending the steps with her small hand tucked in his, ready to offer her support if he needed it. As usual, she had sandwiched him between the railing and herself. From the looks of her, she wouldn't be too much help if he fell, but he knew from experience that she was far stronger than she appeared.

They started walking, counterclockwise, the opposite direction from their usual way. TJ wondered if something was up, she seemed more tense now, when she had seemed less tense before. Maybe it was about the equipment. He *had* been a monumental moron.

A half lap later he tried for an apology.

"Norah, I'm sorry I was such an idiot. But I just knew you'd know what to do. I hope I didn't offend you too much." For some reason his legs felt sore this morning.

"No, it's nothing. I was really rude. I'm sorry."

Again, silence settled between them. The only sounds were the half-scraping noises of their feet on the rough, chipped-rubber surface of the track.

There were several times where he wanted to stop, to grab

the fence beside him and just take a breather. But Norah was a little ahead of him and he wanted to keep up. Something was off. He was certain of it. He just didn't know what it was, or how to get her to tell him.

In little pieces, it ate at him, and he was walking just behind her, his eyes on her feet, his brain churning, when she threw him the curve.

"I'm not pregnant."

He stumbled, but righted himself, then threw in a few stuttering jog steps just to catch up beside her. She gave away nothing, keeping up the pace she had set earlier, and looking straight ahead.

She didn't say anything else, so he pushed. "I knew that. So why are you telling me now?"

"Because I didn't know."

Jesus, the woman was a riddle and she wasn't doing a damn thing to help him solve it. "But you made certain that you didn't get pregnant."

God help him, he was angry about it again. TJ tried hard to shake the feeling and stay the course on this one.

"I didn't take it." She kept walking, still not looking at him.

"That's what you lied to me about."

She shook her head. "I took it."

"Damnit Norah, do we play *Twenty Questions* now, or are you going to tell me what this is about?" He was racing just to keep up with her. She'd been increasing her speed, probably trying to get away from him and he wasn't going to let her off that easy.

Her lips pressed for a moment then she began. "I got the pill, I took the pill. I got sick to my stomach."

Her mouth started shaking and he fought hard against the sympathy that was springing up inside him.

She took a breath, "It wasn't the drugs, it was the thought that maybe I had prevented my own baby. So I did take it, but when I got home I vomited it up."

That was when he did stumble. He went down, hands hitting and scraping the track surface. The burn on his hands and knees was secondary to the one in his brain. The one where she'd wandered around for a week and a half, maybe pregnant with his kid, and hadn't told him what was going on.

"Jesus, Norah."

She turned then, finally making eye contact with him, and he saw what it had cost her to wait. "It took a little while to see if I was pregnant or not."

He rolled himself over to a sitting position, and rested his head in his scraped palm. For a minute he breathed. In and out.

She'd been walking around not talking to him and harboring that.

"Norah, why didn't you tell me?"

She was leaning over him, her hands on her knees, and she was breathing heavily like she'd run too fast, even though she hadn't. "Because you would have brought your opinions to the table, and I was having a hard enough time dealing with my own."

He looked up, for a moment grateful that the track was usually empty. "Why didn't you tell me that you needed me to just listen and keep my mouth shut?"

She threw her hands up. "Oh, I should have dumped this on you and told you your opinion didn't count? How unfair is that?"

"How unfair is *this*?" In anger, he slapped his hand down on the track, only to regret it the instant the pain shot up his arm. "So you just held it all in for all this time? Wandered around like a bottle with a cork in it? I know what you've been through. You could have trusted me a little."

She blinked, and it looked like she was on the verge of tears.

He was on the verge of something, too. He just didn't know if it was taking her in his arms and crushing her to him or tearing her limb from limb.

He wasn't prepared for the next words out of her mouth.

"I told my Dad."

TJ blinked, "I'm sorry. I thought I just heard you say that you couldn't tell me, but you told your Dad."

Norah stood up straight and walked in small circles. She nodded.

"What in hell did you tell him?" His breathing sped up, and he pushed himself to his feet. He towered over her, even though she wasn't short.

"Everything."

The ice that washed through him was like nothing he'd experienced before. Everything was wrong. He'd thought he had her. That she had something on her mind and he had to wait it out. He saw now that he'd never had anything.

"You told your Dad that I busted into your room and seduced you out of your pajamas and that you liked it?"

She gulped in air, her eyes widening as he got angrier, but TJ kept pushing. "You told him that you came apart in my arms, then did it again?"

This time he gulped air. "Did you tell him I felt the condom break but kept going? Did you happen to mention that I didn't know what it was, because I was always a good boy and always wore a condom, but never had one break on me before?"

He was practically yelling, hell he *was* yelling. But Norah stood her ground, even if she did it a little shakily.

Her eyes were wide and wet as she looked up at him and shook her head. "I told him that I threw myself at you and that the condom broke. He told me I was wrong to wait until I knew if I was pregnant to tell you."

At the top of his lungs he turned on her, getting into her face. "Well, he was *right*!"

His hands went into his hair, and he turned away from her, his thoughts and feelings land-sliding through him. He walked away. His breathing was jagged. He had to get alone, and he didn't have any alone right now.

His feet moved, but his brain turned over thought after thought. He only briefly turned over the 'what if she had been pregnant' stone. She wasn't, and she seemed glad about it. It burned him all over again.

It burned that she hadn't come to him. That she hadn't wanted his advice and in fact had worked very hard to keep the opportunity away from him. Worse, she'd gone to her father.

TJ remembered how he'd felt the last time he'd seen her Dad. It would happen again and there *would* be a rifle this time.

What was worse was that he'd have probably gone willingly if she'd been pregnant, but now she'd shown how little faith she had in him. How much she didn't want their lives to mingle, how much she didn't want to share with him.

He stopped about halfway around, the ice giving up its hold to the flood that overtook him. His hands shook against the fence where he'd braced himself. Hot tears started in his chest but didn't make it out his eyes.

More the fool he.

He had decided he was going to make Norah fall in love with him.

Instead he had fallen in love with her.

And she was further out of reach than ever before.

TJ fought the tension around his mouth and behind his eyes. He breathed in the air, admitting that he was an idiot. With a deep sigh he resigned himself to walking again. A quick dart of his eyes told him Norah hadn't moved from her spot, she had merely sat down on the hard surface and put her face in her hands.

She looked to be crying.

Part of him thought, *Good.*

The other part of him realized she was damaged. She'd lost half her family when she'd run off with the man she loved, only to lose both him and their baby in a tragic accident. She'd told him she was damaged. He just hadn't listened. She'd shown him, too. Just in case he was too slow to get it when she said it. She'd refused to go to JD and Kelsey's. The one time she'd held the baby, she'd gone nuts, then gotten so sad.

Still he'd believed that she was functioning on all cylinders when she'd run off that morning screaming that she couldn't get pregnant. Maybe she was functioning on all cylinders, and they just weren't the ones he would have chosen.

Then he got mad that he was feeling sorry for her. She was an adult, and she'd shut him out.

She was still sitting in the middle of the track, her face down and shoulders softly heaving.

TJ planted his feet in front of her and waited the few seconds for her to notice that he was there. When she started to look up he didn't make eye contact, just held his hand down to her. She accepted his help hauling her to her feet. He almost laughed out loud at the irony and symbolism of that action. But he didn't have it in him.

"TJ I'm so—"

He shook his head, a tight, forced movement that cut her off mid-word.

She offered her hand across the track and again he refused.

What a fool he'd been.

He made it up the stairs with only the railing, wanting to collapse at the top, like he wanted to every day. The big difference was most days it was his legs that wanted to give out. His legs were dead, but it was his heart that wanted to give out this time.

She unlocked the car and he pulled open the passenger side door. Reaching down, he retrieved the wallet and cell phone he'd left there. He closed the door and stepped over into the shade of a tree at the edge of the lot.

He wasn't about to give up and sink to the ground until she was gone, so he simply leaned against the trunk and waited.

"TJ what are you doing?" Even her voice sounded like it had tears in it.

Good.

"I'm calling a cab."

He punched at the phone, not thinking about the cab at all. Just thinking that he'd never felt more betrayed in his life—and that it was purely his own fault.

"Don't." She was pleading, and he couldn't stand it. "I'll drive you home."

His eyes found hers, and the tears didn't move him as much as he had thought they would. "Only if you go straight there and don't speak."

She gave a small nod, and he climbed into the passenger seat. He was grateful to be off his legs, grateful that he didn't have to wait. But he didn't—*couldn't*—look at her. Instead he stared blankly out the window, his mind finally, blissfully numb.

He blinked when Norah pulled up next to a sleek green car that took a moment to register as his own. He had the passenger door open and both feet on the ground when she spoke.

"I'll be here at nine-thirty tomorrow to get you to the studio."

His lips pressed. "Don't bother."

Using the sides of the car doorway, he pushed himself upright and slammed the door behind him. He didn't turn or wave, just headed up the ramp to the front door. He fumbled with the key, and it was then that he noticed that his hands had a fine tremor. Lovely.

When he got in the door, he only barely registered the sound of her car pulling away. Seeing the medical equipment in the dining room made him pissed all over again.

She stood here and berated him for not thinking to donate it, when she'd known she was going to drop that bomb on him.

He was half tempted to throw all of it into the front yard and have a bonfire.

TJ turned away, feeling his hands suffering through the shakes, and thinking that it wasn't yet time to burn the chair. He congratulated himself on making an adult decision.

Not since he'd been leaving the bar in his convertible with what's-her-name beside him had his old life looked so good.

CHAPTER 34

Norah drove home without the radio or any conscious thought. When she got there, she turned the key in the lock, grateful that her Dad was out and she had the place to herself.

It would be after she got back from dance before their paths would cross and he'd see her. Even though she'd keep it together for class, he would still know from her expression that she'd told TJ and that it hadn't gone well.

She climbed the stairs thinking that was the understatement of the decade. Her father would hold her and give her a very gentle version of the I-told-you-so. Only when she got to the top, to her bedroom doorway, did she let it come. She threw herself at the bed, great gulping sobs coming in waves as she hugged the pillow.

It had been a mistake not to tell TJ.

But then again, that was only one mistake in a long line.

It had been a mistake to make love to him. And a mistake to do it with her heart involved. And if she was going to do that as she had, then it had been a mistake to not tell him then. At least if she had said *I'm in love with you* he could have shut her down. Instead she'd ridden him right over the edge and fallen off.

But she could go back further. It had been a mistake to let him kiss her and touch her the way he had. She'd known what he was after and she'd been flattered. Stupid.

She shouldn't have kissed him back in the hallway that first night. But she had. Even that kiss in front of rehab with everyone watching had stolen her breath away. She hadn't paid attention to how deep she'd gotten. Mistake number one million, nine hundred thousand, and ninety-two.

Norah cried, deep wailing sobs, until she fell asleep face down in the pillow.

Hours later she woke, knowing that her face told the story of her feelings. Getting it together enough to mask the smearing in her voice, she called Mrs. Kenner to let her know that she'd make it to class but not before.

Mrs. Kenner said "All right." But there was almost a question mark at the end of it. As though she wondered why Norah would call and tell her this. That maybe she didn't really expect Norah to show up much at all as long as she taught her classes.

After all she was only the owner.

Norah sighed and climbed into the shower. The hot water felt heavenly and she stayed in it overlong. It cleared the blotchiness from her skin. But while she stood there, wrapped in her fluffy blue bathrobe, she could see that the puffiness around her eyes would give her away. She grabbed tea bags for her eyes.

Her thoughts wandered, making her want to cry again. But Norah knew the tea bag remedy would only work if she was no longer crying. So she clamped down the thoughts and shut the tears away, and promptly fell asleep again.

When she woke, her eyes were stiff and over-dry. They still didn't look perfectly right, but they weren't puffy any more. She prayed for the miracle of make-up. What she got wasn't a miracle, but it was passable.

Dressing quickly, Norah chose her black leggings and a soft, fuzzy red sweater that was cropped enough to show off her waist. Her waist that would stay just as it was and not expand. The sweater was more for distraction from her face than anything else.

With a great sigh she hauled herself down to her car, passing her father on his way in.

Sure enough, he took one look at her, "You told him."

All Norah could summon was a nod.

Her Dad still carried his side of the conversation. "It didn't go over well."

He held his arms out, offering her a hug, but she refused. "I can't cry now, Daddy." Her voice almost cracked right then and there. "I'll talk to you when I get home."

With that she popped up to give him a quick kiss on the cheek, then turned to get in her car. Only she didn't get in.

Norah turned back to her Dad, knowing he valued honesty above pretty much everything else in the world. "Actually Daddy, I'm going to keep this one to myself. It's between him and me, even if he isn't speaking to me."

Her father nodded at her, understanding. He always seemed to understand. This time something more showed on his face, some small passing of pride in her decision. As she drove off she got the distinct impression that her father had known all along what she was only just now figuring out: in telling him she had betrayed TJ.

She snorted to herself as she pulled up to a red light. It would just figure that she finally understood what she had done to TJ when he had removed himself from the picture.

CHAPTER 35

TJ sighed and climbed in behind the wheel of the new Mercedes for the first time. He'd spent yesterday in a haze. He hadn't even had time to eat. He was too busy waffling between calling Norah to yell at her, smashing every piece of china in the house, or just attempting to forget all of it.

He'd laid on his bed, unable to make a decision, until finally sleep had taken over, keeping him from breaking anything.

At least he'd been able to make a decision this morning. He had a rehearsal to get to, and no ride but his sweet new car sitting in the driveway. He sat behind the console, certain that some of the shine had already rubbed off and knowing that feeling had nothing to do with the car.

He had three hours to get to the studio. So he thought he'd see if he could make it to the end of the driveway, and if that worked, then he'd go around the neighborhood. TJ promised himself that if he felt shaky or accident prone at any time, he'd pull over and call JD.

His fingers caressed the steering wheel, enjoying the feel of smooth leather and independence. Doing things one step at a time, he made sure he was as safe as possible, and that his brain was always engaged in the task at hand. That way it couldn't slip back to more unpleasant thoughts as it was prone to.

TJ started the engine, listening to the low purr of a well-made car. He pushed against each of the pedals, testing their resistance and his strength. Slowly he put the car into gear and let the engine go. As the car rolled down the long drive at idling speed, he wrapped his right hand nervously around the emergency brake.

But he didn't need it. His feet worked, pressing the pedals, feeling them solid and under his control. It was a good thing, too, because no one was scheduled to come get him.

Someone should have been here watching him. Not that there was any way to really kill himself in his own driveway, but if he conked his head he might sit there for a while before he could do anything. However, JD was busy and TJ was *not* calling Norah.

He reached up to click the remote to the gate, thinking he'd be out of the handi-house soon, leaving it available to the next person who needed it. In one week, if today's driving went well. He had no idea if one week was sufficient to allow for a relapse, but he really no longer cared. This place didn't feel like it was his any longer, and he squashed worries that his other house wouldn't feel like it was his either.

Taking a turn, TJ just drove. He kept the radio off, unable to listen to it without analyzing where the current sound was headed and how to keep Wilder out of the pack. None of that was good while he was driving for the first time in months and wondering if he might lose control of his legs when they were most necessary.

He kept going, aimlessly, until he spotted a deserted lot in front of a closed grocery store. Turning in, he did large donuts looking out for potholes amid the weeds. When he was relatively certain that he wouldn't damage the car, he drove to one end of the lot and aimed at the far corner.

TJ floored it, picking up speed and letting go of some aggressions. About half way across he let up on the gas and laid on the brake--hard. There was an immediate noise: the sound of the anti-lock brakes grabbing and releasing in rapid succession. His legs were braced straight in front of him as he practically stood up in the seat. The Mercedes rolled to a soft stop and slowly TJ let off the pedal.

His heart was going a little fast for a set-up situation like that. Yet he turned the car and pulled into another corner, racing up to speed and standing on the brakes again. And again.

After about five times, he figured he'd hold up all right. Only as he was about to leave the lot did he realize he had to turn back around and try something else. This time when he hit speed he didn't use his legs at all but relied on the emergency brake and his arms to control the car. It didn't work as well, but would do in a pinch.

This time he turned around and headed back to the house. He arrived without incident, seeing several cars on the road heading out the other way. Only when he was passed the second time did he realize that he was going far slower than usual. He laughed out loud at himself and fought the urge to yell out at the other driver, *you wouldn't be so impatient if you'd just spent the past four months learning to walk again.* But he didn't.

He hadn't listened before his accident. In fact, JD had told him pretty much just that. Practically everyone who cared about him had.

It felt good to pocket the keys and close the driver's door behind him as he headed up the front ramp. Next week there would be stairs. He'd handle it. It would make him stronger.

He had an hour to kill before he needed to leave for the studio, and he spent it on the phone with first Tim, then the gift coordinator at the rehab center. The woman even asked if she could send a truck out that afternoon, there was a teenaged girl who had a C-6 accident just three weeks before. Her spinal cord had been severed and she had no hope of recovering the use of her limbs like he had. Her family couldn't afford any motorized chair, let alone the souped-up one sitting useless in his dining room.

TJ agreed to be back by four to meet the truck. Then gave all his contact information, before asking that the center get in touch with him when the girl required another chair or this one needed repairs. He asked that the family not be told it was from him in the future.

He hung up and had himself a brief moment of hating Norah. Pushing it aside, he made himself a stacked ham and cheese sandwich and ate the whole thing before leaving the house. Previously, he would have simply eaten it while driving, but then again, previously he had been driving under the influence and getting smacked around by semis because he hadn't had the sense to get out of the way.

When he parked curbside at the studio, he was hitting the door lock when JD pulled up.

"TJ!"

He nodded, but his brother wasn't finished with him. JD took a few moments to get out of the car, reaching into the backseat to pull out his beloved guitar and sling it across his back. "Where's your driver?"

TJ gave a grim smile. "She's history."

"Oh." JD's eyebrows went up, but he knew enough not to ask while they were on the sidewalk or in the hallway, so instead he settled for the more innocuous, "Nice Mercedes."

TJ nodded, "Rides smooth, handles better."

There were other people in the elevator, a few of whom said short hellos before getting off on various floors. The brothers exited to a deserted hallway and quiet, but that didn't mean anything so they stayed silent. The doors led to studios with various names in lettering across the tops. Wilder was one of HeartBeats' first acquisitions back when they were getting started. While the label wasn't a powerhouse, they were certainly eating their share of the market, having expanded every year. Now, you just never knew who would open one of the soundproof doors and pop their head out.

When JD clicked their own door behind them, he simply rested the guitar on the ground by his foot, balancing it with a loose grip around the neck of the case, while he stared TJ down. He didn't need to ask, TJ knew what his brother wanted.

"She isn't pregnant."

"You already knew that." JD pointed out.

"Funny, that's exactly what I told her." He turned away, settling himself at the piano, figuring he'd bang out some aggressions on the keys once he'd brought JD up to speed. "Turns out she barfed up the pill before it could take effect. Then didn't tell me. Seems she didn't want me in the way."

"Ouch." JD picked up the guitar and started liberating it from the case. He was seated and getting ready to make some sound come out of it when TJ spoke again.

"But she told her Dad the whole thing."

"What?" JD nearly dropped the guitar.

"Yeah, I had much that same reaction." He held up his scraped palms, where streaks of small scabs showed. "My knees look about the same."

"Ouch."

"Yeah, you can stop saying that now." He turned to the piano and began to play. He didn't know what it was until he recognized the strains of the piece he had composed the last time Norah was up here listening to him. In a short burst of anger, he stopped, banging out a few bad chords for emphasis.

"All right," Pain was evident in JD's voice. "That was really good until that last part with the chords in F'd-up major. You write that?"

TJ nodded.

"You want to play it for me in the right key?"

With a shrug, TJ rolled into the song, still not sure if that was the right opening chord. With no warm ups he headed into the vocals while his brother sat quietly.

JD looked like he was listening intently, but JD was a master. TJ was certain he was considering alternate keys and rises and falls. Chances were he was already composing a guitar line to lay into the back.

TJ didn't do the final round of the chorus, liking it better lacking finality. He altered the ending notes higher and left the last chord off entirely, leaving the piece hanging in the air. He knew it was just due to his mood today, but he thought it sounded better.

JD was nodding. "Do you want to add violin?"

"Are you serious?" His brother looked serious, but the song had sounded so maudlin to his own ears today that JD was probably just asking to be facetious.

"Yes." He was already getting his out of the case and popping the violin up under his chin. Once he was tuned up, he suggested they record it for later.

"Sorry I took away your practice time. I just wanted to be early because of the driving."

JD laughed at him. "Shut-up, this is exactly what I came early for. You know, you're getting really good with that piano. Way better than me."

TJ felt the jerk from that response as though his brother had physically clapped him on the back, and he was too stunned to say anything.

His world lost its footing and started to topple. Again. He couldn't take any more of this. JD was musically better than any of them. Simply because that's the way the world was. TJ had longed for a chance to be best all his life, but here was his brother, handing it to him, and he couldn't accept it. The sun comes up in the east. Two plus two makes four. JD is musically superior. Just the way things are.

Then he found his voice. "That's not true. You're the musical genius. I'm the front man. You're always better than me at every instrument."

Yet his brother was looking at him like he'd lost his mind. "Do you really believe that?"

TJ nodded, never more certain of anything in his life.

JD was leaning in, and TJ wouldn't have been surprised if his brother's hand had come out and felt his forehead for fever. "Is that why you haven't really composed anything before this?"

TJ shrugged. He'd thought the 'trite and stupid life' was a good enough excuse for not composing, but to be honest he'd never really thought beyond the boundaries of his older brother being a god.

JD started speaking in a disbelieving tone, "I was always better because I was two years ahead of you. You always got in one year what it usually took me two or three."

"This isn't up to par with what you write."

JD snorted. "Yeah, because I started writing fifteen years ago. And it damn sure wasn't as good as that."

He couldn't fight the laugh. "This isn't my first either. I've been writing for a few years now. But it's all been complete trash—rehashed melodies, trite lyrics, no real feeling to any of it."

"Well, that makes me feel better." JD went back to tuning the violin. "Start recording so we can get this down before Alex or Craig opens the door."

God forbid there be a door opening on a first run recording. It reassured him that his brother was still as uptight as always. At least some of the natural order of the universe remained.

They laid down track with JD adding in violin to most of the song. It was still ten minutes before they were supposed to meet when TJ turned the recording off.

JD set the violin down. "Needs work, but we'll get an

opinion in a little bit. You know, I've been wanting to do a two piano piece with guitar and drums."

TJ nodded. "I want a harpsichord. Those things sound freaking cool and no one has used them since like the fifteen hundreds."

JD thought that one through. "I'm sure you'll make it work."

Alex arrived first and spoke only a little before sitting down at his drums and banging out some superior release of tension. It was JD who asked. "What was that about?"

Alex nodded. "I call that one 'colicky baby.' She wouldn't stop crying, and I love her, but I was ready to put her in a room and close the door. Not like it would have mattered, she's got a set of lungs on her that would make me think Bridget had been fooling around with this one," he pointed one drumstick at a surprised TJ, "except that I trust her." He heaved a great sigh and the dark shadows under his eyes mirrored the unshaved stubble that TJ was just noticing.

Craig showed up last, and pulled out his bass, spent one minute warming up and then looked at all the rest of them like *why aren't you ready to go?*

They ran songs and formulated a play list, knowing that they were due back on the road in two months. They also had been planning on releasing a new album in the spring, but TJ's accident had messed that timing up, too. So they talked about what to record and what to leave out of it.

Brenda stuck her head in during one piece, but they were on a roll and didn't stop for her. When they finished, she noted that TJ wasn't on his stool anymore.

"Nope." He smiled, but realized that he ought to be. Especially since he had to drive himself home, and didn't want any lack of energy to affect how he handled the car.

"So, are you ready for a small local show?"

They all looked up at that one.

"When?"

"Where?"

"How long?"

She explained that she had them an in at McMinn's, a local bar where they'd gotten their start. "You could go back for sentimental reasons."

Alex pointed out. "It's not sentimental, McMinn's moved."

"Ironic, isn't it?" Brenda tipped her head. "McMinn's moved because they were getting too big. If they'd stayed in the same place, you couldn't get invited back. You'd violate all the fire codes. It's next Thursday night, if you're up to it."

She looked at all of them.

They all looked at TJ.

He shrugged. "Sure." It wasn't like he was doing anything next Thursday.

"Good." Brenda's voice said the topic was closed, but she didn't move. They all waited.

"If you're up to getting around before the tour dates, there's a Queen Tribute in Central Park. The sponsors have invited you *and,* of the three songs you've been invited to cover, you guys got *Somebody to Love.* And they want you all backing up vocals on *Bohemian Rhapsody.*" She looked straight at TJ. "What do you think of that, Mr. Vocalist?"

"Yeah." The word tumbled out of his mouth before he could think. A Queen tribute? He didn't care if there were only five people there, that was way too cool.

Luckily the others were thinking, and Brenda spilled a long list of celeb names. They hashed out details, got their set list and told Brenda to RSVP for them.

For a brief flash TJ thought about calling Norah, then he squashed it.

JD caught Brenda just as she turned around to leave. "By the way, we need a harpsichord."

"A harpsichord?"

Both brothers nodded, while Craig and Alex made faces and

held up their hands indicating that they'd had nothing to do with this.

She smirked. "All right. Is there anything else I can get you? Balalaikas? Autoharps? Ukuleles?"

JD just shook his head 'no' as though it was all perfectly reasonable, and Brenda left.

It hit him then, TJ felt his jaw unhinge. A Queen Tribute in Central Park.

He had weights to hit tonight.

He'd drive his own ass to the track tomorrow.

And by next week he'd be jogging part of it. He'd be on stage in Central Park in six weeks, and no one would notice a difference.

CHAPTER 36

Norah's feet pounded the surface of the track. Kelsey had come yesterday, this time without Baby Amy. Norah thanked God for small favors. She loved the baby a little too much. And she missed that she hadn't had a jog stroller for Jordan. Every year at the studio, when school started, she missed him. This year he would have been ten, entering fourth grade. Jeff would have been turning twenty-nine in just another month.

Today, no one was here. This was originally her day to pick up TJ and bring him, but he wanted nothing to do with her. She was still telling herself it was for the best, but she was running like she could outpace what she'd done.

She'd come early, lying to herself that she didn't want to see TJ. She hoped she'd miss him. She also hoped she'd see him. Although what good that could bring, she wasn't sure. It was truly for the best. She'd known from the start that she didn't stand a chance with him. Norah didn't fool herself that there wasn't beautiful, willing sex just waiting for him out at a bar, or when the guys hit the road again.

She didn't know how Kelsey stood being married to JD. She

figured she'd ask tomorrow when the other woman was supposed to show up—on TJ's off days. Never mind that all the days were now TJ's off days.

Her feet hit an even cadence, as her brain tried to push out thoughts of JD cheating on Kelsey, although she was certain he wouldn't. He was far too steady. He also wasn't the frontman like TJ, preferring to stay in the background. And, oh yeah, he didn't flirt like a shameless whore with every female nearby.

Norah shook her head and tried again to compose a few exercises to the rhythm made by her feet. After another half lap she gave up, and slowed to stop and breathe for a while. She was always amazed that she could dance, full out, for hours on end, but when she switched to a different exercise she burned out quickly.

When she stood up, she considered calling it quits for the day. She had three classes tonight; she'd get plenty of exercise then running routines with the older girls. But just when she decided to throw in the towel she saw him coming down the stairs.

Norah was at the far side of the track, so it was impossible to make out his features, but it was him. She'd know that physique anywhere. For just a moment, standing there by herself in the cool morning sunlight, Norah lit up a blush like a firecracker. Then she pushed that thought firmly aside.

Only TJ would grasp the railing that ran up the center of the stairs like that. He was in a black sleeveless t-shirt that showed off his arms, and black shorts with white stripes down the sides. His dark hair fell casually, looking like maybe he'd just run his fingers through it.

She wondered if he spotted her.

He did.

Even at this distance she could see him freeze for just a moment, his face, and therefore his gaze, trained right on her.

She didn't move either, waiting to see if he would wave. He didn't.

After that momentary pause, his face went back to looking at the task at hand: the stairs and the gate. He reached the bottom and stretched for just a minute.

Her breathing, which had almost been normal when she'd straightened up, had sped up again. Her heart was pounding and she wondered if he'd even call 9-1-1 if it gave out and she collapsed right now.

She started walking, continuing on the same way she'd been going, her pace slow enough that he'd see her coming. He took one glance and started off in the same direction she was headed.

She'd hoped to make eye contact, but he'd made it impossible.

Norah picked up speed, coming up behind him while he walked, his pace eating a surprising amount of ground. Still, she figured she'd pull up beside him and maybe say something.

Just as she was contemplating what to say, when she was just caddy-corner behind him on the right, his hand shot out. With a quick, casual flip of the wrist he motioned her to go around.

With that one simple gesture, he made it clear that he didn't want to speak to her.

For a lap she was glad that she hadn't told him anything, if this was the way he handled it. Who knew what he would have thought if she'd told him? He might have accused her of trapping him.

This time when her feet came up behind him, he didn't even make the motion. And her brain changed as she passed him.

His stance wasn't arrogant, it wasn't mean. She'd betrayed him, not the other way around. Maybe that was just because she hadn't given him the chance to, but there was no denying that she'd made the first cut.

His head turned slightly away from her as she passed, as

though he couldn't really stand to look at her. Maybe he couldn't.

With a deep breath, she told herself again it was really all for the best. God knew what He was doing, not giving her another baby. Not giving them one to share. She should snap these feelings for TJ at the base. Make it quick and clean.

But there was nothing quick or clean about it.

It had been weeks since they'd been together and she still dreamed of him at night. Hot erotic dreams like she hadn't suffered in years. She dreamed of him trying to hold her afterward, and her own frightened struggles against him.

She had to stop again. She couldn't sustain the pace she'd set, so she made her way off to the outside edge of the track and clung to the fence with her hands on the top bar and her feet braced apart. For long minutes she tried to breathe deeply. She heard TJ pass by her, and wondered if he looked up to watch her.

She stayed at the track the entire time he did. Wearing herself out. Because she needed to. Hair of the dog that bit you, right?

When at last he headed up the stairs, she watched. He was tired, his legs doing too many repetitive motions for too long a distance and then tackling stairs. He'd walked further today than before, but Norah was used to TJ pushing himself.

So she hung back, finishing her lap and reaching the top of the stairs just in time to see his green Mercedes pulling out the far side of the lot. She climbed in her own car and turned the engine over.

CHAPTER 37

TJ had seen Norah three times at the track. Every other morning when he went she was already there. They didn't speak, although he saw that she followed him home each time. Probably worried about his legs giving out on one of those turns.

He had no idea if she was worried about him or protecting other drivers from him. So he tried not to think about it much.

They had no real communication there, and he didn't see her at all anywhere else. He'd tried to hide it, but JD just point blank asked Kelsey one night if Norah talked while they ran. TJ had been sitting right there and considered spontaneous combustion a real option at the time.

Kelsey had turned to him. "Not a single word about you."

Great.

But Kelsey continued on in that woman-logic he didn't understand. "That speaks volumes in itself. She's playing it close to the chest."

If that spoke volumes, Kelsey hadn't pulled any off the shelf to read to him. So he had no idea what to make of it, and wasn't about to turn to JD's wife and ask.

When he was there on the track, he kept thinking Norah might just plant herself in front of him and say something. She had to know that she held those cards. That she could outrun him in any footrace these days if she so chose.

But she didn't choose.

Even when he'd pushed himself to go too fast and he'd stumbled and gone down, she'd only briefly paused, then run on by.

He didn't lie to himself that he didn't harbor images of her stopping and picking up his injured hand and kissing it. But he wasn't that injured because he'd been wearing leather biker's gloves as he'd planned on picking up his feet and jogging a little. And he'd been thinking about the old Norah, not the one who didn't let him in on life-altering possibilities and found it perfectly acceptable to condemn him on her father's shoulder.

He'd gone home each day and showered, thinking that he'd wash it all away. He hadn't been able to scrub hard enough.

He stood waiting, inside the front door of the handi-house. Most of his things were packed up. He'd been to his old house three times taking loads over. Tomorrow, he would actually vacate this place. He hadn't wanted to do it on top of the show tonight at McMinn's. That would just be too much at once.

JD was coming to pick him up, which was good because he was a little more nervous than normal. But that made sense, it was his first time back up on stage. Clearly everyone else was nervous about him, too.

JD pulled up in the SUV and TJ locked the front door behind him, then walked himself down the ramp. He'd warmed up his voice at home, and aside from a few words he remained silent all the way there.

The place was local so it wasn't a long drive, but he just rolled his head from side to side and stretched his arms and legs while his brother drove. He was grateful for the big SUV then.

His brother wasn't a small guy, and TJ was bigger. Well, one inch taller—his pride and joy since he'd attained it at nineteen.

Brenda was off base about McMinn's being nostalgic. They pulled into the back at a loading bay for the stage, not the alley entrance they'd used before. The tables were different, the stage was bigger, the manager was unfamiliar, and now half the audience was there in Wilder t-shirts, which came in too many varieties to count. Their first show here, Kelsey and her friend had showed up in shirts that Kelsey had ironed-on Wilder pictures herself. Only the beer was the same.

TJ glanced through to the crowd. The place was packed already. But that wasn't what he was looking for.

JD's voice caught him from over his shoulder. "Do you think she'll show?"

He shook his head, not bothering to try denying it.

"Kelsey did." JD reminded him.

That only brought a snort. "Kelsey was head over heels for you. And she didn't lie to you, then try to get off on a technicality. It isn't the same."

JD nodded and TJ pulled himself back to look at the other guys. When they finished tuning up, they just nodded at each other like always and he led them out into the glare.

The house lights had dropped, leaving him virtually blind beyond the edge of the stage. With a sense of unreality about it, he took a deep breath and opened his mouth. Like always, the words just happened. He never planned them except to be sure he knew where he was, he just talked to the audience he couldn't see.

He welcomed the crowd and thanked them for coming out and crushing themselves into too little space. He told them he was grateful that he was back up on stage and that he'd worked hard for it. Then he cracked a joke about what they should do if his legs gave out, and he pointed to a tall bar stool that was off to the side of the stage. The crowd laughed and several women promised to fetch it for him if he needed it. Another feminine voice volunteered to help keep him in the chair if he so needed it, and that time he laughed along with the crowd.

"Most of you have seen us before, and it's a real treat to get to perform in a nice little quiet bar like this." The crowd screamed and joked about the 'quiet' part. "As you know, right here is my favorite place to be." His finger pointed at the stage between his feet.

Right then, he realized it no longer was.

For a moment he thought he might pass out, but he sustained himself. Since no one in the audience gasped or even joked about the bar stool, they must not have seen it.

Those words had always been the cue to the guys that he was done talking and they should start playing. Only he barely heard the sound of the chords that were his cue, and he missed it.

He'd never done that on stage before.

Luckily, the guys were pros, and they made a smooth repeat of the intro, which this time he grabbed onto with both hands. He didn't miss a note, but he felt flat all evening. He didn't shine, and it was his job to shine.

Craig outdid him on every beat of *Sand,* which he performed solo with the acoustic guitar. Having the others sing numbers was something usually reserved for longer shows. It was intended to give TJ a rest, and they'd decided to do it tonight in a better-safe-than-sorry measure.

JD and Alex did *Go To Bed Mad,* and outshone him there, too.

TJ went back up after the break the two songs had afforded. He'd used the time to drink water and get back on his A-game. But he wasn't on it.

He wasn't bad. He just wasn't all that good.

For the first time, he was utterly grateful when the lights blacked out and the show was over. The audience screamed for an encore, but he begged out of it and thanked them again before beating a hasty retreat off-stage.

He was walking down the loading ramp, not feeling the damp night air, when a hand clamped down on his shoulder and spun him around.

Craig faced him, still clutching his bass by the neck, the tribalized strap still across his shoulder. "What the hell happened in there?"

TJ shrugged. He really had no clue.

JD found his voice and tapped Craig's hand off TJ's shoulder. "Give him a break, we've all had our bad nights."

It was Alex who spoke up. Since Alex didn't get into the scuffles with the rest of them, they all snapped to.

"No, we haven't *all* had our bad nights. *We* have." He pointed to himself, Craig, and JD. "But TJ doesn't. He's always *on*. He covers for *our* bad nights."

He didn't continue. He'd made his point.

TJ shrugged. "I don't know."

"Is it Norah?" JD's voice hit him like bricks.

"No." TJ protested through ground teeth, not believing his brother would air that here.

"What?" Craig looked back and forth between the Hewlitts. "Tall, hot, dancer Norah?"

TJ just shook his head and stalked off, his hands in tight fists on his hips, denying everything, even to himself.

JD pursued both him and the topic. "It's just the only thing I can think of that's really different. Because we can't play without you up there giving a good show. And you always have. This group can't be tied to Norah."

TJ turned, his fists now in front of him from no conscious thoughts of his own.

"Oh, no." Craig was backing away like TJ had the plague.

The words burst out of his mouth. "That's not what this is. I have just been to hell and back." He lashed out at all of them, verbally clearing a half-circle in front of himself. "Which ones of you just spent months in a wheelchair, a good portion of it not certain if you'd ever walk again? Did your dick not work and you thought it might never again? It was all my own fault, too.

"So I'm sorry if I'm not as good at getting up there and sweet talking a bunch of strangers. That doesn't mean it's about a woman." The hot air left him. "I just have to find my feet again."

JD laughed at him, and instead of getting angry TJ took it for the sign of acceptance that it was. Alex looked satisfied that things were getting resolved, and walked off, his mind always on his sweet wife and his daughter and new baby.

Just like that, they'd all let it go. All had faith in him that he'd resolve it. They packed up and said good-night, agreeing that they had their work cut out for them in the studio.

Later, he showered and laid himself out on the now familiar bed and stared at the ceiling. He thought through the evening and knew it had all gone wrong when he realized that he didn't live for the stage anymore. He shouldn't have made that realization there, with a crowd looking on, but it couldn't be helped.

He was a performer. It was what he did. It was what he was best at. And now it all seemed past-tense.

He wondered if the semi had knocked something more than his spinal cord loose, and if they were only just now beginning to see the effects. For a brief moment he imagined the doctors examining him and concluding that he had broken his stage presence. Or his charisma.

He'd thought he might laugh at the image, but in the end it really wasn't all that funny. He had to find his legs again was all. In more ways that just the obvious.

But in the back of his brain he wondered about JD's suggestion that it was because of Norah.

CHAPTER 38

TJ picked up his feet a little. Norah was coming up behind him. As usual, she passed him without a word.

He trained his mind back on the track in front of him. He stumbled repeatedly when he'd decided to jog. So he only did it for short stretches. It was like his legs were still too new to walking to try another method.

His brain wandered off again to what happened on stage at McMinn's. He still hadn't figured it all out except that what had driven him to perform was gone. The crowd screaming didn't turn him on the way it used to. The women who volunteered to keep him in his seat would have made him grin and think about letting them do just that. But now they were vapid and cheap. Their words didn't mean anything, and he finally saw that.

Maybe that did have to do with Norah.

He took that back, even just to himself.

It had everything to do with Norah. A man didn't just fall in love, really in love, for the first time and have it not change him. Especially when it ended so badly. But either way, he needed to find something else out there.

Maybe what he needed to see was that he was capable. Able

to really love someone. He hadn't truly been sure before. The accolades and adoration he'd gotten from performing had been enough. Now it wasn't.

Maybe the question now was: could someone love him? Not the man on the stage or the one in the papers.

The right woman wouldn't be jogging past him, ignoring him again, in tight black spandex that hugged her dancer's ass.

No, that was really the one place he was certain she wasn't.

This was the seventh time he'd seen her here. She was on the track before him, rain or shine. He'd even skipped a day, leaving three between his return, but still she'd been here, already going, when he'd started.

He'd tried going to the gym and walking their track twice now, but it was useless. The gym was a meat market in the best of circumstances. But being on the track brought out women who wanted to know if he needed a buddy. One had even pulled out a cell phone and called her friends. Fifteen minutes later the track was too crowded to walk, let alone try to jog a little. He didn't need or want a damned audience.

He just needed one person to scrape him off the ground if it came to it. Apparently she was here, spatula in hand, waiting for just that.

Six times Norah had followed him home and waited just behind the neighbor's trees. She must have thought she was actually out of sight. She was either stupid or thought he was. Both possibilities reflected badly on him.

He picked up his pace a little bit and turned it into the lope of a slow jog. He made it to the next mark on the track before he didn't get one of his feet lifted right and the shoe scuffed the rubberized track. Since the track was designed to grip tread, it held his foot and took him down.

TJ felt his hands smack the rough ground. His fingers took it, but at least his palms didn't. The leather gloves had more than done their job, and from the scuffs on them they'd felt every scrape he hadn't.

He knew his neurons weren't still working properly. His doctor had told him so. Apparently he even wasn't supposed to be upright—he was only there through sheer force of will. He didn't have much of the fine muscle control most associated with standing upright and walking.

He felt and forced every adjustment that should have been unconscious. But the jogging was killing him. If he didn't concentrate, down he went. Whatever motor memory he might have had was gone. The doctor made it clear there were three options: find it, re-create it, or live without.

TJ didn't think the third was much of an option, but either of the other two would be fine with him. When he'd asked the doctors how to do it, they almost looked at each other and shrugged comic book style. Of the people who'd done it, no one was sure how. They just had.

So TJ opted for the show-up-regularly-and-throw-yourself-face-first-at-the-track method. With a sigh he picked himself up and dusted off, starting at a walk again. His goal today was to jog a hundred meters without smacking asphalt. The first five tries had all ended the same.

He decided not to even walk the whole loop now. And he just doubled back to the starting line on the inside track, the only place he could accurately measure his hundred meters from.

Only thing was, when he turned around, he was now facing Norah. For the tiniest of moments, she looked up at him and their eyes held. Almost as quickly, she looked away, jogging past.

She was going longer distances now than she had when she started. Not that she needed to.

TJ lined himself up an extra ten meters beyond the start line, walking his way up to it and picking up the jog as he went. He seemed to be having trouble starting. This time he made it about fifty meters before he hit ground.

He turned around and walked back.

This time Norah passed him, and damn if he didn't just glance at her hair, and smack! Hard ground came up to meet him. He sat there with his head in his hands for a minute, realizing what he'd done. He'd distracted himself, and it was with Norah.

He shook it off and tried again, and again smacked down.

This time Norah was up ahead of him taking a breather, and he walked up, noticed her stiffen as he approached. "Why are you here, Norah?"

She was still breathing heavily and it took her a second to respond.

So TJ took it out on her. "I get it. You can jog and I can't. Point made. Go home."

She held up her hand and spoke between still strained breaths. "Just wanted . . . to be sure . . . you're safe."

"I'm good." TJ turned and headed back to the start line, wondering why he'd even started the conversation.

Her voice followed him. "I told Tim I'd do it."

"Oh," He turned back, wondering why she still had the power to stick knives in him. "So it's about Tim now."

She rolled her eyes and jogged off. He hated it, watching her go from a standstill to a leap into a steady pace. A move he couldn't pull off.

He went back to the start line and managed to throw himself at the ground twice before she made it back around. He was on his hands and knees when she approached. He called out. "You going to follow me home again today?"

"Yes." It was all she said as she went by, but he was happy to see that she almost missed a step there. But, of course, even that didn't make her fall.

It took three more tries, but he'd developed a will of steel. He maintained his concentration, thinking about each foot getting off the ground. He was ten yards from his goal when Norah passed him. He paid no attention.

Until her sneakers planted themselves right beside him.

He jogged past.

Her voice shattered his concentration. "I'm sorry."

He went down.

Son of a bitch.

He sat back on the black surface that was getting warmer as the day progressed. "Don't be sorry, just keep your mouth shut. I was five meters away." With an open hand he gestured to the painted white line that marked the end of the dash. Not that he'd been dashing it.

Her feet came closer, but he didn't look up. "I'm sorry, I didn't mean to make you fall. I meant I'm sorry I didn't tell you."

He was not hearing this.

Not here, sitting on his ass, looking at her sneakers.

Her voice carried again. "It was a mistake. A big one. I should have told you."

He heaved a sigh. "Damn right, you should have."

For a moment the sneakers didn't move, then she got the hint and jogged away.

He gave it one more try, and finally made the full hundred meters, collapsing as he went over the end line. This time he sat on the rough surface happy as a little clam.

TJ picked himself up and headed home.

This time Norah followed at a less discreet distance.

CHAPTER 39

TJ rode the elevator up at the HeartBeats studios. No one was on the schedule for today, so he'd have the room to himself. He'd gone to the track again this morning, even though it wasn't his day.

He smacked the ground repeatedly, but made the hundred meters with far fewer tries, then even managed to get one time around the track in a jog, with only one stumble. He was proud that he hadn't gone down. Somehow he managed to untangle his disobedient feet before they completely defied him.

When he'd come back around he'd called it quits early, and was somewhat surprised to see Norah's car behind him on the drive home. She followed him only to the gate, maybe figuring he was safe there. Maybe she forgot she was on the list. Or maybe she had figured he'd taken her off. He hadn't gotten around to it.

Whatever it was, she turned around without entering and headed away.

TJ had spent the later half of the morning at his own house. But the inspiration to be what he had been wasn't there. So here he was walking the silent hallway, and pushing open the heavy studio door.

Sound blasted out at him, momentarily drowning everything out, even his thoughts. He pulled the door closed, thinking that ironically he'd made his way back from grave injury, only to be deafened by one of his band mates.

Craig was letting out his crazy side in there. And he hadn't even seen TJ. That was how Craig composed the harder stuff, and TJ knew better than to mess with it.

Only now he didn't have a studio.

Since he couldn't do the rest of what he wanted, he headed up another floor to see Brenda.

Her door was already partway open when he got there, her secretary having just waved him by, putting her finger to her lips. TJ nodded and pushed his way in quietly, Brenda was on a call, but motioned for him to take a seat.

He wanted to, but it only lasted a second. On his feet again, he prowled the office while she talked. There were pictures wallpapering every non-window surface. He spotted one of the original Wilder posters that Kelsey made. God, they all looked so young.

There were other singers and groups up there. Some wildly famous, some getting there, some already been and gone. She had wedding photos of all sorts of people he worked with. JD and Kelsey were there, and another of them with five kids. That one needed updating. But a separate little photo of newborn Baby Amy was tacked right beside it. Alex and a very pregnant Bridget were up there, with Olivia in their arms. Another with himself and Craig, arms slung around each other. A candid photo at Hailey Watkins' wedding, with Craig and Shay both in the background—the day they'd met.

Her voice from behind him startled him. "I should have known you wouldn't sit well these days. Done enough of it?"

"For a lifetime."

She perched on the edge of her desk. "What do you need?" Her head tilted, perfectly cut brown hair swaying as she moved. She was a very attractive woman for being so much older than he was. He was surprised he only just now noticed that. He'd known her for years.

He sighed. "I sucked the other night."

"Really?" She seemed impressed. Although whether it was because he'd sucked or because he'd admitted it, he didn't know. "I've never heard of you having issues before. Was it neural?"

He laughed at that one. "Yes! But not my spinal cord. My brain. I just . . . I don't know. I lost whatever I had."

She looked at him square. "Are you telling me to cancel tour dates, or are you going to get it back?"

"Hell, yes, I'm getting it back." The determination in his tone surprised even him. "That's what I came up about. I haven't asked the guys yet, I just wanted to know if it was a possibility, but I wanted to ask you . . ."

She didn't tell him to spit it out, she just sat patiently, one of Brenda's greatest strengths.

"Can we play more local dates? Soon? I've got to get up in Central Park for that Queen concert and I've got to be ready." He hadn't meant to sound so desperate.

Brenda's answering smile was all he needed. "Consider it done."

"Thank you." He stuffed his hands in his pockets. "You've always understood and worked with us."

She didn't respond, so he kept going. "When Alex needed time because Bridget's second pregnancy wasn't going well, and this," He gestured to his legs. "This was my own fault. Even back when we hadn't made a penny for you, you worked around JD's schedule with his daughter. Thank you."

She looked at him askance. "You do know why the four of us founded HeartBeats, don't you?"

Sure he did. "You wanted to be a bigger fish in a smaller

pond." He instantly tasted shoe and scrambled to correct it. "That didn't come out right. You needed more control than the big labels were giving you."

Brenda nodded. "I thought so. All this time you missed the point."

TJ waited for her to give it to him.

With a smile she leaned back against her desk, her arms folded. "Eight years ago I got confused about my son's birthday present. He'd said what he wanted, and I mis-heard it. So I went out and got what I thought he said. The problem was, I was so far off base, and I didn't even know it. He was seven years old and I didn't know him well enough to know that.

"I'd been too busy with my job. I didn't know either of my sons. I was just cranking out stars. I lived in a big house that I realized I hated. Didn't know my neighbors. My husband was on the verge of divorcing me, and I think he was in the right. When I took a good look around, I realized nobody was happy. So I left. We founded HeartBeats with the idea that we'd do good work *and* show up at our kids' birthday parties." She waved her hand at him, before continuing.

"So you do whatever you have to to find what you need. We're behind you. There's plenty of money here. If Wilder breaks up, then it was a hell of a great run—"

He jerked back at that. "Wilder isn't breaking up."

"Glad to hear it. But you've done nothing but perform and party for years now. I'm sorry it caught up to you. So you go get yourself together. We'll wait while you get the girl."

He shook his head. "It is *not* about a girl."

She laughed at him. "Methinks thou doth protest too much."

He couldn't stay mad. He tried to. "All right, part of it's about a girl. Part of it's about learning to walk again."

Her eyebrows rose up, "In more ways than one?"

He chuckled. "Yeah."

Brenda went around her desk and started scribbling some

notes to herself. She pulled out her purse and shoved the notes in it. "I'll get on those extra dates in a bit. I have to go see my youngest in his kindergarten play. Walk me out?"

TJ followed, asking what she'd done when she realized she hated her house. He'd been having much the same thoughts. She laughed and said she'd sold the thing to someone just like she'd been, more concerned about the prestige of the neighborhood than being comfortable, and she'd let it go for a hefty profit.

He climbed into the new Mercedes at the curb and drove to his house. He stayed in the driveway for just a moment, really looking at the thing. He didn't really like the arches. And there was no yard.

He let himself in the front door and remembered Norah's mouth hanging open at the fountain. It was too much.

He opened the drawer on the far right side of the kitchen. The real estate agent had put her card there, telling him she was starting his 'junk drawer'. There were two pencils and the card just rattling around. TJ called the agent and put the house on the market. Fifteen minutes later he cut the woman off and hung up on her, thanking her quickly.

He shook his head a little, realizing that he suddenly felt a bit more free.

Winding his way into the living room, and realizing that he'd done zero living in there, he scrounged through his music. Quickly pulling up Queen's Greatest Hits, he thought he'd listen and re-learn the words. He hit the play button then punched another series of buttons piping the music through the entire house.

TJ wandered the house, cataloging what he was going to take with him when he moved, and what he wasn't. As *We Will Rock You* segued smoothly into *We Are the Champions,* TJ found himself singing along, already knowing all the words, and no longer paying attention to the house.

Heading into his small home studio, he reset the music as background, and hit 'record.'

TJ leaned on the wall, not wanting to stand when all his focus was in his lungs and his vocal cords. Two bars in, the room around him dissolved, leaving him with only his own voice and the music.

CHAPTER 40

Norah was uncertain whether she was going to the track again or not. She'd apologized, and TJ had accepted in the worst possible way. She really didn't like running, and he didn't need her any more.

Each time he headed home to all his stairs. As far as she knew, no one held his hand when he climbed to the second floor. Or else there *was* someone there, waiting for him. Either way, she was wasting her time.

Her last class filed in for the night. The later classes had older students, and these were the core of her small dance company. She smiled at each of them as they came in, chattering about boys and clothes and make-up. They'd be normal teenage girls until she put the music on.

They were dressed in various outfits, some all put together with matching pieces bought at local dance shops or from her own little boutique out front. Others were more concerned with not looking so put-together and wore cut-off t-shirts tied in knots here and there. They'd taken scissors to many of the things they wore. No rote black leotards here.

They scattered across the floor, talking in small clusters.

Some of them started warming up on their own, others required a glance from her to get going. It was seven-thirty and they would go until nine.

Norah took her spot at the front of the room and snapped at the music. Sinking to the floor she led the new series of warm-up exercises they were finally getting familiar with. Going through the motions, her mind wandered.

No more track.

She would sleep in tomorrow. The thought brought a smile to her face and when they finished the first series she had the girls space themselves along the barres before they stuffed their feet into pointe shoes.

The class went by without much input from her. A good portion of the girls had been at this studio longer than she had. She watched ankles and corrected posture, led them through turns and leaps and combinations. Then they put together the first three eight-counts of the Holiday Show dance they would do.

Norah danced with them, leading because she knew it and they didn't yet. By nine, she was exhausted, even though she didn't think she'd done anything much.

She did the last two steps and then quadrupled the last turn, thinking at least she'd feel like she'd done something that evening. She used her foot, but she landed in a perfect fifth position as she glanced around. Everywhere girls were falling off their feet, and they'd only had a double pirouette to do. She sighed and turned to Gracie, who'd been brave enough to stand beside Norah for the whole class. "Go write 'pirouettes' on the class board." There was a series of small whiteboards where the teachers made notes about each class. "And Gracie, please spell it right."

Her eyes swept the mirror, taking in her own tired looks, and seeing that most of the girls had pulled it together enough to hold the final fifth position pose, even if they hadn't landed there.

That was when she saw him in the doorway. His dark frame took up most of the space. For that half second, her heart stopped. *What was he even doing here?* Surely he hadn't come to see her, he wasn't speaking to her.

Just as Norah realized she was staring at him in the mirror, he gave a half-smile. In it was a wealth of meaning. He *was* here to see her. He was sorry, too. He missed her.

Or, she told herself, she had simply made all that up because she wanted it to be true.

His eyes broke contact, and in that instant Norah registered the low humming around her. The girls were abuzz. This was Nashville, and they knew who he was.

One even walked up to him, bold as day, strutting and flirting well beyond her seventeen years. "Are you TJ Hewlitt?"

Norah couldn't believe the audacity, and from Leah. Taking a deep breath, Norah consoled herself over disappointment in Leah and in TJ, too, for not looking at the girl like she had no right.

"Yes, I am. I'm here to see Miss Davidson."

That at least made Norah laugh. No one called her 'Miss Davidson'. The term seemed horribly old fashioned coming from his mouth.

The girls seemed to agree.

"Norah!" Several of them called out.

"He's here to see *you*." That was the brunette who'd strutted her way up to him right behind Leah.

Norah sighed. "Thank you, Belinda, for being surprised that Mr. Hewlitt was here to see *me*, of all people." Only then did it occur to her that class wasn't over until she said it was. "Class is excused."

No one moved.

"Go." She looked at each of them in turn.

They lingered, gathering their things, and one by one pushed out the doorway. A bemused TJ had stepped into the room for a brief moment, trying to get out of the crush. It was Leah who looked up at him pityingly. "You can't be in here on our nice wood floors with those shoes. Follow me."

TJ looked across the room at Norah, with panic on his face. She just nodded, agreeing that Leah was right.

He shook his head and followed the girls out beyond the doorway where they attacked him until he slipped out of his shoes and politely fled back into the room. As soon as he found the door, he closed it behind him. Just after the 'click' of the catch came an audible sigh from him.

He caught her gaze. "Thank God I was wearing loafers. You threw me to the wolves."

"They're teenage girls, although I don't know where they got off acting like—"Her voice just quit on her.

"Norah?"

"It's nothing." She shook her head. "What did you want?"

His hands went into the pockets of his leather jacket. "I'm not sure now."

This time when she looked, she searched. Something had just now shifted in him from being here to being ready to turn around and walk out. "What?"

"Are you just going to shut down on me?"

She couldn't help the smile that spread across her face. If he was upset because he wanted inside her head, this time she'd tell him everything. "I just realized that some of them are eighteen, and when I was eighteen I was married and pregnant."

He laughed, then sobered up pretty quickly. "Yeah, but you loved him. They don't know me from Adam."

"Apparently they don't think they need to." She turned back, tucking herself onto the chair behind her and unwinding her pointe shoes. Three faces pressed against the small window cut into the door. Norah glared at them until they left. "Sorry, we still had an audience."

TJ stood close, a frown pulling his brows together. "How are your feet?"

What was he asking about? "Fine?" She pulled off her shoe, flexing her toes.

He looked the foot over, "Because you were dancing on them."

"Oh." She pulled off the other shoe, understanding what he meant. "No, I wasn't dancing on them."

Still looking out of place in his denim and testosterone where there was usually only spandex and grace, he jerked a thumb over his shoulder toward the now vacant center of the room, "Then what were you doing?"

Norah waved his concern away, and pointed her tights-clad toes at him. "That was teaching, not *dancing*. Dancing is when I damage them."

"There are holes in the bottom of your tights." He frowned again.

"Yes, so I can pull them up and down and put toe pads inside if I want." She pulled the gel-filled pad out of the tip of the point shoes and held it up. He reached for it and she snapped it back. "Ew, I've been dancing on it."

He laughed and reached again for the thing, this time quickly removing it from her grasp, "I've bandaged your bloody feet. This is nothing." He held it up to the light and pinched it. "This really is nothing. This can't possibly support your toes enough to stand on them."

"It's not supposed to, your toes have to be strong enough to hold you, this just keeps them aligned and offers a little padding." While she talked, Norah folded and wound the ribbons on her shoes, tucking them in, then she stood and quickly reclaimed the pad TJ was still inspecting, and stuffed it back into the shoe.

She was impressed how easily things reverted to normal, but she was a little suspicious of it, too. It was almost too easy. "I'm sure you didn't drive out here just to check up on my toes."

She saw the words put him just a little off balance, and she watched while he quickly regained it too. "You apologized the other day, and I was an ass. I understand. I don't like the decision that you made, but I understand why you made it."

"So my apology is accepted?"

He nodded.

"Thank you."

He didn't say anything, and she wondered if the girls were still listening in and wondering why their teacher couldn't just bag the guy. "All right, then. I'm glad you stopped by. I will sleep better."

She started for the door, but his hand caught her and her breath caught in her chest.

"Can you promise me that what happened won't happen again?"

She tried to choke back the laugh, but she couldn't, "Of course it won't. I'm not getting in that situation again. The condom won't break again. There won't be any issues."

His jaw clenched and she realized she was being a little slow.

"I *meant*," the word was pushed between tight teeth, "that if you have any issues with me, you bring them to *me*. Not your friends or co-workers or, God-forbid, your father."

She nodded. "What issues could I have with you? You're not speaking to me, remember?" Although obviously he didn't, as evidenced by his very presence. Here she was reminding him. *Fool.*

He used the same tack. "Clearly, I am. And something's bound to come up, I irritate the crap out of you."

"No you don't. Is this why you came?"

He didn't answer her. "Promise?"

"Why does it matter?" *And why was she pushing?*

TJ heaved a deep sigh, "Because I want us to be friends again, but I need to know that you will come to me when you need to. It's called being a friend."

She was such a fool to put herself back here. As his 'friend.' But her brain wasn't allowed a vote, her mouth decided. "I promise."

However, he wasn't finished with her, because he raked his hands over his face, "And no more going to your *Dad* with that stuff. I'll have to face that man again and, God, what he must think of me."

Norah laughed. "Don't worry about that, really. My Dad is very cool. He told me I should tell you everything. He didn't judge you."

"You're his daughter. His youngest!" He put his hands out, and for the first time Norah saw how much it truly bothered him. "How can he not?"

"He was too busy judging *me.* He would never judge someone he doesn't know. Me, on the other hand, he has no issues with condemning."

TJ shook his head, looking even more masculine against the feminine surroundings. "I came by to see if you wanted to go out for a drink."

CHAPTER 41

She pulled her head back. "Drinking?"

"No, I haven't gone stupid. One beer maybe, and no driving until everyone is fine. Maybe something to eat, nothing sticks to you." His hand gestured up and down.

Well, she was too skinny, but God she wanted to go. "I can't. I'm a mess, I need a shower."

"You have one here. You must have a change of clothes." Again he gestured, "I am not taking you out in that."

Of course her knit dance skirt and matching super-cropped top were suspect. She laughed.

He crossed his arms. "I know you don't turn into a pumpkin at ten o'clock. I'll wait."

"All right." She left the room, and wound through to the back to the private shower just off her office.

Norah scrubbed up quickly, jumping at every creak and noise, praying that it was—no make that *wasn't*—TJ coming in to join her. She knew it would be amazing for the few minutes it lasted, then she would be left with nothing but irrefutable proof that he thought she was a cheap lay.

Walking into her office, wrapped in her towel, she

rummaged through her spare clothes. The only things there were black dance pants and a fitted, open necked t-shirt. She sighed to herself, it would have to do.

After towel drying her hair, Norah stepped into the clothes, grateful she had clean underwear. She rummaged through her purse for whatever makeup she could find, cursed her own vanity, and put it on anyway.

She emerged to find TJ standing in the lobby, his face three inches from one of Kelsey's masterpieces of her. There was a large central photo, with smaller ones all around and TJ seemed to be studying each. He must have seen her from the corner of his eye, because without looking over he spoke. "This is amazing."

Norah nodded, coming closer to him. "Kelsey is an incredible photographer."

"Oh, I knew that. What I didn't know," He tipped his head sideways, "was that you could do the splits while standing on one foot."

"It's called arabesque."

"Yeah, whatever." He turned then to look at her. "Jesus, Norah! I can't take you out in public in that!"

She shrugged, "Then I can't go. It's all I have here." He was right, she would feel underdressed out in this, but she was upset she wouldn't be going out with him. She had let her thoughts go a little too far and believe maybe it was a date.

"No, come on, get your jacket. We'll go to a restaurant instead of a bar." He grabbed her blazer from where she'd slung it over her arm, and held it for her. Then he grabbed the bottom hem and tugged it back down, making her laugh.

"I'm sorry."

Taking her hand, he tugged her toward the front door. "I'm not. I'm going to be the envy of every guy there tonight. I would suggest you stick real close. I'm just going to be grateful that you aren't in men's underwear."

He tucked her into the passenger side of the Mercedes, and slid into the driver's seat. "Oooh, this is a change. You trust me driving?"

She nodded.

With a sideways glance, he started the engine. "You didn't follow me home from the track today."

She nodded. "You've been fine. I'd crossed the line from 'concerned' to 'stalking.'" She waved a hand at him to go, and he pulled out of the parking lot, leaving her car there in the corner spot by itself.

He pulled them into an open bar & grill and got them tucked in the back in a small booth. "You want a beer?"

She shook her head.

"You don't drink at all?"

A small smile hit her lips, "I just don't like beer. I'm not the girl that all the guys love because she knows all the sports scores and can pound beers. I never will be, the stuff is nasty."

"What do you want?"

"A margarita, but I have to drive—"

His hand waved in front of her and cut her off. He laid his phone between them on the table. "An hour and a half. One beer for me. I'll get you home safe."

She nodded. "A margarita then. Rocks. Salt."

"You're not so girly." His grin was all fallen angel even though he wasn't trying, and it made her feel girly.

They added insanely greasy cheese bread to the order and chatted most of the way through it. He talked her into a second margarita and she hoped he wasn't talking her out of her pants.

She was feeling the effects of the liquor when she commented, "I couldn't believe the girls tonight just came on to you that way."

Why was she even bringing this up? TJ shrugged, but her mouth got away from her. "I mean they're sixteen, some of them. And they were looking at you like you were chocolate. Like you'd melt in their mouths!"

Oh God. She waited for the universe to swallow her. Instead the blush crept up her face at an alarming rate. Her hands flew to her cheeks as though she stood a chance of hiding anything from this beautiful man who was already laughing at her.

TJ flagged a server and ordered her a glass of water.

Her mouth opened again, "Oh, tell me I didn't just say that."

"You did."

"Agh!" Burying her head in her arms there at the table was only useful for a second.

TJ was talking to her again. "You're fun. What else do you say when you're tipsy?"

Clamping her lips, she refused to speak. He had a sparkle in his eyes that was guaranteed trouble. His beer had disappeared a long time ago and been replaced by soda. He was functioning on all cylinders. Not fair.

She was more than happy when he changed topics. "Are you going to the track tomorrow?"

"Sure." She hated herself even as she said it. Here was a man who picked himself up time and time again, his determination legendary in her mind, and she crumpled in the wind. She'd decided not four hours ago to *not* go to the track. Plus, he'd gotten upset when she'd told JD that she *wanted* to come to dinner. She couldn't lie about this. "No."

She'd confused him. "Which is it?"

"No."

"Oh." His face actually fell, and she was too tipsy to fight the way it took her heart with it. "I was hoping you'd be there."

He might as well have picked a thread on her decision and just unraveled the whole thing. "What do you need?"

"Someone to pace against."

"You're going to outrun me really soon."

His grin was back. "One can only hope. So come with me?"

She nodded and took a sip of water hoping that her heart wasn't showing in her eyes. Norah figured between the liquor and his smiles she was dead-on drunk, and she might as well just sit there and make dreamy eyes. Then she sat up straight. "Oh, I can't. I don't have a car."

He paid the check which had somehow arrived, and showed her the phone timer. One-thirty-five. He offered his hand as he stood. "You are correct, because I am driving you home tonight. But I'll pick you up at nine-thirty and drop you at the studio afterwards."

She nodded, and let him lead her out of the restaurant into the dark, chilly air. Her jacket! She started to duck back in for it only to see that TJ had remembered it.

TJ held it out while she slipped into it. She watched his hand on the small buttons and tried to focus. As she followed its movement, the hand came up and cradled her chin, lifting her gaze to his.

For a moment she went still, certain that he was going to kiss her and uncertain how she should react. What she did know was that if his lips even touched hers, she would launch herself into his arms, all other thoughts be damned, regardless of what she *should* do.

He didn't kiss her. He simply said words.

"You know, I'm going to enjoy being your chauffer tomorrow."

He took her by the hand and pulled her along. Norah noted that the hold was a simple dance-partner, weight-support type of hold, not the interlocked-fingers kind you did with someone you were attracted to.

It was a good thing he was driving. She was too snookered to curb any of her thoughts. She gave him directions to the farmhouse, and he pulled up just to the edge of the less-than-bright circle created by the front porch light and waited.

Again her mouth got ahead of her. "What? You're not going to walk me to my door?"

After it slipped out, she held her ground, as though she had meant to taunt him that way.

"No way. Your Daddy's probably got his shotgun aimed at me right now."

She laughed again. "You'd like my Daddy if you ever talked to him."

"Hard to talk to a man with a gun." TJ didn't move to get out from behind the wheel and she wondered if he was serious.

"Trust me, he'll aim it at me first." She slammed the car door shut with a little too much force, proving to both of them, again, that it was a good thing he'd driven, and she waved a little as she climbed the three steps up to the porch.

TJ did at least watch to make sure she was safely in the house.

CHAPTER 42

TJ fought off the grunt that wanted to escape as he lifted the weight. He was having to really put in the effort to maintain what he'd developed in that stupid chair hauling his own body weight around. For a flash of a moment he considered using the chair as a workout machine, then he sloughed it off.

He had better things to think of: Norah, tipsy and cute as hell, the night he'd taken her out for a drink. He'd almost kissed her there just outside the restaurant. But she hadn't been completely sober and he hadn't been ready for another Norah-here-then-gone moment. So he had settled for watching her sweet ass peek below the hem of that blazer while she'd sashayed up her front steps. She'd given him hope.

She'd also said something about him melting in her mouth, then gotten really embarrassed about it. She'd given him some seriously erotic dreams with that one.

He curled the weight up again and held it.

She'd come out to the track every day and said she was back on his off days, too. Sometimes she invited Kelsey to join her, sometimes not.

He'd showed up on one of those off days, warmed by her happy surprise when she realized he was there. Now he'd had to suppress the urge to go every day. TJ had been startled to find out just how much he loved talking to her. Looking at her. Just being beside her.

He gritted his teeth together, holding the last bicep curl as he admitted that he wanted so much more from her. He also had to admit that he was afraid to go to the track every day—only because he feared smothering her and pushing her away.

At least as things were, they were going well.

Norah had outrun him in every race, but she'd made it worth his while. He'd stumbled once, and she'd automatically put herself in his path. He'd had no chance of saving himself, or her with her right in front of him, and they'd gone down in a tangle of arms and legs that had been worth every bruise.

She'd laid on the asphalt, under him, her mouth open and trying to catch the breath that had been knocked out of her. He'd so desperately wanted to kiss her right there, peel her clothes and make love to her on the almost always deserted track. Instead he'd started talking.

"Norah! Did you'd catch me?"

She looked sheepish. "Kneejerk reaction? By the time I realized there was no way I could support you I'd already made it worse for both of us."

It was still an excellent excuse to feel her for bruises. She'd let him, laughing but not moving away nor pushing at his hands.

TJ changed machines. It was things like that that made him think he might stand a chance with her. Then again, he'd picked her up after her dance classes again more than once. She'd always had jeans and a regular shirt on hand. Which was fine, but meant he couldn't tease her. She also never drank more than just the one margarita again, sometimes not even that much. So maybe the buttons that were done up high enough not to reveal too much, and the lack of liquor was saying he should back off.

But TJ knew he really just couldn't.

He had to get her to want him like he wanted her, and he had to do it before some other guy figured it out.

So yesterday at the track he'd held out the white flag of surrender. Or as close to it as he was going to get at the track.

TJ pushed the leg weights, enjoying that he was moving mass in the hundreds of pounds now. It helped to get some of this off his mind.

Or not, as his brain instantly reverted back to Norah mode.

He'd walked beside her when they had finished their run, and asked before he'd lost his nerve. "So there's this woman I met, that I'm in love with."

Her head snapped his way at that, and she'd met his eyes for just a moment before looking away.

He'd prodded, "How do I tell her?"

Norah was so startled by the whole thing, it made him wonder if he hadn't made as much headway as he'd thought. He figured she had to know it was her, but her suggestion was simply some flowers and the words.

He'd almost groaned and fallen to the track in agony. She'd given him *nothing* he could use. In typical Norah fashion, as she had from day one, she was making him do for himself.

TJ wiped his face, then literally threw in the towel for the day. With no real effort on his part, he walked the motions of showering and dressing and then he hit his studio room. He'd been here every day, belting out his frustrations with Norah and his desire to be on track again.

They had a show tonight, and there would be no bar stool sitting off to the side. The Troubadour had welcomed them back with open arms. TJ was looking forward to being on stage again. He had to find out if he'd reclaimed any of 'it'.

He cued up backup music of Wilder's songs and started changing them up. He altered his volume; he played with starts and stops; he changed his timbre. He'd never really paid attention to it before.

For a brief moment TJ stopped and wondered why anyone had ever let him on a stage, or signed the group, when he had been doing such a poor job. There was a wealth of basic material here that he'd never really considered.

He tried *This Ordinary Man* while at the piano and found that he couldn't do it justice with his lungs hindered from his seated position. He tried again a capella and liked the way it rang. It was hours later before he looked at his watch.

Shit!

TJ forced himself to stop. He couldn't wear out his voice right before a big show. And if he screwed up tonight, too, someone was going to put it in a review.

Thinking that a nap was a good idea, but knowing that he wouldn't sleep, TJ popped himself into the shower again. No sooner was he wet than he realized what he needed to do with his time.

He scrubbed faster than humanly possible and dressed with little care for a man going on stage. Behind the wheel in under five minutes, TJ waited with utter impatience for the long driveway gate to roll slowly back. He peeled out onto the deserted street, and got to the dance studio without much concern about how he'd gotten there. For a moment after he pulled into the lot he stayed still, thinking to himself that he'd better be more careful, Norah would kill him if he hurt himself. Sitting in the silent car alone it made him smile.

What didn't make him smile was the fact that all the lights were off inside her studio, and the parking lot was empty. Then he realized it was Friday. Classes ran Monday through Thursday.

His shoulders sagged, and with a snort of disgust he turned around to pull out, only then did he spot Norah's car tucked against the hedges. With a grin he felt, he popped open the car door and bolted up the steps.

The door didn't give.

Knocking and peering inside, he finally caught a faint light shining through the small cut out window in the far studio. TJ pounded on the door again, knowing she was inside and probably couldn't hear him. He let out a sigh, and stepped back to look for emergency exits, other windows. As he turned, the door clicked open behind him and Norah's voice came to him, "Hold your little horseys."

She was standing in the doorway, four steps above him, and he figured there was something figurative there as well as the literal. She was in those stupid men's boxer briefs and a sport bra, and nothing else.

Her lips quirked into a little smile. He wanted, right then, to tell her he loved her, because he did and he wanted her to know it.

Her voice found him again, "Well, come on in." Norah turned, still holding the door for him, and he realized that he couldn't tell her now. He had a show to do, and if she threw herself at him, he wouldn't be paying attention on stage and it would be even worse than last time.

TJ let a soft chuckle out under his breath. If she threw herself at him, he wouldn't even make it to the show.

And if, God forbid, she said 'no' . . . Well, he wouldn't contemplate that.

"Can you come out tonight?" It fell out of his mouth breathlessly, with no forewarning.

She ducked into the room and must have hit something, because the music stopped just a beat before she emerged again. Her mouth curled and she shook her head 'no'.

"Please." She *had* to come. The longer he stood here the more he realized that he needed her to be there, out in the audience.

"I'm having dinner with my Dad."

He bit back the words, *You owe me something of your father's, he got something of mine.* Instead he tried again, "Please." Before she could protest, he cut her off. "I need you."

Her chagrin turned immediately to concern. "What's wrong?"

"Nothing, but I have a show tonight and I need you there." That just hadn't sounded right.

"I know, but you don't need me, there will be plenty of people."

"I just," *He just what? He just needed* Norah *there, that was what.* "I just have to try something new, and I wanted you to listen to it in the car on the way over and know that you were out there watching."

"I—"

"Please." He put weight behind the word. And waited. His heart was twisted in knots, just wanting to know if she would come tonight.

"Maybe I can come after I meet my Dad."

"Now." He had her hands tucked into his and her gaze caught with his own.

"I'll see." She shrugged and disappeared into the office, emerging with her phone to her ear. "Hi, Daddy. I got invited out tonight. . . . I know, he says it's important though. . . . yes, it is. . ."

TJ imagined that her father had just asked if it was 'that Hewlitt boy,' and he hadn't felt so young in ages.

Norah continued with no mind to him. "Okay, Daddy. I'll be home a little later. We'll do dinner tomorrow . . . Okay, Sunday then. . . . Monday?"

Guilt settled around his heart. Dinner with her father clearly wasn't an everyday occurrence, and he wanted to just tell her he'd find another way. But the thought of going out on stage and her not being there was petrifying, and he wasn't sure why.

He'd never been nervous about it before. There was always a first time, and this was clearly his.

Norah hung up. "It's okay, his girlfriend was going to come anyway it turns out."

"Thank you." His chest unclenched and he smiled, wondering if she could read anything from the curvature of his mouth.

She sighed. "Do I need to go get ready? When do we leave?"

"About five minutes ago?" *Damn,* he was not making any of this easy.

"All right," She sighed and turned back toward the office. "I'll do my best."

TJ puttered around the studio. He was getting to be a pro at showing up and whisking Norah away. And he was getting real familiar with these photos of her on the wall. A few were older, from Houston. One featured her in an overhead lift with some very buff guy; it looked like some kind of sun worship.

He had it bad, and he knew it. The great masters' artwork didn't compare to photos of her in old holey dancewear doing exercises at the barre. He didn't care if he was late for his show, so long as he had Norah in tow.

And he was never late. Because there had never been anywhere else he'd rather be. Before now.

She emerged with wet hair pulled back. Her fitted jeans and a t-shirt left a little skin to show.

He wanted to touch her. He wanted to tell her how great she looked. Instead he talked while he dragged her outside. "Good, let's go. We're at the Troubadour tonight. We start at seven."

"TJ!" Norah yelped and pointed at the dash clock as she slid into the passenger side of the Mercedes. "Are we going to have enough time?"

"Just." He threw the car in gear and peeled out of the parking lot.

He played her various songs while he drove, directing her to change the pieces as he went. "Listen to that, see how the volume changes, it's actually quite an art."

God, he sounded stupid. What had he been thinking?

"You're right. I never really thought of it before." She tilted her head just a bit. "You don't do that."

He'd been thinking just fine. This was Norah, and she understood. "But I need to. I've been trying it out. I just . . ."

He didn't know what to say. So he concentrated on pulling into the back lot at the Troubadour and parking beside Craig's car.

Her hand settled on his arm, stopping him from unbuckling. "You what?"

"I just always performed for the audience. Now I'm discovering I really like singing. I want to be better at it. Does that sound right?"

Her laughed sounded right. "I think we need to get out." She pointed beyond the windshield, at JD and Craig waving him hurriedly in.

Within minutes he was backstage with Norah shuffled off into the audience. By herself. *God, he won the award for not thinking ahead today.* He'd taken her from dinner with her Dad to come see him possibly screw up while she sat in the audience all alone.

He vowed to make it up to her.

Once on stage, he stood in the dark for a moment, just breathing before the lights came up. When they did, he started singing. Other groups did that, but it was unusual for Wilder.

He sang just to be singing, and he added all the mood the song deserved. When he finished, he knew he had to speak. This part was never rehearsed, some sweet-talk bullshit always just fell out of TJ's mouth. Instead, now he introduced the guys without the snarky comments he usually made.

He saw the girls in the front, this time he saw that a lot of them were ignoring boyfriends. He latched on to that. "Ladies,

I'm guessing if some guy brought you here tonight, then this one's from him."

They started into *I am*, an old love song off their second album. For all it was the same as what he'd always done, it felt totally different.

He couldn't see Norah, but rested easier knowing that she was out there.

TJ did what he'd practiced during the day, and faltered only when he picked up the guitar waiting for him at the side of the stage. JD was swapping out for his violin, and TJ and Craig both provided guitar lines.

He made it through the song, wondering if anyone in the audience had noticed. He was supposed to be a pro. Six years they'd been at this, steadily getting bigger and better, and here he was just barely making the notes come out.

After another brief interlude, where JD and Craig swapped out instruments again, he spoke to the audience. He even surprised himself by shading his eyes with one hand and peering out. There were people he'd never seen before. A group of older women sat on barstools across the back wall, they were chattering like the teenagers. A group of guys—actually several of them scattered around the floor.

He knew males made up a good portion of Wilder's demographic, but he'd never put it together before. These people were all fans, and they all deserved the show. Maybe he was stupid.

TJ pointed to the guys off to the right hand side of the stage, they were the rowdiest of the groups, each with a beer in hand, and a few with two. "You guys want a song?"

"Yeah!!!!" The response was almost deafening, and that just from them.

He nodded. "All right, here you go."

Craig took it away with the opening to *Sunday Afternoon.* It was sweetly titled, but about a guy who murdered his girlfriend and buried her in the backyard because she interrupted his football game.

In TJ's head it was clearly one of Craig's pieces, but most of the fans never paid attention to the writer. In the end that was really the correct assessment. It was all just Wilder music.

They closed out the set, then agreed to come back out for one last piece. Having given everything he had, TJ was grateful when his experiment was over.

He was out the back before he knew it. Without being aware how it happened, he was getting kissed by some petite, big-breasted woman who had plastered herself to him. He almost laughed, but didn't want to hurt the girl's feelings. It wasn't her fault she was just all wrong.

TJ peeled her arms from around his neck, and physically set her away from him. She was overly made up and under-clothed. With a smile worthy of a cat with a canary, she leaned up and mentioned a few sexual favors she could do for him; she mentioned them with her tongue in his ear.

Had he ever said 'yes' to this? Maybe the accident had knocked his brain around more than the doctors had thought.

"Thank you, but no." Again he lifted her away, and saw another girl leaning against the back of the building. She looked just as bottle-blonde and gym-body proud as the one he'd peeled away. She made big mushy brown eyes at Craig who offered only a flat grin. Maybe she didn't know Craig was married? Maybe she didn't care. When Craig looked away, she caught TJ's eye and tipped her head in an invitation.

Looking at the two, now three, girls out here, TJ thought the callousness with which these girls picked up men put even him to shame sometimes. He'd never been anything more than another notch on the bedpost.

For the first time, he considered that he could relieve some of the sexual tension he'd built up. But these girls weren't what he wanted.

The guys were talking all around him, he'd done a better job. He knew it. But he still had a long way to go. He was going to work out the kinks, like practicing with the guitar in hand. That a been a stupid mistake. He'd be better the next time they were up.

He talked to JD for a moment, his head popping up and spotting Norah at the back door.

Craig leaned over. "Not about a girl, huh?"

TJ was getting so tired of that. "It's not. The girl is separate."

The girl was beside him then, and he told the guys goodnight, ignored the smile in his brother's eyes, and walked away with Norah right beside him. He held the car door for her, and slipped into the driver's seat. "So where do you want to go?"

"To bed."

His breath caught.

But she corrected quickly. "Home. To sleep." She didn't laugh or even blush at the words that had come out of her mouth.

He might have turned to her and asked about it, but he wanted to get out of the parking lot first. When he turned onto the side street he put voice to his concerns, "What's wrong?"

"Oh, I'm just tired."

"I'm sorry," He scrambled. She wasn't just tired. "I shouldn't have left you out there by yourself. I wanted you to be here and tell me if I was on or not, critique me. Let me make it up to you."

"No. It was a good show. You didn't falter or anything,"

So she hadn't caught that. In the future she would.

Norah's voice continued, flat as a pancake. "I think you did the things you intended, and it worked out well."

"Let me take you out." He glanced to the side, where he could see she was a little cold in her t-shirt that didn't quite come all the way down to her jeans. He caught glimpses of the lines defining her belly and hips.

"No, I just want to go home." Again she had no inflection,

until she pointed over her shoulder. "The studio's back that way."

"I'm taking you home." He wanted to take her to his home, but that wasn't going to happen. He knew better than to think he was going to get the whole Norah package when he wasn't even getting actual speech.

"I need my car."

"I'll get you in the morning."

"I need my car." She couldn't have cut him off more effectively if she'd bricked up the center of the car.

"What did I do, Norah?"

She gave a half-smile that was a smile only in the fact that her lips turned upward. "You didn't do anything, I'm just tired."

He didn't buy that for a hot second, and looked for some way to say that without looking like he was accusing her of lying. In the end she thanked him as she dragged herself from the car, and stepped up to her driver's side door. She gave a small wave as she slid inside. In no time at all she'd turned the engine and disappeared.

TJ sat there wondering what had just happened.

Her eyes had been bright when he'd brought her out this evening. She'd looked amazing in that top and jeans, maybe like she'd been putting some thought into him when she chose it. But then she'd shut down.

All too late, he wondered if she hadn't lied at the end. If the problem was that he *didn't do anything*. But what hadn't he done?

He considered following her home and having it out. Then thought tomorrow would work better. Maybe he could try those flowers and the words she had suggested.

TJ ditched the idea as soon as it came up. It was as stupid as it sounded.

CHAPTER 43

Norah heard her own voice in her head. *It's not you.* She answered it back as her feet hit the track. *It's me.*

The trite line made sense, although not in the usual way. *I'm the one who thought I stood a chance. I'm the one who made all those looks and cheap smiles into something more.*

TJ had dragged her out, away from a reasonable dinner with her Dad, with his face all aglow. He'd wanted *her* there. She *had to* be there. And he'd been so hard to refuse.

Even the rhythm her feet made sounded angry.

After the show, she'd stepped out behind the stage, knowing her face told everything, and for once not caring. Everyone would know she'd gone over the edge for TJ Hewlitt. The only one who saw was the woman pressed against the wall wearing less than most people's underwear.

The woman had assessed her like a piece of meat and apparently found her lacking. Then Norah watched as she kissed TJ on the mouth.

It was like ice water had been thrown on her. What a fool she'd been.

Her embarrassment was only compounded when he saw her

there and turned on the charm. As though she hadn't seen anything.

She now rounded the far corner of the track, trying desperately to enjoy the sunshine. Sadly, the argument in her head obscured most of the world around her.

It wasn't even his fault. He'd never lied, never led her on. He'd hauled her out because he valued her opinion, he truly enjoyed her company. But she wanted something more, and he wanted someone else.

She'd seen the girls who clung to guys, waiting while they screwed other women, certain that the man would come around. The guys already knew that girl as someone who would wait on the sidelines. She wasn't going to be that girl.

TJ, I love you and *Norah, you're a great friend* didn't tip the scales evenly.

He'd called Saturday and she'd ignored it. He'd called Sunday, too, and left a message that he wanted to see her.

He was a persistent little bugger, and no wonder, she'd been a great friend. But she'd have to cut herself off in order to get herself back on even ground.

Norah didn't know how many rotations around the track she'd gone without a break, only that her lungs burned. Slowing, she bent over and opened up her ribs to breathe.

With a start she realized there was another runner on the track. The back of her brain had already registered that it wasn't TJ. This man didn't move like him, didn't pull her like TJ.

Picking up speed, her thoughts clouded over. She wondered if TJ would show up today. She wasn't sure if it was his day or not. She'd ignored him all weekend, and he wasn't keeping a strict every other day schedule anyway.

Maybe he came on the mornings after the nights when he didn't get some activity in that floating bed of his. Her lips pressed together in a grim line. Like everything else, the floating bed was an illusion. At least she wasn't stupid enough to believe that the bed really did float, or that she'd been the only one.

Footsteps came up behind her as the other runner lapped her. For a moment her shoulders tensed. She didn't know this guy from Adam, and she hadn't gotten a good look at him. Well, it surely wasn't TJ, TJ couldn't pass her with that kind of speed yet.

As the guy went by, he gave a small wave, and Norah relaxed.

What the hell was she going to do about TJ?

TJ, TJ, TJ. Agh!

She wanted to go cry on her Daddy's shoulder, tell him she'd been a fool. She'd kept her pants on, hadn't done anything as dangerous or life-altering as possibly getting pregnant, but she had fallen further. And crying on her Daddy's shoulder wasn't allowed. She'd promised.

While she wasn't sure if the promise was valid when she wasn't speaking to TJ, for some reason she'd still feel she'd betrayed him if she did it. And she was speaking to him. Probably. Just enough to tell him that he couldn't haul her away from other things if there was only a rainbow and no pot of gold at the end.

She couldn't ignore that he said he'd fallen in love. Blindly, stupidly, she'd prayed he meant her. But it had been well over a week and no declaration had been forthcoming. Norah would have been happy with the flowers. She wasn't a flowers kind of woman, but it had been a knee-jerk reaction to be rude, before she'd considered the possibility he was speaking of her. Apparently he wasn't.

Norah glanced at her watch. Ten-thirty-two. He was usually here by ten, ten-fifteen if he was late. TJ wasn't coming. It pissed her off to realize that she'd been waiting.

Game over.

On the far turn of the track, Norah looked up. Now grouchy

that she had decided to leave with half the track left in front of her, she bent over to breathe.

After a few moments she stood and started to walk. Maybe she should crawl, she felt seriously depressed.

Footsteps came up behind her, she wished they were TJ's but she knew they weren't. She was berating herself for knowing the man's footsteps so well, when two large arms came into view on either side of her.

For a moment her brain registered that it wasn't TJ. Then, when she understood what was happening, it was too late. The arms clamped around her, one holding her own arms pinned to her side, the other tight across her neck. Time froze. Even as she realized it, she felt a vague sense of the surreal mix with cold terror.

She was almost immobilized, her head unable to turn or even snap back and break a nose. Her hands fought to scratch, but her nails were nowhere near any skin other than her own.

Pinwheeling her legs as he lifted her from the ground, she landed blows to his shins and feet. But her sneakers were rubber-soled and she doubted she did much damage as he dragged her off the track. She could see that he was headed toward the back gate, and ice flooded her veins. There were no good reasons to go out that way.

She tried lifting her legs to get her heels to his kneecaps, but she couldn't seem to cause any damage when she did it.

Kneecaps.

The thought raced through her mind and she acted. Still on the track surface and making it as difficult as possible for him, Norah lifted her legs and hooked her toes behind his knees. Before he could react, she folded, bending double at the waist while pulling her feet forward with force and buckling his legs.

He buckled forward, still wrapped around her, and her head cracked the running surface.

"Bitch!" The word was in her ear, but scream or whisper she

couldn't distinguish. He was up on his feet and moving with her again before she could react.

This time she went limp, becoming dead weight and feeling a good four to five times heavier than a tense person. His arms loosened just a bit as he swore again, and Norah was waiting. She drove the back of her head into his nose.

He let a burbled noise out, but still didn't release her. His arm around her neck shifted though, and she bit down. Hard.

He let go.

Norah hit the ground sailing, racing for the opposite side of the track, she pumped her legs and wished she'd practiced flat out running more.

Then she remembered to scream. Even though her body was tired from the jogging, and desperate for oxygen, she gulped in a big lungful to use for a shriek the likes of which she'd never made before in her life.

She saw the track coming up at her, and it smacked her full body, knocking the sound away, before she even realized he had her ankle. Rolling onto her back and fighting for possession of her limb, she forced him to use two hands to hold onto it.

When he did, she pulled her other foot back and drove her heel into his solar plexus. He went over backward.

Get up.

Then scream.

She was scrambling up even as he did, but she hadn't managed to make any noise. She had to make noise.

His hand came out from behind his back, this time holding a hunting blade.

CHAPTER 44

TJ pulled into the lot, wondering what the hell he was doing there. Norah wasn't speaking to him, and he really wasn't sure why. He was certain it was his fault though, and if she'd just tell him what he'd done, then maybe he could fix it.

He opened the door to the Mercedes and stood up, stretching. The lot was deserted, but no one was here this time of day except maybe Norah. So for just a moment, TJ stood and surveyed the empty track below him.

If she'd come, she'd gone.

He'd really thought she'd still be here though. For some reason he was certain she'd come. Then he shook his head. Clearly she'd given up on whatever she'd wanted from him, and he was becoming man enough to admit it hurt.

Turning, he slid back into the car and backed out of the space. In his rearview mirror he caught a glimpse of a car on the far end, parked beneath one of two trees providing small patches of shade in the open lot.

He frowned. That was Norah's car.

He didn't have to check.

TJ puzzled that for a second. Maybe she'd walked over to the high school to get a drink? He didn't know what she did when he wasn't here. His body ignored the musings of his brain, and was already out of the car. He'd thrown it into park there in the middle of the lot, and he went back over and frowned down at the track again.

Nothing.

TJ figured he'd park himself in the shade and sit and wait, when a glint of light flashed in the trees beyond the track.

In that instant he registered that the back gate was open, the trees were dark, and someone was there.

In a dead terror he didn't fully understand, his feet were already moving, instantly at a run. He didn't feel the stairs—was, in fact, pretty certain that he'd just cleared them in a jump.

Norah!

It screamed in his mind, as his feet took the straightest line to the trees. He ignored the front gate, now all of ten feet out of his way, and went over the fence. His lungs would have burned if he could have felt them, and he hadn't run so fast ever before in his life.

Slamming through the back gate and sending it rattling, his eyes adjusted to the scene before him in the trees. The dead terror he'd felt before congealed into something worse. Norah was pinned under some man whose head snapped up as the gate rattled.

TJ charged, tackling and hauling him off Norah at the same time. Rolling on top, TJ landed blows, his mind in a red rage and bent on murder. He pinned the man, staring into dark eyes and fighting against what he'd seen, what his brain wasn't yet admitting.

He felt his fingers close around the man's neck and begin to choke. Even while he watched the man struggle for air, angry and defiant, TJ thought it was too humane of a death. TJ was larger but he had to fight to subdue his opponent. That was because of the blood, he saw. The man was covered in swaths of red, none of it old enough to be brown yet.

Look out!

He didn't know if he'd heard it or not, but he saw the knife as it came at his side, and in slow motion he watched it arc at him. He considered taking the blow, letting the knife get buried in his flesh, if he could hold on long enough to be sure the man died. But if this monster took him down, Norah would be unprotected.

TJ jumped to one side, taking a deep nick from the blade and then a hook to the jaw that came from the other side. The man was on his feet, and TJ was on his ass. But he was close, and he took the assailant's feet out from under him, landing punches and driving knees into him as he fell.

Norah, run!

He didn't know if he got the sound out. TJ heard ribs crack, and the sick thud of human flesh taking a beating. Some of it was his own. At last he got hold of the man's arm, smashing the forearm over his knee and finding satisfaction, if not enjoyment, in the crack of bone he heard.

This time the other only pushed away, flinging himself backwards as far as possible from TJ and the murder he was certain shown in his eyes. The man found his feet and turned to flee. TJ started to lunge after him, only then feeling his thoughts do a sharp snap to Norah. She needed him.

As he turned his head, he saw the man hike up his pants with his one good hand, and TJ knew what that meant. The rolling started in the bottom of his torso, and pressed upward, feeling like a steamroller on both sides. He'd felt the sensation of his stomach trying to expel food backwards, but this was like his body was trying to expel his soul.

He fell onto his hands and knees, unable to remain upright, and wondered how blades of grass could continue to grow here when *this* had happened. His hands left smears of blood as he crawled, unable to breathe and not wanting to think, to where Norah had started to push herself up to sitting.

She, too, was covered in blood. Smears washed her head to toe, and in a few places it ran in fat drops. Her clothing hung from her in shreds leaving her exposed and virtually naked. He felt the rolling deep inside him again, as though his body had failed to kill him the first time and thus was trying again. But he wouldn't let Norah see that.

His eyes found hers, wide and scared, and he saw her hands reach out to him. He'd been afraid her eyes would go blank, but she was in there, and TJ had only one reaction to that. With no thought he rose on his knees and reached to her, pulling her up, his hands sunk into her hair and he sought to fuse his mouth to hers, the rest of the world be damned.

"Ah!"

He stopped and jerked back, wondering what kind of ass he was to try to kiss her now, but he'd needed it for himself if not for her.

A mewling noise came from her throat.

His hands left her, but hovered near her skin, "What baby, what?"

Her fingers grabbed at his wrists pulling them away, "My head."

All of her—hands, voice, limbs—moved with tremors and only the merest of strength. But she curled herself against him and took long breaths.

Oxygen heaved in and out of his own chest, in time with hers, and slowly his arms closed around her. He didn't know how long they stayed that way, but later he figured it wasn't long.

Warm liquid ran over his fingers and he knew it was blood. Hers. "Norah, you're bleeding."

CHAPTER 45

TJ held her away, wanting nothing more than to pull her close and let this nightmare dissolve away, but he couldn't let her bleed. Her face was swelling on one side, she was cut so many places he couldn't tell where the blood was coming from. Luckily there wasn't that much of it.

Gently, afraid she might break any second, he pulled her back into the circle of his arms and whispered, "Baby, I have to get you to a hospital."

She nodded, then crooked her lips at him. It wasn't a smile. There was no happiness here. "You, too."

That was of no concern.

"Can you stand?" Slowly rising to his own feet, TJ pulled her up with him, ready to catch her if she collapsed, and at no point certain that she, or he, wouldn't.

As she came unsteadily to her feet, he saw ribbons of red down the front of her, long cuts, and his brain worked again, matching the image of the knife coming at him with the almost neat strips her clothes were left in.

He stumbled, as his brain processed that the bastard had sliced her clothes off of her, with no concern for her skin underneath. His feet held, and Norah looked at him, but as soon as her eyes found his, they went unfocused and she wobbled.

His arms found her again, encircling her, holding her to him, the touch of her in his hands the only thing keeping him upright.

What remained of her shirt slipped off one shoulder, baring her further. He had to get her to a hospital, his cell phone was in his car, and it would be faster to drive than to call an ambulance and wait. "Baby, can you stand? Just for a moment?"

He put her arm around his waist and let her support herself, while he peeled his shirt. He damned well wasn't carrying her across the track and into the hospital as naked as she was. Bloody and torn in places, his t-shirt was still whole compared to hers. Gently, he eased the remaining scraps of her clothing from where they hung on her, and pulled the shirt over her like he would a small child. Without talking, Norah complied.

He tucked the pieces of her shirt into the back of his waistband, the thought forming in his brain that he was going to take care of Norah, and then he was going to nail that bastard.

Bending slightly, he scooped her up, one arm behind her shoulders and the other tucking the gratefully too-big t-shirt under her. Her weight felt right in his arms, even if nothing about this was right. She shifted for a moment, getting comfortable while he murmured into her hair before he turned to walk back across the track.

"Wait!"

TJ stopped, it was the first clear word she'd uttered, and one he didn't want to obey. She needed a hospital, soon.

"The knife." Her voice was soft, and he wondered if the blossoming bruises on her neck explained the cause.

Again he felt his gut clench, and again he forced the thought aside, as it would do Norah no good now. She pointed behind him, and when he turned he saw the knife, one small spot of silver, not covered in blood, glittering grotesquely in a wayward patch of sun. He set Norah back on her feet, leaning her on a tree for support while he used the remnants of her t-shirt to pick up the weapon without damaging any more evidence than he had to.

But he couldn't figure what to do with the thing. If he tucked it in the back of his waistband, he might rub at the fingerprints. He couldn't hold it and hold her, but he was tempted to try. Finally, he decided to fling the thing away, Norah was far more important than any evidence and he had to get her to help.

Her hands came out, forming a cup, and it took half a second for him to register that she would hold it.

TJ didn't want to hand it to her. Didn't want her carrying the thing that had been used against her. But he couldn't deny her, and she wanted to bring the knife so he handed it over.

With pain in his heart like he had never felt before, he scooped her up again, walking while she shifted and settled herself against him. The gate to the track stood open and he passed through it, his feet feeling the familiar flat surface beneath. His hurt heart felt grateful that she let him carry her—that after all this, she trusted him.

He went out the gate at the other side, working the latch himself because Norah was growing slowly catatonic in his arms. She was withdrawing, and it scared the crap out of him.

His car was still sideways in the parking lot. TJ pulled the passenger door open and held her, juggling the seat adjuster and her soft weight until he had the seat all the way reclined and he could lay her down.

Immediately he plucked the wrapped knife from her hands, although she didn't seem to notice, and he stashed it on the floor of the backseat.

Norah rolled to face the driver's side, long legs peeking out beneath the hem of his shirt, but her body didn't relax. She needed help. Help he couldn't give her. And his fingers flexed, discovering he had no keys.

He would have to call an ambulance.

His wallet and cell phone were in the foot well that Norah wasn't using. She'd tucked herself into a tight ball, shutting the rest of the world out. TJ didn't want her traumatized by lights and sirens, and he gave himself one chance to find the keys.

They were exactly where he thought they might be, lying in the grass at the top of the steps. He must have dropped them when he'd run toward the suspicion in his head. That moment seemed a lifetime ago. The reality had been far worse than the foreboding, and he knew he still wasn't feeling the truth. It would hit him later, and he wasn't sure he would survive it.

Still, he took the keys and closed both of them into the car. The engine started with a purr that seemed far too normal for this day. He buckled her in, but she didn't respond. Her eyes were closed, but he could tell she wasn't sleeping. She probably just didn't want to talk, and TJ felt much the same way, as he didn't know of a thing he could say that would make even a part of it any better.

He drove with the utmost caution, more concerned with jostling Norah than anything else. Pulling into the drive-up entrance at the Emergency room, he walked around to lift Norah out. She was heavier than she had been earlier, and he wondered if it was him.

Once inside, medical people, doctors and nurses, flooded around him instantly seeing the extent of her injuries. They pulled up a gurney for her, but TJ refused, insisting he carry her to the bed.

He put her on her back, and the t-shirt didn't cover her near as well when she stretched out. Her chest gave one rise and fall, and she rolled over and curled up again.

TJ stood beside her while the nurses ran an IV line into her arm. Norah didn't even flinch, nothing acknowledged what was being done to her. TJ hadn't thought it would be possible, but his chest clenched even tighter. He only turned his back to her to explain to the nurse what had happened. Norah didn't need the recounting.

The nurse sloughed herself off in her tidy pink scrubs and returned carrying an armful of solution-filled bags and syringes and sterile packed tubing. With certain efficiency she briskly asked if either of them was HIV positive, then injected several syringe-fulls into the bag already dripping fluids into Norah's arm. She then turned to speak again to TJ. "I added immunoglobulins and a few doses of anti-retrovirals."

TJ thought he knew what those words meant, and his heart slowly came to a standstill as yet another horror was added to this day.

The nurse kept speaking, "HIV is a real concern in cases like these. She has open cuts as well, and it looks like the two of you made him bleed. Which is a good fight, but brings this other problem."

TJ fought to keep his lip from quivering. He fought to keep himself from shaking.

Continuing her steady cadence, the nurse made it worse. "You're cut, too. You'll need stitches as well, and a host of anti-HIV drugs. We need to start a chart on you."

TJ nodded, thinking that Norah could now be infected with something, when she was entirely innocent.

"Come with me, please." The nurse stood, straight and pink, at the doorway waiting for him. But TJ shook his head.

"I can't treat you without a bed."

"Then don't treat me. I'll come back tomorrow or . . ."

The nurse shook her head this time. "You need these drugs right away."

"Then put me in this bed." He gestured to the one behind him, standing empty.

"This room is for women—"

"I'm not leaving. Forget it."

"Sir—"

TJ didn't look at her, just grabbed a plastic chair from the corner and faced it toward Norah's bed. He sat there, his head even with hers high up on the gurney and folded his hands at the edge of the bed. "She's bleeding, she needs help now."

The nurse nodded, and he was grateful that she let him be, although he feared she'd pushed some sort of panic button and security was going to come take him away. The nurse pulled a pair of scissors from her pocket, and rested a hand on Norah. "Honey, we're going to cut this shirt off of you so we can see what we need to stitch."

Beyond his hands he saw Norah stiffen, and he jumped up to still the nurse. In a hard whisper he added, "Don't! She's had her clothing cut off her once already today."

He didn't know how he finished that sentence, it hurt so much to say the words. But like so many things today, he pushed it aside and turned his attention to Norah. "Baby, can you sit up? We need to get my shirt off you so they can see to help you."

Norah nodded at him. Her eyes didn't connect, but she nodded. Slowly, with his help, she pushed herself to sitting. Gingerly he pulled the shirt up and off her, the nurse held out a gown that he quickly wrapped around the now shivering Norah. While the nurse pulled the shirt along the tubing and over the IV bag, he tried to ignore the almost continuous webbing of bruises and cuts that had ringed her body.

The nurse called for plastic surgeons.

Security showed up at the doorway, luckily only to complain about the car he'd left blocking the ambulance bay. TJ told the man about the knife, sent him after his wallet and handed over the keys, telling him to take the car and do whatever he wanted with it. It was of no importance.

Fortunately, the plastic surgeons only needed to suture.

There were a few spots that needed stitches along her jaw and across her face, and TJ clamped his urge to vomit again when they reassured Norah that there would be little to no scarring. It took them over three hours and fifteen different positions to put all the stitches in her. She had cuts down her chest, on her side, one on her back, her hand, he lost count. Luckily, only a handful of stitches needed to be laid under her skin.

Then they turned on him. Convincing the nurse to admit him to the next bed was a job that took TJ refusing treatment otherwise, as well as Norah's desire to have him there.

TJ would have left in a heartbeat had she asked. She sat on her own bed, IV dangling from her arm and feet dangling over the side in her doubled-up hospital gowns while he was stitched. The plastic surgeons rolled him from one side to the other, trying to both work simultaneously, but he kept his gaze trained on her. He didn't feel the needles poking into him and only peripherally registered the burn of the anesthetic. She looked beautiful and brave and damaged as she watched him get stitched.

When the doctors were finished, the nurses came to work on them like ants on food. They crowded and cleaned blood, and partially pulled the curtain between the two beds. Before he knew it he was covered in gauze. They had parked a serving cart with dispensers of tube gauze that they cut repeatedly, sliding it over his feet, up his arms, around his torso even to hold gauze pads in place where there wasn't undamaged skin to adhere to tape.

Not all of the gauze they cut came his way, and he figured Norah would be at least as covered as he was. When they finished and rolled away the cart, he pulled back the curtain to reveal that he'd been right. The parts of her he could see were half covered with the mesh tubing, much of it with padding tucked underneath.

She lay back, not making eye contact. Words fell out of her

mouth, a whole sentence, and he felt his first ray of hope. "I'm a mummy."

"Yes, you are." He felt the smallest of smiles at his mouth, and pushed himself off the bed only to find he was tethered to the IV and that was looped onto the pole at the end of the bed.

He unhooked the bag and walked over to her. Norah nodded at him when he asked if he could piggyback her IV pole, and he pushed his bag next to hers before taking her hand. She squeezed, that one little contact keeping him breathing.

The nurse in pink returned with another set of sterile bags. She eyed him with disapproval but TJ didn't move from where he stood. Hurricanes wouldn't move him.

"I'm sorry, sir, but I'm going to have to ask you to get back into your bed or step out of the room for a moment."

Out of the room?

Norah's face reflected his puzzlement.

The nurse held up the package with a grim look on her face. Her voice was soft. "We need to do a rape kit, and that involves an exam."

CHAPTER 46

If someone had opened the soles of his feet and let all his blood drain from him, TJ couldn't have felt more empty. He couldn't look at Norah. He just wanted to disappear.

"No!" Norah's voice sliced through him.

"Honey," The nurse used her most soothing tones. "I know that this is awful, but this is how we catch those bastards. You'll likely be glad later that you did."

"No." Norah struggled to sit up, the sheets and her gowns hindering her. She turned to TJ and he waited for her to plead with him to tell her it was okay, that she didn't have to. And he knew that's what he'd say. He'd nail the bastard himself, she didn't have to suffer anymore.

She tugged at his hand forcing him to look at her, and for the first time her eyes met his, and she was really in there. When she had his attention, she spoke. "He didn't rape me." Her head shook side to side, "You got there in time. He didn't."

His legs went out from under him then and he crashed, knees first, to the cold hospital floor, hearing the words falling from his mouth, thanking a God he'd forgotten existed.

"TJ!" Norah shrieked and started to scramble over the side of the bed, only to be stopped by the pink nurse who beat her to his side.

Getting his legs under him, he sat on the floor, his lungs heaving for oxygen as though he'd been underwater this whole time. His eyes blinked, his hands went to his face.

Norah's hand appeared in his vision and, like a drowning man, he grabbed at it and held tight.

"It's okay, it's okay."

It was Norah's voice soothing him. When he was breathing well enough, he looked up to see her still hanging over the side of the bed at him.

But the nurse cut off any conversation, helping him to his feet and pulling his IV bag down, she asked him to join her in the hall. Since he was tethered to the bag and she was leaving with it, he let Norah's hand slip from his, "I'll be right back."

Norah nodded in response.

Once in the hallway, the nurse gave him a stern look. "I don't want to burst your bubble, but women have lied about this. They don't want to believe it happened so they say it didn't."

TJ frowned, but the nurse continued delivering her bad news. "One of the major reasons they lie is because they don't want the men who love them to know. Boyfriends and husbands have left over these situations. Her recovery depends on the truth, whether or not she does the rape kit. And I don't know that what we heard back there was the truth."

The nurse was right, his bubble deflated. "How do we get the truth?"

The nurse looked him square in the eye. "Does it matter to you if she was raped?"

"Hell, yes, it matters. That bastard—" He was near yelling when the nurse cut him off.

"I meant, does it matter about what you think of her?"

"No." It was shorter than a single syllable.

"Then go back in there and convince her of that."

He let out a sardonic laugh. "I'm not her boyfriend. I'm just a friend."

"Are you sure?" The nurse squinted at him.

"I wish it was more, but it's been a fucking bad morning." He put his hands on his hips, and snatched the IV bag from the nurse, before plunging another knife into himself and trying to convince Norah to give them the truth.

In the end, Norah shooed him out of the room, and asked the nurse if the exam would show that she hadn't been raped. "Don't even bother opening your little kit."

TJ left, knowing the nurse still wasn't convinced.

Three minutes later, the nurse emerged. "I didn't even have to do the exam, she's telling the truth."

"Thank you." The words were a whispered prayer to the empty beds and gauze cabinets where he sat on the floor in the hallway just outside her door.

The police came next, and spent far too long interviewing them. They gave statements separately, TJ itching to be beside Norah, but knowing that getting the bastard convicted depended on following the right procedures. He told them everything.

They were both given scrubs to wear, and finally released, no injury was serious enough to hold either of them. Norah was wheeled to the front in a wheelchair, which TJ pushed. He might have enjoyed the irony in another circumstance, but today he was just sick to his stomach. The nurses handed them prescriptions for painkillers, antibiotics, and anti-HIV drugs. The security guard gave him his wallet, keys and directions to where the car was parked.

Holding her hand for support, he led her on shaky legs across the lot. At the car he opened her door and started to hand her in, but stopped halfway through, pulling her into a bear hug. She buried her face in his chest and wrapped her arms around his waist. They clung until his shaking stopped, then her voice piped up from between them. “Ow.”

“Sorry.”

She shook her head lazily, and a little drunkenly. She’d been sedated and it hadn’t all worn off. Nor should it. She was in for a world of pain while she healed. “Don’t be sorry. I needed that.”

“Me, too.” This time he handed her into the car, gently closing the door while she tipped the seat upright and made faces at the blood that had smeared and soaked into the once beautiful gray leather seats.

He tried to slide into the driver’s side and found he was too stiff, that it was more painful than he had expected.

“You need to get home and take some drugs.”

He nodded. “I’m taking you home.”

TJ had no intention whatsoever of going to his own cold house. He had no intention of leaving her side for the near eternity.

“Can I call the dance studio?” Her words weren’t clear; she couldn’t move her face where the swelling and bruising made it difficult for her to talk. Just looking at her made it difficult for him to talk. So he nodded.

“Tell me the number, talking doesn’t hurt me.” He lied.

She dialed and handed him the phone. For a few minutes he understated every truth he knew. Norah wasn’t feeling well, she wouldn’t be in tonight. No, not tomorrow or the next day either. He hung up and handed the phone back to her, “Your Dad.”

This was the phone call he dreaded, and he couldn’t do all of it. If someone told him this had happened to Norah, he would have run down fifteen people on the way to get to her and not cared. “Sir, TJ Hewlitt. First, Norah is all right.” He hoped it wasn’t a lie. “But she’s not feeling well, so I’m going to bring her home.”

“Okay.”

"Are you on your way home?" TJ could tell that Mr. Davidson didn't know why he was getting a call from someone who sounded like he was going to tuck Norah in and give her some chicken noodle soup.

"Yes."

"We'll meet you there in about half an hour." TJ hung up, figuring that mysterious was better than lying or alarming the man too much.

Finally turning the engine over, he headed out of the parking lot. The dash clock read 5:13. He hit traffic every step of the way, his aches settling in with every crawled mile. Norah was asleep within minutes, her bloody sneakers worn barefoot beneath the hem of green scrubs. He looked away, knowing he could stare at her forever, and that it wasn't safe to drive like that. The last road was easier, almost deserted, as it always was here on the edge of town.

He cruised up the long drive, parking as close to the front porch as he could, and forcing himself to unfold. Trying not to wake her, he tucked his arms under her, attempting to not prod or rub any stitches or bruises, and knowing his efforts were futile. There was no place left to touch her it seemed. In the end, he hoped that her medication took the worst of the sting away and pushed his arms behind her, lifting her from the seat.

She mumbled but didn't wake.

With her sleeping bruised and battered in his arms, TJ turned to find her father standing in the open doorway, alarm written all over his face. He was certain that the man would take Norah from him the second they were close enough, and he climbed the stairs dreading the loss of her from his arms.

But Mr. Davidson didn't. He met TJ's eyes and held the door. "Her room is up this way."

He went up the stairs almost backwards, examining his daughter but not taking her. For that, TJ was grateful. The older man grew more worried as they neared the top of the stairs, but again held the door and left the light off while TJ nestled her on the bed and slowly removed her sneakers.

Again he saw the blood on her shoes, so he turned to hand them to her father, "Burn these."

Mr. Davidson set them aside and motioned TJ into the hall. He pulled Norah's door mostly closed but left a sliver of light shining in.

Here it was. TJ had been fearing facing her father, but had never imagined it would come this way. How did he tell the man what had happened? How did he explain that they hadn't called earlier? So he opened his mouth and started with the basics. "She was at the track this morning, and she was attacked. He tried to rape her, but Norah fought him off, sir."

Mr. Davidson put a hand to his face and tried to digest that. He breathed deep for several full minutes before he finally looked up.

TJ braced himself for the blow, the questions, the accusations.

None of it came. "Then who did you tangle with, son?"

"Him." It was the only way to put it.

Mr. Davidson's arms came around him in a bracing hug that he hadn't seen coming. Watery words were spoken at his ear. "Thank you."

TJ nodded, feeling everything drain out of him again. He'd been set for a fight. When it didn't happen, he didn't know what to do.

"You going home?" Mr. Davidson tipped his head.

"No, sir." TJ pointed at the top step, "If you don't mind, I figure this is about as far as I'm headed." He sat.

The older man smiled.

"Oh!" TJ pulled the papers from his breast pocket on the scrubs, "She has prescriptions she needs filled. Can you . . .?"

With a nod, Norah's Dad looked through the small white squares. "Half of these are for you."

Holding up a hand, TJ motioned for them, but he was given a head shake 'no.'

"I'll get all of it. It's the least I can do." He pocketed the pages and turned one last time. "I'll get more details when I get back if that's okay."

TJ didn't meet his eyes, but nodded.

"Is there anything I can get you before I go?"

No, he shook his head, there was nothing anyone could get him.

CHAPTER 47

Mr. Davidson disappeared around the corner at the bottom of the steps, leaving TJ in semi-darkness, the stairwell lit only by the fading light of day. He heard the front door and an engine crank and felt everything break down.

There, on the stairs, five feet from Norah's bedroom door, he put his head in his hands and let the flood take him. It began with shakes, brought on by images he had held at bay until now. His body rolled in on itself again, bringing him to the brink of jumping to his feet to find the nearest toilet to vomit into.

The pressure came at the back of his eyes, and his arms wrapped around his knees. Bruises assaulted him fresh every time he moved and he couldn't get comfortable. The wooden stairs bit into his back, where apparently something was injured. He was stiffening even as he sat there.

Norah was in a drug induced semi-coma beyond the carved wooden door. His cuts and scrapes were nothing. His what-ifs consumed him. What if he hadn't gone to the track today? What if he hadn't caught the glimpse of her car in the rearview mirror? He hadn't gone to look over the track again? Or not seen the single glint of light—that he now knew was likely that vicious knife—in the trees?

What if he hadn't gone to therapy? Or hadn't worked so hard to walk, then run?

He feared more than anything that he would find out that this was a dream—an alternate, more salvageable, ending to the day. That he would wake and find that she'd be dead, or near it.

But she was in the room behind him. He could hear her turning and occasionally making sound and he forced himself to breathe. Only then did the pressure behind his eyes release and he felt the tears on his cheeks. TJ buried his face in his hands and sobbed.

His shoulders heaved with it, and he tried to stop the voice that sought a way out of him. He didn't want to wake Norah, but he couldn't stop.

He didn't know how long he stayed like that, making noises and shaking with uncontrollable cold. He only knew he heard sounds behind him, and with hurried movements tried to dry his face before she saw.

Her bare feet appeared on the step beside him and she sat down. Her voice was thinner than usual and he clenched down on the memory of the web of bruises on her throat. "I couldn't sleep."

He didn't look up. "Your Dad went out to get our prescriptions filled."

Norah ignored that. Her hands found his face and turned him to her, wiping away the wetness that she found. "Is that for me?"

His own voice was a ragged whisper. "I failed you."

"How?" She had nerve to ask that from a cracked and stitched face.

"Have you looked in the mirror?" TJ shook his head, not meaning it the way it had probably sounded.

"Yes." Her hands cupped his cheeks, forcing him to look up

at her. "And I can because of you. You got there in time. Thank you."

He shook his head again, both to tell her she was wrong and to rid himself of the sweet feeling of her fingers against his skin. "You fought him, Norah. Thank God you held him off."

"Yes, I did. But I was losing." Her arms tangled around his neck and her forehead touched his cheek. He heard a small smile in her breathy voice. "You're my hero, TJ Hewlitt."

He felt himself shrink, he didn't feel like anybody's hero. Her battered body attested to that.

The front door clicked, and with a few footfalls her father was at the base of the stairs. "Honey, you're up."

She nodded. "Did you bring drugs?" Her hand going to her side where that ass had put hairline fractures in two of her ribs.

"For both of you." Mr. Davidson held up a white paper bag with a small ream of printed pages stapled to the top. "They didn't want to let me get TJ's, because he's not family. So I told them you're my future son-in-law."

Beside him, TJ felt Norah stiffen. It barely registered. He was glad she was alive. He could love her from afar. At this moment, he would accept anything.

Mr. Davidson reappeared with two tall glasses of water and doled out small handfuls of pills to each of them. TJ swallowed each, grateful for the pain-killers and antibiotics. and not wanting to know which was the anti-HIV drug.

Norah's stomach grumbled, and it seemed so out of place, so *normal* in this mess. Her voice came through the fog. "I'm hungry. I want pizza."

"Okay," It was his own voice, unable to refuse her anything, even a dose of normalcy. "I'll get you pizza. I'll get you whatever you want."

After the words left his mouth, TJ realized that he'd crossed into bad territory. Her father was her family. TJ was nothing but some hanger-on. Probably one of a myriad of men who followed Norah home. Only he'd brought her battered and bloody. He corrected. "If that's okay, sir?"

"I'll get the pizza. Better tell me what you like, and in exchange you don't call me 'sir' anymore. It's Langdon. Or Dad!" He laughed a little to himself, probably to ease the tension. He didn't know that TJ would have been glad to have good reason to call him 'Dad.'

After the pizza was ordered, Norah took his hand and insisted they go for a turn around the backyard. Calling it a backyard was a mistake, it was huge, and even though it was fenced, horses came right up to the other side, begging for carrots and sugar cubes. Norah rubbed their noses, and cried out when one nudged her with his head.

Stepping back beyond the reach of the horses, she rubbed at her side, and TJ watched, helpless. She moved like an old woman, each step careful and precise. She kept walking out of necessity, telling him she was certain that if they didn't it would be worse tomorrow.

TJ couldn't imagine tomorrow being worse. Any amount of physical pain would be better than what this day had brought.

They walked a circle around the yard until the pizza arrived, then beat a slow retreat into the house, with Norah goading him. "Race?"

He wanted to laugh, but the end of the word was slurred due to the damage the side of her face had taken. Still, she made him smile.

He watched as she ate one slice of pizza as slowly as humanly possible, then declared herself full. At her father's concern, TJ mentioned that she'd had three bags of saline and a lot of drugs earlier in the day. Then he jumped on that bandwagon himself. "You'll have to eat more tomorrow, Norah. You need to stay as healthy as possible."

She snorted at that, then added a "Yes, sir" before heading up the stairs to bed.

TJ finished his last slice of pizza, knowing that it tasted good, but unable to distinguish the flavor. While he chewed he wondered how he was going to convince Mr. Davidson that he couldn't go to his own house. He'd never sleep if he was there and she was here.

Mr. Davidson took the conversation on his own shoulders. "Well, I can drive you home. Or you can have the couch. Or Norah's bed is double-sized."

TJ almost choked. "Did you just offer me the other half of your daughter's bed?"

The man simply laughed. "You've already taken good care of her. And I don't think you're going to lift a finger to try anything with the shape the both of you are in. You both might sleep a little better."

He could not believe he was hearing this. So he sat still, digesting what he'd heard.

Mr. Davidson picked up the thread, "You put yourself out there for her today. And you stayed and took care of her. I'm impressed."

"I'm not." He hadn't meant to say it, the words had just fallen out.

"Don't be so hard on yourself. She's beat-up, but she'll come out all right. You saved her from a far worse fate."

"Shouldn't Norah decide who sleeps on the other side of her bed?"

Her father nodded, "Trust me, she'll say something."

TJ laughed, and winced, holding his side. He, too, had cracked ribs. His only satisfaction was that the bastard most likely couldn't use his right hand. TJ had felt and heard bone crack. "I'm sure my reputation has preceded me. Doesn't that worry you?"

"I followed your career, having known you as a kid, but it looks like you aren't living that life any more. Are you going to screw around on her? Break her heart?"

That brought his head up, sharply enough to cause pain. But he met the man's eyes. "Never."

"That's what I thought." Leaning back into the corner of the couch with an ease TJ now envied, Mr. Davidson continued. "You seem like a very determined young man. You've made it into, and then survived, a business that eats people for lunch and spits them out. You walked again when people weren't sure you would. Seems to me if Norah's what you want, then a little slip of a thing like her shouldn't stand in your way."

"This is the strangest conversation I have ever had." TJ rolled his neck, both to keep it from stiffening from the tension he felt speaking to this man and for something to do. "Before my accident, I was an arrogant ass."

No one contradicted him.

"After my accident, I was less of an ass, but my arrogance still knew no bounds. And today . . ." His hands spread out in front of him and he could almost watch everything slide away.

"I wasn't there for her today, but I'm glad you were. Norah will get back up. So will you. Might help if you two lean on each other."

Only half of his mouth twisted, the other half was getting sore and he wasn't sure why. "I've been leaning on Norah a lot lately."

"I'd say any debt has been repaid." He paused for a minute, but TJ didn't fill the space. "You know, I love having her here, but having her to myself is bittersweet. I want her to be loved and love someone in return. She was happy before, and this summer was as happy as I've seen her since. She was excited about something and she was proud of what you did."

"Are you trying to tell me something? Do you know something that I don't?" Was her father saying he knew how she felt? Was that why he was pushing the two of them together?

"I'm not saying anything of the sort. I'm saying if you want something just don't let it go by."

CHAPTER 48

Norah jerked again. The world was hazy around her, and she was just drugged enough that things slid a little when she looked. It didn't help that the room was dark or that she'd fallen asleep a dozen times only to jerk back awake.

The drugs were supposed to help her sleep, but every time she started to fade away she saw arms reaching around her and had that moment where she realized that things were terribly wrong. Sometimes the image she saw was on the track and him standing back up with that green-handled hunting knife in his hand.

She had known then that he was hunting her.

This time had been the worst. She had been pressed into the earth, with her hands held above her head and her struggles useless. She could still hear his voice saying what he was going to do to her.

Each time she woke up, not having slept.

The scrubs were soft, but not what she wanted. So she slung her legs over the side of the bed letting her feet dangle until they brushed the soft rug. The room was too dark to navigate in her slightly altered state. Norah headed for the light switch, briefly entertaining the thought of missing her goal and falling through the doorway.

But her hand reached out, and for a moment it startled her. Much of it was swathed in white gauze, bright in the near dark. She remembered all her cuts and bruises, remembered that actually laughing at the thought of falling through the doorway would just cause pain.

There were feet out in the hallway just beyond her, lit by the pale light coming from the bathroom where the door had been left wide. The feet didn't bother her. They were TJ's, though she thought he would have taken the couch. Norah knew she was frowning, only because she could feel the right side of her face pulling.

Making a conscious effort to smooth out her expression, Norah looked out to see TJ curled into the corner of the hallway with just a pile of bedding. Silly man was going to hurt in the morning. She would have woken him, but he looked peaceful, and this night she wasn't interrupting anyone who found sleep. No point in all of them suffering.

She pulled the door shut softly, then felt along a swath of wall, unable to find the familiar light switch. Eventually her hand made contact in a place that she was fairly certain had been flat wall on the two previous passes. At least she was sober enough to know that light switches didn't move. Sober enough to know that she was drunk, more like.

She had to get out of the scrubs. She felt irritable and for some reason blamed the clothing. If she could just change she was sure she would feel better.

Slowly she picked at the top, taking it straight off in an effort to move as little as possible. She was used to lithe movement, now she had gauze to watch out for. It just clung around her—her left arm, her torso, her right leg in two pieces and left in one, and around her right wrist with a hole cut for her thumb.

She untied the string at the waist of the scrub pants, feeling freer even as she did it. As she stepped out of the pants she realized that she was wearing no underwear.

Slowly she picked her way over to her armoire, and pulled open the left side using both hands as neither worked particularly well right now. She rifled through finding several of what she was looking for—the boxer briefs TJ had teased her about. She chose the softest ones in her favorite color, just because they made her feel a little better, and she was taking every 'little better' she could find.

Norah was starting to step into them when she felt the room spin. She stood, and felt fine. Then tried again, and again watched the wall slide past her. Blinking a few times somehow helped her realize she'd been swaying. Apparently former world-class ballerina Norah Davidson could no longer balance on one foot long enough to get her leg through a pair of men's underwear.

She sat on the bed and pulled them on. Carefully, she held them out away from her skin, pulling them up and over the gauze that coated her midsection and laid the waistband flat on her back and belly.

Ahhhhh.

Maybe now she would sleep. She needed a t-shirt, which was on the other side of the room. Standing, Norah turned and cracked her elbow on the armoire door she had left open. "Ahhhh!"

This time it had sound. It sounded like she had sucked the air out of the room. Pain radiated up her arm bringing tears to her eyes and TJ into the room.

"Baby, what's wrong?"

She gulped the whispered sound out. "Elbow." She pointed at the offending door, the pain keeping her relatively sober.

He frowned, "Did you hit your funny bone?"

She nodded, "It's not funny. Hurts like hell."

He took her hand away from her elbow and examined it. "It

doesn't look like you broke the skin. I know that doesn't make it hurt less."

Only then did she realize that the pain had not made her sober. Her groggy mind had not pushed him out of the room or even motioned to cover herself. She was standing there in only the maroon men's underwear with the little squares.

TJ seemed to realize her nakedness then, too. His breath sucked in.

She looked away. It wasn't the 'oh my god, you are so beautiful' gasp that a man could give. It was the 'oh dear god that looks bad' kind.

His fingers reached toward her as she watched his eyes trace her body. She considered covering herself, but he'd seen her before, and he wasn't looking sexually, that was for sure. She figured she'd have made a different decision if she hadn't been drugged. The best part of the medication was that it made you not care. And she wanted to know what he saw when he looked.

His mouth curled, and she decided maybe she didn't want to know after all. But he told her, in a low whisper that was close to a growl. "Handprints. That bastard left handprints on you."

Norah looked at her arms with new eyes, seeing that some of the darkened areas did indeed look like fingers wrapped around her arms, there was another on her leg. The rest was too much of a mess to distinguish anything, and she was tired of examining her cuts and scrapes. "I need a t-shirt."

"If it's what you want." TJ reached out and closed the armoire door before she could bump it again.

She nodded and found her way over to the dresser. She pulled out the oldest, softest shirt she could find then started to slip into it, only to find that hands had found the shirt and were behind her, holding it up over her head, helping her get her sore arms through.

The nurses had been right. The second day was worse, and she hadn't even gotten there yet.

"Thank you." She turned to see him nod.

"You look sleepy, you should go back to bed."

She wanted to laugh, but couldn't muster it. "I don't need to go to bed. I need to go to sleep. I'm discovering there's a difference.

TJ nodded and turned away. "Good night."

Only then did she realize that he was wearing a white t-shirt but was still in the scrub pants.

Her voice got ahead of her brain. "Are you wearing underwear?"

Turning, he raised his eyebrows. "It's important?"

She shook her head as though that might clear it, but it only made her thinking worse. "I didn't get any from the hospital. I thought maybe you hadn't either."

He nodded. "I trashed mine. I bled on them."

That was all that needed to be said. "Do you want some?"

"I'm already wearing a shirt I borrowed from your father." He plucked at it. "I don't borrow underwear."

"Mine."

Then he laughed. "I've never tried women's underwear before. Today is not the day for it."

She smiled until the right side of her face protested with a shooting pain. That was enough to wipe the expression from her. TJ came at her, worried, but she held up her hand to ward him off.

Walking back to the armoire, she reached in to produce a pack of the briefs just like the one she had tugged on. "I happen to have a brand new pair."

"I can't wear what fits you. But thanks."

"Men's thirty-six. Medium."

"Maybe." He reached out and pulled the package from her hands. "How would you wear these?"

She shrugged and pointed at her own pair. "Your waist, my hips."

Norah crawled across the bed while TJ turned behind her. "Thank you."

She nodded and started to slide under the covers. She felt like crap. But she felt better, fresher, lighter, now.

His hands were there, pulling the covers up over her and tucking her in. It made her want to smile. "Why are you sleeping in the hall?"

He stood, taller now that she was lying in bed below him. "Your Dad offered the couch but I knew I couldn't sleep there. So I grabbed some blankets and camped out in the corner. I think I slept a little. You?"

"Still trying." He hadn't answered her question, but she felt a yawn coming and fought it, knowing it would hurt her jaw.

"Good night, Norah."

"'Night, TJ." She snuggled deep, knowing he would hit the lights as he went.

The room darkened beyond her eyelids, and she heard him go into the bathroom. When he closed the door, for a few scary seconds the room went completely black and she panicked.

Forcing her breathing to slow, Norah talked herself down. She had been attacked. She admitted it. It had been in broad daylight. TJ had come. He had run her attacker off. He was here, just beyond the door. She was safe. In her own bed, in her own home.

She didn't remember the sounds of the door opening, or the light coming back through. She didn't hear TJ shuffling in the hallway. She just slipped away.

She was jogging on the track, only this time Norah felt a horrible sense of foreboding. Her sleeping brain screamed at her to leave. The arms came around her again. She fought like she was in jello. Her blows landed but only made the dark eyes laugh.

Forever, he pulled her into the trees, for every inch she gained toward the track he pulled her two away. He talked to her the whole time, saying foul things he wanted to do. He crushed her lungs to keep her from screaming. Her sleeping brain said TJ would come.

But he didn't.

The man pinned her down and began to do what he'd said.

"Baby." The voice came at a distance. TJ's voice, but he wasn't there. "Baby, please, wake up. Norah, wake up."

I am awake! She wanted to scream, but she couldn't produce the sounds. *Where are you?*

"I'm right here. Wake up, please."

Slowly, she forced her eyelids open to see TJ sitting on the edge of the bed. He looked worried and worn out. "Are you all right?"

She shook her head, and felt the tears. "I keep dreaming it. I can't sleep. Every time I close my eyes it happens again."

"I know. Me, too." His hands went into his already rumpled hair. "I've heard you tossing and turning in here. This time you were crying out."

Norah sat up, not caring about the burn the movement produced in her right side. "This was worse. It was all the same, but you didn't come. You didn't come."

She felt herself dissolve, and had no idea where she went.

Later she found herself in his arms, her legs still tucked under the covers, him still sitting on the edge of the bed. His voice whispering. "It's okay, you fought him off."

"I know that you came." Her breath came in and out in sharp pains. "I know it didn't happen, but when I fall asleep . . ."

Her fingers wound into the soft white t-shirt he wore, her breathing heaving constantly against the wounds to her ribs. She dug her fingers deeper into the cotton knit, refusing to let him leave. "Stay."

He nodded. "Until you fall asleep."

She shook her head. "Just stay. If I wake up, you'll be there. I'll try not to interrupt your sleep."

He nodded, and stood, for a moment petrifying her that he would leave.

But he didn't. He walked around to the other side of the bed, "Is this okay?" He motioned to taking off the scrub pants, revealing the blue men's underwear he had taken earlier.

Norah nodded. Discreetly, he slid off the pants and slipped under the covers beside her but so far away. Ignoring the pain it caused to do so, Norah scooted over closer to him, using his own words. "Is this okay?"

His arms opened toward her. He moved nearer to the middle of the bed and put his shoulder under her head. She was immediately grateful. She felt her body relax for the first time since . . . she didn't even know. She'd been uptight since at least all weekend.

She hadn't been speaking to him. And with good cause, but protecting her heart from doing something stupid was a lot lower on her list now. Sleep was higher. And he smelled so good, like heat and comfort and *him*.

Norah had thought she'd drift off right away, but something kept bothering her, making her squirm. TJ finally asked. "What?"

"My ribs." She was lying on the broken ribs, and figured the drugs had to be pretty good if she wasn't smart enough to get off them.

"Roll over." He motioned with his hand, and she slowly flipped in place.

TJ curled his arm under her head and curled himself up behind her. "Okay?"

"Yes." The sound came out on a sigh as she leaned back into him. Needing the contact, and knowing that she could sleep with him right there.

His arm was restless, pausing across her waist, her shoulders, her thigh. Never touching down in one place.

It was the only thing keeping her from sleep, she was sure. "What?"

"I don't know where to put it. I can't think of a single place that isn't cut or bruised." Then he made a soft noise and his fingers found her hair. Slowly he combed them through, then started at the top again. Over and over, the motion both relaxing and peaceful.

Her eyes fell shut and this time her body let go of every tight muscle, she felt herself falling asleep, her breathing even and getting deeper. But it took so long.

She heard his voice, low, behind her and struggled through the fog of exhaustion and drugs to hear what he was saying, and why it was so beautiful. Her brain put the pieces together, picking out the notes of *This Ordinary Man*.

Just before she fell asleep, Norah wondered if he sang it because it was a good lullaby and he knew she liked it, or if maybe he meant it.

CHAPTER 49

TJ hadn't recognized the number when it showed up on his cell phone. But he was glad now that he picked up. Even more glad that he hadn't taken anything stronger than a Tylenol this morning.

Norah's father had handed her a fistful of medications and she had happily swallowed them. But TJ had taken one look at the older man and assessed his fighting ability and lifting strength and found him sorely lacking. Even knowing it was irrational, he hadn't taken the painkillers. He wanted to be able to drive if need be, and certainly to physically fend off all comers.

He couldn't think of a single thing that could happen here at the house, but he never would have predicted yesterday in a million years. He wondered if his old self who had partied and missed appointments at the gym all the time would have even shown up yesterday to be useful. Then he remembered that she wouldn't have started going to the track if she hadn't been helping him. He'd talked her back into going . . .

TJ shook his head, trying desperately not to connect a chain of evidence to incriminate himself. The nurses had warned him about that, the few times he said it was his fault. They were right, it wasn't. But knowing it didn't ease the guilt taking bites at his heart.

Norah's father took the day off from work, then asked if he could run a few quick errands while the two of them stayed at the house. TJ agreed to stay, thinking it was funny that he'd gotten a formal invite when he had no intention of going anywhere. Not until Norah wanted him to. At least her Dad had seemed okay with that.

When her father left, TJ was glad he hadn't taken the drugs. The pain didn't matter so much. He and Norah had curled up on the couch, her in his arms, and fallen asleep. He kept nodding off then coming around, his ribs would protest when she moved, his leg tensed behind her. But he didn't wake her. She had slept soundly after he'd curled up beside her last night, and he'd slept better, too.

He'd only pried himself away when his phone rang, and was now glad that he'd answered. Norah started tossing, there in the corner of the couch where he'd set her at great pains to himself. Her voice came out in small mews and TJ rushed to gather her in his arms and shush her. He took no small satisfaction in the fact that she had calmed almost immediately when he touched her.

As he worked himself around to a more comfortable position, his hand stroked her hair. Wanting to squeeze her tighter, but knowing it would hurt her, he decided right then to take her father's advice. When she was healed, he would tell her what he felt.

It was probably about a month away, but he wanted to wait. Knowing that it would be difficult to keep his hands off her if she wanted anything at all to do with him resolved him to the time. He didn't want to hurt her, and he didn't want her thinking about the man who had hurt her when it was his own hands on her.

A month.

He could survive a month.

In that month he could do everything in his power to make sure she said 'yes' when he asked.

A car pulled into the driveway, and TJ cranked his sore neck around to see Mr. Davidson pull up. With a sigh, he resigned himself that it was time. He buried his face in her hair and inhaled. "Norah, baby, wake up."

"Hmmm?" Her voice rolled, sweet and stronger than yesterday, through his senses.

"Wake up baby, I have to go—"

"What? No." She bolted upright, and grabbed at the cotton t-shirt he was still wearing. "Please stay."

He grabbed at her wrists, simply holding her there, where her hands had fisted into the shirt. "I'm just going for a few hours. Your Dad is here." He leaned closer. "I promise I'll be back."

She nodded, her breathing relaxing a bit, her hands uncurling from his shirt as her Dad came through the front door. He was burdened with bags, but didn't miss the scene in front of him. "Everything okay?"

"Yes, Daddy. TJ said he was leaving, but it's only for a little bit. He'll be back tonight."

"Of course, honey." Her father continued his path through to the kitchen then went out for another load. This time when he came in, he addressed TJ. "Will you be staying for lunch?"

"No. I have to go now." He kissed the top of Norah's head and pulled his keys from one of a neat series of nails hammered beside the front door. He thanked Mr. Davidson and took the painful steps down the front walk to the car.

The seats were still bloody although it had dried and turned dark. For a moment he stared, knowing that both seats had both her blood and his, and also her attacker's. He slid in, thinking he might leave it there for a while, to remind him of how he was going to make that man suffer.

TJ pulled out of the driveway and drove into town. He'd intended to head straight to the police station, but found himself getting more and more angry as he drove and, knowing his anger would do no one any good, he made a turn and headed for JD's.

He was on his brother's doorstep in no time, knocking and not sure what sight he presented when JD pulled the door wide. TJ spoke first. "I need you. Now. Maybe for several hours."

A hand shot out and grabbed his wrist. JD used surprise and leverage to haul his brother inside the front entry and close the door behind him. "TJ, you look like you lost a bar fight against the whole bar and then slept in your clothes. What happened?"

Again it was hard to put voice to it and he chose the simplest words he could. "Norah got attacked at the track yesterday. She fought him off."

"And so did you?"

He nodded.

"How does Norah look?"

"Worse."

JD took a step away, looking like he didn't want to leave his little brother alone even for a second, and hollered up the stairs. "Kelsey! I have to go out with TJ now. I'll be back in a few hours maybe."

Her voice carried from around the corner as TJ heard her approaching and protesting. "No, I'm going shopping with Bridget, she got a sitter and— . . . What happened?"

Her eyes went wide as she looked him up and down. He repeated exactly what he said to JD.

In that moment JD pulled his startled wife into his arms in a fierce hug, his breathing clearly tight. Whispered words that weren't intended to be heard carried from where his brother had buried his face in his wife's hair. "Kelse, is it wrong for me to be glad that it wasn't you?"

Kelsey kissed him and stepped back, leaving TJ watching the scene with a gaping hole of jealousy in him. He'd always felt it, that's why he'd been so awful to his brother sometimes. TJ didn't want Kelsey, but he'd wanted someone who loved him like that. Norah admitted her envy from day one. TJ, of course, had been slower.

Kelsey looked at him. "I'll call Bridget and we'll reschedule. You two go do whatever you need to do."

"Thank you." Turning from the scene, TJ pulled open the heavy front door and led his brother down the steps to the car.

Startled by the blood when he opened the passenger door, JD looked again at his brother. "What the hell happened?"

"He had a knife. Bastard cut her clothes off her." Again the words clogged his throat.

"Did he . . .?"

Even JD couldn't say it, and TJ felt the combination of rage and helplessness boil up in him again.

"No. I got there just in time. *Just* in time." Still it scared him. If he had been a minute later, or hadn't looked toward the trees . . . "It's not wrong to be glad it wasn't Kelsey. I'd have been glad if it wasn't Norah."

"Let me drive." JD hit a button on his keychain and opened the garage door. They climbed into the huge SUV and JD asked where they were going.

"The police station. They have someone and want me to come ID him."

"Oh shit."

But TJ shook his head. This wasn't 'Oh shit'. "No, I'm just praying that it's him. Not some other fool they picked up."

His brother looked him up and down. "Can we go by your house first? Maybe you should shower, calm down, change clothes."

TJ nodded and JD made the turn, heading the short distance to the subdivision. "I can't shower. Too many stitches in too many places. But I can wash up and change. I'm wearing Norah's underwear."

"I didn't need to know that."

TJ laughed just a little at that, glad for the release of tension, not having realized what he had said. "She dances in men's boxer briefs sometimes, she had a spare pair."

"Sure, sure, little brother."

TJ laughed again. Then the knot in his chest loosened just a touch. "Thank you."

JD's hand lifted from the gear shift and came out to grab his, "Any time."

TJ had to put a manual code into his gate to get it to open, then spent only the necessary time scrubbing himself up and combing his hair, before packing an overnight bag.

JD came in while he was throwing the last things into the bag. "Did I see a lock box on the front door?"

Nodding, TJ zipped the bag and lifted it by the handles, knowing better than to try to use the strap on his battered shoulders. "I put the house on the market."

"Why?"

"It's just a house." He shrugged the best he could. "I need a home."

Speculating even as he opened the side door to the garage, JD climbed into the driver's seat, "And someone to live there with you."

"That may be getting ahead of myself." TJ started then, breathing evenly, knowing what was ahead, and steeling himself for any outcome.

They were almost there when JD asked, "What are you thinking?"

"That if I grab a gun from a nearby holster and empty a clip into him, it will be too humane and only land me in jail. I'm hanging on to that thought pretty tight right now."

"I won't let you."

"I know." TJ tried to let out a breath, to let out some tension. "I think that's why I came and got you."

Without speaking, they parked and walked through the metal detectors at the front entrance. After checking in at the front desk, they were led to a back room with a few chairs lined against one wall and a large window looking into a room with height rulings painted across the back. TJ knew they were on the viewing side of a two-way mirror.

He braced himself for whatever came. A female officer told them that the police thought they might have him but were getting witnesses to ID the man before they went any further.

That was one of the few things he hadn't been prepared for. Hot rage went through him that someone had seen and not helped. He clenched his fists at his side, knowing there was no place to strike out. "Witnesses?"

The officer nodded, her hair pulled back in a severe braid. "Your girlfriend was the seventh that we know of. He's raped six women since January. Again, that we know of."

TJ would have felt better if she'd just slugged him in the gut. And he must have looked like it.

"Breathe." Her hand came to his shoulder and so did JD's. He shook them both off, maybe just a little too violently.

Waiting until he got it together, she then spoke into the radio clipped to her shoulder. "Bring them in."

TJ stood, still focusing on breathing, and felt skin before he realized he'd reached out and clenched his brother's hand.

"Please don't." JD shook him off, thankfully diverting his attention for a moment. "I don't doubt that if you see him you'll crush every bone in my hand. I need that hand. Please."

JD held out two fingers together, looking a little sheepish. "It a labor trick. You can squeeze two fingers as hard as you want and it won't damage them."

He was skeptical. "'Cause Kelsey was in danger of breaking the bones in your hand?"

"Yeah. Clearly you've never been around a woman in labor."

He was grateful for the small distraction, but out of the corner of his eye, TJ saw the men filing in. Five of them, and automatically he grabbed at the fingers, his fist squeezing as hard as it could. "That's him."

It took all the control he could find to hold back and not go through the window and strangle the bastard. Both JD and the cop saw that, placing steadying hands on his shoulders.

She spoke first, into her radio. "Have them turn to face us."

The men did, and TJ was certain that the bastard could see through the mirrored surface to TJ's own fury. The man showed no remorse.

He wished they'd take the man away, get him out of sight, but the cop made him speak the man's number in the line-up and had the ass pulled closer to the mirror for a good look.

TJ hadn't needed it.

The man was bruised, his arm casted, though he didn't look nearly as battered as Norah. The officer nodded. Speaking into her radio again she had the officers take the men out. TJ put his hands on his knees and tried to breathe, but that only hurt the ribs that bastard had cracked.

The voice was soft and feminine and soothing. "Everyone pulled him out of that line up. All the same guy. You make four. He's going away for a long time. We have enough evidence that he'll likely confess. Much of that due to you bringing in the knife. Just so you know, the other prisoners don't take kindly to rapists. He won't have an easy time in jail."

TJ nodded. It was his only consolation for not getting to torment the man himself.

JD asked how he'd gotten brought in.

"A doctor called his local station when the man showed up in his office with the break to his arm and a mismatched explanation. He was almost five hours away."

TJ stood. "Can I get the name of the doctor? I'd like to thank him."

The officer shook her head. "But if you want to write a letter or a note, I'll make sure he gets it."

TJ nodded.

The officer let them out of the room and TJ began to breathe easier. Walking down the hallway he started to feel lighter, but a voice stopped him. "Which one of you is Thomas Hewlitt?"

"I am." TJ started, no one called him 'Thomas,' for a moment he wondered if it was a fan, and knew he just couldn't deal with that now, here. It couldn't be a fan. His brain was fried, maybe it was a cop, they would likely refer to him as Thomas.

It was neither. A middle-aged woman who looked haggard and like she'd been crying came down the hallway, flagging him. "I peeked and read your name off the roster. You and your girlfriend brought that bastard down. I just wanted to say thank you."

"Oh." That startled him. "I didn't really do—"

"He attacked my daughter at college in February. I'm hoping she'll finally get some sleep tonight." With that the woman offered a small smile and went out the building ahead of them.

TJ sighed. "I have another errand."

JD just nodded.

Twenty minutes later they were back at the station, talking to the same female officer. He had borrowed paper and envelopes and written two notes. "This one is for the doctor who called that bastard in." He handed over the first envelope. "And this one is for the woman who flagged me down in the hall. She said that he had attacked her daughter in February."

"I know who you're talking about." The officer took both envelopes.

"Please, make sure they get them."

This time when they left, JD teased him. "I saw how much money was on those bank drafts. I'm impressed."

TJ just shook his head. "It needed to be done. That doctor needs to be thanked, and that woman's daughter probably needs counseling. I told them to donate it if they don't want it."

JD didn't say anything, just started the car and asked where to?

"I'm headed back to Norah's. You can take me back to my car." He was quiet for a minute before he spoke again. "I finally understand why you don't party anymore, don't drink like you used to. I thought you'd just turned stuffy when Andie and then Kelsey came along. But I realize now that you just need to be ready if they need you." He sighed. "I didn't even take my pain medication this morning, just in case something irrational happened."

"Yeah, that's what happens. Are you turning stuffy now, too?"

He couldn't help but smile. "Looks that way."

"It's good to see."

He hugged his brother and thanked him again before getting into his own bloody car. The blood wasn't comforting now, and he figured he'd get it washed out professionally or get a new car. He couldn't put Norah back in here.

He also counted himself damned lucky that the police had found the bastard so fast. He drove back to the farmhouse feeling lighter. Glad they'd found the man, and glad he could tell Norah the good news, and glad he'd been able to maybe help one of the other victims and thank the doctor.

His mouth quirked, the side that didn't hurt. He was becoming a better man. Who'd have thought? He hadn't seen this coming like he hadn't seen the semi. But he liked himself a lot better these days.

Pulling up in front of the garage, he pushed the shift into

park and forced his legs to climb the steps. They were worse than they'd been when he left. Of course, the adrenaline had left him and now he was feeling the effects.

He pushed open the front door, Norah turning to look up at him from her spot on the couch. Her eyes went wide at the sight of him, and they looked even bluer from the black that shaded both undersides and the right half of her face. She stood up. "Are you done?"

Shedding his jacket and carefully hanging it on the stand behind the door, he came up to Norah and folded her into his arms. It hurt his arms and his ribs to do it, but it was worth it. "I went to the police station to ID someone they brought in. It was him. They got him."

"What?"

He got to smile at her. "He's in custody."

"Why didn't you tell me?"

"I didn't want to have to come back and tell you that it wasn't him." He rolled his face so his cheek nestled on top of her hair, he inhaled her sweet smell, wanting her to be his. "If you need to see him, they'll drag him back out for you."

She pulled back at that one, frowning, even though it must have hurt to do so. "I don't know that I need to. Thank you."

"Norah." He reached out as she walked away. "Are you mad at me? I just . . ." *wanted to protect you.* But those words didn't come out.

"No." She shook her head. "I need a drink. The drugs are making me thirsty. Do you want something?"

"Norah."

This time she turned, sensing he had something more to say.

"Baby, you're a hero. He raped at least six women since January. You brought him down. I'm so proud of you."

Her head tilted. "You really believe that, don't you?"

He nodded. He did. "A doctor turned him in. He came in with injuries and a story that didn't match, so the doctor just called the cops. I sent him a thank you. I signed both our names to it. I hope you don't mind."

"Of course not. Thank you."

TJ didn't add that the 'thank you' he'd sent had been in the tune of thousands of dollars. He didn't want her thinking he believed he could throw money at things. And he changed the subject. "Did your Dad make that chicken soup?"

She smiled, not her mouth, that would hurt too much. But her eyes. "We saved you some."

CHAPTER 50

Norah slept when he was here. She would feel him curl up behind her, around her. In the same position every time they went to bed, TJ was an amulet against the dreams. He'd canceled Wilder's show on Wednesday night, although Norah knew it wasn't for her, he just couldn't do it. He couldn't really sing or perform with those ribs. But he sang to her just fine. Every night. Sweet love songs.

Still, he didn't touch her in any way that made her believe he wanted to be anything other than nice. He was fiercely protective, and that, of course, made her fall just a little further in love. And that made her just a little more scared.

The last man she'd loved had been snatched away from her. There one moment, talking on his cell phone, telling her they were on their way. Then, when they should have arrived, the police had, telling her it was all over.

First TJ's accident and now this—she didn't need any reminders that life changed when it felt like it. So she'd sent TJ home for a while yesterday. Her father had been at work, and she'd sat on the couch watching a movie she found. And trying to breathe normally.

Norah had to keep telling herself that she was in her own home. And that man was in jail.

It didn't change the panic. Or the visions that came when she closed her eyes and didn't feel TJ right next to her.

So she sent him home again this evening.

He'd protested, sweet thing that he was. "We both sleep better this way."

But Norah stood her ground. "I know *I* do. That's why you have to go home."

"You're not making any sense."

Her father had removed himself from the room, but Norah knew she did make sense, and she'd make it to TJ however long it took. "I have to be able to sleep on my own, and the longer you're here the harder that will be to learn."

"You're going to be okay tonight?"

"No. I'm going to be awful, but I have to learn."

He protested again, striking at the heart of her argument. "Why do you have to learn to sleep alone?"

Her heart skipped a beat, thinking something more might be coming. But it wasn't. It made sense; she'd seen her reflection in the mirror. No man was going to hit on that. "You aren't going to stay here every night. You're performing in New York in two weeks. After that you're going on tour. What are you going to do? Cancel the whole thing?"

He'd opened his mouth, but this time nothing came out.

It was Norah who filled the silence. "Go home, TJ."

So he had.

As she'd suspected, she was wide awake at midnight and covered in sweat. The thought of a shower was both comforting and terrifying, so she stayed in bed, figuring it was time for professional help.

Again she dozed off and again she jerked awake. But the clock read 1:06. She had actually slept.

Norah lay awake until one thirty with the light on and was

just getting ready to turn it off and try again when she heard the tapping.

Startled, she lay stiff as a board, regulating her breathing, wishing she'd left the light off. Then laughing to herself as she realized what it was.

Rocks. Tiny pebbles, probably from her Dad's rose beds, against the window. There was only one person she could think of who would do that.

Getting out of bed, Norah crossed the room and pulled back the curtain just enough to see the front yard. Sure enough, TJ was standing there with a handful of rocks just below her window. She sighed. It was so close to romantic that she had to shove the window up and look down at him as the cold night air flowed in.

His voice was calm and low. "Your light was on, I hope I didn't wake you."

She shook her head. "What are you doing here, TJ?"

"I had to see if you were okay." He looked chagrinned and ducked his head. "I got worried. I just needed to see you. Good night."

"Good night."

She watched as he turned to go, and pulled the window shut. Her eyes were closing as she turned to go back to bed, and saw the man silhouetted in the doorway.

With a gasp, Norah started. "Dad! You scared the crap out of me!"

"Sorry, honey." He made a face and she knew it was the last thing he'd meant to do.

"What are you doing up?"

"Checking on you." His finger pointed to the window. "Apparently, I'm not the only one."

She couldn't hide the smile that broke loose.

Her Dad always thought if the conversation turned that way, it was a good time for a talk. So at one-forty in the morning he thought nothing of perching on the side of her bed. After all they were awake, right?

"Is he what you want?"

She nodded.

"Looks like maybe that goes both ways."

Norah pointed her finger around her face. "I don't think he'll propose anything anytime soon. Plus, he'll be traveling. He can get anyone he wants."

"That doesn't mean he'll partake." Her father always played devil's advocate. Sometimes it was helpful. Sometimes, like now, she just wanted to curl up with her misbeliefs and go to sleep.

"Daddy, he has no reason not to. Why should I expect him to act according to my wishes?"

"Good point. It's probably hard for him to when he doesn't even know what they are."

"Daddy, I get it. Can I go to sleep now?"

"Good night, honey."

Norah kissed him and sent him to turn off the light after she had tucked herself in. She felt very young asking him to leave the door cracked. Then she curled up with her misbeliefs, and thought happy thoughts.

CHAPTER 51

TJ yawned. He hadn't slept well since Norah had kicked him out. Luckily, she wasn't being rude or refusing to speak to him. She just decided she needed to learn to sleep on her own. Probably she hadn't realized that she was forcing him to sleep on his own, too. Or that it would be just as hard for him to sleep without her. Harder, from the looks of it.

She, at least, seemed to be getting some rest.

He wound up playing the tongue-tied version of Romeo, throwing rocks at her window, and then apologizing for waking her.

The nightmares he had were hard to go back to sleep after. He only stopped going to her house because he didn't want to wake her when she was finally finding sleep. Still, he wanted to be certain the horrors were products of the back of his brain and not reality. Because they sure felt real when he woke up each time.

In one dream. it had been Norah in the convertible with him when the semi hit. This time, when the doctors told him his legs didn't work, they also told him that Norah died. That had been the first night.

The second night, he had dreamed that her attacker had escaped prison and, in revenge, had staked out her house and was casing the place. TJ had actually dressed that night and driven over, sitting vigil at the far end of the driveway, looking for any sort of movement. He'd called the police station and double checked that the man was still locked up. The panic had been that strong.

The third night, he simply hadn't gotten to the track in time. He arrived to find Norah in the trees, staked out and dead. When he finally got back to sleep after that one, HIV had claimed her, and he watched her die a slow horrible death. That had been on his mind all day because the bastard had submitted to a test to avoid attempted murder charges and just that afternoon the results had come up negative.

In the worst, he sat at the top of the stairs watching while Norah was dragged away. In his wheelchair, he was unable to stand, run, or help in anyway.

His brain came up with a new way to torment him every night. TJ didn't need a psychologist to explain to him what it meant. He was petrified of losing Norah. Every time he actually slept he lost her, usually in a slightly different way.

When daylight hours came, he found some way to contact her. He called. He helped her run errands, drove her to the studio to talk to Mrs. Kenner or her dance teachers. She was arranging her own subs now and talking about the Holiday Show that her little company was going to perform. He took her out to see a movie one afternoon.

And he spent his remaining time in the studio. The problem was no one seemed to believe TJ that his change in his music was separate from his feelings for Norah. That was probably because they were in part right. Both had come about from the same accident. But they were separate things. He wouldn't have been able to get up on stage whether or not he'd fallen in love with her. And he would have been finding his way back whether or not he'd been able to drag her into the studio with him and ask her opinion.

There would be no more shows before the Queen Tribute in Central Park, his cracked ribs weren't up for it. In fact, if he followed the doctor's warnings, they wouldn't be doing that show either. But TJ would be damned if he would miss it. Even though he'd almost answered Norah with 'yes'—he would cancel everything to stay beside her. She was right, no matter how much he loved her, they would both go nuts if they didn't learn to sleep alone. It would be a necessity, given his job, even if they did get to have the rest of his time together.

He asked Norah to come to New York with him. It fell out of his mouth one day. She'd been surprised, but maybe not as surprised as he was. He tried so hard to look like he intended to ask. Norah had declined. He wanted to tell her that just because he'd surprised himself didn't mean that he didn't want her to come. The other option was that she was remembering the last concert he had dragged her to. He had left her alone in the audience with no one to talk to, and then something had happened, during or afterward, that had changed her mind and her mood.

TJ still didn't know what that was.

He'd spent the morning in the gym, doing what little he could, then in the studio, singing his heart out to his padded walls and feeling his ribcage protest. Then he'd come to the dance studio. It was usually deserted during the day, except for Norah. TJ had gotten an alarm system installed a week ago, remnants of the paranoia they both felt.

He punched in the code and let himself in. Norah was nowhere to be seen but, as usual, when he followed the music, he found her. She hadn't danced since that morning. TJ was pretty sure that it wasn't a psychological thing. That she hadn't lost her will to dance, she just physically wasn't able.

Even now she was stretching. He'd seen these stretches

before. Over the summer, when she had spread her legs out, she would lean forward until her torso was flat along the floor, her cheek not just touching but resting on the floor and her hands reaching out to her ankles. Now she was leaned over, perched on her elbows—an impressive display of flexibility for anyone except Norah.

She stood and did a short exercise, pointing her toes one way then another, holding herself in perfect form even for these simple movements. When she finished, he kicked off his shoes before knocking and pushing open the door to the dance room. "I waited until you finished your toe-pointing."

She grinned at him, her face less stiff, the swelling entirely gone. The bruises made her look like she'd been in a barroom brawl. "Dancers don't point their toes. You point your whole foot. And it feels good to be able to move again, even if it isn't entirely."

He walked up to her, curious how she was doing and touched the side of her cheek. Her breath sucked in.

"Sorry. It still hurts, huh?"

She looked at him like he was nuts. Pretty much every day, he had checked her out, to see how well she was healing. He had a lot of stake in her healing.

She slapped his hand away, startling him.

"Of course, it still hurts. Look at it. What's with all the poking? You could just ask me, I do know. *Norah, does it still hurt?*"

"I'm sorry." She was right. He was being an ass. "I'm sorry."

"*I'm* sorry." Norah frowned at him. "I'm just frustrated. I want to do so much more than I can, and I didn't do this to me."

"I know, baby." He reached out again, but this time took his hand back. "How are the stitches they took out?" They'd both had sutures removed yesterday. His from his legs finally and her from both her legs and the long cut down her chest. Both of them had received suture strips, so it looked like little pieces of packing tape were holding the still pink gashes together.

She held up her shirt, revealing a sport bra and a long pink line down her chest. It snaked under the bra and out again, ending just above her belly. TJ had learned not to suck in his breath every time he saw it. Again, his hand reached out to trace her wound, but he pulled it back. Of course, it hurt.

"You?" Her voice cut into his thoughts.

He lifted the right side of his shirt then, revealing his own gash where he'd ducked getting the knife embedded into his side. Because he didn't have much movement there and it hadn't been deep like her cut was, he had those sutures out several days ago. The plastic surgeons had insisted that the stitches not be pulled all at the same time. Each had to come out when it was ready, lest it mar their perfect work. For himself TJ didn't mind a few scars. For Norah, he'd drive her back there twice a day if that was what it took to keep the marks from lingering a second longer than they had to.

Norah's hand came out, touching palm down on his side, covering the gash. "You'll heal nicely."

The warmth of her fingers went further than just where she touched him, and TJ had to pull back. He resigned himself again to waiting.

"So, what do you want to do today?" He'd been getting used to seeing her every day, even when he had no good excuse or plan.

Her answer startled him. "Go to the track."

"What?" He didn't think they'd ever go back there.

"I need to. Got to get back up on the horse."

TJ didn't like it, but he understood the idea of facing down your fears, he also understood that Norah could have anything from him. The *I need to* had clenched it this time. "Now?"

She shrugged. "The weather's nice."

"All right." He started to lead her out, and as usual she

stopped at the doorway to the studio and changed her shoes, while he stepped into his own.

She threw on a jacket and followed him out to the car, letting him drive most everywhere, as he had healed faster than she. The blood was gone from the car seats, at a pretty penny and they were a slightly paler shade of gray but Norah didn't have to look at it. They were silent until TJ parked square in front of the steps and turned to her. "You ready?"

She nodded.

Both of them were out of the car in a minute, neither dressed for running, and they met around the front of the hood at the very top of the stairs.

Cold flooded him. It gripped and didn't let go. His breathing faltered and his right hand waved wildly for hers until she grasped it in her own. Lacing his fingers through hers, TJ fought to regain some composure. He hadn't expected this. He'd thought he was here to support Norah. But so many times he'd found that when he expected that, he was wrong.

"What?" Her voice and her eyes were seeking him out.

"I was standing here, having seen your car, and wondering where you'd gone, when I saw that flash of light in the trees. All I knew was you were there and you were in trouble, and I ran. I went *over* the fence. I have *never* moved like that."

In a moment, the nausea passed and he was able to breathe again, but wondered what else was in store for him here.

Norah hadn't moved. "You weren't being nice. You have nightmares, too."

She was only just now figuring that out?

He nodded.

Slowly they descended the steps. Hand in hand they walked one loop. Norah found a dark spot on the far side, and was convinced it was her own blood, still there. She shuddered and eventually stood upright. "He lapped me."

"What?"

"He ran past me. The first time I tensed up, thinking *I don't know this man who's running up behind me.* But he did it several times. He waved once. He made me comfortable that he wasn't going to do anything, that he was just jogging. So when the footsteps came up right behind me I didn't think anything of it until it was too late."

"I wondered." He squeezed her hand. "I wondered how anyone caught you off guard."

"I was in my own head, not paying attention." She shook her head, like she might just shake away the memory like rainwater. "I'm just glad it was me, and not some high school girl. Or Kelsey with the baby."

That turned his stomach again. "I will never be glad that it was you."

"Thank you."

"Can we please get out of here? You are far braver than I." He tugged at her hand and obligingly she followed along.

CHAPTER 52

TJ called her each day he was in New York. They would be gone almost six whole days. He figured that his wanting to call her was a good sign. Both his brother and Craig called their wives every day, no matter what, when they were on the road. Alex was only making periodic check-ins. It seemed the baby yelled all the time. Not cried, yelled. He didn't call home much.

They had been busy every waking moment, each day doing interviews with different radio stations. They went to see the stage that had been finished just prior to their arrival. The rotating platform limited their staging space, but allowed for the bands to switch out quickly, a necessity with so many groups performing. Wilder rehearsed *Bohemian Rhapsody* with all the musicians who'd made it into town early. They picked up another song, from a group that had bowed out.

TJ didn't understand, which is what he told Norah. "I've got it. I mean *It* that I was looking for."

He could hear her smile. "So what is this elusive 'it'?"

"I would have performed this from the chair. It's not about

the show, it's about me. Which is actually less selfish than it sounds."

"Go on."

"I used to do it for what I got out of it. I'm doing the work some justice now. It's actually art." His fingers went into his hair, and he sighed. "I'm preaching to the choir, aren't I? I'm just slow."

She laughed. "I did it because for a while it was the only thing that gave me joy. So, how's this going to play out in the concert?"

"It's funny. We're opening with *Don't Stop Me Now*. I don't know if you remember it. I didn't try it out on you because it came so easy. I finally realize why. Will you be watching?"

"Of course."

"You'll see."

The next day he told her that all that guitar work he'd done had been a waste. JD decided that TJ needed to be on piano and himself on guitar, as it put the best man on each instrument. It meant they had to rehearse the hell out of that, too.

He'd called her from back stage, right before they went live. In the background, another group was finishing up *Crazy Little Thing Called Love.* But TJ had been talking through his nerves with her. He hung up right before they went out, biting back the *I love you* that he wanted to add, sticking to his resolve to wait until she healed.

Positioning themselves back stage, they rotated out with the platform while the lights were black. If he hadn't been so keyed up he would have felt silly.

When the lights blared in his face, for a brief instant he could see people. They flowed out in every direction, literally hundreds of thousands, and millions more watching live on TV. In that same moment, he heard the first note from JD's guitar and he opened his mouth, pushing out the first air and sound. For the first time in his life he had real fun on stage.

There was almost nothing as fun as Queen. He was heaving for breath when he finished the song, his black t-shirt chosen because it didn't show how hard he was working. That didn't matter, because he still had to hold up his first finger to the audience asking them for a minute while he caught his breath.

He'd never done that before. He'd always saved air, believing that the crap he spewed in between the songs was as important as the singing. "I need to know which of you ladies out there has a big backyard." He grinned at the screams and catcalls. "That's what I thought. This is your song."

JD was laughing at him, and they couldn't start. The start was vocal only, all four of them. It took TJ fingering counts for one-two-three to get the two brothers calmed enough to launch. *Fat Bottomed Girls* got as much applause as the first piece.

Hearing them there on stage, TJ agreed with Brenda. They'd been invited and gotten some prime pieces because the four of them had the vocal chops to pull off these numbers.

He didn't speak before launching into their final group song. What would he have said? *This one's for Norah*? But it was. *Somebody To Love* came out hopeful and pleading and as strong as he was feeling it.

He knew if he performed it again it would be different, each time it would be. These people got Norah's version. So be it.

He called her after the show, too. He was exhausted and due at press events and wasn't going to make it without hearing her voice. "So?"

"Wow."

"Tell me what you saw." He braced himself against a wall, wondering what she might say, and knowing that no matter what it was he needed to hear it.

"You used to be good. You put on a great show and you were fun to watch. But this was . . . I don't think anyone could have looked anywhere else. You were suddenly just a singer, who happened to be insanely charismatic. You were right, you enjoyed it."

He let out his breath, but she wasn't finished with him.

"I was even more impressed that you happily faded into the background when the lead came out." He winced. But she was right. Previously he would have drawn attention to himself, played up whatever he'd been given.

"Thank you. That was exactly what I needed to hear. How are you doing?"

"Much better." The sound smiled at him, "I'm drug free, and I did some real dancing today."

He wanted to talk more, but he was getting tugged into a fray of reporters. Norah heard it through the phone and told him she'd talk to him tomorrow.

He didn't tell her she'd see him tomorrow.

Norah replayed the Central Park Queen concert enough times to have it memorized. She was pretty certain her Dad knew what she was doing, though he didn't comment.

He came home late that night and said, "Weren't the Hewlitts on TV tonight?"

She'd said yes, and clicked on the already-cued program. Her father was no dunce, he had to have figured that she'd already watched it several times. But all he said was, "Wow, he's really good."

Norah didn't add, *He's even better than he used to be.*

Mr. Davidson had pulled himself off the couch and gone to bed, but Norah had watched a few more times. TJ was right: *Don't Stop Me Now* was his song. TJ was a 'shooting star leaping to the sky' as the words went. He wasn't playing it anymore, he clearly felt it. Norah chuckled to herself as TJ sang that he was supersonic. Truly he was.

Eventually she shut off the TV and pulled herself up to bed.

She was sleeping better these days, but it wasn't working. Tossing and turning, she was torn between wanting to throw herself at him when he returned and wondering how many groupies he'd screwed while he was out there. She was no fool—just because he was a new man didn't mean he was a celibate one.

Finally sleep found her, but left her facing this day with less than a full tank. She put in some hours at the studio, saying she'd be back on Monday at full steam. She danced off some nerves and considered again throwing herself at TJ.

Being Saturday it was sad her only plans were to sit on her couch and wait for TJ to call. Which was worse than no plans at all, she told herself. Still there she was, cell phone in hand, watching the same patch of recording and trying to convince herself to go for a ride or do something useful when a knock came at the door.

Startled, Norah turned off the show, removing the evidence, when she realized her Dad would never knock. When she pulled open the door her heart flipped over. TJ stood on the other side of the screen, dark hair falling precariously over his eyes, his leather jacket and jeans leaving him with that same disreputable look he'd always had.

CHAPTER 53

Norah launched herself at TJ, pulling back just in time to keep it on the friendly side, reminding herself: *groupies*. "You're back!"

"Yup."

"Come in." She stepped back out of the way, feeling weird inviting him in when he so easily belonged. "Are you headed home to go to sleep?"

"Nope. I slept on the plane. Want to do something?"

She couldn't hide the smile. There were a million answers to his question, but she said, "I was thinking of going riding before it gets dark."

"Yeah? Can I come?"

"Of course." Just like that, she was sliding into her jacket and leading TJ out to the barn. TJ saddled her tall mahogany horse himself, and they were seated side by side before he spoke again. "You look all healed up if you're riding."

She nodded. "You, too."

"Being on stage took the last of the kinks out."

"You were amazing." Kicking her heels, she started Thunder heading up the ridge.

But TJ didn't follow. He looked like he was about to say something, but stopped when Shenandoah sidestepped. He frowned and tried again to follow, but Norah's usually obedient horse didn't listen.

She looked him up and down, unsure what was wrong. The horse wouldn't obey a single command that TJ gave him, and worse, Shenandoah looked nervous. TJ shook his head and pushed forward tugging at the reigns.

"TJ, what did you do to my horse?"

"Nothing. What's wrong with your horse?"

Just then Shenandoah lurched a little forward, just one small leap, and TJ's right hand waved at the front of the saddle finding nothing but air until he eventually gripped the front.

"Oh my God." Norah reached out, "hand me the reins and get down."

"What?" He looked puzzled, which was a pretty calm expression for a man on a big horse that had just given him a warning buck.

"Get off. You can't ride."

"I ride fine." He protested even as he stood in the stirrups and swung his leg over. She noted that he moved easily, without favoring his injuries.

"You ride Western. These guys are trained English."

"There's that much of a difference?"

She shrugged "I wouldn't have thought so, but Shenandoah doesn't like it."

He sighed and held his hands out for the reins. "I'm getting back up, tell me what to do."

She showed him the grip and how small finger movements guided the horse. Tried to push his foot into the proper position. To his credit he tried it before he protested. "How is it that you ride English, Norah? You're from Texas, that just isn't right."

"My grandfather was a Virginia gentleman. I ride English."

"Well, I'm not riding." He dismounted and began to unsaddle the horse.

Norah felt her stomach clench; she wanted to do something silly and romantic with him even if he didn't know it. She wanted to watch the sunset from the ridge.

Then she remembered. "Oh, oh, oh. Don't take off his bridle. We'll both ride him."

She had the perfect solution. Shenandoah, being the larger horse, would bear both their weight better than Thunder would. But she knew there was no good outcome if she just slid up in front of him. If he didn't get turned on, she'd probably burst into tears and flee, leaving the man on a horse that would likely buck him in a minute. If TJ did get turned on, she'd never know if it was from anything other than having her rub her ass against him for the ride.

She pulled the tack off Thunder and set him free, before leading TJ into the storage area. "There." She pointed at, then hauled out, the huge antique saddle.

Seeing her struggling under the weight, he lifted it easily from her hands and put her puny strength to shame by turning it one way then another to see the leather working on it. "Holy shit. A double saddle."

"My grandfather gave me all his supplies. This one's about eighty years old, but Grandpa and I always took care of the leather really well."

TJ again lifted the saddle, easily settling it on Shenandoah's back. "I didn't know they made these."

"I don't think they do. This one's hand-tooled. I have no idea if there were any others like it, or if they survived."

He cinched the saddle under the horse, who protested only a little. "Norah, this has to be worth a small fortune."

"Nope, not selling." She smiled and fingered the scroll-work pressed into the leather, almost invisible after all this time.

He grinned. "I wasn't insinuating that you should." He put

his hands on her waist and lifted her easily into the front, startling her. Then he put a hand against her jeans covered leg. “Stirrups are wrong. They’re longer in front, the back ones are shorter.”

He took a minute, adjusting each, while Norah explained. “Grandpa always rode in front. It’s been years. I would have been the last one back there.”

“What about Lilah?”

Norah shifted forward allowing him to slide up behind her, settling into the half-moon seat that came up right behind hers. “Lilah didn’t love it like I did. She inherited his house, and sold it promptly. I got the horses and the tack and extra money to care for them.”

With her heels, she gave Shenandoah the signal and he started off, albeit a little slow with the weight of two riders. Norah waited for TJ’s arms to come around her waist, for him to lean forward and meet her if she leaned back. But it didn’t happen.

Heading straight for the ridge, she steered them over small rises that led to a ridge with a view of the sunset. It had taken them long enough to get started that they would just barely make it.

Norah covered her bouncing feelings by talking. “Are you going to be back from your first round of touring by the twenty-eighth?”

“I think we get back the morning of the twenty-ninth, why?”

“My friend Mark from when I was in the ballet is coming into town, and he got tickets to the David Parsons Dance Theater. I don’t know if that’s your thing, but I wanted see if you’d like to go with us.” She hoped she made it clear she wasn’t dating Mark.

“I don’t think I’ll be back. But I’ll see you the next day when I get in.”

She nodded, stopping at the top of the ridge, glad that he was planning on seeing her when he returned. Well, more than glad, maybe stupidly ecstatic.

Shenandoah stood, his head turned slightly away from the glare of the huge sinking sun. Tall trees that had been here long before any of them stood sentry in little clusters on either side. A plop sounded, making TJ look over at the pond that was reflecting red and orange.

"Turtle." She said, by way of explanation.

Her breath stopped as his hands finally left their perch on his thighs and slid around her waist. Just as she had wished, he gave her a small tug, bringing her back against his chest. He settled the two of them together, his head tucked just over her shoulder, his cheek against her temple. Norah leaned into him, almost closing her eyes. His breath in her ear whispered the words, "This is beautiful. Peaceful."

She smiled, but he continued, his voice low and soft. "I needed some peace after this last week."

"Yeah, it sounded like it." She was tempted to turn her head and kiss him. It would be so easy. Yet it was so hard.

She just couldn't make her muscles obey. And he made no such moves.

They sat like that, pressed against each other until she couldn't ignore the growing dark and had to turn the horse back before he was likely to turn a leg stepping in a hole or ditch.

Just like that, TJ slipped back away, sitting up straight for the ride home.

He helped her put the tack away and rubbed saddle oil into the leather while she curried the big horse. He walked with her to the side of the house, but said he hadn't even been to his own home yet, he'd come straight here from the plane. He said 'thank you' and 'good night' and disappeared.

TJ Hewlitt was an enigma, and she didn't know what to do with him. She'd given him plenty of opportunities and, she hoped, plenty of signals. She loved the romance—sitting watching the sunset on horseback—but she wanted more. Norah sighed. Her dad was out with his girlfriend and she was frustrated.

She scrubbed up, washing the smell of horse away, and figuring she'd shower later. She stripped naked and pulled on dance-pants and a sport bra then went downstairs into the family room. Her father rarely used it, but it was fully furnished and took a while to clear.

Once she had a smooth expanse of hard floor in front of her, she opened the curtains, allowing the big picture window to act as a mirror, by the dark night beyond it. She found an old set of songs she'd downloaded. If she was right, *I am* off of Wilder's second album was on there.

She let go when the third song started into a mournful melody about bringing on the rain. She danced it modern, spinning and sinking to the floor, and ending on her back with her lungs working overtime. It was the kind of exertion she most enjoyed. When she danced like this, her feelings worked but her brain turned off.

While she lay there on the floor for just a second, she wondered if TJ felt like that on stage. That was her cue, along with the rising notes of the next song to get her ass up and turn off her brain again. This one she did in straight ballet.

Then another.

And another.

And another.

Until she was thirsty and exhausted.

CHAPTER 54

TJ was in pain.

Sweet, horrible, carnal pain.

He'd left Norah after the horseback ride, his mind resolved. Though he'd contemplated just kissing her, he decided against it. He needed to tell her what he felt first. If he had turned to kiss her and was wrong about her feelings, they would have been stuck, on top of a horse and nowhere to go.

So he had driven through a burger joint, and forced himself to eat it on the dark drive out to his house. The agent had an offer, and he was grateful as he chewed the burger he couldn't taste. His brain was bouncing between what words he'd use to tell Norah and deciding that he'd need a house with a barn for her horses.

He'd unpacked. Showered. Changed. Then grabbed his guitar, thinking that he'd maybe sing her something he'd been working on and ask her opinion. He also figured it would be good to have something to do with his hands. Singing to a packed Central Park hadn't made him as nervous as this.

At her house, only her own car sat in the driveway. He let

out a breath, glad that he had her to himself, then hauled his nervous feet up the front steps to knock on the door.

No answer came.

Lights were on, he heard something, but no one answered the door.

He had knocked again. Again, no one.

Certain she was home, and even beginning to get a little worried, TJ circled the house, the guitar his only weapon. Music filtered out to him as he got around to the back and saw light streaming out the large window casting an awkward rectangle on the ground beyond it.

When he peeked in the side door, he could see that Norah had shoved everything out of the way and was dancing. Her hair was pulled up, her black pants clung to her lean form and revealed smooth olive skin from the waistband of the pants to the underside of her sports bra. A long, thin pink line ran up her belly and disappeared beneath the fabric.

He knocked but she didn't hear him, she was that lost in the music. Watching through the small panes, he realized he'd seen her teach, and exercise, and practice. But she was right—that wasn't *dancing,* this was.

TJ had moved around to look in the big window, but still she didn't see him there. He waved and she looked right at him, but continued dancing. When the song ended, she turned away and started into a new dance when the next song came up. He did everything except press himself to the glass, but still she didn't see. Only in the middle of the third song, when she cocked her head and repeated a move while watching out the window, did he realize that she was using it as a mirror and couldn't see him at all.

He looked around behind him wondering if anyone else was watching her. He felt like a voyeur, knowing she didn't know he was there, but he was unable to move.

Norah, as always, defied gravity.

TJ understood how his own gift worked. He knew how vocal cords vibrated, and that his ears, too, were different from other people's. But Norah's dance was beyond him. She moved in ways humans weren't supposed to be able to. She didn't fall off her feet as he'd seen her students do.

She transitioned style with each song, moving easily from ballet into several different styles that TJ could only classify as 'modern'.

He kept telling himself he would leave at the end of the next song, but she was mesmerizing. In this, she put herself out there, thoroughly living her dance. He recognized all of the songs from the radio, and all were at least several years old. He heard a Tim McGraw piece that she danced in the air and on the floor and almost none of it on her feet. He couldn't leave for that. At the end, she reached up and collapsed backward, causing him to leap forward. When she landed on the floor in perfect form, with her knees tucked under and her head tilted back, TJ realized he'd almost gone through the window for nothing.

The next piece she straightened up and did in what appeared to him to be perfect ballet form. He tried to leave, but heard his own voice and turned around.

She danced *I am*. TJ propped himself and the guitar against the tree and stayed for that one, too. She ended with lungs heaving, which surprised him. She'd made the whole thing look so effortless, it was a shock to realize she'd worked for it.

The next song started and she didn't dance. Her head cocked to one side listening to the deep bass line and a sultry voice. Tugging off her dance shoes, she pulled the tie out of her hair, shaking it down. That act alone turned him on, and he was grateful the show was over. But she didn't turn off the music. She grabbed the remote and went back to the middle of the room.

Intrigued, he stared. Norah tossed the remote onto the

couch as the song restarted. Now barefoot, she moved when the song started and her hands skimmed up the sides of her body and into her hair. Her shoulders and hips gave truth to the words about being able to sweep the devil off his red hot feet.

There was nothing stripper-ish or vulgar about it, but every move said 'sex.' Her hands never touched part of her body without skimming it. Never mind that it was a calf or thigh or shoulder or hip—it was hot.

All the blood drained from his head. TJ felt his body shift, thinking again that she didn't know he was watching. There were subtle rolls in her chest and hips. When she turned and reached out toward the window to him, her hands swirling and curling all her fingers, beckoning, he thought about going straight through the glass, but she turned away. He knew she hadn't seen him.

The look on her face was one he'd seen only once before, in bed with her. TJ's mouth opened, dry and wanting, remembering what her skin tasted like. Then her hips ticked in perfect time to the music. She was off, turning and dancing for some imaginary lover, having no idea that he was just beyond the window and desperate to not be imaginary.

The song was slowing, and TJ was grateful, he needed to ease the pain he felt. Norah beckoned again to the man beyond the window, her arms coming in to wrap around herself, as her hips rolled to a final stop with the last note.

She held until the sound faded, then stood up straight and breathed heavily and walked off into another part of the house.

Breathing heavily himself, TJ sat down in the grass, even though it was damp and cold, and tried to get himself together. He'd almost forgotten what he came for. He had to go home. He couldn't tell her he was in love with her with the front of his jeans like that. If he got within five feet of her he'd lose control.

So he pushed himself to standing and walked off toward his car. Music was still blaring and he doubted she'd hear the engine start. Steering down the driveway, his mouth still paper-dry, he tried to concentrate on what little traffic there was.

He made a mental note that the new house would need not only a music studio, but a dance studio. With real mirrors—he was *not* letting his neighbors get an eyeful of that.

After he'd gotten back home, he puttered around, sketching ideas for the house. Maybe Norah's dad would design them a place. Maybe TJ shouldn't let her father near it, because he intended to christen every room with that girl.

He slept a fitful night, waking constantly in either a cold fear that she would say she felt nothing for him or a hot sweat imagining what might happen if she did.

He got up the next morning and worked out. He took JD and Kelsey's kids to the duck pond because it was Sunday and the kids always went. He'd volunteered as a thank-you for the both of them letting him steal JD that day at the police station. Six kids at the grocery store buying bread and then at the duck pond was a handful. But the two oldest, Daniel and Andie, helped a lot with the little ones.

This time when he turned up on Norah's doorstep, she answered and he heard her father in the background. So he told her about his day instead of his feelings.

Her father came into the room a few moments later. "I thought I heard voices."

Though TJ was certain the man could read his face, he was grateful he hadn't actually said anything. "Sir."

"Stop calling me 'sir.'" Mr. Davidson laughed.

Norah sidetracked what little conversation there was. "You probably heard the TV, Daddy, I was watching it."

TJ saw then that a program had been paused on the screen.

Her father nodded. "I'm headed up to bed. Good night."

TJ felt himself frown, and Norah kissed her father and promised to keep the sound low. It was only nine o'clock.

As Mr. Davidson disappeared up the stairs, Norah laughed at

him again. "He was out of town last night, and has to get up for work in the morning. You didn't run him off."

Her head tilted, her feet, cute in white socks, were pointing toward him, flat on the couch. "Did you come for something in particular?"

He shook his own head back at her, lying, and covered her white socks with his own, enjoying the heat of her feet. It was a small intimate gesture that was all he could afford right now, when he wasn't sure how to get the words out of his mouth. "Norah?"

"Yes."

"I—" Okay, maybe not ready enough. But he tried again. "I—"

She waited.

He blurted, "I like being your friend, but—"

"But?" She tipped her head sideways and looked at him, clearly concerned.

He shook his head, thinking he might dislodge his heart from the back of his throat where it was making everything come out wrong. "Don't look so worried." He sighed. "All right, maybe you should look worried."

That only caused her face to reflect greater alarm. "TJ?"

"Norah, I love being your friend but I want to be your boyfriend." It wasn't what he'd intended, but close enough.

He watched her blink, wondering what was going through her mind. He could read the surprise right off her face.

After a moment she asked, "Like a date for national holidays?"

"More." *Like your lover, like 'the one', like you don't notice anyone but me.* But he didn't give voice to any of those thoughts.

Norah sucked in a breath. "TJ, I can't."

"Oh." He froze in place. She'd said 'no.' "Okay." He sucked in a breath of his own, forcing air into his system and knowing he had to get out of here, before . . . he didn't want to think about 'before' what. "Well, now that I've made an ass of myself, I'll be going. Good night."

He didn't know how he'd managed to make that last *good night* sound casual. Knowing it would sink in later, he headed for the door, only to feel her fingers on him. Both of her hands grasped at his and he tried to shake her off.

"TJ." She tugged at him, but he couldn't look.

"Norah, I have to go."

"TJ, don't look so hurt."

How was he supposed to look? But he didn't get it out before she spoke again.

"I can't be your fallback."

"What's that supposed to mean?"

She tugged at him, but he still refused to turn around, certain he couldn't look at her without . . .

"TJ, a little while ago you were in love with someone else. You asked me how to tell her."

He cracked a little, and wondered if this was his way in. TJ had believed that if she said 'no' he'd accept her answer and leave, but now, standing here, he'd take any way in he could get. "Would it make a difference if you were my first choice?"

Her voice was small. "Yes."

This time he rounded and found her eyes. She still sat on the edge of the couch, her hands tugging his, not willing to let him go. "You are my only choice. I asked because I didn't know how to tell you."

Her shock showed. "You didn't say anything!"

"Of course not! I was an idiot! I waited too long, then . . ." He sighed again, letting the pent up air out, and kept talking, because he was beginning to think *maybe.* "Then you were attacked, and all bruised up."

She bit her lip, her eyes falling closed, black lashes fanning her cheeks, black hair framing her face. For a moment he just looked, thinking he'd hold that picture of her in his mind, maybe forever. Her voice pushed him back. "I was pretty ugly."

"Don't go there, Norah." He grabbed her chin and her eyes popped open, startled by the touch. "You were never ugly. You were beat up and bruised and beautiful, and I didn't want to hurt you."

"You wouldn't have hurt me."

His hands went into his hair, only as he moved them did he feel her fingers sliding off his hand. "But I did hurt you. That morning, you were lying there on the ground and you put your arms out to me and the only thing I could think was that I wanted to kiss you. I *needed* to. You were covered in blood, and that's all I could think of. It wasn't even thought."

"You didn't."

"No. Because when I touched you, you said 'Ow'. So I didn't."

"Oh." She blinked again, her pretty blue eyes trying to make sense of it all. "Why now?"

"Because you're healed up."

"Couldn't kiss me when I was bruised? I wouldn't have minded." Her shoulders sank.

"I would have." He saw her jaw clench and fought to explain. He sank to his knees in front of her, finally believing he stood a chance if he could just get her to see. "It feels like so long since we were together, then we fought, and then . . . nothing." He didn't look at her, wasn't sure he could. "After all that, it was important that I didn't touch you and hurt you. I didn't want to have to be careful, and I didn't want to remind you of what he did. And I don't just want what we had back, I want more."

Norah's eyes searched him, but he understood she wasn't going to say anything.

His turn. Again. So he looked up, knowing everything showed in his face and there was nothing he could do for it. "Norah, is there any way you could give us a chance?"

One soft word emerged from her mouth. "Yes."

He smiled, feeling like the sun had opened inside him, and then did it again when she smiled back.

Her eyes turned liquid and heated him from the inside, her lower lip turned in and she chewed on it. She was nervous and it made him laugh, because he finally wasn't. His finger went up to her mouth, thinking he'd get her to stop, but when he touched her lip her mouth opened just a little and he knew he could do more.

CHAPTER 55

Norah watched in awe as this god, a god that she knew for certain was a man, kicked off his shoes again and stood over her. She knew her eyes went wide as he settled one knee on either side of her on the couch. His fingers found her hair and he tipped her back over the pillows. Something sweet and hot flooded her as his lips brushed across her mouth before he settled them over hers.

Norah kissed him back, her hands reaching for his shoulders and finding the hard strength of him under his soft t-shirt. The fabric and the familiar feel of him against her skin was comforting. The breath she sucked in when his tongue found hers wasn't. TJ leaned into her, fusing the front of himself to her, his mouth still seeking more.

When he pulled back, separating their mouths just a tiny bit, he left her feeling open to the elements, even though his body covered hers completely. His eyes found hers and, as she watched, turned a deeper shade of azure before he slowly found her mouth again and kissed her until she thought she'd melt into nothing.

But she didn't melt away. She stayed with him, breathing

him in and feeling the jolt of surprise that he did the same to her. His mouth and nose paused at the side of her face, buried in her hair, and she was so close she felt his chest expand. TJ rolled to the side, fitting her in between himself and the back of the couch, pressed even more fully against him.

Watching her with a small grin, he pulled her arms around his neck and fitted his own around her torso. A soft moan escaped his lips before he pressed them in tiny touches down her jaw and across her lips. Turning her face toward him she searched for more, but he smiled and stayed away from her mouth until she made a small frustrated sound. Then he dove at her lips, kissing her with a vengeance. Had she known that noise would cause that reaction she would have made it earlier. Their legs entangled and her hands found his hair, loving the feeling of touching him and of him wanting her to.

It seemed forever before he pulled himself away, even for just a little breathing room. TJ's breath came hard, and she could feel her own matching his. She felt heavy and weightless at the same time. She was oxygen starved and yet content. His hand came up to push her hair out of her face, and she couldn't remember the last time she'd felt this languid, this safe, this wanted. "Norah, there's something I didn't tell you."

"Uh-oh." But from the look in his eyes it wasn't anything to worry about.

He shook his head at her. "I just realized that I didn't really say it."

"Say what?"

"Norah, I love you."

In the center of her chest, her heart flipped over. Her eyes widened, and her mouth opened. She couldn't help it. He was right, he'd said everything except that.

He softly kissed the tip of her nose and her mouth, before pressing his own lips more firmly to hers, but Norah pulled her head away.

"I love you, too, TJ."

She had to laugh, he seemed so startled. This time he pulled back, looking at her. "Really? You don't have to—"

Grinning, she cut him off. "I love you, TJ."

It seemed to take him a moment to absorb it, so she gave it to him again, enjoying his reaction. "I love you, TJ."

This time he did kiss her, his tongue searching hers out and touching her deeper, now that she knew. He rolled over, taking her under him, one hand pulling at an errant couch pillow and tossing it away to make room for him to lay her flat. His hands wove into her hair, holding her to him. His hips shifted, finding a place between her legs.

They had been making out like teenagers, but it was suddenly steamier. She could feel the arousal he was no longer hiding. One hand slid under the cotton shirt she wore to undo the front clasp of her bra. He pushed the material out of the way, groaning into her mouth as his fingers found her breast, cupping and pressing her soft flesh.

His palm brushed her nipple, making her gasp out. As suddenly as he had started kissing her, he pulled back, but his hand didn't stop. His eyes searched her face while he touched her, his own expression growing hotter by the second. She knew he could see just what he did to her by the way she couldn't stop her mouth from moving even though no sound came.

He leaned back and pulled her up with him, rocking back on his heels, and finally to sitting on the couch. Putting two hands under her shirt on the skin of her ribcage, he straddled her on his lap. He held her against his unmistakable arousal, again causing her to draw a deep breath. His slightest movement sent shivers through her, and he seemed to know it.

TJ laced his fingers into her hair again, and this time pulled her down to him, the movement causing her pelvis to tilt, making her gasp as he met her mouth. This was a slower kiss, her eyes fell shut and her hands found his chest, landing where they fell and almost unable to move.

She didn't know how long they stayed like that, but his voice sent shivers up her, "Norah, I want you."

She answered with only one long breath.

He spoke again, "Are you going to invite me upstairs?"

That cooled her off just a bit. "I can't. My Dad's just down the hall . . . I—"

They'd be too noisy, she didn't think she could make love to him in her bed—

His voice was liquid like his eyes. "Then come back to my place with me." He laced his fingers through hers, but her eyes looked away.

She didn't know what to say. Only that she couldn't go. "My Dad wouldn't know where I was."

"Do you want to?" His eyes watched hers, waiting for an answer.

"Yes!" She felt tears coming at the backs of her eyes. The last time she'd slept with this man, he'd taken her places she hadn't been before. She just didn't know if she could handle what he was offering. "But I can't. Not tonight."

He nodded. "We could find a blanket and go out to the barn, find a clean stall, and have a real roll in the hay."

"Not tonight." Feeling she owed him an explanation, "I need a little time to get used to this."

"Okay. But if this isn't going any further, you have to get off me." He slipped his hands under her shirt, almost spanning her waist, and lifted her off.

For a moment she considered saying 'yes', just to get him to stay, but she bit back the tears and pushed out the words. "I guess you'd better go then."

TJ shook his head. "Do you *want* me to go?"

"You won't want to stay if we aren't going to—"

"Don't tell me what I want, Norah." He leaned over. "Our

tour bus pulls out for twelve days on Tuesday morning at five a.m. Unless you are telling me to go, what *I want* is to spend as much of that time as possible with you. However you want to spend it. If we can't go to your room or to mine then we could stay right here."

She blinked at him. "I can't have sex with you on this couch! My Dad could come downstairs at any moment!"

"I didn't say 'sex', Norah. I'd love that, but that's not going to happen and I'm not going home to my cold bed if I can be here with you."

She loved him and she hated him when he was like that. If he stayed, she was afraid he'd want more. But she didn't have it in her to push him away either, and she leaned her head onto his shoulder.

"I love you, Norah." His hand smoothed her hair, and something clenched around her heart.

"Thank you."

"For?"

"Being understanding." Her arms snaked around his neck, and she leaned in to kiss his cheek. TJ turned at the last moment, giving her his mouth. The kiss was both hot and reluctant. He leaned over, taking her with him, winding up on his back, with her drawn up beside him.

"Forgive me." His voice sounded tight, and he reached down to adjust the front of his pants.

"I'm sorry." She whispered.

"I'm not." His arms circled around her, and Norah let one leg sneak across his, tangling them and liking the feeling.

His hand came up to keep stroking her hair, her arms, her side down to her hip and back up. She sighed, enjoying the feeling of being touched, and the sensation that he just enjoyed touching her.

"I never really got to do this. The last time I slept next to you was just so scary."

Norah shook her head. "No, everything up until you crawled in with me was scary. After that I was okay. And you sang to me." She snuggled herself deeper, enjoying the feeling of his solid arms around her.

"Do you want me to sing to you now?"

"Hmmmm." It came out with a smile. "Do you remember what you sang last time?"

"Yes." There was an extra rumble in his chest, that let her know he was on the verge of laughing, and his next words confirmed that he knew what she'd been after. "I meant it."

Her chest squeezed, and his voice carried softly to her. Norah slipped into sleep and, not paying attention, a little deeper in love with him.

CHAPTER 56

Norah stood in front of the mirror in the smaller studio watching her form. She practiced turns knowing that her girls needed help and wondering what it was that she did that might help them.

That only lasted through two turns, instead she wound up spinning and thinking of TJ. Her father had come through the living room this morning while TJ still slept, his arms curled around her tightly enough that she wouldn't have been able to get up if she had wanted. Her Dad had grinned, "Crazy kids."

It was all she could do not to smile at her father and spout off, "I love him, Daddy." But her father already knew. He kneeled next to her and whispered, "He makes you happy?"

"Yes." The word had come so easy, so true.

Only after she heard her father leave, did TJ stir. He hugged her tighter and kissed her. "I'm glad I make you happy. Good morning."

Together they got up, TJ saying he had an early studio practice and had to go. He kissed her soundly, and told her he wanted to spend as much of the day with her as he could.

She'd showered and eaten breakfast and driven in to the

studio, all with a warm heart and a goofy smile. It was Monday, so she had classes tonight, but she'd see TJ before then.

She had worked her warmup through different muscle groups to her hips and was about to quit when his voice came from over her shoulder followed by an audible click from the closing door. "Morning again."

Her eyes leapt up to find him in the mirror, in his sock feet, his jacket hitting the ground and skidding to the far wall. Her stomach flipped over. "Hi."

TJ's smile matched his eyes, and he turned her to smoke. "Do that with your hips again, only wait until I'm holding you."

His hands circled her waist and his mouth found hers, right there in the middle of the studio. Norah moved her hips against him, enjoying his groan. Then his tongue touched hers and he leaned into the kiss, one of his thighs slipping between hers. She didn't resist and knew that half of the sighs were hers.

He pulled away. "I didn't come over here to pressure you. I'm sorry."

But Norah was having none of that. Her arms wrapped around his neck and she yanked closer. His mouth worked over her eyes and along her neck, while music played on in the background. He brushed aside the straps on her tank top, nibbling at her shoulders. Norah couldn't help the way she clung to him or that her head fell back to give him better access or how she leaned into his touch when he found her breasts. But when he pulled her shirt down further, exposing her, she brushed his hands away. "We can't do that here."

He looked around deviously, "Why not?"

She pointed even as she moved her shirt and straps back into place. "There's a window, and Mrs. Kenner will be in any minute, followed by a bunch of mothers with little babies for a pre-school movement class."

"If they have babies, then they'll understand." He reached for her and she ducked out of his grip, laughing, and shaking her head.

"Then come back to my place with me." His hand and his eyes reached out for her, and Norah didn't know what it was, but something made her stop. Her mouth opened to tell him 'no,' but the sound didn't come. She pressed her back against the mirror wondering what was wrong, why she was shaking.

"Norah, you look scared."

She nodded, only with his words recognizing the emotion behind the chill.

"Norah? Is there something I need to know? Is it because of that morning at the track?"

Now it was him looking scared, and so worried, immediately she shook her head. "No, it's not that."

"You've been with me before, can you trust me? I won't hurt you." Slowly he moved toward her, a worry-frown marring his perfect features, his blue eyes dark this time with concern rather than heat.

"I know that." Her heart raced as though it might actually get away. She wanted to hand it over to this man, but she was so scared. A whisper was all she could find. "The last man I loved died on me."

He smiled, compassion and relief warring in it, "I'm not going anywhere."

Fear-anger flooded her. "You can't promise that! You don't know."

"You're right." He nodded. His hand found his face and scrubbed as though that might make thoughts form. "The irony is a year ago I would have believed I *could* promise that, but a year ago you would never have loved me. I already love you, so it's going to hurt like hell if something happens to you. Why is it going to be worse if we make love?"

"Because," Her eyes pulled away from him, knowing what

she was about to reveal. "The last time I made love to you, I fell a little more in love."

"Last time? You were in love with me then?" His voice held a note of wonder.

She nodded, looking at him only when he put his hand against her face and turned it to him, bringing his own face near. "Me, too."

His eyes searched for something over her shoulder and she wondered what it was until he leaned his mouth closer to her ear, "And I fell more in love with you at the hospital, and that night curled up with you in bed, and last night, too. Making love isn't the only thing that does it."

Norah knew that, her eyes squeezed closed when he looked at her. "I know that. It isn't rational. But one hundred percent of the men I have loved have died on me."

"Do you love me?"

"Yes." It was so fierce, so fast, and so deep, she realized she was slipping further even now.

"Then you're wrong. I'm still here." She felt rather than saw him plant one hand on either side of her head on the mirror. "I'm not leaving this world willingly. Knowing what it's like to be in love with you, I'll bet Jeff didn't either. What I do know, is that if I have to die, or god forbid, you do, I want to know that I spent every moment I could with you, making you happy, making us happy."

Her lips turned in and she chewed on them in an attempt to distract her eyes from making tears. It didn't work. Two fat drops slipped out and down her cheeks.

"Norah," He sighed and kissed them away. "I've had a rough time since June. I've learned how much abuse my body can take, and how much abuse my heart can take, and all I want to learn now is how much you can love me."

"So much." Her arms wound around his neck and she pressed herself to him. "Too much."

He grinned, "Not possible." Then turned serious. "You need to take time to think about it, and get used to it and I understand that. But I also understand you could spend forever thinking about it and not deciding. There's always the possibility we'll both live to be a hundred."

Her heart turned over in her chest and she wondered if he meant to imply that he'd still be with her then. That he might want that.

But TJ kept talking. He pushed away from her and held his right hand out to her, palm up. "My offer's here, whenever you're ready to just take that chance with me, you let me—"

She slapped her hand into his before she could change her mind and even as she did it she felt the bands around her chest tightening, squeezing. "Let's go."

He tugged at her hand, picking up his jacket and settling it around her shoulders and kissing her soundly. Norah snapped twice at the CD player, shutting it off. He laughed "That's cool."

They ran into Mrs. Kenner as they passed through the lobby holding hands. Norah said a brief hello and Mrs. Kenner pointed out that she might want to change out of her ballet shoes before she went out.

Norah felt the heat creep up her cheeks, but broke contact with TJ to rush into the office and grab her purse and street shoes. She reappeared into a chilly wind that did nothing to cool the heat between them. When he had her enclosed in the passenger side and he'd slid into the driver's seat, he turned to her, "I want you so much."

She felt the smile and another blush creeping across her cheeks as he threw the car in reverse and made his way out of the parking lot. Norah shifted in her seat and felt a bag against her feet. Looking down she realized TJ waving at her for it. "What is it?"

"Condoms."

"Condoms!" The bag was full. "What? Did you buy out the store?"

He looked a little red at that one. "Just about. I didn't want another accident, so I checked all the expiration dates."

She laughed at him. "That's romantic."

"You not fleeing afterward and holding back important information is romantic."

She still felt bad about that. "That's not going to happen again. I promise."

"Thank you."

"I'm on the pill." At his expression, she explained. "The doctor wouldn't give me the morning after pill without my consenting to a better form of birth control. So you don't need these." She tossed the whole bag into the back seat.

"This day keeps getting better. Now if I could just do something about the fact that I have been aching, in physical pain, for you for—" he checked his watch. "about thirty-nine hours."

She frowned, "You only showed up last night. I know it feels like longer, but you're off by about a day."

"Oh, please don't be mad at me, baby, but I have to tell you something."

She was apprehensive about what he might say, but nothing damped the heat in her.

"I went over to your house two nights ago."

"No, you didn't."

"Yeah, that's just it, I did." He took a turn, and she could almost physically feel them getting closer to his house, his bed. "I wanted to tell you, but you didn't answer the door."

"Oh!" She said she'd been dancing, and probably hadn't heard.

He looked chagrinned. "I know. I went around back, but you didn't see me. Then I thought you saw me through the window, and that you'd come get the door for me when you finished the song. It took a couple of songs to realize that you couldn't see me at all. I kept thinking I'd go around front and pound on the door after just one more dance—"

Her heart picked up time, if that was possible. *Oh God.* "What did you see?"

He sighed, "I came in at a Tim McGraw song and saw *I am* and I couldn't leave, because it was a Wilder song, and I'd never seen you really dance before, and—"

"And you left?"

He nodded. "Later, after that song about falling for the devil."

This time she said it. "Oh, God."

His chest started moving faster, even though they hadn't touched or anything. He almost missed a turn, "'Oh God' is right. Norah it was so hot, I, I get turned on just thinking about it. I want you to move like that for me, but naked."

She laughed.

"Don't laugh, baby. I've been in pain."

"I'm sorry. You poor thing. You've had a bad time these last months, and now this."

His hand reached across the gearshift as soon as he waved to the guard at the gate. "That's not what I said. I said I've had a *rough* time. I also fell in love with you, and got to make love to you, and intend to do it many times again. I got to perform Queen in Central Park and I grew up. It's been hard, but not all bad."

He parked the car at a sloppy angle in the garage and came around quickly to pull her out of the passenger seat. Closing the door, TJ backed her up against it, his mouth finding hers and fusing. He pressed himself to her and when he finally came up for air, she laughed. "I can feel your pain."

He growled at her, pulling her along, tugging his jacket off her at the same time. He ditched it just inside the entry, and somehow kissed her senseless while he led her up the stairs. When the door to his bedroom opened she was shocked to find her shirt was already half off, straps dangling low across her arms.

As TJ pushed the door shut behind them and locked it, her eyebrows raised.

"JD has a key and so does the maid, and there's a realtor."

"You're selling?" She was shocked, but not for long.

"Yes. Shh!" His mouth worked magic on hers and his fingers tugged the strap of her top down setting one breast free. "God, you don't wear a bra with these."

She started to laugh, but his mouth closed over the tip of her breast and she sucked in air. Her chest expanded with that, and pushed her further into his mouth. TJ took advantage and Norah moaned.

She tried to even the score a little and tugged at his t-shirt, but her hands were ineffectual from the onslaught of sensations he sent through her. She only managed to get the hem untucked before he took pity on her and grinned. Reaching over his shoulders to his back he grabbed at the shirt, tugging it up and over his head. Norah figured two could play at that game and worked the stretchy top off. She was dropping it to the side when he emerged from under his shirt, his grin faded and his eyes went dark as the t-shirt hit the ground. "God, Norah, you are so beautiful."

Her whole body melted against the wall at his words. This from the man with those muscles, those blue-blue eyes, and that sinful mouth. "I could say the same thing about you."

He shook his head, "No."

She grinned, her fingers coming up his arms and loving the feeling of strength there, "Yes. Shh!" Standing on her toes brought her chest to his and cemented the deep feeling that this was exactly where she belonged, in the circle of this man's arms.

His hands skimmed her naked back leaving trails of heat. He pushed her against the wall, again lavishing attention on her now bare breasts. Her hands and mouth found his chest, and she enjoyed the way he quivered under her touch. TJ retaliated by sliding his fingers under the waistband of her warm-up shorts and tights.

He shook his head. "Tights, the new bane of my existence."

Norah laughed at him, while he kneeled in front of her and tugged the clothing down.

His breathing changed audibly. "You're not wearing underwear."

"Of course not."

"Oh, I have changed my mind about the tights."

She would have laughed, but he was reverently peeling them down her legs leaving her entirely bare. Tossing the tights aside, he grabbed each ankle and tugged her feet wider apart. Before she could say anything, he was on his knees in front of her, kissing and nibbling at her belly, and ruining any hope of steady breathing. His hands ran up and down her legs, making her go weak when his thumb found the center of her.

"TJ!" She couldn't get enough air, and she looked down only to find him staring back up, enjoying seeing the way his touch made her move. Then his head ducked and his tongue joined his fingers as Norah's hands found his head.

It was the only part of him she could reach. Her own head tipped back against the wall. She couldn't see anything but stars and didn't know if she'd gone blind or was squeezing her eyes shut so tight in an effort to survive the feelings crashing over her. His tongue laved at her until she came with something between a moan and a scream, and collapsed down the wall.

His arms caught her and he picked her up as though she weighed nothing. He turned, pulling back the comforter before he laid her down, and she slid like syrup across the sheets. Languid, she watched him while he unbuckled his belt and slipped out of his pants and underwear all in one motion. He was rock hard and ready for her, and Norah found the energy to reach out to him as he crawled the few feet across the bed toward her. He was hot to the touch and moaned each time she stroked him.

His knees planted between her legs, and he kissed her breasts, arousing her again, while she struggled to keep him in hand. With a tug, she brought him where she wanted him, and TJ took his weight on his elbows as he nudged at the very core of her.

She arched, bringing her hips closer, trying to take him in, but TJ held back.

"Norah." His hands found the side of her face, and he kissed her long and hard. When he stopped, she lay beneath him, eyes closed, writhing, waiting. She could feel him, poised, ready, but TJ didn't enter her. After a moment she opened her eyes to see what he wanted.

His thumbs stroked her cheeks, "Look at me." His deep blue eyes turned midnight, and he stared right into her while he finally pressed home in one long surge, taking her breath away.

Both of them were breathing through their mouths, lips open, unable to look away as they joined. TJ sank himself inside her completely, his own eyes widening as he did, and Norah knew she was an open book. Her face was a mirror of his own wonder at finding her.

He moved within her, setting up a steady rhythm that she worked to meet. Just the sight of him fighting so hard for just a little more sent her over the edge. Even so, his hands held the sides of her face, keeping her gaze on his, so she saw when he finally slipped beyond his limits and let the feelings dominate him entirely.

His eyes closed as his orgasm at last ended, leaving both of them clinging through the aftershocks. His arms were steel bands around her, holding her pressed close against him, their chests heaving together, their bodies drawing in the same air.

TJ rolled to his side taking her with him. Their legs tangled, and he pushed her hair out of her face before reaching back and tugging the covers up and over them. Still his breathing was heavy, but he managed words. "This is what I want right now. I have waited an eternity for this."

Norah pressed her cheek against his chest, and her fingers along his ribcage enjoying the feel of him against her skin. Then her fingers found a small smooth line in his side. The knife wound. "Does it still hurt?"

"No." His finger traced the scar down the front of her chest, "Yours?"

She shrugged. "Unless I see it, I don't even remember it's there. But you look like yours tugs once in a while."

"It does. But it was worth it."

Her fingers traced the scar again. "Thank you. You saved me."

"Then we're even." He took her hand and led it up to the base of his neck. He placed her fingers along the vertebra there. Norah could feel two more small scars and tiny bumps under the skin that were the permanent screws holding together the bone he'd broken.

She sighed against him, hoping it was true. Because she could think of no other way to pay him back for putting himself in the path of a madman.

Again he reached back to the side of the bed, this time producing an alarm clock. "When do you need to leave to get ready for work?"

She tried to calculate traffic and a shower, "Four-thirty."

"Okay. I'm setting the alarm. Just in case we fall asleep, or just aren't paying attention to the time." He grinned that wicked-angel grin at her, and she felt herself slipping further.

He dipped his head to hers, kissing her softly, stroking her hair, and holding her close. "You know, you were right. It happened."

"What did?"

"I fell a little more in love with you just now." He grinned. "Did you maybe fall a little more for me?"

Norah shook her head and sighed, "No."

"Oh." He stilled.

"A lot."

CHAPTER 57

TJ tossed and turned and checked the clock. Midnight.

Even the clock reminded him of Norah. Not eight hours ago, it had gone off, waking him with her locked in his arms, and reminding them both that she had to go. He'd said as long a good-bye as he could. She wasn't going to be home until well after ten, and he had to be up before the crack of dawn.

It was all a well and good plan. Except it was based on him being asleep. He was here in his big bed by himself, and she was there in her bed by herself. Hopefully she was sleeping. It was the only way them being apart was accomplishing anything.

TJ rolled over pushing his face into his pillow and suffered again. The other thing, the part he hadn't counted on at all, was that the whole bed smelled like her. How was he supposed to sleep with the scent of Norah clinging to everything? Oh, and the bed smelled like sex, too. And his sheets now triggered sense memories of Norah's skin against his. Norah laid out naked on the sheets, the first time he'd carried her over and she'd melted against them. And the second time when he'd thrown back the covers because she'd rolled away from him, then rubbed that hot little ass against him.

Yup. No sleep at all.

He packed everything after she'd left to teach class. Again operating under the false impression that sleep would find him tonight. He thought about getting up and fixing himself a whiskey sour, thinking the alcohol might put him to sleep. But lying there with his hands behind his head and his memories all around him, he realized that he hadn't touched the stuff since before his accident. He'd had two beers at different times in New York and a few out with Norah and that was it.

For a moment, he simply took stock of the changes.

The first was that he wasn't drinking. Not that he'd been bad before. Immediately he amended that. Anyone who didn't react fast enough to get out of the way of a semi when he should have been able to, had been bad.

Second, was the learning to walk again. That had required a level of determination even he hadn't realized he had. And that from a man who had ditched everything and lived fairly hand-to-mouth for a long time just to get started in the music business. Although, that had been four of them. He'd been the last piece of the band to fall into place. So of the four he'd had the least struggles. Also, when things had been tough, they had been four together, and they decided together. Re-learning to walk had just been him.

The third thing was falling in love with Norah. He didn't think he'd been man enough to do it before the accident. He was pretty certain she would have laughed at that TJ and walked away without a care if that man had hit on her. That was a sobering thought. If not for that semi, he'd have seen Norah sooner or later, and she would have never known she was the love of his life.

Fourth, he'd saved her from a horrible fate at the hands of her attacker. It had taken a while to believe that, and he still only believed it in part. If he'd been there or even just been earlier, maybe that bastard never would have come after her.

But Norah had a comeback for everything he said. If she hadn't been attacked, the man wouldn't be behind bars. When she told it, TJ saved far more than her.

Fifth, he'd started writing and found a whole new path to his music. He was a performer, and he was a better one now. He had a big job on this tour to keep improving. It was like being in the chair and knowing he could get up and walk, but not that far. He still had a way to go.

He had scars commemorating the first and fourth things. A great review from the Central Park show, and an invite to perform with the remaining members of Queen that he'd turned down. No matter what the offer, and even though JD had encouraged him to do it, he was loyal to Wilder. Besides, it was obvious from contemplations that he already had too much on his plate. Norah had changed all of him. He wasn't grumpy or bitter or jealous of his brother anymore. Even before they'd fessed up their feelings to each other, he was laughing more and just being better to the people around him.

He didn't want the whiskey sour and he could really only think of one thing that he was certain would make him fall asleep. With a deep sigh he decided to go get it. He had four hours.

Twenty minutes later, he was in his sneakers, flannel pajama pants, and his leather jacket standing just below her window bouncing tiny pebbles off the glass. *Norah, Norah, come on. Wake up.*

Finally, the curtains moved, her hand splayed against the window in what he recognized was a gesture to get him to stop throwing the rocks. He obliged, dumping the rest of the handful back into the rose bed and grinning up at her sleepy face as she poked it out the window. "TJ."

"I missed you, baby."

She grinned, slow and easy, and yawned. "I missed you, too."

"I have four hours and two options. You come out with me or I come up there."

She blinked and he waited, wishing he hadn't dumped all the little rocks so he'd have something to fidget with.

Her voice carried softly down to him. "How are you going to get up here?"

Laughing, TJ told her he'd already figured that out. "Up the front porch post, across the roof and in your window."

The arch of her eyebrows revealed she was both awake and disbelieving. He thought she might make him do it just to see if he could.

He saw her sigh, then she pulled back and closed the window. When the curtains closed, he got really concerned. Had he offended her? TJ went to the rose bed to grab a handful of pebbles to start another assault when the front door opened. Norah stood there in her men's underwear and mussed hair and wide eyes. He couldn't help the smile that spread across his face. Nor could he help that it got wider when she impatiently motioned him inside.

He crossed the threshold, and she carefully closed and locked the door behind him. "You have to be quiet."

Grabbing her, he kissed her with eight hours of pent up longing. His tongue searched her surprised mouth and his hands slipped under the hem of the t-shirt.

She smacked at his hands playfully. "TJ! Upstairs. At least wait until the door is locked." She turned and headed up the stairs and he followed, watching the way her hips swayed as she climbed the steps. He tried to pay attention when she turned and pointed out a few squeaks. But her long bare legs were distracting.

He didn't make it half a second after he closed the door and hit the lock button. He shrugged out of his jacket revealing his bare chest and making Norah laugh that she had her very own stripper. He asked if he could have his very own stripper too, so Norah grinned and peeled her shirt.

TJ wanted to touch her, but instead sent her to set the alarm for four-thirty a.m. Less than four hours. He enjoyed watching her walk around in nothing but the clingy shorts. He begged her to dance for him, and she did, just a little. That was all he could handle before he removed the last of their clothes, pulled her down into the sheets, and pushed into her.

Afterward they clung together, knowing he'd leave shortly, and she fell asleep there in his arms. He re-set the alarm for three-thirty then, wanting to make love to her again before he left.

The alarm buzzed at him almost instantly, waking him as the sound switched to radio. It just had to be his voice coming out at him. TJ whacked at the clock, making himself stop crooning to them, then he grabbed it with two hands and re-set it for four-thirty before rolling over and kissing the back of her neck. Her head rested on his curled arm and she'd spooned in tight against him, and he intended to take every advantage of that.

She was blinking from being rudely awakened by the buzzing. "Do you have to go?"

He kissed her jaw and her shoulder. "In an hour." He kissed down her spine, and moved his hands up her sides, brushing against the swells of her breasts and charging his lust from he-wanted-her to he-had-to-have-her. Norah tried to turn to face him, but he held her in place while he touched her and made certain she was ready for him. In a few minutes she was arching back against him, and he wanted to take longer but he couldn't.

He pushed into her from behind with a groan at how good she felt, hot and wet against him.

"Shhhh!" The shushing turned into a moan in her mouth as he reached around and used his fingers to encourage her to move against him more. Norah obliged, and TJ found himself fighting back loud sounds as he came with Norah bucking against him.

They made love one more time before he left. She kissed him at the front door in the glow of the yellow porch light. Everything beyond was dark, and it felt wrong to be leaving her like this. "You just clear your calendar when I get back, okay?"

"Oh, all right." She laughed.

"Listen, this is what happened when I missed you for eight *hours*. I'm going to be gone for twelve *days*."

She nodded at him. "The planet may crack in half."

"It just might." He grabbed the back of her neck and kissed her soundly again before forcing himself to get in his car and drive away.

He had about twenty minutes to get from the farmhouse to the studio and without traffic, *who else was up at this ungodly hour?* It only took him fifteen.

Craig was already there, his luggage probably already on the bus. TJ squinted at his friend, the easy comfort on Craig's face something he was only just now understanding. Craig and Shay had been up and down for a long time before they figured things out. TJ hadn't understood—until now.

JD was the one who was late. He appeared, looking sheepish and freshly showered, and offered a half-assed apology. TJ made a point to keep his mouth shut. His brother had been up to the same business he had. Only this time it made him happy. Happy for his brother, and happy to see that in seven years he and Norah might still be after each other.

They were all ushered onto the new bus. Their money from album sales had bought them a better bus, but it was still a bus, still taking him away from Norah. Feeling maudlin, TJ tucked himself into his room at the far back and passed out.

When he woke up, the first thing he did was miss Norah. So the second thing he did was call her, but he only got her voicemail. When they'd started touring, they had sometimes done two and even three shows a day, playing festivals and county fairs during the afternoons and opening for bigger groups at night.

But there were no more corn dog fairs, Wilder was too big, and often it was their name headlining the night shows. So they were often still on stage at midnight. Unless he called late, he was going to miss Norah today.

He scraped himself together and went out and put on a good show. It wasn't great though—he could do better.

His cell phone contained a message from her when he got back into his room, but it didn't say he could call late, so he didn't. Eventually he slept.

The next morning, he tried several times to make sure he got a hold of her, and then went around with a goofy grin on his face for the remainder of the day. He didn't care until just prior to that evening's show, when he still wasn't paying much attention, and Craig came up to him, bass guitar slung over his shoulder. "You ready?"

Shit. It hadn't been about Norah before. Not when things weren't going according to plan, but now, when she loved him, he'd almost stopped caring about his performance.

He was the front man. He had to talk and connect with the audience; the others were hidden behind instruments.

Rubbing the heels of his hands to his eyes, TJ tipped his head back and tried to let his brain settle into his current reality. Norah was waiting for him when he got home. Here he was obligated to perform. If he didn't, Wilder's touring days were going to go downhill real fast. It was already his fault that half the year was lost.

He had to get his head in gear. He had to set Norah aside and focus.

He also latched onto his previous thoughts about connecting with the audience. He'd managed to connect with sections of it really well. Recently his performances had been about what he was thinking and feeling, and there was only minimal connection to the people out in front of him. He needed to combine the two and, like at the Troubadour, get beyond those first clusters, find the people along the back walls.

With his brain firmly in his head, TJ made his way out on stage, and put on one of the best shows of his life. He even had a good time doing it.

Norah called the next day, but he didn't listen to the message. He *had* to keep his head on straight. She called the next day as well, and he let it ring, thinking it would be saner to listen to the message and leave her one in return than to get lost in a real phone call. So he listened to the two banked messages that night and left one in exchange when he was certain she would be at dance.

She didn't call the next day. And just the feeling of let-down he experienced was enough to convince him that he had to wait it out. The following day he got another call that he again let ring through, even though he gritted his teeth to do it. He listened to her sweet voice telling him she missed him and she wished she could actually talk to him. His heart turned over.

CHAPTER 58

Norah suffered through not talking to TJ. Now there was a wall of time and real distance between them.

She was counting days until he returned and praying things would be the same. Norah wasn't foolish enough to believe in guarantees of the heart, and he'd made her none. He'd come close, insinuated a lot, but she couldn't say for certain that he even knew he was talking in long-terms a lot of the time.

The last message she'd left him, she'd jokingly said "If I didn't know better I'd think you were avoiding me."

Now she didn't think she could go in and teach class. A text message had popped up on her phone; basically, he *was* avoiding her. He said he couldn't keep his head on straight when he was thinking about her. He loved her, but she shouldn't call.

What the hell was that about?!?

Norah sat with the phone in her hand and looked through the abysmally long message again. The 'I love you' was clear, in exactly those words. So was 'don't call.'

Somehow she made it through her classes. At least she'd done this often enough she could function on autopilot. Then she trudged home to her father who was watching TV. He put the program on pause the instant he saw her. "What's wrong, honey?"

She shrugged. It was all she could think of.

He tried again. "Want to talk about it?"

Yes.

"No." She'd promised. It was the right thing to do. TJ hadn't cut her off completely, he had said that he loved her. Besides, her Dad would probably tell her it was her fault and what she could do about it.

So she showered and went to bed, and thought about crying herself to sleep but couldn't quite muster it. She was just too puzzled.

Somehow the next days passed. She did as she was asked and didn't call. Questions rattled around in her head, causing headaches. Had she been such a horrible conversationalist? Too clingy? Was it all just overwhelming to him? He always talked about the time before his accident as though he'd been some teenager until just recently. He couldn't have been that immature; he had a house and bills and amazing career that had taken some serious work without any promise of payoff.

Norah, who considered herself usually sane and steady, wandered the days not knowing what to do. She got worse as TJ's arrival into town neared, and she was supremely grateful when Mark showed up just as planned.

The knock on her door was a welcome distraction.

She opened it, amazed to see a buff, ripped man standing on the other side. "Mark!?"

He grabbed her and swung her in a huge circle. "Oh, baby, we both look better. You've gained some weight, too." He set her back and looked her up and down. "It looks good on you."

"Wow!" She had to put her hands up and feel the muscles in his arms. He'd always been strong, he had to be to spend his days lifting women over his head, but now it had some bulk, not just whipcord lean strength.

He looked around the farmhouse for a minute. "Is your Dad here? I remember him."

"Of course you do. He came all the time after Jeff and Jordan died."

Mark quit looking at the house and tilted his blonde head at her, his short hair perfect like his creased pants and clingy shirt. "You said it."

"Yeah, I can now. And, no, Daddy's out with his girlfriend tonight."

His arm came out around her shoulders. "I'm proud of you, you know." He led her back out to his gold Lexus, graciously handing her into the passenger seat in a move that harkened back to the days when they danced together. "So, tell me about your dance studio."

She laughed, "It's kids. The youngest are in pre-school and the oldest in high school. It's a double pirouette crowd. But I like it. I have a small company that performs locally."

Over lobster, he told her about his school in L.A. No performances, but he'd sent a handful of dancers back to audition for the Houston Ballet and two had made it, a few more had gone on to other companies. It was clear that he was moving in higher circles than she. Norah braced for the envy or acid that she expected to taste in the back of her mouth. But none came. At some point it had become okay to not be competitive. She finally realized that she *liked* her school. She *liked* helping the high school girls learn to stick their turns, even if none of them would continue with it after they left her school.

Mark told her about his love life and asked after hers. Norah put the napkin down and started at the beginning of the summer. She didn't finish the story until they were seated in the front of the theater with champagne glasses in hand.

"Really?" Mark was fascinated. "Wilder's lead singer?"

Norah had to laugh, and she sipped the champagne

attempting to stay clear of the bubbles. "It's not like that, I've known him since we were kids. We had Sunday dinner at each other's houses."

"Yeah, but it doesn't change the fact that teenage girls have posters of him on their wall."

Norah almost spit the champagne. She didn't know whether to laugh or just be stunned. That thought had never occurred to her. And Mark saw it.

"What? He's just good ole TJ to you?"

"No, he's just TJ with women throwing themselves at him while he's on tour."

That brought raised eyebrows. "And you trust him?"

"Yeah." She didn't mention the phone messages or that she hadn't spoken to him in days. He was due back tomorrow morning. Norah was grateful when the lights went down.

As she suspected, the performance was more than riveting enough to keep her brain out of TJ-mode while she watched. After the show she had to deal with the fact that, while she'd been sipping, Mark had been throwing back drink after drink, and asking questions about dating a rock star.

Norah had laughed and said he was a country star, while she slipped the valet ticket away from him. She paid for the car and tipped, and slid into the driver's seat, listening to Mark while he tuned up a local pop station and yelled "ha!" when Wilder was the third song they heard.

CHAPTER 59

TJ sat in the car with the window cracked, he wanted to hear when she pulled up. He was sitting, waiting, just beyond the glow of the porch light. Initially, he'd parked back here because he wanted to surprise her.

He'd seen her car in the driveway and raced up the front steps to knock excitedly only to get no answer. He persisted, knowing he was early: Norah wasn't expecting him until tomorrow morning. The theater where Wilder had been scheduled to play tonight had suffered an electrical fire, and the show was postponed. It was yet another tour date to tack onto spring, but right now he was glad to be home early.

He had to explain about the phone calls, about how his head wasn't clear when he was thinking about her. He'd knocked on every door, looking for his chance to talk to her and been disappointed by every silent answer.

TJ had the key in the engine and was cranking it, ready to give up and leave, when he remembered that she'd invited him out to see some dance company with her friend. The name of the dance company hadn't stuck, but 'Mark' sure had. Why couldn't this friend have been 'Melissa'?

He realized 'Mark' must have driven and they'd left Norah's car here, so TJ decided to wait her out. Out of the light he dozed a little off and on, waking when cars went by down on the road, but none of them turned into her driveway.

He considered the possibility that her father would be the first one home, and figured there was no explanation like the truth. It was eleven, and he dozed again. This time the headlights did swing into the driveway, and TJ sat up with anticipation, trying not to think how disappointed he'd be if it were her dad.

Stopping right at the front porch, the sedan swung in a perfect arc to back up against the house. It stood aimed and ready to go.

He was surprised to see Norah pop out of the driver's seat, laughing. Her head went back and her throat was exposed to the moonlight, her hair falling in sweet waves over her shoulders. Her blue dress clung to every curve and wrapped across the front, revealing what he knew to be perfect cleavage. The fabric swirled around her legs in a slight wind he hadn't noticed before.

She so distracted him that he was surprised by the blond man, handsome and sharply dressed, coming around the front of the hood. The voice was like honey and he approached very close to her. TJ heard every word through the space he'd left at the top of his window. "Norah, baby, do you have any wine? And will you drink it with me?"

Her smile was wide and genuine. "I believe I do!"

The end of her sentence was lost as the man scooped her up in a dance move that only a professional could accomplish, lifting her high overhead. Norah hit form, moving with him and laughing as she clung to him.

A shot of jealousy pierced him straight through. And his hand flew to the door handle, ready to leap out and protest.

He looked at himself for just a moment, dark where this

man was blonde. He was rumpled and sloppy where this man was sharp and creased. And there was no denying that this man was very good looking. Norah seemed to have eyes only for him.

She was on her feet again, but they had their arms around each other in a way that spelled familiarity. TJ froze. He didn't get the door open. Her words from so long ago came back to haunt him. *I'm a slut*. He hadn't believed it, thinking that she had slept around, but not that she'd cheat on him.

His brain worked far too fast for his own good. Jeff and Jordan had died right after she joined the Houston Ballet, she had said a year later she found sex to console herself. Wouldn't that mean with some of her fellow dancers?

As TJ watched, the man's hand slipped down to her hip, in a gesture that he himself had never done on a woman he wasn't already sleeping with or very close to it. Norah did nothing to discourage him as they headed up the steps.

Norah's voice carried back to him soft and sweet.

"You should stay tonight. You can have the other side of my bed."

TJ felt it hit him like daggers.

Norah looked at her watch, it was past noon and she'd expected TJ in around ten. She'd gotten a sub for this morning's company class, thinking that she wanted to be available when he got in. Now she was glad she was available because she was getting mad and bewildered and wanted to ask him what the hell he'd been thinking.

He hadn't called. Hadn't said the band was running late, and she wasn't going to call, as he'd asked her not to. Mark had left around eight to hit his hotel room to shower and make his plane on time. He'd stood on the front porch in rumpled clothes, finally sober, and told her how wonderful it was to see her again.

So she was sitting on the couch in her jeans and flats and a long sleeved tee, with her keys in her hand trying to decide what to do.

Norah eyed the keys, realizing she'd already made the decision. She went out the front door, seeing her Dad turn in at the bottom of the drive. She waved to him as she pulled out, putting her window down.

He climbed out of his car, "Going over to TJ's?"

She nodded.

Her Dad smiled at her. "Just call if you aren't coming home tonight, okay? I'll see you when I see you."

Norah nodded again, not sure what words she could say. She had a sinking feeling that something had gone wrong, but she didn't know what. She'd suffered through the I-love-you-but-don't-call message and all the waiting. Her chest felt like her eyes did right before she cried.

She managed to stay calm enough to get to his place. She waved at the guard, and he immediately opened the gates for her.

Well, at least TJ hadn't locked her out yet.

Then again, it had taken a good several months for him to take Anna Lee's name off the list. Norah was downright nervous when she pulled up. His gate stood open, and she had to wonder if he was expecting her.

Her brain clicked. If the gate was open, he was home.

Or maybe the maid had come.

She put the car in park, her heart lost in the cavity of her chest as she climbed the three steps up to the double front doors. With her bottom lip between her teeth, she rang the bell and waited.

She heard footsteps and braced herself, hoping it was him and he'd be happy to see her.

The door opened and TJ stood there with a jar of peanut butter in one hand. He just looked at her. "Norah."

No happy hugs, and she had no idea what was wrong.

"You're home."

"It would appear that way." He didn't step back or invite her in.

Norah took a step toward him, forcing the issue. It would have been far too rude to not allow her in, and yet he seemed so indifferent. "I thought you would call when you got in."

TJ stayed in the front entrance. "So did I."

She was just so puzzled, and it didn't help that his eyes glanced away and back, and when they found hers he had lost the façade of non-concern. He looked wounded.

"TJ—"

"Norah, there's something you have to tell me." He cut her off before she could say anything, before she could reach her arms out and touch him.

"What? That I love you? I would have been telling you that all week except you didn't want me to call. I don't understand this." Her hands hung useless at her sides.

"I think I do." He looked at the marble of the floor for a moment, the fountain making an almost peaceful sound while she waited. But Norah waited at the cliff's edge.

"I cut you off. I thought I had to keep performing. So you went elsewhere."

She frowned at him.

"I know, Norah!" He showed real emotion for the first time. "I know what you did. Please, just admit it. Let's get past this. I love you."

Her hands went out, palm up, "Admit what?"

TJ slammed the peanut butter down on the small entryway table behind him. He leaned back against it, gripping the edges so tightly he turned his knuckles white. "I got home early, I went to your house last night to surprise you. I got surprised instead. I saw you."

"Saw me what? You saw Mark? I invited you along to that."

His face turned red and angry, "You slept with him! I saw you!"

"But I didn't." She was still bewildered. Even if he'd seen her, all he could have seen was them getting out of the car, and there'd been no sex there.

"Norah, I saw you two together." His voice was calmer now, but pleading. "We never said we were exclusive, so that's my fault. I love you, I want us to get past this."

"I do, too, but I don't know what you're talking about."

"Just admit that you slept with him!"

"But I *didn't*." She'd said the same line before and he hadn't believed her. "Why do you think I did?"

"I saw you. I saw the way he touched you, and you invited him into bed with you." The last words were hard for him to get out, but he got angry again. "I want you back."

"You've got me."

"Not while you're lying to me!" He turned and stalked off into the kitchen.

Almost against her better judgment Norah followed. "I'm not lying."

He stood facing the counter, his hands braced, his back straighter than she'd ever seen it, and a horrible thought occurred to her. An old saying her father liked, *we can only see in others what we have in ourselves*. She only ever thought of it in terms of herself, but now she was afraid. He'd even pointed it out, *we never said we were exclusive.* "Is this about you, TJ? Is this because you cheated on me and so that's what you saw?"

He whipped around so fast he probably hurt himself. "I didn't cheat on you. *I* was faithful." His eyes bored into hers and there was a world of pain in there.

She could save him all that pain if he'd just listen. She tried saying the words *she* wanted to hear. They were true, her heart flooded with relief. "I believe you."

His voice was low and ironic. "Of course you do. *I'm* telling the truth."

He might as well have slapped her. "If that was the criteria, then you'd believe me, too. I believe you because I trust you."

"You can call any one of them. JD, Alex, Craig, Ben who drives the bus! Every single one of them will tell you I was faithful to you." His eyes blinked too much and the color in his cheeks told her how upset he was, but she was working up a righteous mad herself.

But she had to laugh at that one. "Please, TJ. My sister would call me six shades of stupid if I said 'he was faithful, his band mates swear he was.' I think junior high is the last time us girls stopped believing when guys had their friends vouch for them."

He looked affronted, but Norah continued. "I believe you because I *trust* you! You could try trusting me, too."

"How can I trust you when I saw you? When I saw the way he touched you, and you let him. When you told him to sleep in your bed with you? You slept with him."

"Okay, I did!" She blurted, "I actually slept, as in *sleep,* in the same bed as him. There was no sex, in fact no touching, he was on the other side. It was like having my sister in bed with me. Would you object if I let Lilah in my bed when she needed one?"

"No, of course not, but that wasn't Lilah."

Norah shook her head. "There is nothing between us, TJ. I would never lead a man on by having him in my bed. I offered to Mark out of sheer thought of comfort, and because there never was and never will be anything between us."

TJ didn't look up at her. He just studied the floor for a moment, and Norah noticed the half-made peanut butter and jelly sandwich out on the counter.

Finally, he spoke again. "I want to trust you, but I don't know how I can."

That stabbed at her. Her lips pressed together, and her eyes threatened tears. "That's what trust is. It's what and who you believe when there's no evidence. Or in the face of overwhelming evidence to the contrary. I'm looking you in the eyes and telling you, I did not have sex with him."

He looked at her, but didn't otherwise respond.

Norah almost gasped as it became clear that he still didn't believe her. Desperation made her mouth active if not her brain. Words tumbled out in a plea to make him understand. "You know, Mark and I used to dance together. He touches me like that because dancers touch each other. Because there was never any possibility of anything between us. I have never slept with him.

"And I shouldn't have given him the other side of the bed," Tears were rolling down her cheeks now, one by one. TJ's expression didn't change and she wasn't sure why she kept talking but she did. "That's your spot. I love you and I want you there. And I won't even give it to Lilah, because you're right, I shouldn't have offered it."

She didn't add that Mark was drunk and she didn't think he'd take the couch. Or that she was afraid he'd get up later, still drunk, and drive off. "But I didn't screw him. I didn't cheat on you. I need you to believe that."

TJ took in a breath. "A lot of people think it's not sex if it's just oral sex. Did you make out? Let him touch you?" He gestured at her torso.

Norah cried in earnest then.

He asked another question. "Did you do it to get back at me? I'd understand that, what I did wasn't right."

Her voice shook. "What is this? The damned Spanish Inquisition?"

"No—"

"Sure it is! You've already decided what the right answer is, and if I just confess you'll make everything okay. But I'm not confessing to something *I didn't do!*"

The outburst stopped her for a moment, then she managed to get it together long enough to speak again. "You say that you love me, TJ, but part of that is trust. And you don't trust me do you?"

"I don't see how I can." He leaned against the counter, tears in his own eyes.

In that moment she hated him. Hated him enough to shove it in his face just how wrong he was.

So she walked away, to the front doorway where she still had a clear shot of him standing at the counter, his head down. "Two words, TJ."

TJ looked up at her.

"He's gay."

She slammed the door behind her, hoping the glass would shatter like her heart, but it didn't offer the satisfaction. She shoved the car into gear, making a noise with her tires that would disturb all his snotty neighbors and leave rubber marks on his pristine driveway.

She drove straight home, trying desperately to turn off somewhere, but anyplace she could think of that offered solace was busy. As she pulled into the driveway she realized that even her own home was now occupied by her father.

There was nowhere to go to get away.

She threw the car in park and pocketed her keys, leaving her purse on the floorboards. Norah saw her one escape in the corral, and she grabbed Shenandoah's bridle.

As she did the last buckle on the cinch, blinking back tears, TJ's car turned in at the bottom of the drive. He'd probably come to say he was sorry. But sorry didn't change the fact that he didn't trust her.

Shenandoah finally breathed out and she yanked the cinch one notch tighter, thinking that now was not the time to ride with a loose saddle no matter how tempting it was to just flee. She heard the engine stop on TJ's car, and the door slam as she slung her leg over the back of her biggest horse. She gained the saddle just as TJ came running over to the corral.

All he got out was her name before she was off like a shot.

Shenandoah cleared the fence at the far end and ran hell for leather across the open land. She heard it one last time in the distance, "Norah!" But she ignored it.

CHAPTER 60

Norah ignored his attempts to contact her.

He called. She didn't answer.

He sat on her doorstep. Her father even told her to give the boy a chance. But Daddy hadn't been there, and she wasn't airing their dirty laundry to him, even though it was likely all over. So Daddy didn't know what was going on.

Of course, TJ said he trusted her now. He'd left that much on her answering machine. But that wasn't trust. It was evidence, science. Mark is gay, end of story.

In spite of all the pain, down deep somewhere was a satisfaction that it had happened now. Not later when it would hurt more. Norah wasn't sure how it would hurt more than this, but she was certain that it could.

TJ showed up at the studio before class and pissed her off. "Now is not the time."

He pushed, just like TJ. "Then when is?"

She wanted to hiss out 'never,' but she just bit her tongue and tried to be polite in front of their audience. "I'm at work. Don't do this to me here."

He turned and walked off.

The third day, the flowers arrived. A huge bouquet of purple tulips.

Norah had to go around them on the front porch to get inside and set her things down. It would require two hands and some strength to lift the heavy vase.

She sighed there on her hands and knees on the front porch. Flowers were bad. Flowers were for men who didn't know what to say, to women they didn't really know. But her father's voice echoed in her head to 'give the boy a chance.'

So she plucked the small square card off its stick and sat back on her heels.

Pulling it out of the envelope, she turned the card over and read the words.

Norah, I love you. Please give me another chance. Love, TJ.

Her shoulders slumped. Not only was the wording something they probably had on file, it was *typed*! That made her the maddest. How heartbroken were you if you dictated to the person on the other end of the line?

Fat tears formed in her eyes again.

Everything had gone wrong.

With a deep sigh that let loose another fresh surge of pain inside her, she picked up the vase and carried the whole thing across the driveway to the trash can. Norah let it fall, too hurt to find comfort in the sound of the breaking crystal.

TJ called to check if the flowers had been sent. The shop said they'd been delivered an hour ago. The driver had to leave them as no one was home. So now all he could do was wait.

He was miserable, he tried playing video games, working out, none of it relieved his stress. Then he needed a shower, but wasn't willing to climb in for fear that he'd miss her call. TJ puttered around the kitchen, making himself another peanut butter and jelly sandwich. He'd lived on this crap pretty much since he'd walked in the door after seeing Norah with Mark that night.

He still wondered why he hadn't flown out of the car and stopped them. How he had let some man that he thought was going to have sex with his girlfriend go into the house? All he could think was that he'd frozen. He'd also believed he wasn't seeing the first time, so what was the point?

He wallowed in his string of bad decisions while he ate the sandwich. Ten minutes later he was rewarded for deciding not to climb in the shower. His phone rang, and the name said 'Norah.'

His chest heaved a sigh of relief. He couldn't answer fast enough, and his voice came out riding the wave of his lifted burden, "Baby."

"I got your flowers." Her voice was neither warm nor cold, just matter of fact.

"I miss you." He tried again.

"Flowers don't change facts. Good-bye."

He felt like someone had plunged him into the next ice age, naked. The phone disconnected.

He wasn't trying to change facts. She needed to talk to him, and he had to find some way to make that happen.

He had a list. If all else failed, maybe he could kidnap her and make her listen. Okay, that was a little far . . . but he had to get her to listen.

He spent the afternoon in the jewelry store.

He'd found nothing that he liked, so he picked out something similar to show the jewelers, then had them work overtime. She had to understand, had to at least call. This wasn't flowers. This was something he'd designed for her.

He went back to the jewelers the next morning, with the note he'd written. He checked out the work. It was beautiful and graceful and reminded him of her. And it was just an excuse to get her the note. He'd practically cut himself open and bled onto the paper.

At first he tucked the folded paper into the top of the necklace box, then became afraid she'd miss it. So he settled it over the jewelry and had the store wrap it. With a heart attempting to tear in half from the weight of the dread and the lift of the hope he felt, he drove to the dance studio. TJ was happy to find only Mrs. Kenner behind the front desk.

She smiled up at him like she had no idea Norah had left him. He was glad for that small fact and didn't care if it was ignorance or kindness. "This is a surprise for Norah. Will you give it to her when she gets in?"

The older woman took the box and turned it over. "It looks like jewelry."

"That might be because it is." He didn't add that it was also the plea of a man who was becoming more desperate.

TJ drove home wondering how his heart still beat, and when this would end. This wasn't the kind of thing you just got over. He took a long road around the edge of town, skidding to a halt at a 'For Sale' sign on a large rolling lot. The sign said 4 to 400 acres. Wondering what that meant, TJ dialed the number. While it rang, he noticed houses on either side of the lot. One on the left was still under serious construction, while on the right it looked complete and occupied.

"Can I help you?" The voice on the other end was gruff.

TJ asked about the sign and was told in the same work-rough voice that the man was old and selling off pieces of his own huge holdings along the road. He was willing to sell just the roadside lot, or carve out space behind it, whatever the buyer wanted if the price was right.

TJ told him the price was. Then called his real estate agent and told her the same thing.

Feeling marginally better, he arrived at his own house and shut himself in his studio with his cell phone. Every time it rang his heart flipped. Every time he was disappointed even before he answered it. He fielded calls from JD, Brenda, and Craig. And he waited.

He almost missed the knock at the front door. By the time his brain registered what the sound was, he scrambled to his feet just in case it was Norah.

Throwing open the door, his heart leapt at the sight of her. Her hair was pulled up, and she was in dance clothes, and the necklace box in her hand. She must have come directly here.

"The gate was open." Her voice was soft.

"Norah." He wanted to reach out and take her hands and pull her in, but he didn't know if he had the right to yet. "Come in."

She shook her head. "No."

God, no.

"Norah?"

"Jewelry doesn't cut it. It isn't what I want."

That shocked him. From her. "Did you read the note?"

"Yes. But it's cheap, coming with a necklace." She handed the box over to him and turned away.

He was too stunned to speak, and too stupid to stop her apparently.

It was too cheap?

The necklace hadn't been cheap. It had been anything but. She'd found his poured-out heart cheap? Jewelry wasn't enough?

He shook his head. If she wanted something more expensive, he'd get it. What was the use of his money if not for her? Norah was the last person he'd thought would put a price tag on any of this, but they could talk about that later. He just had to get her back to talking to him.

He made a few phone calls and prayed. Then hit the studio and sang until he collapsed against the wall. Everything sounded heart-broken or hopeful. And he only had a week until they hit the road again. This time for ten days. As he sat there against the padded wall, he began to think in long terms. How would he keep up his assault on her while he was on the road? Because he had to.

TJ was sitting in the same place, almost as exhausted, the next day when the call came through.

"Hello?" He wasn't all that hopeful this time. His heart had been pummeled a few too many times to just hand it over again. And he sure as hell wasn't sure this time was going to work. But he'd tried anyway. He ought to get points for effort.

Her voice bordered on shrill in his ear, and he had to hold the phone away. "You have to stop sending me gifts."

TJ sighed. He could feel yet another attempt biting the dust. "All I really want is for us to talk."

"We did talk. You don't trust me."

"I *didn't* trust you. It was stupid of me. I do trust you now." He was grateful to even get that much out. It was more than they'd said in the times she'd called to tell him various incarnations of 'no.'

"TJ, I can't do this."

"Good, then stop turning me away." He was practically yelling. His insides were boiling. She got him churned up faster than any other person he'd ever met.

So why was her voice so calm? Did she feel nothing for him?

Norah was almost monotonous. "I can't hand you my heart so you can break it again."

"Norah!"

He'd fucked up. Big time. He knew that. But . . .

He was getting ready to say so when she sighed and spoke again.

"TJ, you have to stop trying to bribe me."

"Bribe you!?" God, that was the last thing he'd been trying to do.

"All these gifts won't buy me."

At least there was a little emotion in her voice there. Even if it was anger. He'd take what he could get. This was better than the flat voice.

"I wasn't trying to buy you. I just wanted . . ." He stopped. He didn't *just* want anything. He wanted everything. He wanted them to talk, he wanted to hold her. He wanted her to press herself to him like he was the only one she wanted to be with. He wanted to go back in time and say "Norah, I believe you."

Her voice cut through his wishes when she realized he wasn't going to say more. "I'll return everything you give me." And she hung up.

CHAPTER 61

TJ sat on the floor at the edge of the room, his back against the wall while he looked at the small screen on the phone. It told him that the whole conversation, from his opening 'hello?' to her final hang-up had lasted only a minute and twenty-two seconds.

He sat there for a while, he wasn't sure how long, trying to equalize his breath, trying to vent some of the extra burn inside him.

Eventually, he stood and made his way to the shower, but he wasn't able to scrub away his thoughts.

There had to be another way to her. There had to be.

Part of the problem was Norah. She had been in love before, and she'd lost. TJ would bet good money that she was scared. Just like she'd said at the studio that day. So he had to work around her fear, as irrational as it might be.

The thing was, she'd been right, back at the beginning. Norah had yelled at him that she'd give up her arms and legs to have Jeff and Jordan back. She was right—he'd go back in that chair in a heartbeat if Norah would crawl into his lap like she had.

Just the thought of her curling into him, trusting him, and wanting him, settled a sense of calm into his core. The outside of him—fingers, legs, mouth, and yes, his dick—burned for her. He'd rather watch the sun explode than have her leave him like this.

Something about their conversation nibbled at the back of his brain, but he couldn't catch it. In the meantime, he decided to start his assault. Cold determination had served him well in the past, and he could only pray that it worked on Norah, too. He knew if it didn't, he'd curl up into a ball and stay there for who knew how long.

He cranked off the shower knobs with a purpose and dried himself fast enough to turn parts of his skin pink. He didn't care. He slid into jeans and a t-shirt, and padded barefoot and wet-headed downstairs.

Langdon Davidson was easy enough to find in the yellow pages, and TJ called the office hoping he hadn't gone home early. TJ knew their home number, by heart, of course, but he didn't want to risk getting Norah.

"Davidson." The voice answered.

"TJ Hewlitt, sir."

There was a pause, and TJ wondered what the man was thinking. It became clear in just a second.

"Is this about Norah? I don't know what to tell you. I can see she's upset, but she hasn't really told me anything."

Heat flooded him, and he found a smile. Of course she hadn't. There was hope. She'd promised not to tell their issues to her father, and she still wasn't, even though she sounded like she was washing her hands of him. With a deep breath, TJ forced his thoughts back to the task at hand. "Actually, I'm looking to hire an architect."

"Really?" Surprise wound through the line.

"To be honest, you're the only architect I know, sir. But I like your house, and I figure if you chose it then you might be the best man for the job."

"All right. You want a house?"

TJ nodded as he spoke, smiling, and liking that the cold was at bay for a little while. "Yes, but I have special requirements, too. So if that's too much, or not what you do, then you might refer me to someone else."

"Let's see what you need first. It's best if we talk preliminaries in person, so I can get an idea of what you want. You can come into the office or I can come to you."

"You might want to come here. There's a room in this house that I need duplicated in the new one. It might be best if you just see it." TJ paced while he talked.

"How's this evening look? I'm free after five."

TJ suspected that her Dad didn't usually go out on Friday evenings to meet clients. Then again, this wasn't going to be his usual job either. He bit back a small laugh. "I'm free. My date ditched me."

"I'm sorry about that, son." There was real compassion in the man's voice, although he offered no other information.

"Me, too." He almost didn't say it, then it fell out of his mouth anyway. "You know, sir, you are the strangest father I have ever met."

There was a deep laugh from the other end of the line, and TJ was glad it was taken well, he hadn't thought before the words came out. Then he added, "but probably the best."

"Thank you. I'll see you at five-thirty then?"

"Sure."

"Where am I going?"

TJ gave him directions and instructions how to get through the gate.

Five-thirty was the only thing on his agenda, but it meant he had to turn Kelsey down when she called and invited him over. He got the feeling that she and JD thought he didn't eat well enough by himself. Then he remembered the peanut butter and jelly he'd been consuming with regularity the past week and thought maybe they were right.

He went upstairs and banged on the piano for a while, writing something really melancholy to suit his mood. He kept at it, even though it sounded mad to his ears rather than sweetly sad, which was what he was going for. Maybe he wasn't capable of sweetly sad right now. But his fingers kept pushing at the keys, pushing the time away, until he realized it was five-twenty and he needed to get off the piano, and wait for Mr. Davidson.

As he hit the last notes, TJ heard the lingering chords in the air and his eyes widened. Tomorrow morning he'd hit the studio early before rehearsal and play it on the harpsichord Brenda had found them. A cheap ukulele had turned up as well and JD was threatening to compose Brenda a song on that. Quickly TJ played the piece through one more time, using the piano sounds only as a cue for what his brain converted to harpsichord. He'd have to hear it on the real thing to be sure, but he thought he finally had both this piece solved and the answer to what to do with the harpsichord.

He pounded down the steps, not wanting to be late and wound up puttering around waiting for Norah's father. TJ managed to get in the first of what he suspected would be a series of calls. Norah didn't answer, nor had he expected her to. So he waited for the beep and said, "Norah, I love you" then hung up. Mr. Davidson arrived five minutes late with a briefcase and an apology in hand.

"No worries." TJ let him in and led him into the dining room to the over-grand table and chairs for ten that he never used.

Mr. Davidson hardly saw where he was going, he was too busy looking around. He didn't sit, and his expression was a little odd. "Nice McMansion you have here."

"Yes." TJ answered, "It's the finest cheap construction and unimaginative architecture money can buy. You can see I had it decorated in generic opulence to keep the whole place unified."

The laugh that came out of the man put a smile on both their faces. Mr. Davidson finally pulled off his coat, settling it across the back of the chair before he sat. "All right. I think we can work."

"Thank you." TJ pulled out the adjacent chair and got as comfortable as he could in the for-looks-only furniture. "I didn't realize until recently that I really hate this place."

He pulled out grid paper and a keen looking mechanical pencil. "So, start talking. What do you want?"

For someone who knew what he wanted, TJ found he couldn't really put it into words. "Not this."

"That's a good start. Style?"

"I like your farmhouse. I hate A-frames. The land I just bought rolls, I want the place to look like it fits. No modern angles. I like the windows that come out of the roof."

"Dormer windows."

"Those."

The man was scribbling frantically. "Bedrooms?"

"Yes." *What a silly question.*

"How many?"

"Oh! Three or four."

"So," Mr. Davidson jotted more, "two to three bathrooms? Anything special for the master bath?"

"Yes. The big white bathtub with the . . ." TJ motioned with his hands.

"Claw feet. Good choice."

"Do they come big?"

Norah's Dad tilted his head to the side. "Big enough for two?"

Oh, shit. Maybe this wasn't such a good idea. But TJ squared up and looked him in the eye. "Yes, sir. Do they make them?"

There was a small grin with his nod. "Yes, I'll design it, and a good contractor can get you just about anything if you're willing to pay for it."

"Let's see how unreasonable it is, before we decide."

"Fair enough." He jotted more. "Any special rooms?"

"Oh, yes." TJ stood up, pushing the chair back and attracting the architect's attention from his papers. "Come with me."

He showed the studio, and discussed minor changes to the one for the new house, saying that some of the pieces here could be moved. The acoustic padding he had would come down and could go to the new place, he pointed out the special carpeting that would have to get replaced.

They trailed back down the stairs this time with Mr. Davidson leading. "Any other special rooms?" he asked over his shoulder.

"Yes, sir. A dance studio."

The older man stopped at the bottom of the stairs and turned to face him, leaving TJ a few steps up and curious if her dad was going to point out that he was betting a lot on an uncertain future.

"Do you want a packed foam floor like she has at her school now?"

No beating around the bush there. And no question as to why he wanted it, or for what. TJ answered. "Yes, sir, she loves that floor."

"That she does. It'll change the options for where it can go in the house."

"So be it." TJ followed as Mr. Davidson headed back through the kitchen scribbling frantically again while he walked. TJ threw out another gambit. "And a barn."

"Let me guess. Three horses?"

"Make room for five, sir. I need a western trained horse to go out with her. She rides English and it's just wrong."

Langdon Davidson let loose a deep, head-thrown back laugh, and TJ could see where Norah got it.

He added another contingency. "Oh, and no windows in the dance studio."

Her dad frowned at him. “That’s not right. It won’t look consistent on the outside of the house and there won’t be any natural light. Why are you insisting that there not be any windows?”

“The back of the house is open to range, sir. The land isn’t entirely fenced. There are houses on either side, and while there are trees, there aren’t enough to keep someone from watching her.”

“Would someone have perhaps done this while she was dancing at my house?”

TJ swallowed. “Yes, sir. Accidentally, sir.”

“Well, then we’ll have to come up with a solution. But I’m going to get around that ‘no windows’ thing.” Mr. Davidson sat back down and began sketching frantically.

CHAPTER 62

TJ worked frantically on the 'Norah problem' as he had now deemed it. He called several times a day, even though she never picked up, always leaving the same four words. His brain tracked the last conversation they'd had several different ways, knowing that there was some inherent clue in what she'd said.

He did the homework her father had given him, and wondered if the man had mentioned any of this to his daughter. TJ suspected not, but was uncertain if there was some code of architect-client confidentiality. Still he faithfully jotted down other ideas he had for the house. He included hardwood floors, everywhere, thinking that Norah could spin and turn through the house as she had when they had lived together. He wanted a fence around the property—to keep people out, dogs in, and be low enough for a good horse to safely jump.

Sunday morning TJ photographed the land he'd bought and emailed the photos, before hitting the studio and the harpsichord. He managed to make the song a little sweeter, but only after closing his eyes and imagining Norah in their new house. He refused to imagine an empty dance studio. He was building it. He'd wear her down if he had to.

Monday morning, he woke up and rolled over, going back to sleep. It was maybe the best thing he'd ever done, because when he woke the second time the clock said 10:53 and he remembered what it was about their conversation that had been eating at him.

He ate cheerios, not tasting a single bite. By noon he knew what to give her.

He showered and dressed frantically before realizing he had no idea where to get what he needed. He speed dialed JD, who gave him Kelsey's cell number.

"TJ?" She had answered. He never called her.

"Kelsey, I need help. Where can I get pretty boxes and tissue paper and that kind of thing?"

Norah lay on the couch, watching soap operas. She didn't answer TJ's calls' and he called about three to five times a day. *Norah, I love you.*

She could hear it in her head. It sounded a little different each time. Her phone logged when the calls came in. She hadn't been able to bring herself to delete them. Saving them would have been too active, so she simply hung up after listening.

This morning she had been stupid and played through her 'skipped messages,' tormenting herself with *Norah, I love you* in fourteen different shades. So she sat on the couch with the TV playing and some woman crying because her soap opera lover had done her wrong.

Norah should be eating lunch. She should be at the studio dancing. She could have run errands if nothing else. Instead she was on the couch with her phone in her hand like a lovesick fool.

She reminded herself that he'd be leaving again in four days, and felt overwhelming relief mixed with overwhelming sadness at that. So she figured she deserved some good old-fashioned self-pity on the couch. She contemplated eating a lunch of nothing but ice cream.

The door clicked as the show ended, and Norah bolted upright. "Dad, what are you doing here?"

"Apparently, I'm catching you guilty of something. Want to tell me what?"

"Not particularly." She lay back down, sinking into the pillow and down comforter she'd hauled out.

"Are you sick?" He shrugged out of his long coat, hanging it on the stand behind the door.

"No." *Yes.* She was heartsick.

Her Dad came over to the couch and shoved back part of the bedding, finding a seat for himself. Norah made room, knowing he was going to talk to her, because they were both here and awake, right?

"Actually, this is why I came home. I thought I might find you here."

"Daddy, I'm often here during the day."

His eyebrows lifted. "On the couch in your jammies?"

She didn't say anything, but mentally she conceded.

He pushed. "So you and TJ had a fight?"

"He screwed up, Daddy." She did not want to be having this conversation.

"Norah, we all screw up."

"Big time."

"We all screw up big time."

Damn the man. "Too big."

"Norah, he's determined. And he loves you."

That made her sit up. "How do you know that?"

"Well, for starters, I found this stuck in the screen just now."

He held out a three-by-five index card with four words: *Norah, I love you.*

She almost laughed, except for the part where she wanted to cry.

Her father shrugged. "Maybe you should give him another chance."

"I *did,* Daddy."

"There's always another."

God, her father could be exasperating. "What am I supposed to do? Keep letting him break my heart? Just keep handing him chances? I don't see you handing Mom any more chances."

He tipped his head, like he was conceding. His words did anything but. "The difference is I don't want to be with your mother. And I don't think your mother ever really tried to save us."

"Daddy," She sighed the word. "He sent me flowers, and then jewelry! He tried to buy me."

"You know, baby, he may have been trained by past women that that's an appropriate apology. I know your mother thought the more I'd screwed up, the bigger the diamond she deserved. You have to tell him that's not what you want. I'll bet if you told him what you do want he might very well come around."

Norah sat up again. He always judged her, always told her how she could fix the situation. But she didn't want to hear it. "Why are you on his side?"

His face hardened up really fast and Norah knew she'd struck a nerve. "I'm on *your* side, Norah, always."

"Then why are you pushing me to do this?"

He sighed. "You weren't a happy child, Norah. You didn't do well with the limits your mother and I put on you. Lilah did fine with them and so we did the same thing with you and looking back I don't think it was the right thing."

Norah rolled her eyes. "Daddy, Lilah broke every rule you guys set."

"I know that. I think breaking them made her happy. Now she seems happy living much like your mother does, all about the rules. You weren't happy that way. I think dancing gave you some satisfaction out of life, but you weren't happy until you started dating Jeff."

Her father paused here and blinked. "Your mother and I had so many fights about that. She thought you were too young to be serious about him and that we should stop you. I thought we were a day late and a dollar short on that one, because you already were serious about him. I knew from my own experiences that parents aren't very successful at keeping kids apart. And, the thing was, he made you happy.

"When you got pregnant, and got married, I thought you were too young. But I was wrong. You were so poor, but you both stayed in school, and then when he was going to graduate early and you were accepted to the Ballet, I couldn't have been more proud." He shook his head. "And then Jeff and Jordan died."

Norah could see that he had loved his son-in-law and grandson more than people probably knew. And he missed them both to this day.

"When they died, it was like someone flipped your light switch off. I tried so many ways over the years, but I couldn't make the light come back." He didn't look at her. "And then, at the beginning of the summer, you left. When I saw you again, several weeks later, it was on. I was so shocked. I'd become afraid it wasn't going to happen for you again." Here he faced her down. "He makes you happier than I think I've ever seen you. And that's probably why he makes you more upset. He deserves another chance. And *you* deserve another chance. If nothing else, do it for me. So I can see my little girl happy again."

She *hated* when he did that. The worst part of it was that he made sense.

So she heaved a sigh and decided she needed lunch if she was going to have the energy to haul herself out of the doldrums. As if he were reading her mind, he patted her arm, stood up, and said he had come home to reheat lasagna and did she want a piece?

He left her there with her thoughts.

Her Dad was right. TJ shouldn't be vilified when most women would have been ecstatic to get a bouquet like that. Most would have thought that an adequate apology. She groaned and covered her face, realizing for the first time that she was partly to blame. Hadn't she suggested he woo some girl with flowers, when she had been angry and thinking that he was in love with someone else?

He was persistent, too. TJ hadn't gone off to console himself with someone else when she turned him out. When things were good, he did make her happier than she'd been.

She heard the microwave ding, and she pushed the comforter off, revealing that her father was right about the jammies. He set two plates on the table, and she ate every bite of hers, knowing that she might be on TJ's doorstep for a while. If she couldn't get him today, she'd go back tomorrow. She could be persistent, too.

There were definitely things to straighten out. But for the first time she was willing to give it a shot. And horribly afraid it wouldn't work.

With a small smile on her face, she showered and dressed and actually put on some make-up. Her footsteps were light going down the stairs, and she threw on a jacket and was startled by the knock at the door.

Frowning, she opened it, her eyes widening at the sight of TJ standing on her porch. He was holding some sort of cube tucked under one arm and his face looked ready for battle. "Norah."

"TJ—"

"Please, let me in Norah, or come out here." The 'please' sounded more like a command.

Without a word, she stepped back, ushering him into the living room, thinking she didn't have a silly little entryway with a fountain.

He closed the door behind him and held out the cube. "This is for you."

She could see now that it was a decorated gift box, complete with perfectly fitted lid. It was beautiful, but it was another gift, and Norah pushed it back at him.

"TJ. I don't want gifts. I—"

"No, please, just listen." He looked away and took a breath, he hadn't even bothered to take off his jacket. "All those gifts, they weren't attempts to solve anything. They were just a gesture to tell you I was sorry, and try to get you to talk to me. I screwed up, Norah. I know it. I should have believed you."

She started to open her mouth, but his hand went up, palm forward, stopping her. "I know you've been in love before, and this is scary. But this," He gestured between the two of them, "doesn't grow on trees. If you feel half of what I feel for you, and you had that before, then you're the luckiest person on this earth. I don't ever expect to find this with anyone else. So, I'm warning you, I'm going to keep at this until you can either swear to me that you don't love me at all, or until you give in."

Without giving her a chance to respond he again held out the gift box. "This is for you."

Her voice was soft. What he'd said was about the sweetest thing she'd ever heard. So she didn't get mad. "I get it. I'm dating a very wealthy man, but I don't want your money."

He nodded. "I know. You said you'd return everything I gave you."

She meant it. The gifts were tainted by the fact that he had given them out of desperation, not joy.

He put the box into her hands. "If you want to return it, you can. But you should see it, so you know what you're giving up."

Norah sighed, resigned to opening the damn thing. It felt so light, she shook it. "It feels empty."

He almost snorted. "It's not empty."

She turned a little. There was nowhere to set the box, so she went into the living room with her jacket still on, unsure what the outcome would be, and knelt in front of the coffee table. TJ followed her, setting himself carefully on the edge of the couch. She looked at him, noting he looked stoic, almost expressionless.

Inside the box was another box, identical, only slightly smaller. Norah frowned and set aside the first lid reaching for the other box. TJ stopped her hands, directing her back to the lid. Wondering what he wanted, she picked it up and held it while he turned it over.

She blinked. Set into the lid was a beautiful piece of paper with writing on it. Quickly, she rotated the lid to get the words upright.

LOVE in big hand-written letters went across the top. His scrawl filled the rest of the page: *I love you I love you I love you I love you I love you I love you I love you I love you I love you I love you I love you I love you I love you I love you.*

Norah looked up at him, surprised. He just nodded at the next box for her to continue.

She pulled the second box out and opened it, only to find another box. But this time she flipped the lid and looked inside, sure enough there was writing here, too.

This time *FAITH,* and under it, *I have faith in you. I have faith in us. We've been through so much. We can get through this and anything else that comes our way. As long as we're together.*

Her heart lurched into her throat, and she dove for the third box. She saw the fourth box inside, but was already checking under the lid. *HOPE. I have hope that we will have years and years together. That we will grow old together. Live to be 100 and die in each other's arms.*

She fought back tears and tore into the fourth box. Under the top was the word *FIDELITY* followed by *You are the one I bring my problems and my solutions to. You are the only one I'll make love to and with. What is ours is ours alone.*

The fifth lid said *DESIRE. I want you. You are the only one I want. You turn me on. You are the one.*

She was swimming in boxes and lids. And fighting back the urge to just throw herself at him. But he looked so walled off.

As she lifted the lid of the sixth box she saw that it was the last. This lid she could span with her fingers, and she turned her hand and read. *TRUST. I trust you, above all others. Beyond all evidence. You are my truth.*

Her eyes were full, glazed with tears. As she looked at him, TJ grew blurry, but still he didn't move toward her. At a complete loss, and flailing as she slid down a sharp slope, falling head over heels further in love with him even though he showed no expression, Norah held up her hands asking him what she should do.

His voice was gravelly. TJ's voice was never gravelly. "You know what you said you'd do with any gift I gave you."

"I said I'd return it, but I don't want to return this." She'd been the world's biggest fool to think she could or should walk away from this man.

Still he showed no expression.

CHAPTER 63

Her heart stopped, she'd thought he would be happy that she wanted to keep it.

Suddenly she understood. He'd given her love, faith, hope, fidelity, desire, and trust. She was *supposed* to return them. "Wait!"

Frantically she settled lids on the right boxes, stacking them inside each other, screwing it up and having to unpack two of the boxes to get the missing one inside. She didn't look up until it was repacked, and she handed it to him, startled to see the smile on his face. Laughter even. "I'm returning it."

His eyes caught hers. "Only if you really want to."

"I do." This time she did launch herself into his arms, and he set aside the box just in time to catch her but he held her back.

"Norah, sometimes I'm an idiot. And I'm sure I will be again in the future. You'll have to tell me. I'll listen."

She nodded yes, and leaned in to kiss him, needing his mouth on hers and so much more. But still he held her away.

"I need your word, Norah."

She was ready to give it, whatever he wanted.

"You can't just run away when things scare you. This is twice now you've completely shut me out from how you're feeling. Not again. I need you to know, that no matter how bad things may seem, I never want to hurt you." His fingers wound into her hair, holding her at a distance from his face and yet near. "I should have trusted you more. But you should have trusted me, too. I wasn't trying to bribe you. I was trying anything I could to get you to speak to me. It shouldn't be that hard."

Her voice came out on a wet whisper, "I'm sorry. I love you."

"I love you, too, Norah."

This time when she pushed toward him, he let her, his lips sealing over hers. His tongue searched her mouth, and his hands held her to him. For a while she just clung, needing his touch, enjoying making out on the couch again.

Eventually she pulled back. "There's something you should know."

"Uh-oh."

"No," She grinned, "Not uh-oh. I was on my way out the door when you came in—"

He looked worried. "Is there somewhere you need to be?"

"Yes. I was on my way to camp out on your doorstep so we could talk." She offered a smile. "I guess I thought life would be better if you couldn't hurt me. But then I realized that I was already hurt and maybe I had the power to end it. That we couldn't possibly make things okay if I didn't at least talk to you."

Leaning his forehead in toward hers, he touched her—her hair, her face, her arms. "Don't leave me again, Norah. You were right. I'd give up my arms and legs in a heartbeat to have you back."

She shook her head as she spoke. "You don't have to. But I do have a dance school to run, and classes to teach tonight. You have a tour to go on in a few days, and I want you so enslaved to me that none of those groupies are even half tempting."

He laughed at that and Norah thought it might be the best

sound in the world. "Baby, I already am, but if you want to try a little more just to be certain, I'm not against that."

She left her jacket on the couch and slipped him out of his before tugging on his hand and leading him upstairs. He tugged off the clothes she had just put on, and she left his in a pile on the floor. Then she found him again. How could she have forgotten this?

Afterward, she set the alarm to get her up in time to teach class, and curled up in his arms. When their breathing steadied, she figured she'd go to sleep, but TJ sat up a little straighter. "Listen, there's something you need to know."

"Uh-oh, that doesn't sound good." She smiled, thinking there wasn't much of anything that could destroy this day.

"It's not. But you should know it, and it would be bad if you found out later."

This time she sat up a little, too.

"Norah," he sighed. "You remember at my house that morning you walked out, you asked if I was accusing you of cheating because I had."

She nodded, not liking where this was going. Her hand, which had been making lazy circles on his chest, stilled. "You said you hadn't."

He covered her hand with his, "I didn't. I didn't lie to you, and I didn't cheat on you. But you struck a nerve. Maybe I thought you were sleeping around on me, because I figured I deserved it." He tucked a finger under her chin and met her eyes. "I've never been faithful to anyone before you."

"Anyone?"

He looked down and shook his head. "I'm not proud of it. But it never mattered. I never cared if anyone found out and left me because of it. You should know about my past though and that I won't cheat on you. This is different."

Slowly she nodded. "Is this some kind of record?"

He nodded, and Norah pushed away, sitting bolt upright. "Three weeks is a record for you!?"

"Probably." He looked sheepish, and Norah started thinking back. He must have read her mind because his arms tightened around her. "Don't think that way, I hit three weeks of being faithful to you long before we even kissed. There hasn't been anyone else since before the accident."

That soothed her but she had to clarify. "TJ you weren't faithful to me then. There just wasn't anyone else around. There's a difference."

"Yes, there is. And I was faithful to you. I wanted, I got turned on, I fantasized. It was all about you, so don't go thinking I settled."

Smiling, she curled into him. This was where she belonged. Her heart rate slowed, and she knew other women would warn her about her decision, but she believed him. More importantly, she believed *in* him.

TJ sat on the tour bus almost two weeks later. He called Norah every day this time. His head was still in the clouds a lot of the time, but he managed to pull it out for the shows. He was getting better at it, too. It was turning back into fun. He was meeting all sorts of people, fans he'd never considered before.

He and Craig were working up the song with the harpsichord. They meshed sounds better than he'd even expected. Though his best friend was intensely private, TJ finally understood the emotion behind the words. He understood what Craig had meant in *Sand*—his hit from a few years ago.

He told Norah all of this. Even about the women in the bars that he pushed away, suddenly finding them garish. He told her about him and Craig finally being on the same page. So he wasn't surprised to see her name across the front of the phone. "Hi, baby."

"TJ?"

"What's wrong?" He worried, simply because she was upset.

She started rambling, and he'd learned that was a sign that she was nervous. "So I was here, at your house. I got the mail, and," there was a sigh from her. "There's this woman who keeps calling the house, if I answer she says she lost your cell phone number and will I give it to her? Then sometimes she leaves messages saying she's thinking what she wants to do in the bedroom and she talks about the marble enclosed bathtub. So she's obviously been in there."

Norah quit with the rambling, and TJ smiled. "Norah, that's Lisa, and you can give her my cell number. She's buying the house."

"Oh!" Then she laughed again. "Please don't hate me for being worried. But I called you. I asked."

"You did, Baby. Just so you know, I'd be asking, too, if I ever heard anything like that on your machine." He fingered the velvet box again.

"When do you have to move out?"

"End of the month."

She sounded surprised. "That's soon. Where are you going to go?"

He shook his head, even knowing that she couldn't see him. "Right now, I don't know, but eventually the new house will be built."

"You're building?"

"Yeah, you should see the plans, baby."

Norah sounded far more content than she had when she started the call. "You'll show them to me when you get in?"

"Why don't you go ask your Dad? He's designing it." He didn't say much more than that, just listened to her surprise and told her, "I miss you. I'll be home in two days."

CHAPTER 64

TJ hit his speed dial for Norah's number. "Hey, I'm home."

Her indrawn breath was music to his ears. "You're two hours early. Do you want me to come over?"

He turned up the driveway. "Come over where? I said I'm *home*. That means I'm less than fifty feet from you. I'm looking at your front porch."

"Just a minute." She hung up on him.

TJ turned off the car and climbed out, opening the velvet box, wanting to see her eyes when she realized what he was holding.

Instead he saw Norah in the doorway, underdressed for the chill in the air, decked out in a series of knits that were mismatched and clingy enough that they could only be dance clothes. Ballet shoes raced across the front porch and over the driveway, and she almost threw him off balance when she wrapped her arms around his neck and her legs around his waist.

She sighed out the words. "I missed you." But she didn't climb down him.

He hugged her to him one-armed, "Norah, I have a present for you."

"Don't care." She kissed his neck.

"I'll bet you do." He smiled.

"Nope." Her kiss landed on his mouth and she hit him like wine. She seeped in through his tongue, and everywhere she touched him. Spreading like wildfire throughout his system, she warmed his core and invaded his extremities, left him feeling just a little drugged.

He pocketed the ring and kissed her back.

CHAPTER 65

Five months later

TJ stood at the side of the church. Everyone was inside. Everyone except Norah.

JD found him standing there playing with his cufflinks just for something to do with his hands. "Cold feet?"

"Try 'cold fear.' Norah's not here."

His brother nodded. The ceremony was due to start in five minutes and the bride was missing. "She'll come. She loves you. That much is obvious." He sat on the bench and watched while TJ paced.

TJ nodded. "This scares the crap out of her."

"Well, there's some sense in that. The more you commit yourself the more you have to lose. I know that first hand. So do you."

He knew that part made sense, but . . . "She says it's like by marrying me she's making me more likely to die. It's irrational."

"Of course it is. But it's all she knows. Marry a man and he dies."

He conceded. "I know this is taking a supreme act of bravery and sheer faith on her part."

JD put a hand on his shoulder, and it calmed him a little.

"You know, JD, this is a big day for me, so it's a good time to say big things that might not otherwise get said. Thank you. Before Norah, you were the only one who always believed in me and accepted me for who I was. And I didn't always treat you well enough."

JD shrugged. "I didn't always treat you well enough either. We're brothers, not angels." He laughed and embraced TJ in a hug that meant the world. "Speaking of angels, little brother, look."

TJ felt his shoulders get turned.

Norah was walking toward him, dressed all in white, her dark hair partly up, partly cascading down her back and over one shoulder. She held a bouquet of purple tulips down at her side and wore the necklace he had designed for her. Her beautiful face held wide eyes that seemed to see only him.

TJ looked to thank JD, but his brother had disappeared.

He couldn't tell from Norah's face whether she had come to tell him she was ready or that she couldn't do it.

When she was close, she stopped but didn't touch him. Her voice was low enough that he had to strain to hear what she was saying.

"I had to tell you something first."

He nodded, waiting.

"I am so scared. I lost so much when I lost Jeff."

He knew. The sun had risen and set on Jeff, and he only hoped one day she looked back on her years with him with the same fondness.

She continued. "But my Dad reminded me of something a

while ago. When I was with Jeff, I was a kid. I loved him like a kid. I hadn't ever lost anybody, and I took a lot of it for granted.

"You told me that I'm strong. And I survived it before, so the worst case scenario is that I survive it again. But you're wrong. This," She gestured between them, "is already so much more than what I was even capable of then. I have never loved anyone like I love you and I don't think I could survive losing you. So I figured I'd come here and tell you I couldn't do it."

TJ held his breath.

"But on the drive over, I realized I was already too late. I already love you too much, and I can't back out now. I'm sorry I'm late. But I wanted to come and tell you, you have your bride. One very scared bride, if you'll still have me."

"Of course." It came out as a whisper. TJ Hewlitt, who belted songs before a packed Central Park and always had something to say, could only whisper. He wondered how he'd ever get his vows out. "I'm scared, too. Norah, you're my world."

Searching for words, he shook his head. "It's this big cliff and we just have to hold on and jump and hope it's tall enough that we don't ever hit bottom."

He held his hand out to her.

Slowly, Norah put her hand in his.

EPILOGUE

Nashville Music News
Maggie Jacobson

These days having a Wilder single at the top of the country charts is little cause for excitement. Wilder hitting the top of the pop charts is also something we've seen before. So when their latest single *Jump* hit #1 on Billboard's Top 100 no one was surprised.

Jump has stayed at #1 for sixteen weeks now. A harkening to their heavier side, it blends deep guitar riffs and wild drum solos. The first hit written by lead singer TJ Hewlitt, *Jump* has an unusual vocal track that blends all four members' voices and is simultaneously both mellow and intense. Only when you listen to the words do you realize that *Jump* is a love song, with our liquid-voiced lead encouraging us to take his hand and take a chance.

One has to wonder if this is any reference to Hewlitt's new bride, Norah Davidson Hewlitt, formerly of the Houston Ballet. Hearts broke everywhere when Wilder's front man wed

Davidson here in town last spring. The former playboy has been mostly out of the limelight since recovering from a crippling car accident just over a year ago.

The band has been back on the touring circuit for nine months now and TJ Hewlitt seems better than ever. Wilder remains one of the few groups to record only music of their own writing, so it's amazing to see a band this tight take a chance like this and add a new writer. TJ Hewlitt's style is clearly his own and, while he maintains Wilder's trademark sound, any fan who listens will be able to distinguish his music from the other band members' pieces as well as from group efforts.

On stage, the band remains technically amazing and just plain fun to watch, however this new tour shows a maturity in their music that wasn't previously there. Anyone who gets a chance should pay whatever price is asked to see them in one of the smaller local venues they've taken to playing lately.

As a Wilder fan from back in the days before they were signed, it would be tempting to believe I've heard everything they have to offer, but truly these guys are just getting started. Even with only two singles released, the aptly titled *Leap of Faith* has been their best and biggest selling album to date, and deservedly so.

AFTERWORD

Dear Reader, I hope you're swimming in all the happily-ever-after that Norah and TJ finally found. When I was about 3/4ths of the way through writing Our Song, I suddenly just *knew* I had to write TJ's story. *Love Notes* is actually the second *Wilder* Book that I wrote. Norah and TJ were in for so many surprises in their story, but they both had a lot of healing to do. I loved writing this one and I hope you loved reading it.

If you did, I'd love if you'd leave a review! Reviews can be short and take only a minute. A simple "I loved this book" will make any author's day!

PREVIEW OF MUSIC & LYRICS (WILDER - BOOK 4)

Alex was sitting on his couch with a beer when the woman went stomping past him. She didn't say a word. She didn't have to, her face said it for her.

Her orange hair was scraped back into a tight knot, and her sensible shoes shook the floor as she went by. She was done. He'd seen that expression before. Hadn't he just been trying to ignore the yelling coming from the other room himself? Of course she'd had enough. It was really a miracle she'd lasted this long.

She came back into the room, luggage packed and in hand.

Well, shit. She'd been ready, he realized. Still, he listened to her words.

"Mr. Beaumont, I'm resigning my position here." She handed over a typed and signed paper. It wasn't dated, so she hadn't known she was leaving today. As he scanned it, he saw the words even as she spoke them. "Effective immediately."

By the time he looked up, she was already gone from the room. Then he heard the back door slapping shut behind her. Not that it was a good sound, but it was far better than the discordant yells coming from Sophie's room. That awful sound was probably the worst thing a musician could hear.

He tipped his head back and poured in the beer as though it would seep in and fill all the cracks in his life. It didn't, but the slight buzz of the expensive, local beer made him feel just a little like it did.

It worked, too, until the yelling went quiet and he sat sharply upright at the sign of impending doom. There was no telling what Sophie was up to when she was quiet. But he sat still as though he would hear something, or a crash would come, or maybe she would *say* something.

The last one was never going to happen. Well, not in the lifetime that he could foresee. Probably the reason for the beer. Nothing filled the cracks of failure like a good cold one.

For so long, things had been fine. Golden even. He toured, his wife ran the show here, his daughter was perfect, and things were great. It had all gone to hell one unknowing step at a time. Just one day he woke up and everything was wrong. He could see the path he'd taken to get here, but he hadn't seen it when he'd been walking it. Now he was stuck between the worst options a father could have.

Then Olivia stuck her head into the living room. "Daddy?"

Her voice was sweet, the tones dulcet, her smile soft. She was his perfect girl. "What baby?"

"You need to get Sophie." She began to frown, her lips pressing together.

He nodded and stood up, only then realizing the beer had been a little more potent than he'd figured. He shouldn't have drunk it all. Then again, he couldn't have predicted that Mrs.... Mrs....

Shit. Her name wouldn't come to him. Then again, did it matter? The woman had quit. That's what he couldn't have predicted.

But if he'd been a little more sober, a little more on the ball, a little better of a parent, he *would* have seen it coming. She wasn't the first one to leave. She wasn't even the first one to stomp out with no notice.

Then again, if he'd been a better parent, they probably wouldn't be in this predicament in the first place. Maybe it was Bridget's fault. He liked to believe that was possible.

Perfect Alex and Perfect Bridget had made Perfect Olivia.

Then they'd had Sophie and everything had gone wrong.

Catching his balance, Alex followed his older daughter into the back room, just as the discordant yelling started up again. He didn't know if that was a good sign or a bad one.

Looking down at Olivia and thinking he shouldn't leave her in charge of her sister as much as he did, he said, "We'll have to get another one."

She seemed to understand that he meant 'another nanny' and nodded up at him.

But in the meantime, it was all up to him.

He had to go face his two-year-old daughter.

Mariliz Jennings sat across the desk from her last hope.

The stern, older woman frowned down at Mariliz's resume and then frowned harder. It was understandable.

Maraliz had a degree in psychology with a focus on abnormal childhood development, with minors in French and creative writing. It was as though she wanted to be sure she had a career that required she ask people if they wanted fries with that? Oh, and loads of student debt, too.

To say she was having a bad month was an understatement. She was about three weeks away from running out of rent money, and that wasn't an exaggeration. She had the notice—two weeks and five days to be exact. Then she had to either break into the savings she swore she wouldn't touch or find a new craphole to live in.

On the upside, she'd once been a teacher. Not qualified to teach in a real school, because she'd quit before getting the state certificate. She'd worked in a retail shop once—luckily not serving fries—before she completed her degree. Then, after that one year of teaching, she'd been a wife. Which didn't look all that impressive on a resume.

To be fair, her work hadn't been all that impressive as a wife, if her recent divorce was anything to measure by. She'd been told to be pretty, plan parties, play house. She'd done all of that exceptionally well, if her friends were to be believed. She'd also gotten her nails done, spent an exorbitant amount of time prepping home-cooked, organic meals, and filled her boring down time with lunches and more romance novels than a person could shake a stick at. Well, there were no more sticks left; she'd read so many books that all the trees had likely been killed. She was grateful when she got an e-reader and could better hide her habit from Reynold, who thought she should be reading loftier things.

Looking back, maybe he was right. Had she been reading something educational she might have been able to put it on her damn resume. Or, she might not have needed the resume in the first place, because she never would have realized her marriage was so lacking. She might never have found strength from the women behind the pretty or racy covers who stood up for themselves. And Reynold might never have told her she was crazy and should be happy with the good life she had.

She might never have looked further.

She might never have decided to take charge and plan a special trip. That was when she found out her husband had been taking special trips all along—just not with her. Still, he'd told her she should appreciate the nice life he gave her. Mariliz didn't.

Well, until now, when she was her own woman, on the verge of getting evicted from her crap apartment. A woman who had gotten a very nice car in the divorce and not enough alimony to cover everything. Her lawyer hadn't argued well enough that she'd put as much into the marriage as he had. Maybe she hadn't.

At least she learned along the way to sit still and smile when the pressure was on. She used that now. And her nails looked fantastic. She had a lot of free time being unemployed and nail polish was cheap. So she faked calmly lacing her fingers and crossed her legs under the skirt that was only vaguely professional, but definitely not cheap.

She was the best-dressed woman at her apartment complex, that was for sure. So she smiled wide under the last smidge of her expensive lipstick. She needed another tube of it. She needed rent. She needed a paycheck about two weeks ago.

Mrs. Purvey, of the Purvey Child Care Agency—which Mari thought was a terrible name for anything with children—pointed down at the bottom of the print copy she'd been asked to bring. Apparently, Child Care was not part of the electronic age.

"It says here you speak sign language?" It was a question, despite the fact that she said it all wrong.

"I was a certified interpreter in American Sign Language. But I'm not at the medico-legal level anymore." She offered a sad smile. It had been years. Another cool skill that Reynold thought was another way his wife could be crass. Ya know, *working*. Had she tried to get reinstated, she would have surely failed the test now. But, as with many things, at one time, she'd showed promise.

"You do or don't speak the language?" The woman stared at her harshly.

"As a nanny? Perfectly fine." A deaf kid? The thought had no sooner occurred to her than Mrs. Gray was voicing it.

"We have a family in need of a live-in starting tomorrow. The younger daughter is deaf." Another harsh stare, as though she was daring Mariliz to take the job.

"That sounds fantastic." *Tomorrow?* She hardly paid attention as Mrs. Gray listed the stats. Number of kids, ages, genders, etc.

Mari blinked. She could live in. No more worries about rent, or money. Not if she had a place to stay. Then she blinked again. She'd better pay attention or she was going to lose the job before she even got it. In her hand was an info sheet still warm from Mrs. Gray printing it out for her.

"Do you have any questions?" The older woman asked in a tone that brooked no uncertainty that no, Mariliz Jennings did not have any questions.

"I can't think of any." She said, then realized that made it sound like her brain didn't work. She motioned with the fact-sheet. "This looks very thorough."

At last, the older woman looked pleased.

Mari filed that away. She'd gotten very good over the past years at learning and cataloging who liked what, who'd vacationed where, and how to remember factoids as though she actually cared.

Three minutes later, it was over. She was dismissed from the office and found herself on the front steps. She was expected at the address at eight p.m. tonight to introduce herself before the children went to bed, then she would start tomorrow at eight a.m. suitcase in hand.

Holy shit. She had a job. One that paid her for a real skill. She drove off with a smile on her face. It stayed there even though Nashville traffic piled up around her. It stayed all the way to the crappy apartment on the other side of town. Never mind that East Nashville was up and coming. She was too far east and her place was definitely down and going.

Once she made it home, she took one look at the brown, metal front door to her apartment and put the car back in gear.

She was a good cook, but the thought of cooking in that awful little kitchen, with the glitchy electric burners that she hated, was more than she could handle. It was a good news day and there was a meat-and-three down the street. She and her Lexus would stick out like a sore thumb, just like they always did. But they knew her there. They knew she would show up in her designer skirt and happily eat green beans cooked with bacon fat. They would wink and give her extra banana pudding, too.

The meatloaf tasted better with a side of freedom. She read up on the family while she tried to keep banana pudding smears off the page. The address looked nice, Brentwood area on the south side of town, not too far from the agency. That made sense, the agency would be located where there was a high density of families that could afford live-in help.

Once, she'd been that kind of wife. Now she was the help. Maybe she should have had kids. For a moment, she looked up at the old acoustic ceiling and thought about that path. Nope. She would have been tied to Reynold, and even her crappy apartment, with the eviction notice taped to the front door for everyone to see, was better than being tied to a man who cheated on her and didn't even see a reason to be sorry.

She looked back down at the page. Father—Alexander Beaumont. Mother—Bridget Beaumont. Children—Daughter-Olivia-Age 8 and Daughter-Sophie-Age 2.

Fun ages, Mari thought. She had plenty of brothers and sisters and cousins. She understood what a two-year-old and an eight-year-old might be like. She also understood that every single one of them was their own person, even at those ages.

No pets. *Good.* Mari wasn't even fond of goldfish.

Live-in space—mother-in-law suite with private entrance on ground floor. Her own suite! It was probably bigger than her crappy apartment!

At the noise of her spoon hitting Corian, she looked at the plate to find she'd cleaned it. Then she pulled her phone to discover that she had barely enough time to change, fight traffic, and show up at seven-fifty.

Folding the paper into her purse, Mari breathed deeply of the smells of fried chicken and cooked-within-an-inch-of-their-lives vegetables. There would probably not be a mom and pop place like this on the other side of town.

Thank you for reading! I love romances with real love and believable characters, and I hope you found all that in these pages. I want to fall in love right along with the characters, and I do, while I'm writing it.

About Savannah

I started writing when I was eight--I hand wrote an 80-page novella that I believed to be (adult) romantic suspense. I'm proud to say, I've gotten a lot better since then. I've grown up to be a nerd at heart! I love neuroscience and people watching, and if you look, you'll find some of that in each Savannah Kade book. Most days you'll find me in my office, looking out my window at a handful of the neighbor's cows, or watching my dogs or my cat roam the backyard.

Follow me, find me, ask me questions! I would love to hear from you.

www.SavannahKade.com
Savannah@SavannahKade.com

www.ingramcontent.com/pod-product-compliance
Lightning Source LLC
LaVergne TN
LVHW050915080826
845145LV00001B/97

* 9 7 8 1 9 4 8 0 5 9 4 9 7 *